Margaret T̶̶̶̶̶̶̶̶̶̶̶̶̶̶̶̶̶̶̶̶̶̶̶̶̶̶̶̶̶̶̶̶ lived there all her life. She is a qualified teacher but has retired to concentrate on her writing. She has two children and five grandchildren. Her previous Blackpool sagas, *It's a Lovely Day Tomorrow*, *A Pair of Sparkling Eyes*, *How Happy We Shall Be*, *There's a Silver Lining*, *Forgive Our Foolish Ways* and *A Stick of Blackpool Rock*, are all available from Headline.

Wish Upon A Star

Margaret Thornton

HEADLINE

First published in 1998
by HEADLINE BOOK PUBLISHING

First published in paperback in 1998
by HEADLINE BOOK PUBLISHING

10 9 8 7 6 5 4 3 2 1

ISBN 0 7472 5690 X

Typeset by Avon Dataset Ltd, Bidford-on-Avon, Warks

Printed and bound in Great Britain by
Clays Ltd, St Ives plc

HEADLINE BOOK PUBLISHING
A division of Hodder Headline PLC
338 Euston Road
London NW1 3BH

For my agent, Darley Anderson,
and my editor at Headline, Clare Foss.
My thanks to you both for your help,
advice and encouragement.

Chapter 1

'So you think it's going to happen, do you, Sally?'

Ellen Hobson's dark brown eyes were anxious, and Sally felt that she would do anything, if she could, to allay the fears of her mother-in-law. But she knew that she couldn't. To do so would only be evading the issue. War, as they all knew, if they would face up fair and square to the facts, was inevitable.

Sally smiled back at her a trifle sadly. 'I'm afraid so, Mam. It looks that way, doesn't it? All we can do now is wait until they tell us it's definite.'

'Mmm . . .' Ellen nodded resignedly. 'It's only what I've known, deep down, for ages, of course. But I kept telling myself that it couldn't happen again, not so soon. Hitler's never had any intention of giving way over Poland, and now that he's invaded . . . well, that's that, isn't it?' Ellen leaned forward in her armchair, staring intently at Sally. 'Sal, d'you think that if – when – it happens . . . d'you think George'll have to go into the Army?'

A spasm of fear gripped at Sally's heart, as it had done several times already, at the thought of her husband having to go to war – again. George had served in the Great War, as it was now being called, and had returned a very changed young man. Sally hadn't known him then – she had met him some four years later – but she had heard from George's own lips of how he had had a very serious drink problem, brought on by his horrific experiences in the trenches of France. Sally liked to think that it was she, in the main, who had helped to cure him of his addiction and to banish the ghosts from the past which, at that time, had still haunted him. George hardly ever touched a drop of the 'hard stuff' now and never spoke of his gruesome memories. But Sally knew that they were there, though deeply hidden, and she knew, also, that the idea of going to war again would be abhorrent to the tender-hearted George.

'I shouldn't think so, Mam,' she replied now, as casually as she could, in answer to Ellen's question. 'Certainly not at the beginning, at any rate. George is pushing forty now, isn't he? They'll be wanting the younger men first. Besides, George has done his bit serving King and Country in the last lot, and in my opinion one war's enough in any man's lifetime.'

'I couldn't agree more,' replied Ellen emphatically. ' "The war to end all wars" they called it, didn't they? And now, well, I can hardly believe that it's all starting up again.'

Sally nodded thoughtfully as she stared into the fading embers of the fire. She had tried, along with the majority of the British people, to believe in Neville Chamberlain's 'peace for our time'. Then, as news began to filter through, first about Hitler's out and out betrayal of Czechoslovakia, then about his designs on Poland, she realised they had all been deluding themselves.

Far more real to the ordinary folk than the reports of happenings in far-off countries were the leaflets that began to drop through their letter boxes. The one entitled *The Protection of your Home against Air Raids* urged the man of the house to take on the role of 'captain of the ship' and to conduct air-raid drills as he would lifeboat drill on a ship. *Masking your Windows* was another one and *How to use your Gas Mask*. Now they had all been supplied with the infernal things. The full-scale use of poison gas, it seemed, was a dreadful possibility; and an immediate aerial bombardment as soon as war was declared. Vague, and possibly unsubstantiated, estimates were being thrown about with abandon, one being that 100,000 tons of bombs would be dropped on London in the first fourteen days – a massacre of such proportions that one couldn't even begin to contemplate it; and Sally couldn't entirely believe it.

All the same, the evacuation of children from the major cities had already begun. The first trainloads, from the Liverpool and Manchester areas, had arrived at Blackpool Central Station only that day, Friday, 1 September. Ellen had been one of a small group of women, members of the WVS, who had volunteered to meet them on arrival, handing out to each child a stick of Blackpool rock, a sizeable amount of which had been donated by Hobson's, their own rock factory. Ellen had come home almost in tears. The sight of the poor little mites, she said, some of them only five years old, looking so lost and bewildered and many of them weeping, had touched her heart as much as anything she had ever seen. Which was why Sally decided now to broach the subject which was at the forefront of her mind.

'Yes, I'm afraid it is all starting again, Mam,' she said now, answering Ellen's previous remark. 'At least, it will be before very long, barring a miracle, and I can't see one of them happening, not at this stage. I've been wondering . . . how would you feel about us having a couple of evacuees?'

Ellen stared at her for a few seconds as though she couldn't comprehend what Sally was saying. Then she began to chuckle delightedly, shaking her head from side to side. 'Well, well! They say great minds think alike, don't they, dear? Do you know, I was going to suggest the very same thing myself, but I didn't know how you would feel about it, Sally. After all, you're working full-time at the shop and you don't get much time to yourself.'

'I don't think it really matters how we feel about it,' replied Sally. 'It's what we must do, isn't it? We've all got to do our bit. But I was a little doubtful about mentioning it myself, Mam, because I feel that the bulk of the work would fall on you. And you must admit that you're . . .'

'I hope you're not going to say "you're knocking on a bit". ' Ellen frowned at her daughter-in-law in mock reproof. 'There's life in the old dog yet, you know!'

Sally laughed. 'Of course not. I wouldn't dream of saying that. I was going to say that you must admit you are very busy. And with me being at the shop all day, as you've just said, most of the time the children – whoever they are – would be with you.'

Ellen, at the age of nearly sixty, was still in overall charge of the family rock firm, regularly visiting the two shops and the factory, as well as serving on various charitable committees, and she had recently joined the WVS. Both Sally and George worried about her at times, fearing that she was doing too much, but they always hesitated to tell her so. She was fiercely independent and resentful of any suggestion that she was growing older. Neither did they want her to feel that they were trying to wrest the control of the firm from her hands. Hands that were still very competent; her family knew that they would have to wait until such time as Ellen herself was ready to let go of the reins.

'I'm not so busy that I can't offer a home to a couple of kiddies,' replied Ellen. 'A boy and a girl I think, don't you, Sally? Perhaps a brother and sister. It'll take me back to the time when our Rachel and Georgie were little . . .' Ellen smiled reminiscently. 'I doubt if we could cope with any more than two.'

'Yes, I think that's about right,' agreed Sally. 'A boy and a girl . . .' She was pensive for a moment. Yes, she liked the idea very much.

'Of course, we haven't asked George yet, have we?' said Ellen. 'Here we are making all these decisions, and we haven't asked the opinion of the man of the house.'

'Oh, we don't need to worry about him,' replied Sally, smiling confidently. 'You know as well as I do, Mam, that George is only too happy to go along with whatever we decide to do.'

4

Sally knew that her husband was by no means a 'yes man', but that he was usually amenable and ready to fall in with suggestions, particularly those concerning the home. At work it was a rather different matter. George had plenty to say with regard to the running of Hobson's rock factory. This had, in the past, caused more than a few sparks to fly between him and his brother-in-law, Harry Balderstone. But that was history now and the two men worked quite amicably together. Following the disastrous fire at their Euston Street premises they had started again, early in 1924, at a brand new factory on Elizabeth Street. It was round about the same time that they had acquired their second shop on Bank Hey Street, near the Tower, strategically placed to catch the trade from holidaymakers going to and from Central Station, just as their Dickson Road shop was a favourite popping-in place for those visitors using North Station at the other end of the town.

'Er . . . as a matter of fact, I've already mentioned the subject of evacuees to George,' Sally went on. 'I was asking him if he thought it might be too much for you,' she hastened to add, not wanting her mother-in-law to think they were taking matters into their own hands without consulting her. 'But he said just what you have said, that you would be only too delighted at the idea. And George thinks it's a splendid idea as well.'

'Hmmm . . . So you'd got it all cut and dried, had you?' said Ellen with a touch of asperity. But the smile on her lips and the twinkle in her eyes showed Sally that there was no malice in the older woman's words.

There never was. Sally knew that she was blessed, indeed, to have a mother-in-law such as Ellen. She had taken to her straight away when they had been introduced, way back in 1923, and when George and Sally had married the following year they had been happy to make their home with her.

The house in King Street, near to the town centre of Blackpool, had been far too big at that time for just Ellen and George. But Sally knew that the place held many happy memories for Ellen and that was why she had never wanted to move to somewhere smaller. It was the house she had bought in 1904 when, as a young widow, she had moved from Preston to Blackpool. She had lived there with her two children, Rachel and George, and her mother, Lydia; and then with her second husband, Ben. He had died, very tragically, soon after the war ended, so Sally had never met him. She wished that she had. She had heard so much about him and he sounded to have been a quite remarkable man. Sally knew that the memory of him was still very much alive in Ellen's heart and mind.

George and Sally had not intended, at first, to stay in King Street for ever. They had every intention of buying a place of their own, but somehow the years had gone by and they had not done so. The old adage about two women in one kitchen was not true of Sally and Ellen. They got on very well together, two busy women sharing the household tasks with a little help from a daily cleaning woman. And after Sally's own parents had died a few years ago – neither of them had ever fully recovered from losing their only son in the Great War – Sally and Ellen had grown closer than ever. Often when George was out of an evening, as he was tonight at his Liberal Club, the two of them spent a happy couple of hours together, knitting, listening to the wireless or just quietly chatting.

The years had been kind to Ellen, on the whole. Her fair hair had turned almost entirely to grey and she had lost a little weight. Probably because she was so very active, thought Sally, although Ellen had always been of a slight build. But her warm brown eyes were still as sparkling and alert as ever and she had not lost the spring in her step and her general air of enthusiasm. Sally did so wish that she would take things a little more easily – there were times when she looked very tired – but it was no use trying to tell Ellen that. She had worked hard all her life and, as she frequently said, it was what kept her going.

As for Sally, she felt that she, too, had not changed very much over the years. Her mirror told her that her curly auburn hair was a little less bright than when she had first met George. There was a sprinkling of grey there, which was only to be expected, she supposed, as she approached the age of forty. She had put on a little weight, to her consternation, and it showed most particularly in her plump cheeks and the dimple which appeared when she smiled, which she did, quite a lot. Her blue eyes were still clear and bright and she didn't yet need glasses, as George already did for reading. Not that it would worry her overmuch if she did. Nothing worried Sally unduly, and she knew that she was a good complement to her husband, who had always been something of a worrier.

Her biggest disappointment had been that no children had come along to bless their very happy marriage. Sally had no idea why this should be. Heaven knows, they had tried hard enough, especially in the early years, she often thought with wry amusement. But nothing had happened and neither she nor George had bothered to consult a doctor as to the reason why. Neither had they seriously considered adopting children, although the subject had been discussed between them once or twice. But without any serious conviction. The truth was that they were quite contented as they were, with one another, with their busy life and their happy home. And Sally had always taken a great interest in her three nieces, Rachel and Harry's children. She was very fond of Pearl, Ruby and Emmie and she believed that the affection was returned, particularly by Ruby, the middle one, who worked with Sally at one of the family shops on Dickson Road.

'Those bedrooms have been spare for too long,' Sally said now. 'It will be good, won't it, to see them in use again – one of them, at any rate. The small one's just a lumber room, isn't it? Yes, it'll be grand to see a couple of kiddies around the house.'

Sally's and Ellen's eyes met in a look of complete

7

understanding and empathy. Such was the accord between them that each knew exactly what the other was thinking. Sally was becoming aware now of how she had missed having children far more than she had realised. And Ellen knew and understood.

'I'm glad we're both agreed that it's something we would like to do,' said Ellen, 'because even if we didn't like the idea we might very well find that we had no choice in the matter. I was watching them this afternoon, a crowd of poor little mites, being trailed from door to door to see how many the woman of the house would take. In Regent Road it was, not far from here. They may very well be knocking on our door before long. Not tonight, of course, but when the next lot arrive.'

'Good gracious, that sounds dreadful!' exclaimed Sally. 'Poor little kids, being hawked around like that, as though they were parcels or something. Is that the way they're finding homes for the evacuees? Just knocking on doors and asking somebody to take them in?'

'One of the ways, I believe,' said Ellen. 'Or you can go to one of the reception centres yourself and choose your own. I've promised to do a stint myself on Monday – with the WVS, you know – at the Central Methodist Hall, making the kiddies welcome and giving them tea and buns, so I could choose a couple of them at the same time. Perhaps you'd like to come along too, Sally? I'm sure Ruby could manage on her own at the shop for an hour or so, and it's only fair you should be there to make your choice. Dearie me,' Ellen shook her head sorrowfully, 'that sounds awful, doesn't it? Choosing them . . . as though we were choosing a new hat or a coat.'

'You're too sensitive, Mam,' said Sally, smiling fondly at her. 'You can be sure the other women will be doing just the same and there's nothing wrong in trying to find kiddies that we feel would be happy with us. Yes, that's a good idea. I'll come along on Monday. It'll give us the weekend to get things sorted out.'

'Yes, this is just a lumber room,' said Ellen, closing the door of the small room above the front door. 'There are all sorts of odds and ends in there – your sewing and knitting things and George's fishing tackle. There's a single bed in there, though, that we could use if we needed to.'

It was Saturday now, and the evening meal over, Ellen and Sally were getting ready for their expected guests. 'I thought we could use just the small back room,' Ellen went on. 'There are two single beds in there . . .' She frowned thoughtfully. 'D'you think, Sal, if we took a brother and a sister, it would be all right for them to share a room?'

'I'm sure it would.' Sally smiled ruefully. 'If you ask me, some of those kiddies will have been sleeping four to a bed, or even more, where they've come from, Manchester or Liverpool or wherever. Not all of them, of course. You can't lump 'em all together, but I bet some of them'll think they've come to Buckingham Palace, having a whole bed to themselves. To say nothing of a bathroom.'

'Mmm. Yes, of course, I'm sure you're right, Sally love.' Ellen looked thoughtful for a moment. 'D'you know, it sounds dreadful, but sometimes I forget just what it was like to be poor. I've enjoyed my share of this world's goods for quite some time now. More than my fair share, if I'm honest. I feel really guilty about it sometimes, when there's so much poverty elsewhere.'

'I'm sure you don't need to feel guilty, Mam,' Sally told her. 'There are not many people who do as much as you do for those who are less fortunate. And you've worked hard all your life. No one could begrudge you what you've got.'

Ellen leaned against the banister rail, her brown eyes thoughtful. 'Yes, I've worked hard, that's true enough. And my mother before me. I remember when we lived in Preston – such a poor little street it was, Sal, near to the covered market – my sister, Mary, and me, and our mam. It must have been a struggle for her, being left a widow with two children to bring up. But she did it. She earned her living selling sweets on the market, her own home-made sweets. That's how the business started, of course, from that first sweet stall . . .'

Sally smiled to herself as Ellen's eyes grew misty. She had heard it all before, of course, but she wouldn't have dreamed of saying so.

'Yes, we were poor right enough,' Ellen went on. 'Well, comparatively poor, I suppose. There were a lot worse off than we were. But my mother used to say, "It costs nowt to keep clean; all you need is a bit of soap and water." It wasn't easy, mind you. We'd only cold running water. No bathroom and just an outside lav. But there were the public baths round the corner, and Mam insisted that we went there regularly, as well as using the zinc tub in the kitchen. Yes, I'll bet our Mary and me were the two cleanest kids in the neighbourhood.

'D'you know, Sally, you might think I'm dreadful for saying this, but I don't think I could take into the house any children who were dirty. Poor, of course . . . but I would prefer them to be clean.'

Sally nodded. She agreed with Ellen. She would prefer to look after clean kiddies – who wouldn't? – but they would just have to wait and see. Sally, who came originally from the Oldham area, as a child had seen a good deal of poverty in the surrounding streets and at the school she attended. But she had been considered to be 'quite well off' because her parents owned their own business – a newsagent's shop which also sold sweets and tobacco. She had worked there before she met George, and her knowledge of the retail trade had been a good help when she later started to work for Hobson's.

'Well, let's hope we can find some kiddies to suit us,' said Sally. She knew that it was a gamble taking strangers into one's home, but what else could they do? There was a war on, or there would be before very long, and they all had to play their part. For the first time since she had made the decision Sally began to feel a tremor of apprehension – which she immediately quelled by thinking of all those poor little children, miles away from their homes and families, all wanting somebody to love and care for them.

'Come on,' she said now, opening the door of the spare room that Ellen had indicated. 'Let's get these beds made up, then we'll be ready for them on Monday, or maybe before if they come knocking on our door.'

'Are you and George not going out tonight?' asked Ellen, as they spread the clean sheets over one of the beds.

'No, not tonight,' replied Sally. 'I don't think either of us are in the mood for picture-going.' They sometimes went to the cinema on a Saturday evening, when the week's work was finished. Ellen sometimes accompanied them, but more often she preferred to stay at home reading or listening to the wireless. Sally knew that her mother-in-law, ever tactful, was giving them the chance to be on their own, to relive the days when they were courting or newly married.

'No, I don't think any of us are in the mood for enjoying ourselves, are we?' replied Ellen. 'Not until we know what's in store for us – and they'll be telling us that in the morning. I never would have believed it could happen again, not so soon.'

Ellen had said that so many times over the past few days, and Sally noticed that her eyes were sad as she stared unfocusedly out of the bedroom window, her hand clutching tightly at the winceyette sheet. Sally guessed that she was remembering Ben, her dearly loved husband, who had survived the war, but who, nevertheless, had been a victim of that terrible conflict. Just as she, Sally, couldn't help thinking about her brother Billy. Memories of loved ones had become particularly poignant over the last day or two as the inevitable climax grew nearer. Sally had found herself wondering just what the future would have in store for them all.

'Come on, Mam,' she said now. 'There's no time to stand

brooding.' She straightened the sheet, then proceeded to hump one of the pillows into its pillow case. She grinned cheerfully at Ellen. 'Let's finish getting ready for our visitors. I wonder what they'll be like? Exciting, isn't it?'

Chapter 2

Gloria Mulligan dipped the nib of her pen in the inkwell, then she began to write, painstakingly copying in 'real writing' on to the sheet of lined paper the list that the teacher had chalked on the blackboard.

Clothing required: a warm coat or mackintosh; skirt or gymslip (it also said 'trousers' as half of the class were boys, but the teacher had told them to use their common sense, 'if you have any', and to write only just what applied to them); pullover or cardigan; blouse; two pairs of knickers; two pairs of socks; four handkerchieves . . .

Gloria's pen nib spluttered and made a bit of a splodgy mess which she quickly blotted with the pink blotting paper. The children of Standard Two had only recently started writing in ink, just a few weeks before the long summer holiday from which they had just returned. Less than perfect work, therefore, was only to be expected; even so, untidiness was frowned upon by Miss Butler, their strict teacher. This missive, however, was not for her eyes; it was to be taken home and given to the parents. Gloria gave a little sigh as she started to write again, well imagining the response she would get when she presented the list to her mam.

'Night attire', she continued to write. (She supposed that meant pyjamas or a nightdress, neither of which she possessed; she slept in her vest and knickers.) Brush and comb; facecloth (goodness, the list was endless!); toothbrush; spare pair of shoes, if possible.

It was a good job Miss Butler had added the words 'if

possible', thought Gloria, glancing down at her black lace-up shoes – her only pair – which were scuffed and broken down at the heel, and the soles of which were worn right through. She did have a pair of shabby wellies though, which she wore in the rain – very frequent rain in Manchester – so she supposed she could take those.

'Gas mask to be carried', it said at the end of the first list. But on the adjoining blackboard there was a second list, this time of suggestions of food for the journey.

Egg or cheese sandwiches; packet of nuts or raisins; dry biscuits with cheese; apple or orange; barley sugar (this was supposed to be better than chocolate).

When she had finished, Gloria put down her pen in the ridge at the top of the desk and watched her friend, Wendy, the other occupant of the double desk. It always took Wendy longer to finish her work. She was as neat and precise with her schoolwork as she was in her appearance. Gloria was slightly envious of her friend's shining blonde hair, well brushed and formed into two tidy plaits, each finished off with a navy-blue ribbon to match the colour of the school uniform. Not that the headmaster and teachers fussed too much about the wearing of school uniform. They knew it was no use as only a few of the more well-off families could afford it. Wendy Cooper belonged to one of those families. Gloria didn't waste too much time and energy, however, in envying her friend. She liked her too much for that and she had learned ages ago, even though she was only eight years old, to accept things as they were.

To accept her lank, dark brown hair – not long enough to plait, as Wendy's was – which often felt itchy because it wasn't washed as frequently as it should be. She had been made to have it cut short earlier that year, when she was in Standard One, because the visiting nurse, 'Nitty Norah', had discovered that she had these little creatures living in her hair. Gloria hadn't been the only one in her class, not by any means, but there had been no end of a fuss made by Mrs

Cooper, Wendy's mother, that lady insisting that her daughter could no longer sit next to the scruffy child she insisted was her 'best friend'. That was several months ago, however, and as Miss Butler, the teacher of Standard Two, hadn't been informed of the edict, the two girls had drifted back together. And Gloria's hair had grown, almost to her shoulders, and was feeling itchy again.

She knew that her mam was fighting a losing battle – she had often heard her say so – against poverty and grime, hampered by a husband who coughed up only as much of his weekly wage as he felt inclined. To hear her mother talk it had been an uphill struggle throughout her married life, and she had been married twice. The older children of the first marriage, to a builder's labourer, who had died when a wall collapsed on him, were all married now and living in their own homes; except for Frankie, Gloria's fifteen-year-old brother who was a telegraph boy. Then there was Arthur, only a few months younger, who was a grocer's assistant. Arthur was not Gloria's real brother, though. He was her stepbrother, the son of Bill Mulligan. Bill had married her mother a long time ago. Gloria wasn't sure just when; she only knew that Bill wasn't her real father – although she called him Dad and had taken his name – and that she didn't much care for him. There were three younger children now, two girls aged three and two, and a baby boy of six months. So Gloria came right in the middle, between the married and working ones and the babies. She felt at times as though she were something of a misfit, as though she didn't really belong at all . . . but she couldn't have explained why.

She just knew that this was the way things were and she had to put up with them. She had to put up with her shabby clothing, the stodgy, uninteresting food her mother dished up, the bed – often smelling of urine – that she shared with her two little sisters, and the feeling that her mother thought she was rather a nuisance.

Gloria felt far happier at school than she did at home,

even though their new teacher, Miss Butler, seemed stricter than most. School was exciting. Gloria loved learning new things. All about kings who had lived ages ago; how King Canute had tried to hold back the sea, and how another king, one called Alfred, had burned the cakes. About other countries, far, far away, where people with black and yellow skins lived. She loved adding up columns of figures, multiplying and dividing and reciting tables, and writing compositions in a red exercise book. Gloria knew that the teachers considered her to be a clever little girl. Her last teacher had told her mother so on a rare occasion when Mrs Mulligan had visited the school.

'Bloody hell, I hope not!' had been the woman's reaction. 'I can't be doing with kids that are too big for their boots. She'll have to work for a living soon as she's old enough, like all t'others have had to do. We've no money for fancy schooling, I can tell you, miss!'

And at school, of course, there was Wendy. Gloria and Wendy had been friends ever since they were in the babies' class; only at school, of course, because they didn't visit one another's homes. Well, Gloria had been once to Wendy's home, ages ago, but she hadn't been invited again. Her friend had finished writing now and turned to speak to her, in a whisper, because they weren't supposed to talk in class.

'When d'you think we'll be going, to be 'vacuated?'

Gloria shrugged. 'Dunno. Can't be today, can it, 'cause we haven't got all this stuff, have we?' She pointed to the list. 'P'raps it'll be tomorrow.'

'I don't want to go, do you?' Wendy's pale blue eyes looked fearful and Gloria knew that her friend might well be experiencing some qualms at leaving her comfortable home and her doting parents.

As for Gloria, she felt no such trepidation. 'Oh, I don't know,' she answered. 'I think it might be quite exciting, going on a train. I've never been on a train. Anyroad, we'll be together, won't we?' She nudged her friend. 'You and me.

16

Don't worry, Wendy. I'll look after you. We'll tell 'em – we want to stay together.'

'Gloria Mulligan and Wendy Cooper, stop that talking at once!' The teacher's authoritative voice broke into their chatter. 'You know I don't allow talking in class . . . although I suppose there might be some excuse at the moment,' she added, a little more gently. 'I expect you're all wondering about the evacuation. Well, I don't know when it'll be any more than you do. All I know is that we have to be prepared, and we have to practise so that we'll all know what to do when the time comes.

'Right, Standard Two, put your pens down whether you've finished or not and line up at the door.'

They filed to the cloakroom and put on their coats, as they had done the day before. Then they marched, with their teachers at the side, barking instructions, two by two in crocodile form, through the streets of Salford. Not as far as Victoria Station, which would be their ultimate destination, but far enough to ensure that they knew how to cross roads safely and walk in an orderly fashion.

Turbanned women in flowered pinnies came to the doors of the houses that opened directly on to the street, waving to the children.

'They're going, see. Aah . . . bless 'em. Look at 'em, poor little mites.'

'Aye, it's enough to make you weep, i'n't it?'

'Hey up . . . Our Peter'll be among that lot.' One woman dashed from her doorstep, running frantically alongside the line of children. 'Where the devil is he? They might've told us!'

'Don't be so daft, Alice.' Her next-door neighbour caught hold of her arm. 'They're not going. They've not got no luggage, look – only their gas masks.'

'That's right, madam,' said one of the teachers, in passing. 'It's not today; it's just a practice.'

'But p'raps tomorrow it'll be for real,' said Gloria. She

17

took hold of her friend's arm as they turned back towards the school, unable to suppress a tremor of excitement.

'And how the bleedin' hell are we expected to find this lot?' Daisy Mulligan stabbed angrily at the list that Gloria presented to her, as the child had feared she would. 'Do yer teachers think that money grows on trees? I'd like to see them bring up half a dozen kids on a few bob a week. God knows how I'm going to find all this. We'll have to see if yer dad can scrounge some odds and ends off them posh folk he collects from.'

Bill Mulligan was a bin-man and, from time to time, brought home booty that had been left near the dustbins to be taken away. An umbrella with only one or two broken spokes; chipped enamel saucepans; a set of brass fire-irons; and a wireless set which only needed new batteries – these were some of Bill's recent finds. As Daisy said, some folks had more money than sense, chucking out good stuff like that. And a few of the women had, occasionally, given him clothing that their own children had grown out of.

'And what the hell's this?' Gloria looked anxiously at her mother as she scrutinised the second list. 'Egg sandwiches, cheese and biscuits, barley sugar . . . Holy Mother of God! What do they think this is – the bloody Co-op café? You'll take jam and bread, my girl, and like it. Don't suppose you know when you're going, do you?'

'No, Mam, they didn't say.'

'No, they wouldn't. They tell us nowt. They're keepin' us in t'dark, like they always do. Anyroad, I don't suppose it's your fault.' She looked a little more kindly now at the child – as kindly as Daisy was capable of looking, which wasn't saying much – shoving the lists into her apron pocket. 'Get yer coat off, then you can peel them spuds for yer dad and the lads while I nip out to t'shop. Yer dad'll murder me if I forget his tomato ketchup again. And keep yer eye on them two. Baby's asleep, thank God . . .'

18

Gloria cast a cursory glance at her two little sisters before she went into the scullery to begin her daily chore. Rose and Lily seemed contented enough playing on the rag rug with an assortment of building bricks and rusting toy cars; more of the bin-man's spoils. They were both rather silent children – it wasn't often that anyone spoke to them much, except for Gloria – with the same sandy hair and watery blue eyes as their father, and the same lumpish features. Not much like the flowers for which they had been named; but neither was their mother, Daisy, much like her namesake. The very few photographs that Gloria had seen showed that her mother had once been slim and quite pretty. Now she was fat, with a shapeless drooping bosom, and her once black hair was almost entirely grey, wispy and as untidy as a bird's nest. Gloria didn't know how old her mother was; such things were never mentioned. But as their Monica, the eldest daughter, was twenty-five – Gloria had overheard that – then she supposed her mam must be forty-something or other. All Gloria knew was that her mam looked a lot older than most of her friends' mothers, easily as old as Wendy's gran who sometimes came to meet her friend from school.

Gloria also knew that she, herself, wasn't 'much of a Gloria'. She had heard an outspoken aunt say so to her mother, ages ago, and though she hadn't known exactly what the woman meant, the remark had hurt. Gloria's mam had told her that she had been called after a famous film star . . . But as the child stared now at her reflection in the broken mirror behind the sink – her dad washed and shaved there – she realised that what her Aunt Molly had said was true. Film stars didn't have nasty greasy hair – itchy hair – that hung down like rat's tails, neither did they wear blouses with frayed collars and jumpers with holes in the elbows. She bet that Shirley Temple didn't. Gloria had seen her once on a rare visit to a Saturday matinée, but she had been unimpressed by the little girl's saucy smiles and shining sausage curls. She looked what Gloria's mam called a 'proper little madam', and it was Gloria's opinion that she thought she was 'it'. I bet she doesn't have to peel the spuds, she thought now, plunging her hands into the mucky water in the sink, but there was very little rancour in her musing. This was just the way things were and she had to get on with it. Besides, maybe tomorrow or the day after, she might be getting away from all this.

Her dad said nothing about the lists she had brought home from school, and Gloria guessed that her mother hadn't told him yet. He said very little anyway when he came home after a day on the bins. He was usually surly and uncommunicative, unless he had had a spectacular find. Gloria tried to keep well out of his way whilst his wife fussed around getting the menfolk's dinner on the table. Bill Mulligan, Frankie and Arthur dined separately, after Daisy and the younger children had finished their tea of bread and jam. They had a dinner of sorts at midday, when Gloria came home from school, but it was invariably a makeshift sort of meal, nothing to compare with the hefty spread produced for the men of the house, the workers.

Gloria knew that her mam would have to ask her dad about the clothes sooner or later, because she wanted him to scrounge off those posh ladies he visited, although there was precious little time left; they might be going in a day or two. Perhaps she was waiting till he was in a more affable mood, as he might be when he returned from the pub. That was where Bill Mulligan had gone after he had finished his meal of sausage, beans and chips, smothered in tomato sauce and swilled down with two cups of strong tea, and had had a read of his evening paper and smoked a couple of Wills Woodbines. It was where he went every evening without fail.

Daisy did, however, mention the list to Monica when she came round later that evening. Monica was the eldest of Daisy's children, although she wasn't a Mulligan. She had been a Reardon, which was the name of Daisy's first husband; now she was Monica O'Brien and she had two children of her own. She often visited her mother of an evening as she lived only a couple of streets away.

'Hi there, kid,' Monica greeted Gloria, as she trundled the huge black pram containing her two sleeping boys into the already crowded living room, always referred to as the 'kitchen'. 'Here y'are. Don't say I never give you nowt.' She tossed a copy of last week's *Dandy* comic into Gloria's lap. 'Gerry's finished with it, so you might as well mek use of it. I know you like books, don't you, kid?'

Gloria nodded and smiled. 'Yes. Ta very much, Monica.'

The *Dandy*, the favourite reading matter of Monica's husband, could hardly be classed as a book, thought Gloria. It certainly didn't compare with the books they had read at school as class readers, like *Peter Pan* and *Alice's Adventures in Wonderland*, or even with the Enid Blyton books; she knew her friend, Wendy, had a whole shelf-ful of those. But it was better than nothing, she reflected, settling down in the depths of the sagging armchair to enjoy the latest doings of Korky the Cat and Keyhole Kate. She wasn't fully engrossed though – it didn't take much concentration to 'read' the pictures and the words in the balloons – and more than half of her attention was centred on the conversation going on between her mother and Monica.

'You've managed to get 'em off then?'

'Aye, them two don't need much rocking. I'll pop 'em straight into t'cot as soon as I get back. They'll not even know they've been moved.' Monica sat down at the kitchen table and lit a cigarette, then she tossed the almost empty packet to her mother. 'Here y'are, Mam, it's the last one . . . Little 'uns in bed, are they?'

Gloria's mother nodded. 'They are, thank the Lord.' She, too, lit a cigarette and took a long drag. 'His Lordship's gorra darts match and I dunno where t'lads are. Off gallivanting somewhere or other. There's only 'er here.' She jerked her thumb in Gloria's direction. 'And she won't be here for much longer,' she added, mouthing the words behind her cupped hand. As though I'm stupid or something, thought Gloria, her eyes ostensibly glued to the page. Does she think I'm deaf, or daft?

'Here, tek a look at this.' Daisy delved into her apron pocket, then tossed the two sheets of paper, now very crumpled, across the table to her daughter. 'Brought it home from school today, 'er did. They've got a cheek, I must say, them teachers.'

'What's this, Mam?' Monica blew a smoke ring, then tapped the ash into a saucer on which rested a cup half full of cold tea; the table had not yet been cleared after the evening meal. Her eyes rapidly scanned the page, then she looked curiously at her mother. 'You're letting her go then?'

Gloria lifted her eyes momentarily from Korky the Cat to look at her sister. Monica's pencilled eyebrows were raised questioningly and her red-lipsticked mouth was set in a tight line.

'Looks as though I've no choice, don't it?' said Gloria's mother. 'I reckon they'll all be going. It's that lot as I'm bothered about.' She pointed to the offending list. 'How the hell do they expect us to find—'

'Never mind that, Mam.' Monica shook her turbanned head dismissively. 'I'll help you out with that – you know I will, if I can. But you could've talked it over with me first. Poor little mite. Have you thought of what it'll be like for her, being sent away from home?'

'She'll be all right. All her pals'll be going and she's a tough little kid, you know she is. She won't come to no 'arm. And she might do if she stayed 'ere. It'll be for t'best, our Monica . . .'

Daisy stopped, casting a wary glance towards Gloria, who quickly lowered her eyes again to the pages of her comic. 'Gloria, nip into t'back kitchen, there's a good lass, and put t'kettle on. Mek us a fresh cup of tea, and see if you can find some of them Nice biscuits. They're in the Coronation tin, I think.'

Gloria obeyed without demur. She knew they wanted her out of the way because they were talking about something private. As if that would stop her from listening! They must think I'm stupid, she thought again, lighting the gas, then filling the whistling kettle and taking the mugs from the pot cupboard as quietly as she could, all the while with one ear cocked towards the open door. Gloria's hearing was as acute as an animal's, but they didn't seem to realise that.

'Anyroad, don't you start telling me what I must do and what I mustn't do,' her mother was going on. 'I've had it up to here, I can tell you, with all this lot.' Gloria could imagine her mother putting her hand to her head. 'An' it'll be one less mouth to feed. Eat me out of house and home, they do.'

Gloria opened the rusty tin with the picture of King George and Queen Elizabeth on the lid and the two little Princesses on the side, and took out the half-eaten packet of biscuits. Her mam had called them 'nice' biscuits, as though that was what they were; biscuits that tasted nice. But Gloria knew that you should say 'nees', all posh, like her Aunt Molly tried to talk. She had heard her aunt correct her mam once about the biscuits and her mam had told her to, 'Mind yer own bloody business. I'll talk 'ow I like, you stuck-up cow!' That was why Gloria remembered.

'What about the rest of 'em?' Monica was asking. 'Our Rose and Lily and t'little 'un? Are they going an' all?'

'Don't talk so daft, our Monica! How can kids of two and three go, and a six-month-old babby? Use yer loaf, girl.'

'Hold on, Mam, don't jump down me bloody throat. I was going to say that you could go with 'em, couldn't you? I've heard as how whole families are going. Well, the women and kids anyroad. I was thinking I might go meself for a bit of an 'oliday. We might get sent to the seaside. That 'ud be nice.'

'Don't talk so daft,' said Daisy again. 'How the hell can I go? It's all right for you if you want to go gallivanting off. Your Gerry's too soft with you, but I've got His Lordship to see to and them two lads. No, I'll have me work cut out here, an' if that Hitler starts dropping his bloomin' bombs, well, I reckon we'll just have to take a chance, won't we, same as lots of other folk? At least she'll be out o' t'way. I thought you'd be glad about that. I know you're fond of her,' she added grudgingly.

'Aye, happen it's for the best.' Monica sounded thoughtful.

Gloria decided it was time to make her reappearance. She hadn't heard much that she hadn't heard before. She knew about the bombs. The kids at school had all been talking about how the Germans would start dropping bombs as soon as the war started. But Gloria knew that it wasn't really because she was concerned about her safety that her mother was sending her away; it was because she would be glad to get rid of her, although Gloria wasn't sure why. Don't care! thought Gloria defiantly. I shall be bloomin' glad to get away from here, from the whole flippin' lot of 'em. No, that wasn't quite true. She would miss their Monica. Monica was the only one who seemed to care two hoots about her. Not that she was all that lovey dovey with her – they were not that sort of a family – but her big sister gave her a comic or a packet of sweets now and again, and a card on her birthday, which was more than the others did.

Gloria put the tin tray down on the table, clearing a space amidst the debris of the evening meal, then handed a mug of tea each to her mother and sister, at the same time proffering the half-packet of biscuits. She knew there was no point in putting them on a plate, all posh, like her Aunt Molly did. Her mother would only accuse her of making 'more bloody washing up'.

'Thanks, kid,' said Monica, without even glancing at her, and her mother took the offerings with not a word of thanks. Gloria cast them both a baleful look, which went unnoticed, as she flopped into the armchair again with a Nice biscuit and a mug only half full of dandelion and burdock. It was the last drop in the bottle and had gone flat, but there didn't seem to be another bottle. Daisy often forgot to buy the things that she knew were Gloria's favourites. Gloria kept very quiet and still and she moved on to the doings of Pansy Potter (the strong man's daughter). If she made her presence felt her mam might send her off to bed and she wanted to know what was going on, especially if they were talking about her.

'I can let you have a bob or two to help with this lot, Mam,' Monica was saying. 'At least you could buy the kid a new gaberdine – well, new second-hand, you know what I mean, from Mickey's market stall. And I'll ask Connie next door if she's got any bits and pieces that Betty's grown out of. She's a year or so older than our Gloria.'

'Aye, thanks, lass. That'll be a help.' Daisy sounded distracted. 'An' I'll have to ask His Lordship to do a bit of scrounging an' all. I'm waiting till he's in a better mood. He hadn't half got the hump at tea-time, I can tell you. Don't know what's up with 'im, I'm sure.'

'Happen it's all this talk of war. It's getting to all of us, isn't it? Nobody seems to talk about owt else these days. D'you think he'll have to go, if it happens?'

'What . . . Bill? Shouldn't think so. Surely not! He's forty-six, y'know – he's a year or two older than me – an' he was in the last lot. One bloody war's enough in any man's lifetime, isn't it? I dunno though . . .' Daisy stared thoughtfully into space. 'It 'ud give me a bit o' peace, wouldn't it? I've told 'im, if he gets me up the spout again . . . What about your Gerry? He'll have to go, won't he?'

'Bloody hell, Mam! They'll be hard up if they take him, won't they? He wouldn't know which way up to hold his bloomin' rifle.'

'He's the right age though, our Monica. They take all sorts when there's a war on. They have to. An' I don't know why you've always got to be so flamin' rude about him. He's a good lad is Gerry O'Brien, I've always said so. Catholic lad an' all. He married you, didn't he, when he knew your Sam was on the way? That's more than that other 'un was prepared to do.'

'All right, Mam. Leave it alone, can't you?' Gloria held her comic up in front of her face as Monica glanced in her direction. 'You never let it rest, do you? I know Gerry's a good husband, as husbands go. A darned sight better than the one you've got anyroad, Mam. At least the lads and me don't go short of much. He might not have to go, come to think of it, with him being at the mill. They'll have 'em making uniforms, won't they?'

'Huh! They'll have t'women doing it, more like, same as they did in the last lot. The womenfolk were damn near running the country till the fellows came back, and it'll be the same again, you mark my words. And to think they said it was the war to end all wars. A fat lot they know, them bloomin' politicians. Anyroad, our Frankie and young Arthur are not old enough to go, thank the Lord. And we'll have to pray to the Holy Mother that it'll all be over before they are.'

Gloria became aware of a sanctimonious tone creeping into her mother's voice. She lowered her comic and, peering over the top of it, saw Daisy cast her eyes in the direction of the statuette of the Virgin Mary which held pride of place on the cluttered sideboard. Surrounded by the mess and muddle of day-to-day living – piles of ironing, undarned socks, tarnished photo frames and chipped ornaments, a cracked fruit bowl containing a wizened apple and two blackened bananas, and a pottery jug stuffed to overflowing with keys, pencils, string, sealing wax, odds and ends of wool, and unpaid bills – the Madonna smiled serenely from beneath the folds of her bright blue gown. She was reverently dusted each day, whatever else around her might be ignored, and piously appealed to in times of crisis or despair. Like now.

'You think it'll happen then, Mam? It's not just a lot of eyewash? You know, them trying to put the wind up us?' Monica's eyes, clear grey, like Gloria's, were fearful as she, too, glanced at the statue of the Virgin, then at her mother.

'It'll happen, sure as eggs are eggs.' Daisy nodded grimly. 'Let's just hope it doesn't go on as long as the last bloody lot did. Come on, lass, you can give us a hand with these pots before you take the lads home. It's like washing up after a bloomin' army. And you, 'op it.' She nodded curtly in Gloria's direction, pointing her thumb towards the door. 'Up the wooden hill. Let's be having you.'

Gloria closed her comic and got up without any argument. 'G'night, Mam. G'night, Monica.' She didn't make any move to kiss them or anything like that. They didn't go in for that sort of soppy stuff in her family, as she knew Wendy's family did.

'Goodnight, lass.' Her mother was already halfway into the kitchen with a laden tray and didn't even glance at her.

But Monica smiled at her, rather sadly, her grey eyes looking the tiniest bit moist. 'Goodnight, lovey. Take care of yerself.'

Glora nodded back at her. 'All right, Mon. See yer.'

Monica had been quite nice to her tonight, Gloria thought. She pulled off her skirt and blouse and, still wearing her vest and knickers, climbed into the double bed at the other end from Rose and Lily. They slept top to tail, the three of them, and Gloria had to position her legs carefully between the legs of the two little ones. Yes, she would miss Monica more than any of the others . . . and Sam and Len, Monica's two little boys. They were quite good fun, much more lively than Rose and Lily.

Gloria gabbled a quick prayer for her family, trying to include them all. But her mind soon wandered. Maybe tomorrow, or the next day, she would be leaving them behind.

Chapter 3

It was Monday, 4 September, before the children from Gloria's school embarked on their great adventure. At least, that was what it was to Gloria although she knew that many of her class-mates didn't see it that way.

'Stay with me. You won't leave me, will you, Glor, me and our Michael? Mummy says Michael and me have to stay together.' Wendy's pale blue eyes, to Gloria's concern – and slight exasperation – were filling up with tears again. She had been crying on and off since they arrived at Victoria Station. Now, some ten minutes into the journey, squashed in the window seat next to Gloria, she was still at it.

''Course I'll stay with yer, and your kid. I'll look after yer. I've promised, haven't I?' said Gloria, squeezing her friend's arm again. 'Only . . . for God's sake, stop yelling, Wendy.'

Wendy's brother, five-year-old Michael, sitting opposite her, didn't seem nearly so worried. He turned his wide blue eyes, just like his sister's, upon Gloria now. 'It's *her* that has to look after me, Mummy says.' He pointed a thumb in Wendy's direction. 'Our Wendy, not you, Gloria Mulligan. Mummy doesn't like you. She says you're mucky and you'll give our Wendy nits and she hasn't to—'

'Shut up you, our Michael!' Wendy landed out with her foot, daintily clad in a black patent leather ankle-strap shoe, kicking her brother none too gently on the shin. 'I'm staying with Gloria. She's me friend. Anyway, Mummy's not here.' The words caught in her throat and, to Gloria's horror, she started to sob in earnest, worse than before.

'Oh, come on, kid.' Gloria put an arm right round her friend. 'It won't be so bad, you'll see. It'll be fun. I wonder where we'll be going? They haven't told us yet, have they? 'Ere . . .' She delved into the brown-paper carrier at her feet and drew out a crumpled bag. ' 'Ave an 'umbug. Our Monica gave 'em to me. D'you want one, Michael?' she added, though a trifle reluctantly, and she didn't smile at him.

His words had hurt her although she wouldn't show it. Gloria knew only too well Mrs Cooper's opinion of her. She had known it ever since she and Wendy had been in the babies' class. Wendy, though, to give her her due, had never let her mother's attitude influence her at all. She had still clung to Gloria even this morning amidst the milling throng at the station, in spite of Mrs Cooper's awesome presence. That lady always acted as though she had a nasty smell under her nose whenever she set eyes on Gloria and she had acted no differently today. She had said very little, however, no doubt not wanting to upset her precious little daughter even more.

Gloria couldn't help but feel peeved that her own mother was nowhere to be seen. They hadn't been told which day they were going, so she supposed there was some excuse. Nevertheless, word had been passed round the maze of little streets surrounding the school that 'today's the day'; and a lot of the mothers had appeared at the school or at the railway station, many still wearing aprons and with curling pins under their turbans.

For three days – Thursday, Friday and today, Monday – Gloria and her class-mates had carried their luggage to school. Most of the items on the list had been procured, one way or another, by Mrs Mulligan and bundled into a carrier bag. The string had cut into Gloria's fingers as they tramped through the streets to Victoria Station and her gas mask, in its cardboard box, bounced rhythmically against her legs. It was quite good fun at first when, on arriving at school, they

29

were issued with luggage labels to tie round their necks – like parcels – and they realised they were actually going at last. But Wendy was turning out to be such a pain – nobody else in their class was making so much blooming fuss – and Gloria had been glad that parents were allowed no further than the barrier. Then, just as Wendy was being prised from her mother's neck by a harassed teacher, Monica had arrived, trundling her huge black pram with two jammy-faced infants inside, right into the middle of the mêlée.

' 'Ere y'are, kid. Be a good lass, won't yer, and take care of yerself.' There had been time only for Monica to shove a bag of sweets into her hand and give her a quick peck on the cheek – most unusual, this – but Gloria had been glad to see her. At least there was someone who cared about her, if only a little.

'Suck yer 'umbug and look out of the window,' Gloria said now to her friend. Thankfully Wendy's tears subsided a little as the sweet was rolled round and round in her mouth. 'Look – them's cows in that field. I've seen 'em before, of course,' Gloria added nonchalantly. She had, in fact, seen these creatures only a couple of times before, on infrequent Sunday School outings to the plains of Cheshire.

' 'Course they're cows. Anybody knows that!' chirped up Michael. 'We've seen 'em millions of times, haven't we, Wendy?' Wendy nodded glumly, but she did seem to be taking more interest in the scenery now. 'Bet you've never been on a train before, have you, Gloria Mulligan?' Michael went on. 'We have, haven't we, Wendy? Millions of times.'

Gloria didn't reply, although it was true that she had never travelled on a train before – the Sunday School treats had been on charabancs – and she was finding it very exciting. She knew, though, that the churned-up feeling in her tummy was not due entirely to excitement. She wouldn't want to admit it, but she was just a teeny bit frightened. She had never been away from home before, and though the folks there largely ignored her, it was still . . . home. That was why she had been so pleased to see their Monica. Gloria had promised she would take care of Wendy, but she did wish, deep down, that there was someone who would take care of her.

Stoically she sucked her minty sweet and looked out of the window. They had now left Manchester far behind and a place called Bolton – Gloria had heard of that before – and were bowling along through open countryside. Mile upon mile of green fields, stretching in every direction, with here and there a patch of darker green formed by a clump of trees silhouetted against the blue sky. Gloria had never imagined there could be so much green in the whole world. She remembered when she had been in the Infant School a favourite teacher telling them that green must be God's favourite colour because it was the colour He had chosen to paint most of His world. Gloria hadn't really believed it because she hadn't seen it for herself. Salford was all grey – grey streets and pavements, grey slated roofs and thick grey smoke belching from chimneys – and dingy red brick, with just a small area of green at Peel Park, a place Gloria had visited only a couple of times. Now, feasting her eyes upon all this superabundance of greenness she realised that what her teacher had said was true. It was a truly beautiful world.

Here were some more black and white cows, and in the next field a flock of woolly sheep, grazing quietly. A red-roofed farmhouse, a farmer driving a tractor, towering haystacks and a pond around which waddled some fat white geese. Gloria, lost in her own thoughts, was unaware of the chatter of the rest of the children in the compartment as she gazed at all these wondrous sights she was seeing for the first time.

'Now then, we've all settled down, have we?' Miss Butler, their teacher, poked her head round the door. It was a corridor train and the teachers were continually patrolling up and down. Miss Butler's face was red – redder than usual – and sweaty and she was smiling cheerfully. 'I think it would be a good idea if we had a sing-song, don't you? It'll help to pass the time. Now, what shall we have?'

' "Ten Green Bottles", miss . . .'

'No, "Old MacDonald" . . .'

'No, "One Man Went To Mow" . . .'

'All right then – "One Man Went To Mow". And when you've got to ten men, then I think you could all eat your sandwiches. Come on then, let's start: One man went to mow, Went to mow a meadow . . .' Miss Butler began singing in a hearty voice, waving her hand in time to the rhythm, before disappearing into the next compartment. Gloria had never seen her in such a jovial mood, though her voice was shriller than usual and sounded a bit odd, as though she couldn't control it properly.

Soon, hundreds of raucous voices raised in song echoed up and down the train. Then, quite soon afterwards, there was comparative silence as paper packets were opened and sandwiches and biscuits were munched.

'I'll swap you one of mine for one of yours,' said Wendy. She had stopped crying now and was tucking into her sandwiches with some relish, whilst casting sidelong glances at Gloria's feast. 'Mine's salmon paste, some of 'em, and the others are cheese. I like jam butties best, though, but Mummy doesn't let us have them very often.'

'No, she says they're what poor kids have,' chirped up Michael, 'and you've not to say "butty", our Wendy. It's common; that's what Mummy says.'

'And she says you've not to talk with your mouth full neither,' retorted Wendy, scowling at her brother's bulging cheeks. 'Aw, go on.' She turned to her friend. 'Can I have one, Glor?'

''Course you can,' said Gloria, eagerly swapping a 'door-step' into which the plum jam had run, all gooey and messy, for two dainty triangular offerings, one salmon paste and one cheese. Wendy gave her a few nuts and raisins too and a

32

barley-sugar sweet. Obviously Mrs Cooper had obeyed the instructions on the list to the letter.

The children fell silent after they had finished their meal, for the most part staring moodily at their pals sitting opposite and shuffling around in their seats. They still hadn't been told where they were going. Soon after they had passed through Preston Station Miss Butler popped her head into their compartment again.

'Listen, boys and girls, I've got a surprise for you. Guess where we're going?' Her face, red as a boiled beetroot, was beaming and her eyes, behind their steel-framed spectacles, were wide with surprise. 'We're going to Blackpool! Just imagine that! Aren't you lucky boys and girls?'

Even Gloria, who had hardly ever left the environs of Manchester, had heard of Blackpool. She knew there was a tower there, and sea and sand.

'Hurray! Hurray!' Two boys on the seat opposite now started jumping up and down with excitement, cannoning into one another and enjoying an amiable game of fisticuffs, whilst the girls next to Gloria began to tell one another that they'd been to Blackpool before. One had had a ride on a donkey and the other had had a stick of Blackpool rock.

'I've never been, have you?' asked Gloria, turning to her friend. Wendy silently shook her head. 'Ooh, I say, kid, isn't it going to be fun?' But Wendy was staring out of the window. She was sucking her thumb and the tears had started to flow again. Gloria decided it might be best to ignore her.

Soon the green fields gave way to rows of red-brick houses, rather bigger and posher though, Gloria observed, than the ones in Salford. Then they passed through a station called St-Annes-on-Sea, and through gaps in the houses they could actually see the sea in the distance, beyond a vast expanse of grass and sand.

'Them's sandhills,' said a knowledgeable girl sitting next to Gloria. 'I've seen 'em before. And look – that's the Big

Dipper at the Pleasure Beach. I've been on it – it were dead good. Made me feel right sick though.'

Gloria wondered at the sense of this remark. How could you enjoy feeling sick? Then, as she stared at the towering heights of the roller-coaster, a carriage came hurtling down the steep slope. Goodness! Fancy being brave enough to ride on a thing like that! And yet Gloria knew she would like to have a go. She had heard of fairgrounds, of course, but she had never visited one. And this one, at Blackpool, seemed to be enormous. What an exciting place Blackpool must be. Gloria's tummy started to feel all churned up again, but the feeling was not entirely unpleasant. Perhaps that was how you felt riding on the Big Dipper, only more so.

There was a squeal of brakes and a loud hiss of steam as the train finally stopped. They had arrived, and resounding cheers from the children echoed along the corridor. Now was the time for the teachers to start getting all bossy again. The children were pushed, two by two, into a long crocodile, then they marched along the platform, through the barrier and out on to the station forecourt. Then the orderly crocodile broke up as hundreds of pairs of eyes gazed up at the gigantic ironwork structure looming above them. Blackpool Tower!

'Hey, look! Ain't it big?'

'Yeah! 'Normous, i'n't it?'

'Looks as though it's moving.'

'Crikey, yer don't think it's going to fall on us, do yer?'

'Don't be so daft! Will it heck as like!'

'I've seen it before. I've been up it . . .'

The teachers frantically tried to usher their charges into some sort of formation again; but there was yet another diversion as a group of ladies went up and down the line handing each child a stick of rock.

'Hey, look! Mine's pink!'

'Mine's yeller!'

Some of the children's voices were getting louder with excitement, their fears and their homesickness forgotten for the moment in all this welter of new experiences. But Gloria was feeling very quiet now. She smiled at the kind lady and said, 'Ta very much,' then pushed the rock into her bulging carrier bag. When order had been re-established they were on the move again. But they didn't go far; only across the road to a red-brick church behind which there was a Sunday School hall. Ladies in flowered overalls and green hats gave them each a cup of tea and a bun; then they sat on long benches and waited. Waited and waited for someone to choose them; to walk up to them and say, 'Would you like to come and live with me?'

Gloria stared around. This room was very much like ones she had been in before, like her own school, in fact, with green walls and dark brown paintwork and a wooden partition separating it from the room next door. At the front was a table where some ladies were all busy, consulting lists and talking in voices that sounded very posh to Gloria. They weren't taking much notice of the children; nobody seemed to be taking much notice of them at the moment.

Gloria wanted to go to the lav, although she had been once on the train, but she didn't know who to ask. And her legs were feeling all hot and sweaty. Monica had given her a pair of Gerry's socks to wear as her own were all in holes, and they were prickly and uncomfortable. She pulled at the tight elastic garter below her knee; it had left a nasty red mark. It wasn't just her legs that itched; her head, beneath its woolly pixie hood, was itching too. She untied the strings and pulled it off. Then she just sat there, hoping it wouldn't be too long before they all knew where they were going, her and Wendy and little Michael. Michael was a blooming nuisance really – a real clever-clogs – but Gloria knew she would have to put up with him because she had to stay with Wendy. Thank goodness Wendy had stopped crying now, though she was still snivelling a bit, from time to time wiping her coat-sleeve against her nose. Gloria knew that Mrs Snooty Cooper wouldn't approve of that! But Gloria was not all that

35

bothered about Wendy at the moment. She was so very, very tired.

She yawned, opening her mouth wide and not bothering to put her hand in front, as she knew she should. Then she heard a kind voice speaking to her and she looked up. She saw a pretty lady – not a young lady; she looked quite old, in fact, but she was very pretty – with curling greyish hair under a green hat. She was one of the helping ladies and she had warm brown eyes and a lovely smile.

'Hello, dear,' the lady was saying. 'Would you like to come and live with us? And your little brother. He is your brother, isn't he? He looks just like you.'

Then Gloria, to her horror, for the very first time that day felt tears coming into her eyes. Because the nice lady wasn't talking to her at all. She was speaking to Wendy.

Chapter 4

The Sunday morning service at the Methodist chapel that Ellen and her family attended had been shortened so that they could all get home in time to listen to the Prime Minister's broadcast.

'. . . I have to tell you now that no such undertaking has been received and that consequently this country is now at war with Germany.'

Ellen, on hearing the words of Neville Chamberlain, gave an involuntary gasp of horror. They had known what was coming and yet it was a shock. Sally glanced concernedly at her, giving a little sad smile of understanding, then they listened in silence to the rest of the broadcast.

'It is the evil things that we shall be fighting against – brute force, bad faith, injustice, oppression and persecution – and against them I certain that the right will prevail.'

Sally quickly turned off the set. 'So that's it. Now we know.'

'Yes . . . now we know. I always think it's better to know – even to know the worst – than to live with uncertainty.' Ellen glanced apprehensively at her son George. He had hardly spoken since they came home from church and now he was gazing abstractedly into space. Possibly this news had hit him even harder than it had his wife and mother. After all, he had actually been there, had seen for himself the horror of it all. 'Are you all right, Georgie?' Ellen asked, although it was rather a pointless question. And she had used, automatically, the pet name by which he had been known as a little lad – one he now scorned.

'All right, Mam? How the hell can I be all right? How can any of us?' His blue eyes were more puzzled than angry as he stared at her for a moment or two, then rose to his feet. 'I'm going out. I need to clear my head. I'll go and have an hour or two on the jetty.' He turned to his wife. 'You don't mind, do you, Sal?'

'No, of course not, dear.' Sally knew, as Ellen did, that George's quiet, contemplative hobby of fishing, usually from the jetty at the end of North Pier, was a source of comfort to him when he was troubled.

'What about your dinner, though?' asked Ellen. 'We've got a chicken in the oven, haven't we, Sally?'

'It'll keep.' George shook his head a trifle irritably. 'I'll have it at tea-time if I feel like it. Don't worry about me, Mam. I've got to be on my own for a while, all right?' He stood in the kitchen doorway, his broad shoulders and his height of nearly six foot almost filling the space. 'Look, if it'll make you happier I'll take a sandwich. We've got some cheese, haven't we? No, don't fuss . . . I'll make it.'

He almost, but not quite, smiled as he disappeared into the kitchen. Sally shook her head at Ellen, saying under her breath, 'Best to leave him alone, you know what he's like. He'll be as right as rain when he's had some time on his own.'

Ellen nodded. At one time she would have feared that George would bolt to the nearest pub to drown his sorrows. But that was now a thing of the past, and for that she had Sally to thank. 'Let's all have our meal at tea-time, when George comes back,' she said. 'Chicken's just as nice cold, isn't it, and today certainly isn't an ideal day for cooking roast potatoes and three veg. It might have cooled down a bit by this afternoon.'

For Sunday, 3 September, the first day of the war, was a glorious day of cloudless blue skies and hot sunshine. A day on which it was almost impossible to believe that anything awful could happen.

There must have been a couple of hundred children in the hall at first, but they were gradually being thinned out now as they were chosen, in ones and twos, or taken out in small groups to billets where they were expected. It was for all the world like a cattle auction, thought Ellen when she emerged from the kitchen where she had been boiling kettles, filling teapots and putting rock buns on plates, to say nothing of washing up what seemed like hundreds of cups and saucers. She had had little time as yet to observe the children, but now, as she cleared yet more cups and saucers from the trestle tables she took time to look at what was going on. It made a lump come into her throat, watching the kiddies' faces light up with expectancy as they were approached, only to settle into a look of resignation again as they realised that they were not the chosen ones. For it was the prettier little girls – Shirley Temple facsimiles, some of them – who were being picked out; or bigger, sensible-looking boys and girls who gave the impression that they would cause very little trouble . . . or would possibly provide an extra pair of hands in a busy boarding house, wondered Ellen.

Many of the children appeared to be from poor homes. Their clothes were shabby, thick socks wrinkled around skinny ankles and shoes that were scuffed and broken down. A lot of the boys were clutching school caps in their hands, whilst the girls, in spite of the warm day were, in the most part, still wearing woollen berets or hand-knitted pixie hoods. Quite a few, Ellen couldn't help but notice, were far from attractive, with running noses, spotty faces or lank greasy hair. But they all belonged to somebody, she thought, feeling a pang of remorse. There was somebody, somewhere who loved each one of these children. They were all part of some family or other, and now they had been wrenched away from that family and brought here to make their home with complete strangers.

She was watching a little boy and girl – brother and sister, she guessed from their similar appearance – sitting dejectedly at the end of a long form. The girl looked as though she was some two or three years older than her brother, but it was the boy who seemed the less disturbed of the two. The little girl was clearly upset – sad and bewildered and homesick, Ellen surmised – as so many of the children were, although there weren't many now who were actually crying. This child was not weeping openly, just sniffing and rubbing her nose occasionally against her coat-sleeve. Ellen smiled to herself. She guessed this little girl would have a nice clean hanky somewhere – she looked a well-cared for child – perhaps tucked up a knicker-leg, which was a favourite place, but that she was just too weary to retrieve it. The boy was looking anxiously at her, his head on one side, now and then bending forward to say a few words to her – of comfort, maybe, although he looked only five years old or so. He seemed a self-possessed little lad, one who wouldn't be afraid to stick up for himself, although he, too, must be feeling the pang of parting from a loving mum and dad. Ellen guessed they belonged to loving parents. The pair had well-groomed fair hair, the girl's in two plaits, each tied with a neat blue ribbon, and they were wearing matching navy-blue gaberdine rain-coats, stiff with newness, and shiny black shoes.

These two will suit us fine, thought Ellen. She decided she would point these children out to Sally when she arrived. She glanced at the clock on the wall; nearly three o'clock. Sally should be here any time now and she was sure her daughter-in-law would approve of her choice. Nice clean seemingly well-brought up children . . . Then she felt a stab of self-reproach. She was proving to be just as guilty as the rest of the women in choosing attractive-looking children. That little lass needs comforting though, she excused herself. She needs a warm and friendly home, like the one she has no doubt left, with kindly sympathetic people to care for her . . . and who better to do that than herself and Sally and George?

The brother and sister were still there when Ellen had carried several laden trays into the kitchen, and by then it was time for her to knock off. She had been there for three hours and another group of women were scheduled to do the rest of the washing up. And Sally had just arrived. Ellen could see her hovering a little hesitantly in the doorway. She went across to greet her.

'Hello, dear. I'm glad you managed to get here. No problems at the shop? Ruby can cope all right, can't she?' Ellen didn't wait for an answer to what were rhetorical questions. She hurried on to say, 'I've been taking a quick look around and I've noticed two kiddies over there. I think they might suit us just fine. Look – a brother and sister, at least I should imagine they are. What do you think, Sal?'

Sally didn't answer at first. She raised her eyebrows slightly as she looked first at Ellen, then at the children her mother-in-law was pointing out. She opened her mouth as if to comment, then seemed to change her mind. Sally looked, if anything, bewildered and a little sad, as Ellen had been when she first set eyes on these ranks of lonely, homeless children. And there had been far more of them at first, when Ellen started her afternoon stint. She realised, belatedly, that she had been somewhat presumptuous. She had invited Sally here to help her with the choice and now it must seem as though she already had it all cut and dried. Maybe that was why Sally was looking a little perturbed.

Hastily she added, 'Of course it's up to you, dear, as well. But they do seem nice and . . .' she had been about to say 'clean' but she changed it to '. . . pleasant.'

To her relief, Sally smiled. 'Yes, of course, Mam. Why not? They look just fine; very suitable. Whoever we take it's something of a gamble, isn't it? We can't tell what any of them are really like . . .' Her voice petered out. 'I'm sorry, Mam. I know I seemed a bit hesitant. I just felt so sad – horrified, really – when I came in and saw them all.' Ellen noticed there were tears in Sally's blue eyes. 'Yes, we'll take those two,' she said. 'Come on, Mam, let's go and talk to them. You ask them, will you, if they'd like to come and live with us?'

Ellen realised that she might have to do the talking at first. Sally was such a tender-hearted lass and she seemed to be quite overcome. She couldn't help but notice as they walked across the room the girl sitting next to their two evacuees; that was how she was already thinking of them, as theirs. A scruffy, neglected-looking child with dark greasy hair that badly needed washing and combing; it hung like rat's tails almost to her shoulders. Her coat, in contrast to the spruce pair next to her, was shabby and well worn, her thick grey socks were concertinaed round her ankles and her shoes couldn't have been polished for months, the leather on the toes almost worn through. Poor little kid, thought Ellen. I do hope she manages to get a nice home . . . but not with us, she added quickly to herself. No, not with us; we've only got room for two. The scruffy girl yawned, her mouth opening wide enough to show her breakfast – that was what Ellen had always used to say to her own children when they yawned in that unmannerly way – and her shoulders slouched in utter weariness. Ellen found herself turning away.

'Hello, dear,' she said to the little fair-haired girl. 'Would you like to come and live with us? And your little brother. He is your brother, isn't he? He looks just like you.'

The little girl looked at her shyly. 'Yes, please,' she said, after a moment's hesitation. 'Yes, I think we would.' She gave a deep sniff before turning to the little boy at her side. 'We would, wouldn't we, Michael? We'd like to go with this lady. But what about . . . ?' She turned to her other side, to Ellen's dismay, towards the neglected-looking girl. 'This is me friend, Gloria. We're together, y'see, me and Gloria – and our Michael – and we've got to stay together.'

'Yes.' The girl, Gloria, spoke up now. Just imagine, thought Ellen – *Gloria* of all names! She couldn't imagine anyone less like a Gloria! 'Wendy's me friend, like she's just

42

said, and I've got to go with 'er. I promised I'd look after 'er
. . . and she can't go without me.'

Ellen smiled sympathetically at the child, and she saw, to
her horror, that the girl's eyes were glistening with unshed
tears. Fancy that! She seemed such a tough little customer.
Lovely eyes they were too, grey and luminous, fringed with
dark lashes, and they were gazing intently at Ellen. 'I'm
sorry, dear,' Ellen began. 'We've only room for two children,
a boy and a girl. But I'm sure someone else will be able to
find room for you. And your friend will be all right with us.
I promise you we'll look after her.'

'No!' The girl shook her head. 'I've got to stay with
Wendy. I promised. She's me friend.' To Ellen's dismay two
tears overflowed and began to run down the girl's sallow
cheeks. 'She can't go anywhere without me.'

'That's right.' Wendy grabbed hold of Gloria's arm. 'If I
go with you she's got to come with us. I shan't go without
Gloria.'

'It'll be all right, Wendy.' Her brother – Michael she had
called him – was pulling at her sleeve. 'Never mind about
her. Never mind about Gloria Mulligan. You know what
Mummy said about her. We'll be all right with this lady, just
you and me.'

'No!' Wendy shook her arm away from her brother's grasp.
'And you can just shut up, our Michael, saying nasty things
about her! I won't leave Gloria . . . and that's that!'

Sally had been standing to one side, listening quietly to
this interchange. She hadn't spoken yet and Ellen knew that
she had been trying to regain her composure. The sight of
the evacuees had seemed to affect her even more than it had
affected Ellen.

Sally spoke now. 'Mam,' she took hold of Ellen's arm,
'let's take this little girl as well.' She turned and smiled at
the child. 'Gloria's a lovely name, isn't it? Don't cry, dear.
It'll be all right.' She looked back at Ellen, saying in a
whisper, 'We've plenty of room, Mam, you know we have.

43

There's the little spare room as well, and we can't possibly turn our backs on her. Just look at her, poor little mite. And how kind of her to want to look after her friend.'

Ellen felt a tinge of irritation. Now it was Sally taking matters into her own hands. It was all very well, but the child was so ... 'Yes, I know all that, Sally,' she said, whispering back. 'I understand what you're saying, but she's so ...'

'Yes, maybe she is.' Sally looked almost angry for a moment as she stared at Ellen. Then her glance softened. 'I know how you feel, Mam, honestly I do. But I'll look after her. She can be my responsibility. How's that?'

Ellen nodded slowly. 'Very well, dear,' she said. After all, she had no choice. The girl had already heard Sally offer to take her. 'You're right – of course we must take her. But I'll look after her as well, you know. I wouldn't want you to feel that I didn't care.'

Ellen looked down then at the trio in front of her and her heart almost burst with compassion. You horrid, snobbish woman, she berated herself. How could you? A poor little neglected girl, in need of love and understanding, and you were actually thinking of turning your back on her. She smiled at them, placing a hand gently on each of the fair heads. Wendy and Michael; it seemed as though their mother was a devotee of Peter Pan. Then, a trifle more timorously, she touched the dark head. 'All right, we'll take all three of you, won't we, Sally? Will that make you happier?' She looked at each of the girls in turn and was gratified to see, for the first time, smiles appear on their faces. Wendy was such a pretty little girl, all pink and white. And Gloria ... Ellen looked at her in amazement. Why, the child was quite beautiful when she smiled!

'What about you, Michael?' Ellen turned to the little boy. 'Is that all right? We'll take you and your sister ... *and* her friend.'

'S'pose so.' Michael shrugged his shoulders, then he

grinned. 'Yes, she'll only start yelling again if we don't take Gloria.'

'Very well then, that's all settled.' Ellen smiled confidingly at him. 'Come along then, gather up all your belongings – don't forget your gas masks – and we'll go and tell the lady in charge that you're coming with us; with Sally and me. We live quite near here. It's not far to walk . . .'

Gloria took a deep breath when they stepped out into the street, filling her lungs with the fresh, tangy, salt-laden air. That was one of the first things she had noticed when they arrived at Central Station, when they had got away from the smoky, sooty smell of the huge engine, of course, although that had been exciting as well – her first train journey. The air smelled so clean and sparkling, and the sky was a clear blue, not dirtied and darkened by dozens of factory chimneys as it was at home.

They walked up a long street of tall red-brick houses, much bigger than most of the houses Gloria was used to seeing in Salford. Some of them had fancy names above the doors – like Rest-a-While, Cosy Nook or Tower View – and notices in the windows saying *Vacancies* (or *No Vacancies*) so Gloria supposed these must be hotels where people stayed when they went on holiday. Gloria had never been on holiday, and today was the first time she had seen the sea, from the train window. She thought they were walking away from the sea now.

Michael was walking in front with the older lady, holding on to her hand, because he was the smallest, and the two girls were following behind. The lady called Sally had disappeared when they got outside and Gloria gathered from the hurried conversation between the grown-ups that she had gone back to work – in a shop, Gloria thought, and she would be back home in an hour or two. Gloria had liked her straight away and she had known it was the Sally lady who had persuaded the older lady to take her as well.

Gloria quickened her steps now to catch up with her and Michael and Wendy did likewise.

'Will we be able to see the sea again?' asked Gloria. 'It's over there, i'n't it?' She pointed back over her shoulder. 'We're going away from it, aren't we?'

'Don't worry, dear. It'll still be there another day.' The lady smiled at her, so very kindly. 'And you can be sure we'll go and see it, all of us, the sea and all that lovely sand. You'll be able to make sand-castles and have a paddle, perhaps.'

'Tomorrer?' asked Gloria. 'Can we go tomorrer?'

'I don't know about tomorrow,' said the lady, 'but soon – I promise you we'll go very soon. You'll have to go to school tomorrow, won't you, or the next day? All three of you.' She frowned slightly. 'I'll have to see about it. Didn't they tell you?'

'Nope. They didn't say nothing about school, did they, Wendy?' Wendy shook her head. 'We've all got separated, haven't we, all us kids? We're all going to different places like, but our teachers came with us on t'train, so I 'spect they'll sort us all out, won't they?' Gloria looked up at the lady who was smiling, but staring at her a bit sadly, as though she was going to start crying. 'What's yer name?' asked Gloria. 'You haven't told us, have yer?'

'Oh dearie me! How dreadful of me,' said the lady. 'How very rude you must think I am.' Gloria didn't think so at all. She thought that she and the Sally lady were just about the nicest, kindest people she had ever met, especially now they had decided to take her as well as Wendy and Michael. 'I know all your names, don't I? Gloria Mulligan, and Wendy and Michael Cooper, but you don't know mine. I'm called Mrs Hobson . . . but I think you'd better call me Auntie Ellen. And the lady who was with me is Mrs Hobson as well – she's my daughter-in-law – so you can call her Auntie Sally.'

'All right.' Gloria nodded. 'We'll call you Auntie Ellen, won't we, Wendy? When'll we be there, at your house? You said it weren't far.'

46

'It isn't very far now, just round the next corner,' said Mrs Hobson. 'Why? Are you tired, dear? I suppose you must be.'

'Just a bit,' said Gloria. She had perked up a little when she had known that she and Wendy had been chosen, at last – it had been awful, sitting there waiting – but now she was feeling very, very tired, and hungry too. All she had eaten since breakfast was a few sandwiches and a bun at the church hall.

They turned into another long street and then they came to an iron gate between two red-brick pillars, each topped with a large concrete ball. 'Here we are,' said Mrs Hobson. 'This is where we live.' She opened the gate then stopped for a moment, rummaging in her handbag. 'Just wait till I find my key.'

Gloria stood there and stared. The path, edged with rose-bushes in full bloom, led to a glossy-painted green front door. There were curtains of cream lace hanging at the windows, upstairs and down; and such a lot of windows, big ones, too. And there was a tree – just fancy that, a real tree! – growing in the garden. Wendy lived in a nice house. Gloria had been there, just once, but it was nowhere near as posh as this one. This looked like a bloomin' palace, although Gloria noticed that the houses on each side were almost the same. Gosh! Mrs Hobson must be a very rich lady to live in a house like this.

'Come along in.' She ushered them through the front door and when she closed it Gloria saw that there was a window in it, all pretty coloured glass making a picture of a ship sailing on the sea. There was a red carpet on the floor and the same red carpet going all the way up the stairs. The room at the back of the house where Mrs Hobson led them now had a nice carpet, too, brown with yellow and orange flowers with a border of polished wooden boards surrounding it. Gloria had never seen such luxury. Their living-room floor at home was covered with cracked linoleum with just a peg rug in front of the fireplace, and the stairs had no carpet at all.

Here there was a great big sofa and two massive chairs on which there lay pretty embroidered covers. There was a flowered cover on the huge sideboard as well, underneath the glass fruit bowl, filled to the brim with rosy red apples, oranges and bananas, the silver-framed photographs and the little golden statue of a lady with no clothes on. Gloria looked at that in surprise for a moment, then she looked away. She thought it was rather rude; they had the Virgin Mary on *their* sideboard.

She turned round, still staring, at the curtains at the window, brown and yellow and orange to match the carpet, at the polished table and four big dining chairs with brown leather seats, the pictures on the wall – one of hairy cows with big horns standing in front of some mountains, and another of King George and Queen Elizabeth – then up at the ceiling from which was suspended, on three chains, a yellow and white glass bowl. Gloria let out a great sigh of wonder, almost of disbelief. 'Ohhh . . . heck!'

'What's the matter, dear?' Mrs Hobson was at her side, an arm round her shoulders. 'Is there something wrong?'

'No, there's nowt wrong,' said Gloria. 'But . . . i'n't it posh? I've never been anywhere as posh as this before.'

Mrs Hobson laughed, but Gloria knew that she wasn't laughing at her, as though she had said something stupid, but along with her somehow. 'Oh dear! We don't think it's posh. It's a bit shabby really. We've had this furniture for ages, and the carpet too. We're happy with it, though.' She stopped, looking seriously at Gloria. 'But – yes, I suppose it might seem a bit . . . posh.' Again Mrs Hobson looked as though she might be going to cry. Grown-ups were very hard to understand at times. Gloria couldn't see anything to cry about, especially when you lived in a place like this.

She suddenly thought of something. 'Auntie Ellen, can I go to the lav?' She had been wanting to go in the church hall, but in all the excitement she had forgotten about it. Now she realised she did want to go, quite badly.

'Of course, how very silly of me,' said Ellen. 'I was going to put the kettle on, but first things first. Come along upstairs, all of you – bring your things – and I'll show you where you're going to sleep.'

'But . . . the lav,' persisted Gloria, by now almost crossing her legs and making for the kitchen door.

'Yes, dear, it's upstairs.' Ellen smiled. 'In the bathroom. Come on, I'll show you.'

'A bathroom? You've got a real bathroom?' Gloria picked up her carrier bag and gas-mask case and followed her hostess up the stairs, Wendy and Michael trotting behind.

'Er, yes, we've got a bathroom, dear,' said Ellen.

'So've we,' chimed in Michael. 'We've got one an' all. How can you have a bath if you haven't got a bathroom? P'raps that's why you're so mucky, is it, Gloria Mulligan, 'cause you never have a bath.'

'Michael! That's very rude.' Mrs Hobson stopped at the top of the stairs and turned round, looking severely at the little boy. 'Don't you ever let me hear you speaking to Gloria like that again. And you're *all* going to have a bath, after we've had our tea. Now, just say you're sorry to Gloria.'

'Sorry,' mumbled Michael. 'Sorry, Gloria. But it's only what me mum says. She says—'

'That will do, Michael,' said Mrs Hobson quietly. 'If you're going to live in my house then I want you to all get along nicely together, or else it isn't going to work, is it?'

'Never mind him, Auntie Ellen,' said Gloria. 'Take no notice of him – I don't. He's always rude to me. It's Wendy that's me friend, not him.'

'Yes, I know, dear. But we can't have him being rude, can we?' Ellen pushed open the door at the top of the stairs. 'There you are. Use the toilet and wash your hands, then Wendy and Michael can go. And I'll show you all where you're going to sleep. Give me your carrier bag, Gloria, and your coat.'

The bathroom was another lovely surprise. There was a

huge white bath on little feet, a gleaming wash-basin with a special place for the soap – nice lavender-scented soap – and a lavatory with a polished wooden seat. And there was proper paper, too, in a little box thing at the side. Gloria pulled the chain, which had a wooden handle to match the seat, then washed her hands and dried them on a fluffy white towel that was hanging on a rack.

'This is your bedroom, Gloria,' called Auntie Ellen. 'Come and see where you and Wendy are going to sleep.'

There were two beds, each covered with a pink flowered eiderdown, a dressing-table with a pretty pink skirt all round it and a white painted wardrobe. And a bookshelf with a row of books. Gloria went over to it and, kneeling on the floor, she looked at the titles. *Little Women*, *Alice's Adventures in Wonderland*, *What Katy Did*, several school stories by Angela Brazil and a few other more grown-up books.

'Those belonged to my daughter,' said Ellen. 'She used to have this room, a long time ago. She took a lot of her books with her when she got married, but she left a few behind. Do you like reading, my dear?'

'Yes, I love it,' said Gloria, 'but I haven't got any books of me own, only comics. Wendy lends me hers sometimes, but she daren't let on to her mum, and sometimes the teacher lets us take a book home from school. Only the best readers though, like me . . . and Wendy. She's a good reader an' all.'

'I think you'll get on well with my granddaughter then,' said Ellen. 'Our Emmie is a real bookworm. We'll have to ask her if she'll lend you some of her books, you and Wendy.' Wendy and Michael were now in the bathroom and Gloria was pleased to have Auntie Ellen to herself for a few moments. 'I expect you'll be meeting Emmie very soon,' Ellen went on. 'Pearl and Ruby and Emmie – they're my three granddaughters.'

'How old are they?' asked Gloria. 'I'm eight and so's Wendy, and Michael's five. I 'spect they're older than us, aren't they?'

50

'Yes, they're all quite grown-up now,' replied Ellen. 'Emmie – the one that likes books – she's fifteen and she's still at school. But the other two are working.'

'Where do they live then? They don't live here, do they?'

'No, they live with their mum and dad – that's my daughter, Rachel, and her husband – in a house near Stanley Park. That's a nice big park, Gloria, with a lake with ducks on it and lovely flower gardens and two putting greens. Have you ever played putting?' Gloria shook her head. She'd never even heard of it. 'I think you'd like it, you and Wendy, but I don't know if Michael could manage it. I used to love playing putting. I remember taking Pearl when she was a little girl, soon after the park opened.' Auntie Ellen was looking all pleased and excited and her eyes were shining. 'We'll have to go to Stanley Park one of these days. There are all sorts of things we can do now you've come.'

'Who lives here then, with you?' asked Gloria. 'Have you got a husband?'

'No, I'm afraid not, dear. He died, a long time ago. My son, George, lives here with me, and his wife, Sally. You know, the lady you met at the hall. You'll be seeing her again soon, and George, when they come home from work.'

Gloria was still gazing round at the most beautiful bedroom she had ever seen. There were a teddy bear and a black doll sitting on a little basket chair between the beds, pictures of fairies and toadstools and rabbits on the walls, and some pink glass things on the dressing table; a tray and two candlesticks and two jars to put things in. It was all too lovely for words and Gloria felt tears coming into her eyes. She didn't know why because she didn't feel unhappy, not a bit.

She dashed over to Ellen, putting her arms round her waist and hugging her, something she hardly ever did with her mam. 'Oh, Auntie Ellen, it's lovely. It's really, really lovely. I'm ever so glad you said I could come and live here.' She knew it was really Sally who had made the decision, but she also realised that she couldn't have come if this lady hadn't agreed.

'I'm pleased you like it, dear,' said Ellen very quietly. Her voice sounded a bit husky. 'I'm sure we're going to be very happy together . . . all of us, aren't we?' Wendy and Michael had now returned from the bathroom. 'Just dump all your things on the bed and we'll sort them out afterwards. Now, I'll just show this young man where he's going to sleep.' She beamed at Michael, then opened the door of the smallest bedroom.

'You'll be in here, Michael. A room all to yourself, for a big grown-up boy. It's a bit of a tip at the moment, I'm afraid, but we'll tidy it up for you. That's my son's fishing tackle. We'll have to see if it will fit in his own room.'

'Gosh! Does he go fishing?' Michael stared goggle-eyed at the assortment of rods and lines and waterproof clothing. 'D'you think I could go with him?'

'I don't see why not,' said Ellen cautiously. 'Have you been fishing before, Michael?'

'Me dad goes fishing in the river,' said the little boy. 'He takes me with him sometimes. Not very often though,' he added.

'Well, George fishes in the sea,' said Ellen. 'It can be very rough sometimes. You'd have to be very careful, but I daresay he might like a companion now and again, if it's a nice day. We'll have to see.'

'That's what Mummy says,' said Wendy. 'We'll have to see.'

Ellen laughed. 'I think that's what mums always say. Now, what about some tea? You must be ravenous, all of you. What would you like? Beans on toast? Egg and chips? Or I've got some chicken left from yesterday. We could have that with chips.'

'Gosh!' said Gloria. 'It's like a bloody café, i'n't it?' The word had slipped out without her noticing it, until she saw Auntie Ellen look at her sharply.

'Don't swear! It's naughty to swear, isn't it, Auntie Ellen?' Michael looked up at her self-righteously. 'Mummy says—'

'Yes, Michael,' Ellen interrupted him with a warning glance. 'I suppose it is rather naughty. It isn't something I like to hear, but I don't think Gloria meant to say it, did you, dear?'

'No, sorry. It just slipped out,' said Gloria, covered with confusion. 'Sorry, Auntie Ellen.' They all swore in Gloria's house, her mam and dad and her brothers. Sometimes you couldn't help saying naughty words, you heard them so often.

'Her mam swears. We've heard her,' said Michael. 'We see her at the shops, don't we, Wendy? And she's always—'

'That will do, Michael. I don't want to hear another word about it. Do you understand? Not one more word!' Ellen looked sternly at him, then her glance softened. 'Now, let's go and see about some tea, shall we? Perhaps you could all help me to set the table.'

Whilst they ate their meal, chicken and chips with a whole big tomato each – Auntie Ellen said they were special Blackpool tomatoes, grown on a place called Marton Moss – they told her all about their families back in Salford; and Mrs Hobson, in turn, told them about her own family here in Blackpool. Gloria was thrilled to bits to hear that they owned a rock factory. Just imagine that! Living with a lady who actually made Blackpool rock; and, not only that, they had two shops as well. Wendy, too, seemed quite pleased and excited at this news, so much so that she didn't cry even when she talked about her mum and dad. In fact, she hadn't done any crying at all since she came here to Mrs Hobson's nice house. Gloria thought she would be very silly and babyish if she did; there was nothing to cry about now.

When they had almost finished their tea the other members of Auntie Ellen's family came in from work. Sally arrived first, and Gloria grinned at her as though she was an old friend, which she already seemed to be. What a pretty lady she was, with ginger hair and such a merry smile. Then

George came in, a big man with black hair that was turning a bit grey and bright blue eyes, who looked a lot more serious than his wife. He was very nice though, and said how pleased he was that Gloria and Wendy and Michael had come to live with them.

It was Auntie Sally who helped the three of them to write their postcards to send home. They had all been given a special postcard, stamped and printed with their home address, which they had to return to let their families know where they were. Gloria didn't need much help with hers.

Dear Mam and Dad, she wrote, *I have arrived safely and I like it here. There are two ladies called Mrs Hobson and a man called Mr Hobson and they make Blackpool rock. I hope you are well. Give my love to Monica. Love from Gloria.*

Sally wrote the Blackpool address on all three cards and said she would slip out to the post-box with them straight away. She cast her eyes over the message that Gloria had written, in her best, neatest 'real writing' and she smiled.

'I'm glad you like it here, dear,' she said. 'It's bound to feel a bit strange at first, but we want you to be happy here. It's not like living with your own mum and dad, I know, but we've got to try and make the best of all sorts of things now the war's started. We'll all get along just fine together, I'm sure.'

Sally turned to Wendy, Michael having gone upstairs with Ellen to have his bath. 'Won't we, dear? We're all going to be real good friends.'

But poor Wendy, who had been doing so well, at the mention of her mum and dad had started crying again.

Chapter 5

Ellen leaned back in the easy chair and closed her eyes. It was incredible that coping with just three children could make her feel so very exhausted, and this was only the first day! Goodness knows how she would feel when they had been with her a week or a fortnight. On the other hand, it might get easier.

'Tired, Mam?' asked Sally, in a gentle voice, echoing her thoughts, and Ellen opened her eyes and smiled.

'Yes, dear, I must admit I am feeling a bit tired. Ridiculous, isn't it? I manage to cope with the shops and the factory – not on my own, of course, but I do try to pull my weight – to say nothing of the WVS and church committees, and never stop to think about it. But three little kiddies and . . . well, to be honest, Sally, I'm feeling my age and that's a fact!'

'You're bound to be tired, Mam,' said Sally. 'It's not because of your age – don't you believe it! – it's because of the trauma of it all, trying to settle three strange children into a new home, and it's going to take some time with that little Wendy, if I'm not mistaken. Poor little lamb! She was crying as if her heart would break when we went upstairs, but I've managed to calm her down, I hope. I gave her Rachel's old teddy bear to cuddle and I've told her her mum'll be writing to them as soon as she gets the postcard. And Gloria promised she'll look after her.'

'Yes, Gloria.' Ellen sighed. 'That poor little girl. And she's such a grand little lass, isn't she? I'm glad you suggested that we should take her as well.' Ellen realised she had just said 'suggested', but she knew that Sally had wellnigh insisted upon it. And Ellen had to admit now that her daughter-in-law had been right. 'How any mother could let her child get into a state like that is beyond me,' she went on. 'I must confess, when I first set eyes on her in the school hall, so scruffy and bedraggled-looking, I just didn't want to know. You know that, don't you, Sally, and I'm ashamed of feeling like that, but there it is. And then, when we found out she'd got nits . . . well, if you hadn't been there, dear, I don't know how I would have coped, I'm sure.'

They had discovered at bath-time that not only had Gloria got nits in her hair, but that several of the little white eggs had hatched and her scalp was crawling with head-lice.

Michael had had his bath first with just a little help from Ellen – he didn't seem at all embarrassed by this – and had put on his blue striped pyjamas. There had been two pairs in his luggage, one red and one blue, neatly ironed and folded, just as in Wendy's luggage there had been two winceyette nightdresses, one with pink and the other with blue sprigs of flowers. Wendy had bathed, too, in between intermittent spells of weeping, then they had both been settled by the living-room fire with a cup of cocoa and a comic each, bought earlier that day by Sally in readiness for their new guests.

Then it was Gloria's turn for the bathroom and Ellen had agreed to see to her whilst Sally took charge of the other two. Ellen was trying so hard to overcome her earlier aversion to the child which she realised had been entirely a reaction to the little girl's appearance and nothing at all to do with her personality. When you got to know her she was a dear little thing, and Ellen guessed that she had not only charm, but guts as well. Far more than the weeping Wendy.

'Does Mummy wash your hair over the sink, or in the bath?' asked Ellen, eyeing somewhat dubiously the greasy matted tresses.

'Don't know,' said Gloria. She scratched her head. 'What

56

I mean is . . . well, I don't have it washed all that often. And we haven't got a nice bath like you, Auntie Ellen. We've got a tin one what hangs in the scullery and Mam fills it up with hot water and then we all get in. Not all at once – the three little 'uns first, and then me. But when it gets to my turn the water's gone all cold and a bit messy.'

'And your hair?' Ellen prompted, fighting back a feeling of repugnance. 'Does your mum wash your hair in that same water?'

Gloria didn't seem any too sure. 'No . . . The last time she washed it, when I had it cut right short, she did it in the kitchen sink. But that's ages ago.'

'Very well, dear,' Ellen smiled at her. 'You can have your bath – you can manage on your own, can't you, if I run the water for you? – then I'll wash your hair in the wash-basin upstairs.'

The child had had no nightdress to put on when she came out of the bath. 'We don't bother with nighties,' she explained. 'Me and Rose and Lily – them's me sisters – we sleep in our vest and knicks. It said we had to have one on that list, but I don't suppose me mam took any notice of that. I'll be all right, Auntie Ellen, honest.'

Ellen was looking askance at the grey vest, full of holes, and the faded navy-blue knickers that Gloria had put on again. 'No. I'll give these a wash, dear, and I daresay I can find you something to wear for tonight, until we're able to get you a nightie. I know – I've got just the thing. Wrap yourself in this big towel, there's a good girl, while I go and find it.'

The child was overjoyed with the pink celanese underslip that Ellen unearthed from the bottom of her chest of drawers. It was too big, of course, but as it had built-up shoulders and not flimsy straps it did manage to stay pretty well on Gloria's thin frame. It had been knee-length on Ellen, worn in the days when skirts were shorter, but it came down to Gloria's ankles.

57

'There! It'll keep your feet warm,' laughed Ellen, 'and tomorrow we'll get you one in your own size.'

'Oh no, you don't need to,' said Gloria, reverently stroking the silky fabric. 'I'll wear this – it's lovely. I've never had anything as lovely as this.' She picked up the skirt, daintily holding it out on either side of her. 'Look, Auntie Ellen. It's just like one of them posh dance dresses, i'n't it? Like them film stars wear.'

'Yes, dear. Perhaps it is.' Ellen swallowed again at the lump that kept coming into her throat. 'Let's get your hair washed, shall we? I've got some nice Amami shampoo here.'

The child bent her head over the wash-basin, then, just as Ellen was about to pour on the first jugful of water, she saw it. Something crawling on the scalp. She parted the dark hair then jumped back in alarm – she just couldn't help herself – because the child's scalp was positively alive with head-lice.

'Oh! Oh dear!' Her cry was involuntary and she could have kicked herself, but Gloria seemed unperturbed.

'What's up, Auntie Ellen?' The child turned her head to look at her. 'Have I got summat in me hair?'

'Well, dear, I rather think there might be,' said Ellen carefully.

'I've got nits again, 'aven't I?' Gloria sounded quite unconcerned. 'I thought I had. The nurse came to look at us the other day, but I heard her say to t'teacher that it was too late to do owt about it 'cause we'd be going away soon. She said they'd be able to do summat at the other end, when we got where we were going.'

Ellen felt indignant for a moment. Why on earth had the nurse bothered to look at the kiddies then, if all she was going to do was pass the buck to somebody else? Lack of time and resources, she supposed, and the fact that evacuation was imminent. What did a few nits matter compared with Hitler and his bombs? Better to have a lousy head than be blown to smithereens. At all events, it wasn't this poor little girl's fault.

58

'They'll happen come out if you wash it,' said Gloria cheerfully, before adding, much more anxiously, 'but you won't cut all me hair off, will you, Auntie Ellen, not like me mam did the last time. It were dead short and all the other kids laughed at me.'

'No, I'll try not to, dear,' replied Ellen, 'but I think this is going to need more than Amami shampoo. Just wait here a minute.' She went to the top of the stairs and gave a shout. 'Sally, could you spare me a moment?'

'Nits!' she mouthed when Sally came dashing up the stairs. 'The poor kid's crawling with them.'

Sally nodded. 'Actually, Mam, it's what I expected when I first saw her.'

But it didn't put her off taking the child, thought Ellen, realising anew what a generous, fair-minded person Sally was.

'But what can we do?' said Ellen. 'It's going to need treatment, isn't it, not just shampoo.'

'Hang on a minute,' said Sally, 'and I'll pop next door. D'you remember, Molly had the same trouble with their Shirley a few weeks ago?'

'Oh, yes, Molly was horrified, wasn't she? She said Shirley must have picked them up from the girl she sat next to.'

'She soon managed to get rid of them, though, with some special stuff. I'll go and see if she's got some of it left.' Sally popped her head round the bathroom door. 'Don't worry, Gloria love, we'll soon get you sorted out.' She winked at the child then turned back to Ellen. 'There's no point in us whispering, Mam. She knows very well what we're on about, don't you, love? I'll just go and check that the other two are OK first. George'll have to keep his eye on them for a minute.'

'Auntie Sally, don't tell Michael, will you?' pleaded Gloria as Sally turned to go downstairs. 'You know, about the nits. He'll only start going on at me again.'

'Bit of a nosey parker, is he?' Sally tapped her nose with her forefinger and grinned at Gloria. 'Don't you worry, kid; it's our secret.'

She was back in a few moments with a bottle of greenish-black shampoo. 'It's all right, Mam, I'll see to her,' she told Ellen as she unscrewed the cap from the bottle. 'Crikey!' She drew back a little. 'This stuff doesn't half pong. It's bringing tears to my eyes. I tell you what, Gloria, if this doesn't kill the little blighters then nothing will.' She gave the child's shoulder a friendly squeeze. 'Now, just put your head over the bowl again, there's a good lass.'

Ellen hovered in the background realising that Sally might need some help. 'Spread a newspaper over the bed, will you, please Mam?' Sally said as she brought the child, her head wrapped in a towel, into the bedroom. 'Molly lent me this as well.' She produced a fine-toothed steel comb from her apron pocket. 'Now then, Gloria, let's see what we can do. Just lean over the paper and put your head right down.'

Sally combed and combed and the nasty little creatures, for the most part struggling in their death throes, dropped on to the newspaper. She tried not to tug too hard, but the hair was matted in places and Gloria winced as the comb refused to go through the tangled mess. Some of the worst knots had to be cut out and Gloria drew back in alarm when she saw the scissors.

'Oh no! Please, Auntie Sally, don't cut it all off, will you?' she begged. 'I've been telling Auntie Ellen how me mam made me look dead ugly. It were shorter than a boy's even, and everybody laughed at me.'

'No, of course I won't,' said Sally soothingly. 'But it is rather too long, Gloria, and that front piece keeps flopping into your eyes, doesn't it?' She stood back, putting her head to one side as she looked at the child. 'I think you would suit a fringe, and we'll cut the rest to just below your ears – how's that?'

'All right,' said Gloria, still rather diffidently. 'It feels better now, though. Not as itchy. Did you wash Wendy's hair an' all? And Michael's?'

'No, dear. They said their mum had washed it last night,' replied Sally hastily. 'Now, hold still – ever so still – and I'll see what I can do.'

'I'll go and make her some supper then,' said Ellen, smiling gratefully at her daughter-in-law. 'You're doing splendidly, dear. I just don't know what I'd have done . . .' She blinked rapidly before hurrying out of the door.

'There, what do you think of that?' Sally turned the child round to the mirror, standing behind her with her hands on her shoulders.

'Mmm, it looks nice.' Gloria nodded approvingly. 'I'm a bit cold, though, now.' She rubbed at her bare arms, protruding like thin brown sticks from the flimsy makeshift nightgown.

She was certainly sunburnt. She had most likely spent most of the long summer holiday running wild in the streets of Salford, Sally surmised, but the poor kid could do with a good deal more flesh on her bones. 'Here, put my bed-jacket on,' said Sally, nipping into the next bedroom and returning with a fluffy blue garment. 'It'll keep you nice and warm. Now, we'll go and dry your hair by the fire and I expect Auntie Ellen will have made you a drink of cocoa.'

Michael looked up curiously from his comic as they entered the living room. 'She's had her hair cut. Why has Gloria had her hair cut? Did she have—'

Sally silenced him before he could get the word out. 'She's had it cut because it was too long. Like somebody else's nose.' Playfully she tapped at Michael's freckled nose. 'Now, shove your chair back a bit then Gloria can sit on the rug and dry her hair. And something tells me it's nearly bedtime.' For Michael had just given an enormous yawn.

Now they were all in bed and Ellen was feeling as though she had had charge of them for five weeks, not just five hours. 'Yes, Gloria is a grand little lass, isn't she?' she said again. 'And not really as rough as she might have been, considering her background, if you know what I mean. Not that we know much about her background, do we, but reading between the lines and from what she's let slip it sounds as though it's pretty awful.'

'It's probably helped her having Wendy as a friend,' said Sally. 'Some of Wendy's nice manners are sure to have rubbed off on her. Chalk and cheese, aren't they, those two? And yet they are inseparable. It's amazing the odd friendships that children make. They don't seem to notice the same things that grown-ups do. It's probably never occurred to Wendy that her friend is . . . well, a bit scruffy, because she's so fond of her.'

'She clings to her,' agreed Ellen. 'They wouldn't be parted, would they? But I'm glad we've brought both of them here,' she said again. 'And Michael, of course.' Ellen grinned. 'He has no illusions about his sister's friend. A bit of jealousy as well, more than likely.'

'Yes, he's certainly got all his chairs at home,' replied Sally. 'And he seems a very well-adjusted little lad. He went off to bed without so much as a whimper.'

George looked up from his newspaper. 'I must admit it's good to have a few kiddies about the place. That little Michael's a knock-out, isn't he? He wants me to take him fishing. What d'you think of that?' George looked very pleased at the thought.

Ellen gave a chuckle. 'I'll tell you something. I bet Wendy and Michael's mum won't be all that pleased when she knows we've got Gloria as well. From what Gloria was saying she's not very popular with Mrs Cooper.'

'Then it's just too bad,' said Sally forcibly, 'because that's the way it is and that's the way it'll stay. The woman should be glad Wendy's got such a good friend. And Gloria'll not go short of anything while she's with us. It was nice of you to give her that underslip, Mam. She's thrilled to bits with it, though she could really do with a proper nightie.'

'Yes, I'll go to the Co-op tomorrow and get her some decent clothes,' said Ellen. 'A skirt and jumper and some strong shoes. And underwear and nightdresses . . . she's going to need the lot. I've never seen such a tatty collection as was in that carrier bag. There's a cardigan and blouse that aren't too bad, but the rest of the stuff's only fit for a jumble sale. Not even fit for that, if you ask me.'

'I daresay that's where it came from, Mam,' said Sally. 'From a jumble sale. She said her coat was new. New from a second-hand stall, I suppose she meant. Her sister bought it for her. "Our Monica", she calls her.'

'Do you think they're Catholics?' asked Ellen suddenly. It was something that had only just occurred to her. 'Monica's a Catholic name, isn't it? And what did she call her baby brother? Our Vinnie . . . Vincent. Yes, I suppose they must be. There's enough of them, heaven knows. The older ones are all married, she says, and then there are three more younger than Gloria, and two more brothers at home. Oh dear.'

'It doesn't matter what religion she is, does it, Mam?' Sally was looking at her curiously.

'No, I suppose not,' said Ellen. 'I was thinking we should send her to Sunday School, that's all – well, all three of them, of course. But if they're of a different faith . . . You didn't ask them if they said their prayers, I suppose, when they went to bed?'

'No, I didn't bother with all that,' said Sally decisively. 'Not at the moment. I told you, I had enough to do settling Wendy down. I shouldn't worry, Mam. I'm sure we'll be able to sort it all out.'

'Mmm. Better having a Catholic child than a Jewish one,' said Ellen thoughtfully. 'No, I'm not prejudiced,' she added, seeing Sally's look of astonishment. 'You know me better than that, I hope. But it can cause all sorts of problems, things you wouldn't even think about.

'They were talking about it at the church hall today,' she

went on. 'Apparently quite a few Jewish children have come with the Manchester lot – they've been arriving since last Friday, you know – and I heard tell of two little brothers who refused to eat bacon or pork; it's against their religion, you see. And Mrs Murray – she's a staunch Catholic, of course – she's got a little Jewish girl who nearly had hysterics when she saw their picture of Jesus on the cross. She said her mother would go mad if she knew she had to look at that while she was having her dinner. So Mrs Murray took it down off the wall. All credit to her, I say, although I don't know why she wanted it there in the first place. Morbid, if you ask me.' The view of Ellen's church was that the cross was empty because Christ had risen. But she knew that there were so many different ways of looking at things – not only religion – and the arrival of the evacuees already seemed to be throwing all kinds of issues and problems into focus.

'There's day school to think about before Sunday School, isn't there?' Sally pointed out. 'What are you going to do about that? Have you been told?'

'No,' said Ellen. 'I'll sit tight, I think, and wait until the billeting officer contacts us. The kiddies deserve a few days off, surely, and we've some shopping to do tomorrow for Gloria. I won't be able to get into the rock factory or the shops for a while, that's for sure.' Ellen was realising, in fact, that she would soon have to hand over the reins almost entirely. Looking after three evacuees was going to be a full-time job.

'I'll go up and see if they're asleep,' said Ellen in a little while, when she had drunk a welcome cup of tea that Sally had made. 'No, Sally, you stay where you are. You've done more than your fair share tonight. It's my turn now.'

Michael was fast asleep and so were the two girls, but Wendy and Gloria were now both in the same bed. It looked as though Gloria had crept across to comfort her friend because she was the one nearer to the edge, her arm resting protectively over the other girl. Ellen smiled and decided to leave them as they were. If Gloria awoke and decided she was uncomfortable – or fell out of bed! – then she was sensible enough to sort herself out. Besides, Ellen guessed that in the crowded household she had left the child was no doubt used to sleeping in decidedly more cramped conditions than this.

At least she was sleeping in the bed and not under it. Ellen had heard that afternoon another story of two little brothers who had insisted that they always slept on the floor. They had been terrified of climbing on to the high flock mattress, and after their new 'auntie' had pacified them and tucked them up she had found them, an hour later, fast asleep underneath the bed.

When Ellen went into the girls' room the following morning Gloria was still in Wendy's bed and was just opening her eyes. It was turned half-past eight and George and Sally were getting ready to go off to work, but Ellen had decided to let the children have their sleep out. Poor little mites; they certainly needed it. She drew back the pink curtains and pulled up the blackout blind.

'Hello, dear. Slept well, have you?' she asked. 'Wendy's still an old sleepy-head, I see.'

'She took ages to get off,' said Gloria, sitting up and looking seriously at Ellen. 'She was crying, y'see, and she kept saying she wanted her mum, so I got in with her to give her a cuddle. She was all right then, but I didn't want to leave her. So I'm still here.' She grinned at Ellen.

'Yes, so I see. You're a very good girl to look after her so well,' said Ellen. 'But you'll be more comfortable in your own bed, you know. And Wendy has to get used to being here. So, if I were you, I'd leave her on her own tonight. OK? Here she is, look, just waking up.'

As the morning sunlight began to stream into the room Wendy opened her eyes. She gave a startled look at Gloria, then at Ellen, before her mouth began to pucker.

'Good morning, Wendy,' said Ellen brightly. 'And what a

lovely sunny morning it is. Now, you two big girls can decide who's going to use the bathroom first, then you can get yourselves dressed, can't you?' She decided upon a matter-of-fact approach with Wendy, who looked as though she might turn on the water tap again, and she would no doubt be better if left alone with her friend. 'I'll go and see how Michael's getting on.'

Michael was sitting up in his single bed looking very worried and fearful, not at all the cocksure little character he had seemed the previous day. When he saw Ellen his big blue eyes filled with tears and his lip trembled. 'Auntie Ellen, I'm all wet.' His pyjamas were soaked, as was his sheet and the foam-rubber mattress. 'I didn't know, honest. I'm sorry.'

Oh no, not that, thought Ellen as, for the first few seconds, she closed her eyes in vexation. Then, almost immediately, she put a comforting arm around him. 'Never mind, dear,' she said. 'We'll soon get you sorted out. Just hop out of bed and I'll see if there's enough hot water for you to have a bath when the girls have finished.'

But she couldn't help frowning a little and had to bite back an exclamation when she saw the state of her nearly new mattress. She and Sally and George had invested in the new Dunlopillo mattresses for all the beds not long ago, to replace the old feather and flock ones. And now this one looked as though it was ruined, Michael's little accident having soaked right through the thick twill covering. This was something Ellen had never anticipated, not with a child of five – it wasn't like a toddler – but she supposed it had been foolish and remiss of her. There was a rubber sheet somewhere in her chest of drawers that she had had since her children were small. It would have been so easy to put it on the bed, but she had never given it a thought. Oh well, it was too late now; the damage had been done, but she would make sure she used it tonight. In the meantime she would have to dry this as well as she could. Ellen was more annoyed with herself than with Michael.

'Has this happened before, dear?' she asked him, helping him out of his pyjamas. 'At home, have you had any little . . . accidents?'

Michael shook his head but he didn't answer and Ellen decided that the least said the better it would be. 'Well, never mind,' she said again, wrapping her own woollen dressing gown round his little body. 'Come and sit in my room until the girls have finished, then you can have a bath. And tonight I'll leave a potty under your bed, just in case you need it. But don't worry about it, Michael. Do you hear? You mustn't worry.'

Michael was staring down at his feet as though he were too ashamed to look at her.

It happened three more times that first week, but the rubber sheet helped to prevent the worst excesses. All the same, there was a sheet and a pair of pyjamas to be washed most mornings. Ellen was glad of the continuing warm weather as she constantly had a backyard full of washing. Comparing notes, as she did, with friends of hers from chapel and the WVS she learned that bed-wetting was a very common problem. The organisers of the evacuation scheme were now, somewhat belatedly, providing rubber sheets to households with young children, but in many cases it was too late to prevent the ruin of mattresses and bed-clothes.

During the day, however, Michael was, on the whole, a chirpy little fellow, doing his best to jolly his sister out of her still frequent bouts of weeping. When Wendy wasn't crying she was a pleasant little girl, eager to help Ellen with jobs around the house. Jobs such as washing up, setting the table and making her own bed seemed to be a novelty to Wendy, and Ellen guessed that she and Michael had been spoiled by a doting mother who had waited on them hand and foot. This was a pity, Ellen reflected, because they were only too willing to help. At times, though, they were a hindrance rather than a help because they took ages to complete a task she could have done in a fraction of the time.

67

Not so with Gloria. Ellen soon realised that the child had been used as a drudge in the household she had left. There was very little that she wouldn't tackle with a will; washing and drying the pots, peeling the potatoes, buttering the bread, shelling peas, topping and tailing gooseberries. These last two tasks, however, appeared to be unfamiliar to Gloria. Ellen gathered that in her home, peas were solely the vivid green variety that came out of a tin, and fruit pies, on the rare occasions they had them, were bought from a local shop. Indeed, Gloria told Ellen that she had never seen a gooseberry before, and both she and Wendy had enjoyed preparing the fruit for the pie that Ellen was making, and then each concocting their own little tart from the bits of pastry she gave them.

It took Ellen back to the time when Rachel was small and she had encouraged her to 'help' in the kitchen. She recalled, though, that she hadn't likewise encouraged Georgie, and she was only giving Michael jobs to do so that he would be fully occupied and not fret for his mother. Ellen believed it was a woman's privilege to care for her menfolk. It was true that her own dear husband, Ben, had helped her around the house – that was before he went off to fight in that dreadful war – but then Ben had been one in a million.

Gloria even offered to bring in the coal, to lay the fire or to scrub the kitchen floor. But Ellen refused to allow her to do such menial tasks. She was only a little girl and in Ellen's view all children had the right to behave as such. Childhood was precious and so very fleeting. But Ellen was realising that there were places not too far distant – homes that many of these evacuees had come from – where children were made to grow up far too quickly.

All the same, Ellen was relieved when the three children were able to start school. They had been given a few days' grace, the Blackpool schools this year having started a week or so later than usual as many of the teachers were involved in the evacuation scheme. And when the term finally did get under way, education was operated on a rota basis – local children in the morning, evacuees in the afternoon, turn and turn about – as the schools were unable to cope with practically double their usual numbers. So it meant that the children were still at home for more than half the day; and with Sally working full-time at the shop they were Ellen's responsibility during the daytime. She began to realise, more than ever, that it was time for her to make some changes.

Chapter 6

When the evacuees had been with her for just over a week
Ellen decided that it was time for a family conference – the
nearest the Hobsons ever got to a 'board meeting' – as she
wanted to set out her plans for the future running of the
firm. She was gratified that her family still looked upon
her as the head of what had remained, throughout the years,
entirely a family firm. She was the Managing Director, she
supposed, although Hobson's had never gone in for high-
falutin names and high-powered board meetings and the
like. The shares were held solely by herself and her son and
daughter (the children of her first husband, William) and
their spouses, and, in fewer numbers, by Ben's (her second
husband's) two sisters who had long been associated with
the firm.

They met together in Ellen's spacious lounge when the
three evacuee children had gone to bed; Ellen, George and
Sally, Rachel and Harry and their three daughters, Pearl,
Ruby and Emmie. Emmie was the only one who was not
working for the firm – and Ellen didn't think it likely that
she ever would – but she had as much right as any of them to
know what was happening.

'Right, everyone,' said Ellen, when they were all settled
with the habitual cup of tea and a digestive biscuit. 'The
time has come, I believe, for some changes. I have decided
that I will no longer be taking such an active part in the
running of Hobson's. As you know, my circumstances have
changed rather drastically over the last week or so and, quite

frankly, I just haven't the time that I used to have to devote to the firm.'

There were murmurs of agreement and it was obvious that Ellen's words were no surprise to any of them.

'I should think not, Mam,' said Rachel. 'We certainly don't want to see you wearing yourself to a shadow.' She turned to smile confidently at her husband. 'I'm sure that Harry will be only too happy to take over . . .' Rachel faltered momentarily, and Ellen was aware that Harry had frowned and shaken his head, though almost imperceptibly, at his wife, before casting his eyes, again quite unobtrusively, towards George. And George was looking fixedly at her, Ellen. Ellen was aware, too, of Sally's slight 'tut' of exasperation along with her keen, but amused, glance at her mother-in-law. A glance that Ellen, at this moment, did not return. She was careful never to be seen to be taking sides and so she continued to look impassively at Rachel.

'I mean Harry . . . and George, of course,' Rachel continued. 'I'm sure they'll be only too pleased to take over the work you've been doing, Mam.'

Ellen was gratified to see a glimmer of a smile now on her son's lips as he nodded meaningfully in her direction. George knew, as Ellen did, that Rachel looked upon her husband, Harry, as the second-in-command at Hobson's; and at one time it had, indeed, been Harry who was the more forceful of the two young men, the one with more initiative and 'get up and go'. Harry had been very successful in all his enterprises. Ellen was grateful to him for the sterling help and advice he had given her in the running of the business, especially after Ben had died, and for his comforting presence and assurance in times of trouble – and there had been quite a few of those over the years.

But the rivalry between George and Harry was now a thing of the past, George having more than proved his worth in the firm. It was only Rachel who was inclined to be defensive of her husband's position, probably because his name was Balderstone and not Hobson, which was indisputably one of the famous 'rock' names in Blackpool. Ellen sensed, at times, a certain friction between Rachel and Sally and she thought she knew the reason; or reasons, rather, because she felt that there was more than one. It was obvious that Ruby, the middle girl, who worked with Sally, seemed to lean to her aunt rather than to her mother. Sparks often flew, it had to be admitted, between Rachel and Ruby, whereas the girl got on famously with her Aunt Sally. And Sally, also, took more than a passing interest in the other two girls, Pearl and Emmie; an interest that Rachel, who considered that her way was always right, might well resent. Also, and perhaps even more significantly, Ellen knew that Rachel was somewhat jealous of the rapport that had grown up over the years between her, Ellen, and Sally, although her daughter tried hard to hide this. Yes, family relationships were difficult, indeed, mused Ellen, aware of the various currents swirling around her.

'Yes, I was coming to that,' she said now. 'To who is going to take over from me.' She looked steadily at her daughter then frowned slightly. 'In fact, you've taken the words out of my mouth, Rachel. George and Harry . . .' she looked at each of them in turn '. . . I want you to take over the running of the firm. *Jointly*,' she added, putting just the slightest emphasis on the word. 'Which will mean, of course, that you won't be able to spend as much time on the factory floor. I know that you are both very good at your job. There couldn't possibly be two more experienced sugar-boilers in the town, but I think it's time now to pass on those skills to others. I know you've always done so; training has been an important part of your work. But I'm thinking more now of . . . women. It seems very likely that in the near future there may not be many young men to train.'

'I take it that you're thinking of the young chaps being called up?' said George. Until then George and Harry had listened without interruption, as they always did when Ellen was speaking. 'Yes, I see your point, Mam, but they come to us at fifteen or sixteen, y'know. They'd not be joining up for two or three years, surely. It might be all over by then. Who knows?'

'Exactly, George. Who knows?' said Ellen. 'None of us knows how long, or how short, this war is going to be. The way I see it, we've got to plan ahead, as much as we are able. We don't know, for instance, if we're going to be hit by shortages of supplies. We may well be.'

'But there's nothing much happening at the moment, is there?' said Harry. 'If you ask me, this war is just one damned big anti-climax. All these preparations, and then what? Nothing at all. All those kiddies have been dragged away from their homes for fear of the bombs, and nothing's happened. Not that we want it to, of course,' he added hurriedly. 'They've even closed all the bloomin' theatres.'

'They've opened them again now, though,' added Sally. 'Blackpool would've felt the pinch, wouldn't it, if there'd been no entertainment places to go to.'

Ellen sighed. 'We're getting off the point, aren't we?'

'Not really, Mother-in-law,' said Harry. 'I was going to say that George and I were fully expecting our call-up papers, weren't we, George?' He grinned at his brother-in-law. 'But now it seems to have gone quiet.'

'It wouldn't be yet, though, would it, for either of you?' Ellen gave him an anxious look although her concern was mainly for George. Harry had served in the Great War, too, but he was a different 'kettle of fish', as the saying went, from her son. Harry had returned home relatively unscathed, ready to marry his sweetheart, Rachel, and ready to embark upon a new career at the rock factory. Ellen had no doubt that Harry would go to war again, if need be, with the same resolute intent with which he tackled everything.

'No, I was exaggerating,' agreed Harry. 'It wouldn't be yet, but it might well come eventually. As you've already said, who knows? For the moment, I've applied to become

73

an ARP warden. I feel I've got to do my bit even though there's not a lot happening.'

'And I'm thinking of applying to be a Special Constable,' said George, to his mother's surprise. It was the first she had heard of it, although he was certainly of the right height and physique. And if he did that, it might well help to keep him out of the forces, she thought, with a feeling of relief.

'Yes, it might be a good idea to train a few women,' George went on to say now, 'if you think they could cope. Handling the "lump" is pretty strenuous work, you know. It weighs well over a hundredweight when it's transferred to the batch roller, and it needs two men to support the weight. I fail to see how women could do that. It's always been considered a man's occupation. There are some things women could do, of course,' he added, sounding, Ellen thought, just a little condescending. 'Rolling and wrapping, as they do now, and I daresay they could tackle the sugar-boiling . . .'

I should jolly well think they could, thought Ellen with wry amusement, looking back to the time when she had done the sugar-boiling in her own kitchen at home, when George and Rachel were little. But she didn't mention this. Instead she went on to put forward her idea that they should make smaller sugar-boilings, which would produce a smaller 'lump', more easily handled by the women, and that instead of making just rock, which involved a great deal of manual pulling and kneading, they should diversify and make a variety of boiled sweets; fruit drops, barley sugars, humbugs and the like, all made from the same basic boiling.

It was also agreed that Harry would be responsible for getting the orders for Hobson's, the young man they employed as a sales representative having already enlisted in the Army, whilst George supervised the factory and the shops, taking over the role that his mother had formerly held. And in between times they would endeavour to employ and train more women to add to the workforce.

'What about your chocolates, Gran?' asked Pearl. 'You're

not going to give that up as well, are you?'

'No, that's my "baby", and I'm holding on to that for as long as I can,' said Ellen, smiling. 'Hobson's Chocolates – The Only Choice', were almost as famous in the town and throughout the north of England as Hobson's Rock. It was an enterprise that Ellen had started soon after the Great War when she had been in the depths of despair following the death of her beloved husband, and it had gone on from strength to strength.

'Yes, I shall continue with my chocolates, and Dora and Millie seem happy to carry on making the toffees and fudges.' These two women were the sisters of Ben, Ellen's husband, who had carried on with the work that their mother, dead some years now, had once done.

'And what about you, Pearl, dear?' Ellen looked enquiringly at her eldest and, she had to admit, her favourite granddaughter. 'You're not thinking of leaving us just yet?'

Pearl had confided in her, just before the outbreak of war, that if the inevitable happened then she might consider joining the Land Army. 'Would you mind very much, Gran,' she had asked, 'if I gave up my job in the office?' Pearl had left school at sixteen and after taking a course in book-keeping, shorthand and typing had started work in the office at Hobson's. She had now been there for three years and was competent and quietly efficient. 'I mean to say, if there's going to be a war, then rock-making won't be terribly important, will it? Not as important as doing something to help your country.' Pearl's deep brown eyes, so like her mother, Rachel's – and, Ellen knew, so like her own – were serious.

Ellen tried to reply sympathetically, although she couldn't help but give voice to some of her misgivings. 'The Land Army . . . Mmm, yes, I see. I know you like the country, dear, but I shouldn't have thought that working on a farm would be quite your cup of tea?'

'It isn't really what we *want* to do in wartime, is it, Gran?'

Pearl had replied earnestly, using almost exactly the same words as Sally and Ellen had used in their discussion about taking the evacuees. Yes, thought Ellen again, their own feelings shouldn't matter; it was doing their duty that was important. 'Anyway, like you've just said, I love the country. I think it would be grand to work on a farm.' Pearl sounded almost defiant in her enthusiasm.

Ellen didn't want the girl to think she was throwing cold water on her plans, tentative though they might be at the moment. It wasn't exactly disapproval that she was feeling. How could she disapprove of Pearl's desire to do her bit for her country? It was more a loving concern that she was feeling. Pearl was such a delicate-looking girl. Not that she had ever ailed much in her eighteen – almost nineteen – years, but she was slightly built and pale-complexioned, her fragile appearance enhanced by her soft golden hair which waved gently like a halo around her small face. Such a purposeful little face, thought Ellen, as she tried to nod encouragingly.

'Of course I wouldn't mind you giving up your job in the office,' replied Ellen. 'We would miss you, though, you can be sure of that. But do think carefully, Pearl. You're a town girl, aren't you, born and bred.'

But Pearl had repeated how much she liked the country, adding challengingly, 'And I'm *not* afraid of cows!'

Ellen thought, although she didn't say so, that there was a vast difference between not being afraid of cows and actually having to milk one of the creatures. She couldn't for the life of her imagine the dainty and graceful Pearl milking a cow or mucking out a stable or driving a tractor. If it had been Ruby, now . . . Ruby had a toughness and a devil-may-care attitude to life that her elder sister lacked.

'Anyway, Gran,' Pearl went on, 'I thought I may as well volunteer for what I want to do, rather than wait until they call me up. They might call girls of my age up before long, don't you think so?'

'I shouldn't have thought they'd be calling on the women just yet, dear,' replied Ellen. 'And surely not girls of your age? You're only eighteen. Don't you think you're jumping the gun somewhat?'

'I'll be nineteen at Christmas. Besides, if I wait I might get pushed into something I don't want at all. If I join the Land Army I might be sent to a farm on the Fylde. That'd be great, wouldn't it? Then I could perhaps get home on my days off.'

'You'll just have to wait and see, won't you, love?' Ellen smiled, imagining her granddaughter being sent to far-off Devon or Cornwall or the distant wilds of the Scottish Highlands rather than the Fylde. 'That's all any of us can do for the moment, wait and see. What about Ruby?' Ellen had asked. 'Has she any startling plans?'

'Not that I know of, Gran. She's not really old enough yet, is she? And she seems quite happy working in the shop with Auntie Sally. But I haven't told Ruby about all this – you know, the Land Army. As a matter of fact, I haven't told anybody but you.'

Ellen had felt gratified that she was the one to be taken into Pearl's confidence. She knew that the two of them, grandmother and granddaughter, had a unique relationship and that the girl sometimes told her things that she didn't tell her parents or her sisters. Ellen loved all her granddaughters, but Pearl was the one who was somehow . . . special. She reminded Ellen so much of herself at the same age; quiet-natured, a little unsure about the ways of the world, although she, Ellen, had already been married at eighteen with a baby daughter.

She knew that Pearl had told her parents now about the Land Army – Ellen had insisted that she must do so without further delay – and that they, surprisingly, had not seemed as alarmed as Ellen had been. A different attitude of the next generation, she supposed, although Ellen considered herself to be quite go-ahead in her thinking.

'No, not yet, Gran,' said Pearl now. 'I've decided, after all, that I won't be leaving you, not just yet. I agree with Dad. It all seems to have gone very quiet, so I think I'll just sit tight and wait. There's no point in rushing into anything until I see how things are going. I shall no doubt join up eventually, but at the moment – yes – I'll still be working in the office.'

It went without saying that Rachel would continue as the manageress of the Bank Hey Street shop, and Sally of the Dickson Road shop. Ruby, too, would continue to work at the latter branch, as it was well known that she worked along with her aunt far more agreeably than she would have done with her mother.

'For the time being at any rate,' Ruby said, with a slight shrug, when she was brought into the conversation. 'I don't suppose I shall stay there for ever.' There was a spirited gleam in her eyes as she turned to grin at Ellen. With her bright blue eyes, rosy cheeks and almost black curly hair Ruby really was a beautiful girl, thought her grandmother. Undoubtedly the pick of the bunch as far as looks were concerned. 'Like Pearl, I might join up,' she said. 'But I shall go into something proper when I do, not just the silly old Land Army.' She stuck her tongue out at her elder sister.

'You'll do no such thing, not yet awhile,' retorted her mother. 'You're only just seventeen, so you'll have a long wait, my girl.'

'Not as long as *I* have to wait,' said Emmie plaintively. So far, Emmie, the youngest of the three girls, had been very quiet, but then all this talk of Hobson's didn't affect her very much as she was still at school.

Ellen turned to smile at her. Emmie was the one that you tended to forget about, unintentionally, of course. She was often reading or studying and had far less to say than Ruby, or even Pearl. Ellen had thought it was somewhat fanciful of Rachel and Harry to name all their daughters after jewels; but oddly enough the girls did resemble their namesakes.

With Emerald – always known as Emmie – they had taken rather a chance. Her eyes, an indefinite greyish-hazel shade at birth, could well have turned out to be brown. As it happened, they were now a clear bright hazel, glinting more greenly, like the jewel of her name, whenever the girl was enthusiastic or excited, happy or angry. Emmie, at a first glance, didn't seem to be as striking-looking as either of her sisters. Her hair was wispy and of a mousey brown shade, waving back gently from a high forehead, and her round face was pale with unremarkable features. Until you looked at her eyes; Emmie's eyes were truly lovely. The eyes were the mirror of the soul, so Ellen had heard, and if this were so, then Emmie must have a profound one. She was, indeed, the brainy one of the family. Ellen knew that her parents had great hopes that the girl would become a teacher or even go to university.

'It'll be ages before I'm eighteen, won't it, Gran?' Emmie said now. Her hazel eyes were glowing greenly – intensely – as they did when she was thinking hard. 'Ages and ages. You're all talking about what you're going to do in this war.' She glanced round the room at them all. 'And what can I do? Nothing . . . only go to school.'

'You've your studying to do,' said Rachel, quite curtly. 'You know that, Emmie. It's School Certificate year for you and we want you to do well.'

'And then you'll be going on to college or university, won't you, dear?' said Ellen gently. 'There's such a lot for you to look forward to.'

More than for any of us, most probably, thought Ellen, although she didn't say so. Emerald was the 'high flier' of the family and Ellen was sure she would go far. Rachel had already made it clear that she had no intention of letting her youngest daughter go into the family rock firm. And Ellen, in spite of her loyalty to the firm she had founded, was inclined to agree. Intellect such as Emmie's had to be fostered.

Emerald, though, at that moment, was looking thoroughly disgruntled at the thought of the years of studying that lay ahead.

Three daughters, mused Ellen. What a responsibility they were, to be sure. What a responsibility any family was, for that matter, none more so than her own. Her son and daughter, and their spouses, and their children, each with their own hopes and ambitions, likes and dislikes, doubts and fears . . . all so very different. And now there were three more little individuals to be considered in this family of hers; and Ellen didn't intend to forget about them, not for one moment. They had been invited into her home and she would make sure, whilst they remained with her, that they would be just as much a part of the family as any of the others.

Chapter 7

Gloria had to admit that it was good to be back at school and to see all her old Salford friends again. It had been nice to have a few extra days' holiday and to see some of the sights of Blackpool – it really was a wonderful town – but Gloria had always enjoyed going to school, and the return to normality was helping Wendy to settle down and stop crying. Gloria was glad about that. It had been getting on her nerves and she was sure it had got on Auntie Ellen's nerves as well, although she didn't say so. She was a very patient lady.

Gloria thought, also, that Michael had now stopped wetting the bed. Not that Auntie Ellen had ever said that he had done so, but Gloria had guessed. Why else would there be sheets and pyjamas flapping in the breeze every morning? Gloria hadn't taunted him about it, even though she knew he would have done so to her had it been the other way round. She was aware that both Michael and Wendy were still missing their mum and dad very much, whereas she, Gloria, had never been so happy in all her life. Michael didn't make rude remarks to her any more. He was much more subdued these days. Besides, there was no need, because Gloria knew that she had changed, in outward appearance at least, almost beyond recognition.

They had started school again the following Monday at the red-brick building tucked away behind the shops, not far from King Street where Gloria now lived. It was, in many ways, very similar to the school they had attended in Salford so the children felt quite at home. And the girls and boys of

Standard Two found that they had the same teacher, Miss Butler!

'Hello, Gloria,' she said in some surprise, quite pointedly staring at the child, when she saw her again for the first time. 'I hardly recognised you . . . You do look nice, dear.'

Gloria knew that it wasn't a very tactful remark, but she didn't mind because she, too, was very surprised and pleased at her new appearance. She couldn't help looking in the mirror time and time again at her neat fringe and shining dark brown hair which fell in a straight bob to just below her ears. It didn't itch any more, and all those horrid nits seemed to have vanished after two more applications of that magic shampoo.

She had lots of new clothes too – including a smart navy gaberdine mac, just like Wendy's and Michael's, and some soft comfy woollen knee-socks and shiny black shoes. Not those patent leather ones with an ankle strap like Wendy wore, but lace-ups with a fancy pattern punched in the leather. Gloria had looked rather longingly at the ankle-strap shoes when she had seen them in the shop, but Auntie Ellen seemed to think they were not very suitable for everyday wear and had persuaded her to have the more sensible ones. Gloria hadn't argued. She knew she was a very lucky girl to be having new shoes at all. And Auntie Ellen had half promised that she would buy her some of the fancier ones later, then she would be just like Wendy. Wendy had been talked into wearing her patent leather shoes only on a Sunday now, not every day; so when the two girls walked along Church Street together on their way to school you could hardly tell them apart, except that one was dark and the other fair.

The gymslip that Gloria was wearing wasn't exactly new, neither was the white blouse, but they were almost new, having belonged to Auntie Ellen's youngest granddaughter, Emmie. With them Gloria was wearing a red and blue striped tie and a matching woven girdle round her waist. She kept touching the girdle lovingly, running her fingers through the fringed ends. It was just like new and Gloria couldn't believe it was really hers. She had never had a proper uniform before and now she was one of the very few who had the correct uniform for this Blackpool school. The colours were the same as the Salford school, navy blue and red, so there wasn't much difference, but Gloria knew that the items she was wearing were the 'real thing'.

She was pleased to own something that had belonged to Emmie, for Gloria had liked her as soon as she had met her, a week or so after she had come to live in Blackpool. Sally had taken Gloria and Wendy to Rachel's house one evening when Michael was getting ready for bed. He had made a bit of a fuss, saying that he wanted to go as well, but Ellen had persuaded him that he wouldn't be very interested in hearing a lot of ladies chattering, Rachel's being a largely feminine household. George had promised to read him a Toytown story so Michael was pacified; he was becoming very fond of Uncle George.

It wasn't dark when they set off, but the light was beginning to fade in a rosy glow in the direction of the sea. Sally took her big silver torch; they would need it when they were coming home, she said, as all the streets were now blacked out after dark.

Gloria stared around wonderingly at the wide tree-lined streets and the enormous houses, each set in its own spacious garden. Some of them were even bigger than Auntie Ellen's. The house where Rachel and Harry and their three daughters lived was near the gates of Stanley Park in a quiet leafy avenue. There was a tree with pretty leaves, some of them just beginning to fall, by the garden gate, and Sally told them it was a sycamore. That was why the house was called 'The Sycamores'. Just imagine living in a house that had a real name and not just a number! Gloria gaped in awe, although she was getting quite used to seeing posh houses now, both at the outside and then, when Rachel opened the door for them, at the inside.

Rachel seemed quite nice, very much like Auntie Ellen to look at, but much younger of course. But she wasn't quite as friendly or as warm as either Auntie Ellen or Auntie Sally. She didn't invite Gloria and Wendy to call her Auntie Rachel, so they didn't call her anything.

'Hello, Sal.' She kissed Sally on the cheek, a peck rather than a kiss. 'And these are our two visitors, are they? I wondered when we'd be meeting you. Now, let me guess.' Rachel stood back, looking at them with her head on one side. 'You must be Gloria . . . and you're Wendy. Am I right? Your little brother's in bed, I suppose?'

Wendy nodded. She seemed to have lost her tongue, as Gloria had. But Wendy did manage to say, 'Pleased to meetcher,' when Rachel said 'How do you do?' and held out her hand, whereas Gloria could only mutter a feeble 'Hello.'

Gloria soon realised what Auntie Ellen had meant when she had said that their own house was a little bit shabby. Gloria didn't think it was – not at all – but even she could see the difference in the two houses. Auntie Ellen's house was comfortable and homely, the sort of place where you could dump your belongings on a chair if you wanted to; but this house seemed altogether too grand and certainly too neat and tidy. It wasn't very big – Gloria knew that it was what was called a semi-detached house – but everything in it was so swanky.

In the living room at the back of the house, where Rachel now took them, the red carpet with a pattern of grey and white leaves filled every inch of the floor, and the long curtains hanging at the windows, in exactly the same shade of red, looked like real velvet. The dining table and chairs and the matching sideboard were not as dark or as heavy as Auntie Ellen's. They were made of shiny orangey-coloured wood, very plain and modern-looking. Gloria had seen some just like them in the window of a posh furniture store in Blackpool.

There was a crocheted mat in the middle of the table on which stood a cut-glass vase filled with huge yellow and white chrysanthemums, the sort that looked like mop heads. Gloria knew they were called chrysanthemums because her mam had bought some last year when Grandad had died, to take to the funeral. It was the first time she had seen these flowers since then and Gloria decided that she didn't like them. They brought back memories of Grandad who had been the only person who had seemed to care about her, apart from Monica. She missed the smell of his pipe and the feel of his bristly moustache when he kissed her, and the tiny scented floral gums he used to give her.

For the first time since she had come to live in Blackpool Gloria began to feel a little bit sad. She didn't feel at home in this swanky house and for once Auntie Sally wasn't taking any notice of them. She was chattering away to Rachel about grown-up things – the shop and the factory and those WVS ladies that Auntie Ellen sometimes helped – while she and Wendy just stood there. Gloria tried to think what it would be like living here instead of in King Street and she couldn't imagine it at all. Ellen or Sally usually covered the table with an old brown, sort of velvety cloth when they weren't eating off it, so that she and Wendy and Michael could do jigsaws there, or draw and crayon. Sally had once let them paint, using an old paintbox of George's that she had found tucked away in a cupboard. She hadn't minded even when Michael had spilled the water and it had soaked right through the cloth. Gloria couldn't imagine being allowed to do that here. There wasn't a single thing lying about like there was at home – Gloria already thought of King Street as her home – such as Auntie Sally's knitting or Auntie Ellen's favourite magazine or Uncle George's newspaper and packet of cigarettes.

The room felt a bit chilly, too. There was no glowing fire like Auntie Ellen always had, even when the day was quite warm, just a cheerless-looking electric fire set into a surround of cream-coloured tiles, and over the mantelpiece two wall lights – unlit – shaped like the shells that you found on the beach with a rectangular mirror in between.

Gloria shifted uncomfortably from foot to foot. She didn't like to sit down without being asked. Besides, she would almost be afraid to sit on one of those pale grey armchairs. She might make the seat all mucky or crease the lace-edged cover on the back.

Just then the door opened and two girls came in, young ladies, really, because they were much older than Gloria and Wendy. Gloria guessed these must be two of the grand-daughters she had heard about. Which ones, she wondered. She knew there were three of them. One of them was dressed ready to go out in a grey costume with a saucy little red hat perched on top of her black curls. She had ruby red lips and rosy cheeks and Gloria guessed at once that this must be Ruby.

She was right. 'Off out again, Ruby?' asked Rachel. 'Where are you going this time?'

Ruby gave an exaggerated sigh. 'Anybody 'ud think I'm always going out. Hello, Auntie Sally. It doesn't seem long since I saw you.' She smiled at Sally in a very friendly way and Gloria remembered that Ruby worked with her in the shop. Then she turned to the two little girls. 'Hello, you two. You're Gran's little visitors, are you? And Auntie Sally's, of course. She's treating you OK, is she? You let me know if she doesn't.' She winked and gave an impudent grin at Sally before turning back to her mother. 'Yes, Mum, I'm going out . . . *again*. I'm going to the pictures with Mavis. Anything else you'd like to know?'

'Don't be so cheeky, Ruby.' Rachel frowned at her. 'I was only asking. I like to know where you're going, especially now. I don't want you wandering around in the dark. The pictures, you say? I thought the cinemas were closed.'

'They're open again, Rachel,' said Sally. 'It was in the *Evening Gazette* the other night – didn't you see it? Due to public pressure, it said.'

'No, I didn't see it,' said Rachel. She cast an aggravated glance at her sister-in-law. 'When do I ever have time to read the paper from cover to cover?' She turned to her daughter. 'What picture are you going to see anyway?'

Ruby sighed again. 'Will Hay in *Ask a Policeman*. It's on at the Palace. Flippin' heck, Mum, it's like the Spanish Inquisition with you! And no, I won't be late back. And yes, I'll get a tram to the end of the road. And yes, I've got my gas mask, although goodness knows why we've got to carry the bloomin' things around everywhere. Now, are you satisfied, Mum?' She turned to her aunt. 'Honestly, Auntie Sally, did you ever know anybody nag as much as she does?'

Sally raised her hand. 'Leave me out of it, please, Ruby. Your mother's only concerned about you, and I would be just the same if you were my daughter.'

Gloria, who had been watching and listening to this interchange rather carefully, thought that Sally looked a bit sad for a moment, and Rachel glanced at her sharply.

'You'll have to hurry, won't you, dear, if you want to get in for the first house,' Sally said quietly. 'Seven o'clock, isn't it?'

'I'm not sure. I think it might be continuous,' replied Ruby, giving a casual shrug. 'It doesn't really matter what time we go in. We can watch it round again. Cheerio, Auntie Sally, see you tomorrer.' She waggled her fingers in a cheeky wave. 'Bye, Mum. I won't be late, honest. Bye, you two. Oh, bye, Pearl,' she added as an afterthought, nodding towards the other occupant of the room.

Then Ruby was gone and it seemed as though a whirlwind had passed. She's good fun, thought Gloria, although she had been a bit shocked at the way the girl had been so cheeky to her mother. If she, Gloria, had spoken to her mam like that she would have got a clout across the face, or her dad would have belted her if he had been there to hear. But it hadn't been often that Gloria had answered her mother back, like the lads did, and Daisy Mulligan seemed to take it from them with scarcely a comment. At all events, Gloria thought now, it was obvious that Rachel cared about her daughter in a way that Daisy had never cared about her. All the Hobsons and the Balderstones (which was the funny name that Rachel's family had) seemed to be caring, loving people, though they showed it in different ways.

Rachel shook her head now and sighed. 'She's so cheeky and rude I don't know what to do with her at times. She's too big for a good hiding, not that I have ever smacked any of them much; I don't believe in it. But she's a real handful.'

'She's all right,' replied Sally fondly, and Rachel looked sharply at her again. 'Yes, I know she's a bit cheeky, Rachel,' Sally went on, 'and I'm not excusing her, but I daresay it's her age, isn't it? A phase she's going through. And you've never been really worried that she'd step seriously out of line, have you?'

'No, I suppose not,' Rachel muttered. 'It's just her manner.'

'She's a grand little worker in the shop,' said Sally, 'and the customers like her. She's always got a smile and a cheery word for everybody – and that goes a long way when you're trying to sell things.' Sally chuckled. 'I sometimes think the customers go out with loads of stuff they'd never intended buying. She's great at pushing our new lines.'

'Yes, I'm well aware that she's a good saleswoman,' replied Rachel, a little sharply. 'That's not the point. I just wish she could be a bit less difficult when she's at home. She's not at all like the other two and that's for sure.'

Rachel turned now towards the other girl in the room, who was curled up in an armchair flicking over the pages of a magazine. She had fair hair and brown eyes and looked very much like her mother. 'Pearl's never given me half as much bother, have you, love? Nor has our Emmie. Come on, Pearl. Aren't you going to say hello to our little visitors?'

Pearl smiled warmly at them. 'Hello, Wendy. Hello, Gloria. I know both your names, you see. I was just waiting till the storm had died down. You can't get a word in when our Ruby's around.' She uncurled her slim legs and rose to her feet. 'Come on, you two. I'll take you upstairs and introduce you to Emmie. You don't want to stay here, do you, listening to these two chattering? All boring stuff!' She wrinkled her nose. 'And Emmie's a little bit nearer your age than I am. She's a few years older, of course. She's fifteen and you're eight, aren't you?'

Both girls nodded, although Gloria added, 'Nearly nine, acksherly.'

'Well, only six years then,' said Pearl, nodding seriously. 'Emmie said she was going to do some homework, but I daresay she'll have finished by now.'

'Thanks, Pearl. Yes, take them up to Emmie.' Rachel sounded as though she was quite glad to have them out of the way. 'Off you go, girls, and I'll bring you up a drink of cocoa in a little while, when Sally and I have our cup of tea. You're not going out then, Pearl?'

'No, I'll listen to the wireless. I think Jack Warner's on tonight.'

'You'll have to go in the front room then; Sally and I are talking. Our Pearl's a real stay-at-home, not a bit like her sister,' Rachel was saying as the two little girls followed Pearl up the richly carpeted stairs.

She pushed open a door at the end of the landing and the girl who was curled up on the bed reading a book looked up in surprise. Gloria realised at once that this youngest girl, Emmie, was not as pretty as either of her sisters, Pearl or Ruby. Those two reminded Gloria of the fairy story about Snow White and Rose Red because one was so dark and the other so fair. But this girl was neither. Her hair was a mousey-brown, waving back from a wide expanse of forehead and, at first appearances, she seemed to be rather plain and ordinary. Gloria felt an immediate kinship with her. She knew what it was like to be the unattractive one although, in Gloria's case, the comparison that was sometimes made was with her friend,

Wendy, not with her sisters. Emmie was wearing her school uniform – a navy-blue skirt and white blouse and a pale blue and navy striped tie, but her feet were bare. Then she smiled, and Gloria wondered how she could have thought she was not very pretty. Her eyes, greeny-brown and fringed with dark lashes, positively glowed, lighting up the whole of her round face.

'Hello! You're Gloria and Wendy, aren't you? I've heard a lot about you from Gran and I've been dying to meet you. Come on, sit on the bed with me and we'll have a natter.' Emmie put down her book, then swung her legs across and made room for them. 'Are you staying, Pearl?'

'No, I don't think so. I'll go and listen to the wireless. I haven't disturbed you, have I, Emmie? You've finished your homework?'

'Yes, we didn't have all that much tonight. No doubt we will when term gets going properly, but it's bound to take some sorting out, sharing the school with the girls from Manchester.'

'Manchester?' Gloria's eyes widened at the word. 'You've got 'vacuees at your school an' all, have you, like us?'

'Yes, from the Manchester Central High School for Girls,' replied Emmie. 'We're starting school earlier, quarter to nine till quarter to one, and the Manchester lot have the building in the afternoon, from one o' clock till five. And we're using the cricket pavilion in the park as well – it's only down the road – and some rooms the Co-op are letting us use. It makes a change.' Emmie grinned. 'Livens things up a bit.'

'Which school do you go to?' asked Gloria as Pearl quietly left them.

'The Collegiate School, just round the corner,' said Emmie. 'I'm in my last year now – School Certificate year, unless I stay on for the Sixth Form. Mum and Dad want me to, but I don't know.' She gave a slight shrug. 'We'll have to see.'

Gloria nodded, but rather uncertainly. It all sounded very

grown-up and appealing, but quite out of her sphere of experience. Gloria had always been told that she would have to leave school and go out to work as soon as she was old enough. 'We're at St John's School,' she said, 'aren't we, Wendy?' trying to draw her tongue-tied friend into the conversation. 'I've got some of your clothes, 'aven't I? And your tie and girdle.'

'Yes, I believe you have,' said Emmie. 'Gran said so.' She smiled at the little girls. 'You look nice in your uniforms, both of you. I liked it at St John's, do you? It's one of the oldest schools in Blackpool. Mum went there when she was a little girl, and Uncle George.'

'Yes, we like it, don't we, Wendy?' Gloria persisted. 'We've got our old teacher from Salford. She's a bit strict – well, a lot really. She doesn't let you talk, but she's all right, I suppose, isn't she, Wendy?'

Gloria and Emmie exchanged understanding glances over the head of Wendy, who seemed to have completely lost her tongue. 'And what do you like doing best at school, Wendy?' asked Emmie. 'No, let her tell me,' she whispered as Gloria opened her mouth to answer. 'Reading, or doing compositions, or sums?'

Wendy pulled a face at that. She admitted, shyly, that she wasn't very good at sums. She quite liked writing stories, but what she liked doing most of all was drawing and painting, something they hadn't done very much of since coming to Blackpool. When it had been established that they both liked reading they all knelt down to look at Emmie's selection of books on the shelves at the side of her bed.

'It's only a small room,' said Emmie. 'Pearl and Ruby share a bigger one at the back, but I like to be on my own – I have my homework to do, you see. There's not much room, but I had to have my books in here.'

The room was certainly not very big, not nearly as big as the one that Gloria and Wendy shared, with scarcely enough space for the single bed, small wardrobe and dressing table.

Gloria noticed a hockey stick and a tennis racquet propped up in the corner and a few pairs of shoes – black school shoes, white plimsolls and a pair of fluffy bedroom slippers – flung untidily around. On the wide window-ledge there was a collection of china rabbits, all with impossibly round heads and long ears, in colours of green, blue and yellow, and some mugs with pictures on them of the Princesses Elizabeth and Margaret Rose, when they were quite a lot younger. There was a hairbrush and a mirror with embroidered backs on the dressing-table, and some more of the little animals, cats and dogs this time, sitting amidst a jumble of hair-slides and grips, letters and papers and half-eaten packets of sweets.

Gloria thought how nice it would be to have a collection of little animals – or a collection of anything – but she also thought how untidy it all was, compared with the room downstairs. The eiderdown, a billowy shiny pink one, had been taken off the bed and was lying on the floor; Gloria guessed that Emmie didn't want to get it all creased by sitting on it.

'Doesn't yer mum get on at you to keep yer room tidy?' she blurted out now, as her eyes alighted on the various objects, such a lot to be contained in such a small space.

Emmie laughed. 'Sometimes. I'm not the tidiest of persons as you can see, but you should see our Ruby's room, her half of it at any rate. It drives Pearl barmy and Mum's always on at her. We have to keep our own rooms tidy – it's only fair – dusting and making the beds and all that, but Mrs Greaves, that's our cleaning lady, she comes in to do the hoovering and polishing. Mum's a real fusspot, though, forever tidying up and moving our things out of the way. That's why I spend a lot of time up here when I can. Not in the winter though; it's too cold. Now, would you like to borrow some of my books to take home? Just help yourselves, then when you've read them you can come back for some more.'

'Ooh, can we really?' said Wendy, who was much more cheerful now. 'It's like a library, isn't it? Thanks ever so much, Emmie.'

Wendy's eyes scanned the shelves, then her hands reached towards the collection of *Picturegoer* and *Film Review* annuals. 'Can I borrow one of these?' She drew one out and quickly turned the pages. Gloria guessed that she was looking for pictures of her idol, Shirley Temple. Mrs Cooper took Wendy to see every one of the child star's films.

'What about you, Gloria? What would you like?' asked Emmie. 'School stories? I've got quite a lot of those.' She pointed to the row of Angela Brazil books and *Girl's Crystal* annuals. 'I used to get one of those every Christmas, but I'm a bit old for them now.'

Gloria wrinkled her nose. 'I don't think so. I've read one or two of 'em, but . . .'

'But you don't like school stories very much?'

'They're all right, I s'pose. But they're not like us, them kids, are they? Not like me, anyroad. I mean, they're dead posh, aren't they, and they live in swanky houses, and they all say daft things like, "Oh golly, Belinda, that's absolutely spiffing!" ' Gloria pursed up her lips and half closed her eyes as she spoke in a pseudo-refined voice, and Emmie burst out laughing.

'Oh, Gloria, you are funny!'

'Well, they do, don't they?' Gloria retorted. 'All them bloomin' midnight feasts and French mamzelles, and girls who are princesses from India or somewhere. 'Tisn't real, is it? 'Tisn't like our school anyroad,' she added thoughtfully.

'That's because they're boarding schools,' said Emmie. 'Yes, I do know what you mean, Gloria. I never really thought about it when I read them – I just enjoyed the stories – but we've been reading a book called *Pride and Prejudice* at school. I don't think you'll have heard of it; it's by a woman called Jane Austen and she wrote it – oh, about two hundred years ago. But when I read it, I thought just the same as you did about those school stories. I thought, Goodness, these people aren't like us at all. They have servants and enormous houses and they have so much money they don't even need to go out to work. And the women just spend their time visiting people, or painting and embroidering, or going to parties and balls, or just ... gossiping. They never do anything real. I know it all happened hundreds of years ago in that story, but I suppose there are people like that today. And I'd never even thought about it till I read that book. We're doing it for School Certificate,' she added.

Gloria looked at her in surprise. 'But *you're* rich, aren't you? You've got a big house – well, yours i'n't all that big, is it? Not as big as yer gran's – but it's dead posh. And you've got servants an' all.'

Emmie laughed. 'Only Mrs Greaves to do a bit of cleaning. No, I can assure you, Gloria, we're quite ordinary. Gran's not poor, I'll admit, but that's because she's worked hard. And there's nothing very posh about a rock factory, is there? No, we're only ordinary folks, the Balderstones and the Hobsons.'

I bet your mum doesn't think she's ordinary, thought Gloria. That Rachel woman, she thinks she's *it*! But, of course, she didn't voice these thoughts to Emmie.

Gloria's eyes returned to the bookshelf. The Toytown books, *Swallows and Amazons* and some more big thick books by Arthur Ransome, *Pinocchio*, Winnie The Pooh, the *Just So* stories and the *Jungle Book* ... simply loads of children's books, and some grown-up books with *Everyman* printed on the paper covers. Of course, Emmie was not a child any more. There was here a veritable feast of literature, and Gloria was mesmerised.

'Gosh, have you read 'em all?' she gasped.

'Yes, some of them a few times,' said Emmie. 'It's one of my favourite things, reading.'

'Mine an' all,' breathed Gloria, gazing admiringly at her new friend.

'Which d'you want then? Can't you decide?' Emmie smiled at her. 'Shall I help you?'

Gloria nodded. 'Mmm. Pick one of your favourites, an' I 'spect I'll like it as well.'

Emmie deliberated for a moment then handed her a copy of a Mary Poppins story. 'I think you'll like this.' She grinned. 'The kids in it are a bit posh, I'm afraid – they have a nanny – but they do all sorts of exciting things. I remember I loved it.'

'And can I lend a film book an' all, like Wendy's doing?'

'It's "borrow", not "lend", ' chimed in Wendy, looking up momentarily from the pages of *Picturegoer*.

Gloria gave her a withering glance. 'All right, Miss Clever-Clogs, I know it is.' Gloria knew she got words mixed up a bit sometimes, but she was trying hard to speak 'proper' since she had come to live with Auntie Ellen and Auntie Sally. Wendy liked to show off because, just before they came away, she had started having elocution lessons where they learned you to talk all posh. 'I know it's borrer. Can I *borrow* . . .' she exaggerated the word in a mincing tone before sticking out her tongue at Wendy. 'Can I borrow one of them film books, please, Emmie? I want to see if there's any pictures of that lady what I'm called after.'

Emmie gave a little frown, then, 'Oh yes, I see,' she said. 'Of course. Gloria Swanson it'll be.'

'Yes, that's 'er.'

Gloria finally settled on the annual of her choice and Wendy chose *Ballet Shoes* to read in addition to her film book. Then they all enjoyed a drink of cocoa from china cups with roses on them, carried up by Pearl on a tray with a lace-edged embroidered tray cloth. Pearl stayed with them and they all shoved up to make room for her on the bed. Emmie had pulled down the blackout blind and drawn the pink curtains, and with the glow from the pink shaded light it was all very friendly and cosy.

'It's like one of them midnight feasts, i'n't it?' said Gloria, but rather shyly. She didn't know Pearl as well as she did Emmie.

'Yes, just like those posh girls have,' said Emmie, and the two new friends grinned at one another.

'There's a lot of yer mum's books at home, at Auntie Ellen's,' Gloria told her. 'In our bedroom. I've started reading *Anne of Green Gables*.'

'Oh yes – that's mine, not Mum's,' replied Emmie. 'I left it there once when I was staying with Gran. It's too difficult for you, surely, Gloria? I must have been ten or eleven when I first read that.'

'Mmm, there are some big words,' Gloria agreed. 'But it's about a kid like me, i'n't it? Anne didn't have anybody what really cared about her, did she, till she met Marilla and Matthew? Like I've met your gran and Auntie Sally . . .' And you, Emmie, she added to herself. 'An' I like all that stuff about kindred spirits,' she ventured, feeling shy again. 'I think I know what that means . . .'

It was completely dark when they set off for home and Harry insisted on walking with them as far as the big main road. It was the first time Gloria and Wendy had seen him and they were a little in awe of him. He looked a bit like Uncle George, with dark hair going grey and blue eyes, but he was shorter and slimmer and you couldn't chatter to him like you could to George. But maybe that was because they didn't know him as well.

Along the main road, the edge of the kerb was painted white so that you could see it in the dark, and there were white stripes, like a zebra, round the trunks of the trees which loomed menacingly above them. These same trees had seemed quite friendly a couple of hours ago, gay and colourful in their early autumn foliage. Now, in the darkness, they were towering giants, black sinister shapes silhouetted against the dark grey sky. Gloria was glad of the shining beam from Sally's torch, illuminating the way ahead. A huge double-decker bus passed them, casting a bluey-purplish glimmer from its dimly lit interior. It looked spooky and scary, but Gloria didn't feel frightened. She had had a lovely, lovely evening and she felt all warm and happy inside.

She was thinking of what she had mentioned, somewhat timidly, to Emmie about kindred spirits. Gloria decided that she had met two real kindred spirits since coming to Blackpool. Wendy, walking at her side, her arm tucked companionably through Gloria's, was her best friend. She had known her for ages and she looked after her. But Wendy wasn't a real 'kindred spirit'. Sometimes she and Gloria didn't think the same way about things at all.

Auntie Ellen wasn't one either. She was lovely and kind and Gloria liked her a lot, but she was quite old and, like Wendy, Gloria guessed that Auntie Ellen sometimes looked at some things a little bit differently. As for Pearl and Ruby, Gloria didn't know them very well yet, and she didn't even consider Rachel. But Auntie Sally and Emmie, now they were definitely kindred spirits.

Sally turned, smiling down at her. 'You're very quiet, Gloria. Are you all right, dear? Just tired, I expect.'

'No, not tired, Auntie Sally.' Gloria shook her head decidedly. 'I'm not tired at all. I was just thinking . . . how much I like living here, in Blackpool.'

Chapter 8

'I hope this isn't going to unsettle her, that's all,' said Ellen, looking down at the letter in her hand.

It had arrived that morning from Mrs Cooper, Wendy and Michael's mother, saying that she would be coming to Blackpool on a day excursion train from Manchester, the following Saturday, and would like to take the two children out for the day. There had been two letters, in fact, one addressed to Ellen and the other one, tucked inside, for Wendy and Michael. Wendy had been overjoyed at the news, more so than Michael, and had gone off to school skipping and dancing along the pavement, with a more subdued Gloria following behind her.

'Wendy has settled down so nicely now,' Ellen went on. 'We haven't had any tears for ages, have we? And Michael has stopped wetting the bed, thank goodness. But it's Wendy I'm more concerned about. It's bound to upset her, seeing her mum again – well, not seeing her so much as saying goodbye to her at the end of the day.'

'You can't blame the woman, though, can you,' said Sally, 'for wanting to come and see her kids. She must be missing them as much as they're missing her – more, probably. Like you say, Mam, they've settled down pretty well now. What about their father, I wonder? She doesn't mention him, does she?'

'No, she doesn't.' Ellen put the letter back in its envelope and pushed it behind the wooden clock on the mantelshelf. Sally had already read it that morning. 'She writes a good letter, I must say. Nice notepaper and a well-formed hand. Obviously quite a well-educated woman.'

'Mmm. Well, I daresay she is,' said Sally, a little broodily.

Ellen sat down again, looking concernedly at her daughter-in-law in the opposite fireside chair. 'What's the matter, Sal? There's something troubling you, isn't there?'

'Well, you can guess what it is, can't you, Mam?' said Sally. She tucked her knitting down the side of her chair and leaned forward earnestly. 'It's Gloria. It's her that I'm concerned about, to be honest, more than Wendy or Michael. What is this going to do to Gloria, her friend's mother coming over and not a word from her own family? You saw her this morning, how her little face dropped when the letter arrived. I've never seen her look so dejected, not since that time we first set eyes on her in the church hall. I could have wept for her. And no mention, of course, of Mrs Cooper taking Gloria out as well. Just the two kiddies, she said.'

'You can't hold that against her,' said Ellen. 'It's her own kiddies she'll want to see, it's only natural.'

'And Gloria never went down very well with her, I know that,' added Sally quietly. 'But she's sure to notice how much the little lass has changed, bless her.'

Ellen's eyes softened as she continued to look steadily at Sally. 'You're getting very fond of her, aren't you, dear?'

Sally stared down at her hands folded serenely in her lap. She was silent for a moment, then, 'Yes, I am . . . very fond of her, Mam,' she said. 'I like the others as well – I think we've got ourselves three grand kiddies; we've been very lucky – but Gloria, well, I must admit she's rather special to me.'

'You chose her. I've not forgotten that,' said Ellen quietly. 'I'm so glad you did, dear. And I know it upsets you that her family don't seem to care about her.'

Sally shook her head. 'I don't understand how they can behave like that, never even writing to the poor little kid. I know her mother is probably not very much of a scholar, but she could make an effort – a postcard or something. And that Monica that Gloria goes on about – not as much as she did at first, mind you – her sister, you'd think she could get in touch.'

'Perhaps you could take the child out for a treat on her own sometime,' suggested Ellen, 'seeing that Wendy and Michael will have their mother here.'

'I might,' said Sally. 'Although I'm always careful not to show favouritism. It's Gloria's birthday, isn't it, in October, so perhaps we could do something for that. Surely her family will get in touch with her then.'

'I certainly hope so,' sighed Ellen. 'When Mrs Cooper comes I think we'd better ask her to come back for tea, hadn't we, before she gets her train home. Saturday'll be October the seventh, won't it, and Gloria's birthday's the next week. So maybe we could have a birthday tea on Saturday . . . What do you think, Sally?'

'No, I don't think so, Mam,' said Sally, quite vehemently. 'Invite the woman to tea by all means – it's only polite to do that – but I somehow don't think that Gloria would want Mrs Cooper at her birthday celebration. We'll make that a separate occasion, shall we?'

'Yes, of course you're right, dear,' said Ellen. 'But then you usually are,' she added, smiling.

Gloria had stayed out of the way, reading in her bedroom – like Emmie did, she had said – when Mrs Cooper came to collect Wendy and Michael the following Saturday morning. Ellen hadn't argued with her, understanding full well how the child must feel. Having checked that Gloria was all right she waited with the two excited children, their noses pressed against the front-room window, for the arrival of their mother.

Ellen didn't warm to Mrs Cooper. She was fair-haired and blue-eyed, like Wendy, quite tall and slim with neatly chiselled features and an air of aloofness. She greeted her children effusively, of course, hugging and kissing them and saying how much they had grown and how well they looked (Ellen was relieved to hear that). But she was rather taken aback when the woman proceeded to tidy Wendy's already immaculate hair and to re-fasten Michael's gaberdine coat, pulling it into shape. She then peered at herself in the hall mirror, adjusting her tiny veiled hat to more of an angle on top of her flaxen curls.

'There, all spick and span,' she said, giving both children an appraising glance. 'Put your shoulders back, Wendy. Don't slouch, there's a good girl. Thank you, Mrs Hobson,' she added, as though, Ellen thought, she was a menial. 'We'll be back for tea. Five o'clock you said, didn't you?'

She didn't say thank you for the invitation though, but as Ellen recalled, she had already done so in a letter so perhaps she didn't consider it necessary.

'You'll be out for your dinner, of course,' said Ellen. 'I was wondering if – er – perhaps I should have made you some sandwiches. It won't take more than a few minutes if you'd like some.' The younger woman, to her annoyance, was making her feel all flustered, something that Ellen, an experienced businesswoman when all was said and done, was unused to feeling.

'No, thank you all the same.' Mrs Cooper smiled sweetly. 'The children and I will have our lunch in a café. I expect we'll be able to find a decent one in Blackpool?'

'Any amount of them,' replied Ellen, a little tartly. She had noticed the woman's slight emphasis on the word 'lunch'. All right, Mrs Snooty Cooper, she thought to herself, echoing in her mind the words she had heard Gloria use (out of Wendy's hearing!). It's 'dinner' to us here in Blackpool. Dinner is what we have in the middle of the day, and I'll bet you do in Salford as well if you're honest. Lunch indeed! So she didn't make any suggestion to Mrs Cooper as to a nice café where they could eat their 'lunch'. Let her find one for herself, thought Ellen, although she knew she was being somewhat churlish.

She watched as the trio walked down the street, Mrs Cooper's high heels clip-clopping on the pavement and the head of her fox fur staring glassy-eyed over the shoulder of her stylish black costume. She was chattering away to the children though, and they were all, very obviously, happy to be reunited. Ellen's thoughts flew to Gloria. Poor little girl. She would give her a treat this afternoon. Perhaps they could go and have an ice-cream at Pablo's. So far, the war didn't seem to have made any difference to the production of their delicious confection.

Sally left the shop earlier than she usually did on a Saturday, leaving Ruby and the other assistant in charge, because she wanted to be present at the tea-party and to meet Mrs Cooper. George was there as well. The factory was closed on Saturday afternoon; besides, as the son of the firm, and especially in his new position as co-Director of Hobson's, he would have been justified in taking the odd hour or two off when necessary.

Wendy's normally pale cheeks were flushed with excitement as she recounted the delights of their day out. '. . . An' we went on the pier, right up to the jetty, then we went on a tram up to the Boating Pool and we had a ride on them wooden animals . . .'

'Those, dear,' corrected Mrs Cooper, ' "those" animals.'

'Yes, well . . . like I was saying, I went on a lion . . .'

'An' I went on a hellefunt,' said Michael. 'And we had a bottle of red pop, all fizzy, didn't we, Wendy, and an ice-cream . . .'

'The ice-cream was after your lunch though, dear, wasn't it?' said Mrs Cooper. 'You mustn't let Mrs Hobson – Auntie Ellen – think that I let you have ice-cream and pop at the same time. You'd be sick, wouldn't you? We had a very nice lunch, actually.' She turned to the grown-ups. 'At Jenkinson's café, very nice indeed, considering. Roast lamb with mint sauce and ice-cream for dessert, as Michael says. That was

102

after we'd been to the Boating Pool. The children loved it there. Such a nice little place for kiddies, isn't it, in the more ... *select* part of Blackpool.'

Sally felt herself bristling. 'Yes, isn't it? I took the children there myself, soon after they arrived ... *actually.*'

'Yes, we've been there, all of us.' Gloria, who had been very quiet, spoke up now. 'It were dead good. We went on them animals, didn't we, Auntie Sally?' She moistened her finger, determined not to let any of the tiny hundreds and thousands from the top of her iced bun escape. She scooped them up and licked them off her finger. 'Then we went on a paddle-boat an' all. You went with Michael, and Wendy and me went in one on our own, didn't we, Auntie Sally?'

Sally smiled her agreement. 'That's right, dear.'

'You didn't say, Wendy. You didn't tell me you'd been there before.' Mrs Cooper looked as though the wind had been taken out of her sails, and Sally instantly felt sorry. It hadn't been her intention to upset the woman, even though she was something of a stuck-up madam.

'They probably didn't want to spoil your surprise,' Sally smiled. 'Or they may not have even thought it was worth mentioning. It was just a little treat to help them to settle down.'

Mrs Cooper smiled back, rather frostily, but seemingly mollified. 'But I don't suppose you'd been to Fairyland before, had you? Wendy, Michael ... you hadn't been there, had you?' The children shook their heads. 'Oh, they loved Fairyland, they really did.' Mrs Cooper clasped her hands together ecstatically. 'I was quite fascinated myself by all those dear little fairies and goblins. It made me feel as though I was a little girl again.' She gave a tinkling laugh. 'I'm not very keen on that part of Blackpool, of course. At the end of the Golden Mile – such a vulgar area, isn't it? I would never have gone, you can be sure, if I hadn't heard about it from my next-door neighbour. She told me her children insist on going to Fairyland every time they come to Blackpool, and I thought, Well, if it's good enough for Mrs Adams then it's good enough for me. Her husband's a solicitor,' she added, preening herself, as though it were her own husband she was talking about. 'He's with a very good firm in Manchester.'

Which reminded Sally that they hadn't heard very much about Mr Cooper. Wendy had once told them that he worked in a shop, but had seemed vague about the details.

'Perhaps you could bring the children's daddy the next time you come,' said Sally. 'Wasn't he able to accompany you today?' But if he was a sales assistant he would probably be working on a Saturday, she thought.

'Daddy's joined up,' said Mrs Cooper brightly, a false brightness, Sally felt. 'Hasn't he, dears? Daddy's joined the Army. That's one of the reasons I came over today, to tell Wendy and Michael. Yes, they should be very proud of their daddy.' Her eyes were glistening and her prim little mouth was trembling slightly, but she kept on talking. Sally couldn't help but admire her.

'He didn't need to have gone. He's turned thirty – but he's not quite as old as you, of course, Mr Hobson,' she added, to Sally's amusement. George raised his eyebrows questioningly and with slight annoyance, although he was well aware that he looked his age and more, and had done ever since he had finished with 'the last lot'.

'No, Daddy didn't need to have enlisted. I doubt if they'll be calling his age group up yet awhile, but he felt he wanted to do his bit. Well, you've got to, haven't you, Mr Hobson?' Mrs Cooper looked challengingly at George. 'We've all got to do our bit. What was it they used to say in the last war – "Your Country Needs You"? Of course, I'm hardly old enough to remember all that; neither is Daddy. We were only children.' She gave another falsetto laugh. 'But that's what he felt. His country needs him. We're very proud of Daddy, aren't we, children?'

Doesn't 'Daddy' have a name? thought Sally irrationally, as her husband struggled to make some sort of a reply.

'Mmm, yes, well . . . good for him,' muttered George. 'Yes, Mrs Cooper, as you say, we all have to do our bit – and I won't shirk it, I can assure you, when the time comes.' His voice and his face were impassive, but he was looking keenly at the woman. 'But some of us remember the last lot only too well. Some of us were there . . . and it isn't an experience we want to repeat, believe you me. But I'll do my bit, you can be sure of that. As a matter of fact, I've applied to become a Special Constable.'

Sally didn't register her surprise. She had known it was in George's mind, but not that he had already made the application. Neither did Ellen react in any way. She was busying herself pouring out their second cup of tea, the 'chatting cup', as she always called it.

Mrs Cooper appeared a little discomfited. 'Have you indeed? Well, I think that's wonderful. Very commendable. I wasn't suggesting . . . Please don't think that I . . . I didn't realise you'd been in the war . . .' Her voice tailed away. 'Of course, I should have known. And one war's enough in anybody's lifetime, isn't it?'

That's just about the most sensible thing the woman's said so far, thought Sally, recalling that those were the very words she and Ellen had uttered that first weekend of the war. It seemed ages ago although it was hardly more than a month, but there was still very little happening. Men were joining up, like 'Daddy' Cooper, and thousands of children were living away from home, but there was still no sign of any real conflict. Sally felt herself thawing slightly towards Mrs Cooper. She must be feeling the strain, living on her own, with both her children and her husband away.

'You must be lonely then, Mrs Cooper,' she said concernedly. 'What do you do? I don't suppose you work . . . go out to work, I mean?'

Mrs Cooper shook her head although she didn't seem offended. Sally was wondering, belatedly, if she might have put her foot in it. Women didn't, as a rule, work away from home, unless they were involved in a family business, as she and Rachel and Ellen were; or if they were desperate for money, as she knew many of the mill-workers were in the Manchester area.

'No, I've never needed to work,' said Mrs Cooper. 'Daddy had a very good job. He was in charge of the furnishing department in Lewis's, you know.' Her smile was just a mite self-satisfied as she straightened the starched collar of her crisp white blouse. 'I was always very happy keeping my home nice and looking after my husband and children, but now . . .' her composure seemed to slip . . . 'the place seems like a morgue. No, I don't mean that exactly,' she amended. 'That's a frightful expression. What I mean is, the house seems so empty, so . . .'

'Desolate?' suggested Ellen. 'Not lived in? Yes, I can understand how you must feel.' She nodded sympathetically towards the younger woman. 'But if it's any consolation to you, I think you've done the right thing in letting the children come away.'

'You really think so?' Mrs Cooper sounded, for once, unsure. 'I have wondered . . . We panicked, I suppose. Well, it was the politicians who panicked and made us feel it was what we must do. But nothing's happening.'

'No, it's the "bore war" sure enough,' said George. 'That's what they're calling it.'

'But we never know when it *might* happen,' insisted Ellen. 'And if – *when* – it does, then it's the big cities that'll cop it. Not much consolation to you, my dear, I know.' She smiled understandingly at Mrs Cooper. 'But you want your children to be safe, don't you? And you can rest assured that we'll look after them for you, for as long as you want us to.'

'Yes, thank you. I can see you're doing a good job,' replied Mrs Cooper. 'They're obviously very happy here.' Sally was well aware how much it must pain her to say it, in one way, although she must be relieved they had found a good home.

The woman turned to Gloria, almost the first time she

had addressed the child apart from a lukewarm 'hello'. 'And I certainly wouldn't have recognised this young lady. So smart and . . . such a pretty dress.'

The dress was one of Emmie's, a red and black check in a fine wool which looked well with the little girl's dark shining hair. Sally was glad that Mrs Cooper hadn't said 'so clean and tidy', which was obviously what she was thinking. Although Gloria must be used to remarks like that by now. Her school-teacher had commented on her changed appearance, as had the billeting officer and a few more of Ellen's WVS ladies who had noticed the sorry little figure that first day at the church hall.

'Thank you, Gloria, for looking after Wendy,' said Mrs Cooper quietly and, it must be admitted, a trifle grudgingly. But at least she had said it, and Sally realised what it must have cost her in pride to do so. 'She's been telling me how kind you were to her when she was a bit upset.'

'Sorlright,' said Gloria cheerfully. 'She's not upset now, are you, Wendy? She likes it here – we all do – and she doesn't cry any more.'

'Yes, well, thank you,' muttered Mrs Cooper. Then she spoke to Sally and Ellen in a low voice. 'I miss them so much. But if I can convince myself it's for the best . . . and I'm trying to keep busy. Time hangs so heavy. But I have joined the WVS.'

'Oh, that's good,' said Ellen. 'I'm in the WVS.'

'But that doesn't fill the void. I'm even thinking of going out to work. There's a munitions factory, I believe, not far away, and it would be . . . well, I'd be doing my bit, wouldn't I?' She smiled a little uncertainly at George.

Sally was wondering how they should handle the departure of Mrs Cooper. It was sure to be upsetting all round. Farewells on railway stations were always horrendous, but, on the other hand, they couldn't let the woman walk back to Central Station on her own. In the end, Sally and all three children accompanied her, and Sally and Gloria stood back whilst the family said their goodbyes. Mrs Cooper, by this time, had regained her poise and there was no frenzied bout of weeping from Wendy, which was what Sally had feared. The child's eyes were just the slightest bit moist when, holding her little brother's hand, she met Sally and Gloria again at the platform barrier.

'P'raps my mam'll come soon,' said Gloria thoughtfully. 'D'you think so, Auntie Sally?'

'Perhaps,' said Sally, squeezing her hand. 'You never know.'

Sally was more than a little surprised, but very relieved, when a letter arrived during the following week. It was not from Gloria's mother, however, but from her sister, Monica O'Brien, saying that she would be coming to see Gloria on Saturday and she was bringing her two little boys with her.

'Our Monica, and our Sam and Len an' all? Gosh, that's super!' said Gloria, her grey eyes shining with joy.

Sally felt a pang of . . . what? she wondered, as she looked at the excited little girl. Could it be jealousy? Surely not. It was only natural that the child should want to see her sister again, and her nephews. Don't be so peevish, Sally admonished herself.

'Yes, isn't that good news?' said Sally, smiling at Gloria, then at Ellen. The letter had been addressed to Ellen who had read it first then passed it to Sally over the breakfast-table. 'Here, you can read it for yourself, Gloria. I think they'll be coming on the same train that Wendy and Michael's mum came on. It gets in about ten o'clock.'

'So they'll be here all day,' said Gloria, eagerly seizing the letter. Her eyes quickly scanned the contents. 'It says she's coming 'cause it's my birthday. Isn't that nice, Auntie Sally? And can they come for tea, like Wendy and Michael's mum did? Can they, please, Auntie Ellen . . . Auntie Sally?'

'Of course they can, dear.' It was Ellen who replied. 'We intended having a special birthday tea for you. It was going to be a surprise, but we'll let you into the secret now. I think it might be a better idea to have it on Saturday, not on Thursday, don't you, then your family will be here as well. Isn't it exciting?' Ellen beamed at the little girl while Sally thoughtfully pushed the letter back in its envelope.

There hadn't been a separate letter for Gloria, as there had been for the children in Mrs Cooper's missive, but three birthday cards arrived for the child on Thursday. One from Mam and Dad, one from Monica, Gerry and the lads, and another one from a couple called Patrick and Sheila and the kids. Sally didn't think she had heard of them before.

'That's one of me brothers,' Gloria explained. 'The one next to our Monica; she's the oldest. We don't see 'em much. They live in Gorton, but it's nice of him to send me a card, isn't it, Auntie Sally? I 'spect Monica reminded him. I don't think he's ever sent one before.'

No presents had arrived, but Sally assumed that if there were any Gloria's sister would be bringing them on Saturday. But Gloria seemed very satisfied with the three Manchester cards, plus a few others from the Blackpool folk. One from Ellen, one from Sally and George, one from Rachel and Harry and their family (which, Sally guessed, Emmie had insisted they should send), and one from Wendy and Michael. Most of them bore a shining gold figure nine, together with posies of flowers, dressed-up cats and dogs and cute Mabel Lucy Atwell characters.

'Seven cards!' cried Gloria excitedly, after she had impatiently ripped them all open at the breakfast-table. 'I've never ever had so many, never in me whole life.'

She was overjoyed, too, with her presents; a red pixie hood and gloves knitted by Sally, a card of red hair-slides, shaped like bows, from Wendy and Michael (Wendy had had a secret excursion to Woolworth's with Ellen after school one day) and an Enid Blyton book from Ellen. Gloria was rendered speechless by all this bounty, but her shining eyes and her rapt expression were all the thanks that Ellen and Sally required. She did manage, eventually, to breathe a whispered, 'Thank you,' then she fell silent, staring down at her gifts and cards, overcome by the wonder of it all.

There was another treat that evening, for all the children, so that Wendy and Michael wouldn't feel left out of things. Sally took them to see *The Wizard of Oz* at the Odeon cinema.

'It's the best birthday I've ever had, Auntie Sally,' said Gloria as they walked home through the dark silent streets. What wonderful times she had had since she came to live in Blackpool. Sometimes it was hard to remember Salford and her mam and dad and all the kids. But she had never quite forgotten Monica and she was looking forward very much to seeing her again on Saturday.

This time it was Gloria waiting impatiently with her nose pressed up against the window, whilst Wendy and Michael were drawing and painting at the big table in the living room. Ellen decided it would be their turn for an ice-cream treat today, while Gloria was with her sister. But this time she had prepared sandwiches, salmon paste and cheese, neatly wrapped in greaseproof paper, and a few chocolate biscuits, guessing that Monica O'Brien wouldn't have much money to spare for 'lunch' as Mrs Cooper had. Ellen only hoped that the day would be fine and warm enough for the little family to eat their meal on the sands, or on a bench on the prom. The nights were drawing in now and there was a definite nip in the air in the mornings and evenings. Still, there would be a handy promenade shelter should it rain, and she fancied that Gloria's sister would be well used to 'making do'.

Gloria jumped up and down with excitement when the young woman pushing the huge black pram appeared in the distance, and when the door was opened she flew down the path to meet her. Monica wrapped her arms round the child in a bear-like hug, lifting her off her feet then swinging her wildly round.

110

'Gosh, it's good to see yer, kid,' Ellen heard her exclaim as she put her down again. ''Ere, let me 'ave a look at yer.' The young woman stood back, surveying the child intently. 'Goodness, you've fair shot up, 'aven't yer? It must be this Blackpool air, or are they putting horse manure in yer shoes? And don't you look a bobby-dazzler, eh, in that frock?'

'It's Emmie's,' Gloria explained, casting an apprehensive look in Ellen's direction. Ellen was purposely standing back to let the sisters greet one another.

'And who's Emmie when she's at home?'

'She's Auntie Ellen's granddaughter. She's given me quite a lot of her things.' Gloria turned round, beckoning anxiously to Ellen. 'Come here, Auntie Ellen. This is me sister, Monica, and them's the boys, our Sam and Len.'

'How d'yer do? Pleased to meetcher,' said Monica cheerfully, at the same time giving Ellen a keen look.

This one doesn't miss much, thought Ellen, but she immediately felt that she would like the young woman. 'Hello, Monica,' she said warmly. 'I'm so pleased you could come. We've heard such a lot about you.'

She was more or less what Ellen had expected. A bit 'rough and ready', but dressed neatly enough in a tweed coat and headscarf and flat-heeled shoes. Far more suitably clad for a day at the seaside than Mrs Cooper had been. The boys, two round-faced, rosy-cheeked youngsters with balaclava helmets on their heads, were sitting one at each end of the big pram. They looked almost the same age and size, but Monica said that Sam, who was two and a half, was the elder by ten months. He would be able to walk part of the way until he got too tired. She was extremely grateful for the sandwiches Ellen had prepared, and Ellen said goodbye to them feeling very gratified that, at last, Gloria had someone of her own family to show some interest in her.

Sally was getting fond – probably too fond – of the little lass, she mused as she went back indoors. But sooner or later – who could tell when? – the time would come when Gloria

111

would have to go back home. It wouldn't be right to distance the child completely from her home and family, no matter how unsatisfactory one might consider them to be. Which was why she was glad that Monica had turned up today. In the end 'blood was thicker than water'.

Chapter 9

'It's good to see yer, kid,' said Monica again as they set off down King Street, Gloria holding on to the handle of the pram. 'Now, where are we going? You'll have to be in charge today; you know the place better than I do.'

'You've been here before though, haven't you?'

'Oh aye, once or twice. But you're – what d'yer call it? – a resident of Blackpool now, aren't you? You like it here, do you? She seems a nice woman, that Mrs Hobson. A bit posh-like, but very nice.'

'Yes, Auntie Ellen's nice, so's Auntie Sally and Uncle George. You'll see 'em at tea-time. We're having a party for me birthday.' Gloria grinned up at her sister.

'Oh yes, yer birthday. I haven't forgotten. There's a couple of presents in there.' Monica pointed to the black bag swinging on the pram handle. 'You can have 'em later. One's from yer mam and the other's from me. Cards arrive all right?'

'Yes, ta very much, Monica. How's me mam?' Gloria had only just remembered to ask. 'She didn't want to come and see me?'

'No, well, it isn't that she didn't want to, lovey. But you know how it is. She's got Rose and Lily and Vinnie, hasn't she? Then there's the lads to see to and yer dad, of course. So I said I'd come. I 'spect she'll be in touch soon. They all send their love.'

'Mmm.' Gloria was quiet for a few minutes. Memories of her family, apart from Monica who was here, seemed very hazy.

113

'What's up, love? You don't want to come home, do you?' Monica was looking at her rather worriedly.

'No, of course I don't,' Gloria replied quickly. 'Why? I can't, can I? We've been 'vacuated.'

Monica shrugged. 'S'pose you could if you really wanted . . . or if Mam wanted. A few of the kids have come back, but it's not a good idea. There's no schools for 'em to go to; they're all shut. No, I reckon you'd best stay put for the time being. It 'ud be different if you weren't happy, and I can see you are. Now, where are we going? It'll be the sands first, I suppose.'

They had reached the end of Albert Road and they were quiet for a few moments negotiating the pram across the busy road near Central Station, then across the tram-track to the slope that led down to the sea. Monica had come prepared for the sands with a big striped towel for them to sit on and to wipe the children's feet should it be warm enough for them to paddle. It wasn't. The day was cloudy with only a fitful sun, but the boys were warmly clad and they were soon happily engaged helping Gloria to build a sand-castle. Monica had also brought two little wooden spades. There were only a few late-season holidaymakers on the beach and a smattering of children who were, no doubt, local or evacuees. The last time Gloria had been here with Sally and the Cooper children, a couple of weeks ago, it had been much more crowded.

'Wendy's mum came last Saturday,' Gloria told her sister as they tucked into Ellen's sandwiches and drank beakers of hot tea from the Thermos flask that she had also thoughtfully provided, with enough milk for the two boys. 'But I don't think they went on the sands. Don't see how they could've done.' Gloria giggled. 'Mrs Cooper was dressed up like a dog's dinner. You should've seen her.'

'Oh aye, Mrs Snooty Cooper.' Monica nudged her and they both laughed. 'I'm glad you've got Wendy with you though. She's a nice kid and you look after her, don't you?'

'Don't need to so much now,' said Gloria. 'She's all right. Her dad's joined the Army. She didn't seem all that bothered though. But 'er mum did. She looked as though she was going to cry when she was telling Auntie Ellen.'

'Yer don't say! He's already gone, has he, Mr Cooper?'

'Yes, I think so. I think he's just gone.'

'Good grief! He must've put his name down straight away, as soon as the war started. Unless he was in them Territorials. He might've been. It usually takes a few weeks before they get their papers. Gerry's put his name down, but he hasn't heard anything yet.'

'Your Gerry's joining up? He's going in the Army?'

'Yeah, that's what he says.' Monica didn't seem all that concerned about her husband enlisting. 'Happen Mr Cooper was glad to get away, eh, kid?' She nudged Gloria again. 'I meanter say, it must be murder living with a fussy woman like that. I bet he daren't hardly put his bum down on one of her posh chairs. A fellow likes things a bit more free and easy. One thing you can never accuse me of is being house-proud, nor me mam neither. 'Course, we've never had the brass to chuck around like some folks, have we?'

Monica could only be guessing what the Cooper house-hold was like because she had never been there. Gloria, from her one visit, remembered it as being overly clean and tidy – very much like Rachel's house – a vivid contrast to the house where she, Gloria, lived. Daisy Mulligan's home was decidedly shabby and dirty, and Monica's was not much better, something that hadn't occurred to Gloria before she came to live in Blackpool. There were some homes, though, that were clean and comfortable without being so spick-and-span that you daren't hardly breathe in them. Auntie Ellen's house was like that; it was a real home. Monica would see it for herself soon.

'What's up with you? You've gone all broody.' A poke in the ribs from her sister brought Gloria back to earth. ''Ere, 'ave a look at yer presents.'

Monica rummaged in the black bag, bringing out two parcels hastily wrapped in brown paper. One contained a skipping rope, a very nice one with brightly painted blue handles, and the other one held two puzzles where you had to jiggle little silver balls around to get them in the holes.

'The skipping ropes are from me and yer mam sent the puzzles,' said Monica. 'Well, she told me to choose summat for you from the market,' she added. 'Hope you like 'em, kid. Oh, and Gerry's sent you these.' There were two copies each of the *Dandy* and *Beano*, Gerry's standard reading matter, only slightly thumbed. 'He's been keeping 'em nice so as you could 'ave 'em.'

'Thanks, Monica.' Gloria smiled at her, more than pleased. It was the first time she could ever recall her mother giving her a real present although Monica sometimes did.

'Now, where are we off to? The tide's coming in, see. We'd best be sharp.' Monica started to bundle up all their belongings, including the two little boys, depositing them in the huge pram. 'Have you decided where you want to go? The day's yours, you know.'

'Could we go to Fairyland, please?' asked Gloria. 'Like Wendy did. Her mum went on and on about it.'

'OK, Fairyland it is,' said Monica. 'Anything to oblige.'

The pram was something of a handicap, but a willing attendant kept an eye on it whilst the little party was transported through the dark caverns where fairies were flitting in flowery dells, goblins were digging for diamonds and woodland creatures cavorted around red spotted toadstools. Then they walked back along the Golden Mile and, again, Monica left the pram outside while they had a go – several goes – on the slot machines (an occupation of which Mrs Cooper would definitely not have approved!). They lost far too many pennies when the balls disappeared down the wrong holes, and several more when the silver hand with rubber fingertips failed to pick up any of the varied enticing prizes on offer – celluloid dolls, furry monkeys, glittering bangles and brooches, even bars of chocolate. It did eventually grasp hold of a tiny box, dropping it through the opening of the machine into Gloria's eager hands. It contained a big furry spider on a string, a 'jokey' thing, not much to Gloria's liking, but she was pleased to have won anything at all and decided she would give it to Michael.

There wasn't time for them to go to the Boating Pool as the Coopers had done. They couldn't take the pram on a tram and it was too far to walk there and back before teatime. But Gloria was quite content to walk along the promenade, breathing in the salt-laden air and listening to the raucous cries of the seagulls whirling and diving above their heads. They were amusing creatures and she had become very fond of them since she came to live here. They seemed to symbolise Blackpool – the seagulls, along with the golden sand and the dark grey neverending expanse of sea. She laughed out loud as three of the comical birds alighted on the green-painted railings just ahead of them, heads cocked slightly sideways, observing them with their black beady eyes.

'Let's give 'em some bread, Monica,' said Gloria. 'That's what they're waiting for. You've got some left, haven't you?'

'I think there's a crust or two that the lads left.' Monica handed them to Gloria who threw them high in the air, laughing again as the sea birds swooped after the largesse with shrill cries, angrily shoving one another out of the way.

'That's the lot, you greedy rascals,' said Monica, depositing the paper bag in a nearby litter bin. 'The next time we come we'll have to be better prepared, won't we?'

'You'll come again then, will you, Monica?' asked Gloria as they turned the pram round, heading for home.

' 'Course I will, you fathead,' Monica grinned. 'We're not going to desert you, you know, just because you've come to live among the nobs,' she added quietly. 'Anyroad, it's good for the lads to get a bit of fresh air into their lungs. Yes, we'll come again. Can't promise when, mind you. We'll have to see. Now, let's get off to this tea-party, shall us? I bet there won't 'alf be a spread. I 'ope so, I can tell yer. I'm so hungry I could eat an 'orse.'

'I've done sausages and chips, seeing as you had sandwiches at dinner-time,' said Ellen when they were all seated round the table.

Len, the younger boy, who was used to a high-chair, sat in his pram, whilst Sam managed on an ordinary chair heaped up with three cushions. Gloria's eyes were positively shining with joy as she looked round at all the people who were sharing in her special birthday tea. Sally felt her heart expand with love as she watched her. She knew that it was the first time the child had ever had a party solely in her honour. Gloria had told her so. She probably hadn't been invited to many parties either, back home in Salford. Sally guessed that for children of Gloria's background, birthday parties were an undreamed-of indulgence.

Sally's eyes moved to Monica, the member of Gloria's family she had heard so much about or, to be more correct, the only one of the child's family that Gloria ever spoke about at all. She was very much as Sally had imagined her, but she had obviously taken some pains with her appearance for her trip to Blackpool. Her royal-blue marocain dress, her 'best one' Sally guessed, was rather tight in places, straining across her well-shaped bust and hips. She wasn't fat, however. Apart from her shapely bosom the young woman was slender with slim legs, and tall, as Gloria was. Sally noticed that her hair had once been dark, again like Gloria's – you could see the dark growth at the roots when she bent her head – but now it was blonde, bright and brassy, carefully arranged in corrugated waves. Had the young woman's hair retained its natural dark colouring, the resemblance between her and Gloria would have been even more striking. As it was, they were very much alike with the same wide-spaced clear grey eyes, rather long nose and determined mouth.

118

Monica, suddenly becoming aware that she was under scrutiny, looked across at Sally, giving a quizzical half-smile. Sally felt a little embarrassed. She hadn't meant to stare, but she had found herself struck by the resemblance of the two sisters, giving a glimpse of what Gloria might look like several years hence. Underneath the powder and paint, generously applied, and the dyed hair, Monica was really a very attractive person.

Sally hastened to explain herself, smiling in a friendly way at the young woman. 'I was just thinking how very much alike you are, you and Gloria.'

'Well, we should be, shouldn't we?' Monica's reply was brusque and Sally was somewhat taken aback. Maybe she had been staring too closely at their guest; she recalled her mother telling her, as a little girl, that it was 'rude to stare'.

'I meaner say, we're sisters, aren't we?' Monica went on, more reasonably now. 'Her and me, we're proper sisters, y'see. That's why we've always been close, me and our Gloria.'

Hmmm, so close that you didn't get in touch with the child for over a month, thought Sally, but of course she didn't voice her thoughts. At any rate, the young woman was here now.

'Me mam's husband, Bill Mulligan, he's not me dad,' Monica went on, 'nor is he Gloria's. So Rose and Lily and Vinnie, the little 'uns, they're Gloria's half-sisters and brother. Her and me, we belong to the first lot, the Reardons – that was me mam's name when she was married before – but she changed Gloria's name to Mulligan when she married Bill. And our Frankie's an' all; he was a Reardon.'

Sally felt a mite confused in all this plethora of family relationships. What a lot of them there were, to be sure; Mulligans, O'Briens and Reardons. She had known, however, that Mr Mulligan was not Gloria's real father. And, reading between the lines, the child didn't seem to reckon much to him at all.

'Yes, I see,' said Sally. 'Gloria has told us a little about your family.' It was, however, only a very little; the child seldom talked about them.

'I'm the eldest of the lot,' said Monica, quite chattily now she had got over her initial abruptness. 'There was me, then our Patrick and Shaun and Mickey. They've all left home now; our Patrick's married, so's Shaun. Frankie's still at home with Mam though. He was the youngest of the Reardons . . . till Gloria here arrived.' She broke off to grin at the little girl. 'Quite a lot later that was, of course. She was an afterthought, you might say.'

'Yes, she told me she was just about the middle one of the family,' said Sally, still somewhat bewildered by all these various brothers and sisters.

'Aye, she's a right little piggy-in-the-middle, aren't you, luv?' said Monica. 'Me mam had no more sense than to start again when she married Bill Mulligan. She'd no choice though, had she, once she'd wed the chap? Babies come along and there's nowt much you can do about it, is there?'

Sally cast an apprehensive glance towards Gloria, Wendy and Michael. She was unused to quite such outspoken remarks, certainly not in front of the children. But Wendy and Michael seemed unconcerned, tucking into the red jelly with banana and peach slices, which had followed the sausage and chips, as though their lives depended on it. They were probably not even listening, though Gloria had one ear and eye cocked towards her sister as she, too, enjoyed the delicious dessert.

Monica's remark about babies coming along had touched a raw nerve in Sally, one she had thought she had put behind her. No babies had 'come along' for her and George, more was the pity. But if they had, then she was sure that they would have had the good sense to limit their family to two or three, as the Coopers had done, rather than go on producing hordes of unwanted children. She was quite certain that not all the later offspring of Daisy Mulligan were wanted or loved as much as they ought to be; Gloria certainly wasn't. But who are you to judge? she reproached herself, aware that her hackles were rising again, as they always did, in defence of her dear little Gloria. When all was said and done the family was a Catholic one, and therein lay the difference. Which reminded her that there was a matter she had to bring up with Monica before the young woman departed.

'Me mam 'ud have been better to call it a day when me dad died,' Monica was saying now. 'I've told her so time and time again, and I think she knows it now. She was all right as she was. Me and the lads were at home then and we all pulled our weight, then she has no more sense than to go and get wed again. I told her she were a bloody fool, but would she listen? Would she hell as like!'

Sally glanced warily at the children again before saying, sympathetically she hoped, 'Yes, I see. What about your father, Monica – Mr Reardon? When did he die? Gloria must have been only a tiny girl.'

'Yes, she were only a few months old when me dad died,' said Monica. 'A wall fell on him,' she added quite unemotionally, 'so that were that. But life has to go on, hasn't it? You've got to take the rough with the smooth, I suppose.'

'Yes,' said Sally, not knowing what else to say. 'I daresay you do, yes.'

It was Ellen, who had been quiet for a while, who spoke next, taking the words out of Sally's mouth. 'We know that your family are Catholics, Monica,' she said, 'so we feel we must tell you. Gloria is going to Sunday School – so are Wendy and Michael – but we are Methodists, you see, and so – well, that's where they are going, to the Methodist Sunday School. Gloria said she didn't think her mother would mind, but we thought we'd better explain.'

Fortunately, Monica seemed quite complacent about the situation. ''S all right. She's going somewhere, ain't she, and that's what counts. I'd rather she went to t'Catholic church, I must admit, but not to worry. Don't suppose 'Im up there minds.' She cast her eyes in the direction of the ceiling. 'She used to go to Our Lady, the Catholic Sunday School, at home, that's to say when she went at all. More often than not she was looking after t'little 'uns on a Sunday afternoon, weren't you, kid?'

'But the day school she attended wasn't a Catholic one, was it?' asked Sally. She had been rather puzzled about this. 'It couldn't have been, because Wendy and Michael were there.'

'No . . . me mam fell out with one of the teachers at Our Lady, years ago when our Gloria was in the babies' class. Me mam's always falling out with somebody or other, y'know. Can't remember what it were about. Anyroad, she took her away and sent her to t'school round the corner. It were nearer and me mam thought it didn't much matter where she went. She never goes to church now, me mam, but she's had all t'little 'uns christened. Our Gloria's got her saint's name an' all, you know. Gloria Bernadette, that's what she's called.'

'And what about you, Monica?' asked Ellen. 'Do you still go to church?' Sally considered that it was not really any of their business, but such things were important to Ellen.

'Oh yes, I go,' replied Monica. 'Not every week, mind, but I go, and Gerry an' all.' She gave a careless shrug. 'It gets you, don't it, religion? It's part of me; I can't seem to get rid of it. Don't suppose I ever will.'

'And that's no bad thing either, my dear,' said Ellen. She smiled warmly at Monica, but her decisive nod conveyed that this particular subject was now closed. 'Now, I think we might all make room for one of these,' she handed round a doyley-covered plate holding dainty little fairy cakes each topped with a cherry, 'before we have a piece of Gloria's special cake.'

The guests quickly demolished the buns – they were scarcely a mouthful, but a very delectable one – while Ellen, beaming proudly, carried from the sideboard the *pièce de résistance* of the meal, a fruit cake covered with white icing, piped in pink with the words *Happy Birthday, Gloria* and holding nine pink candles.

'Now – let's all sing for Gloria, shall we?' said Ellen, placing the cake in the centre of the table. 'Come on, everybody. "Happy Birthday to you . . ." '

And while they all sang George fetched the matches and lit the candles.

'Now, Gloria, are you going to blow out your candles?' asked Sally, feeling a decided lump in her throat at the sight of the little girl's rapturous face and shining eyes.

'Yes, come on, luv, blow 'em out,' urged Monica. She, too, seemed pleased at her little sister's happiness.

'And make a wish,' said Ellen. 'You must make a wish.'

So Gloria puffed out her cheeks and blew. Once . . . then a little extra puff till all the candle-flames were extinguished.

'Now, I'll cut the cake,' said Ellen. 'We must all have a piece, just a little one; I think we're too full up to eat any more. And Monica must take a few pieces home for Gloria's mother and her brothers and sisters, seeing that they can't be here to share Gloria's birthday.'

'What did you wish for?' asked Wendy in an audible whisper as Gloria, red-cheeked and starry-eyed, sat down again. She leaned close to her friend, holding on to her arm. 'Go on, tell us.'

Gloria shook her head.

'She can't tell, Wendy,' explained Sally, smiling. 'You can't tell wishes, or they might not come true. That's right, isn't it, Gloria?'

'Mmm.' Gloria nodded. The joyous, but conspiratorial smile the child gave her made Sally's heart overflow with love, to be followed almost immediately by a feeling of foreboding. When the time came, as it surely must, how would she ever be able to part with this little girl? Sally glanced across the table at Monica, but that young woman's eyes were downcast as she nibbled at her slice of birthday cake. Sally couldn't see the expression in them.

Chapter 10

Are we *really* at war, Ellen was tempted to think as she turned the pages of the *Gazette & Herald* in mid-December, 1939. Life seemed to be going on as normal with complete disregard to what might, or might not, be happening overseas. Moreover, there was a superabundance of seasonal goods on offer. There was a huge advertisement for the Toy Fair at the Co-op, an annual event, as well as adverts from various local stores proclaiming that they had in stock everything that the conscientious housewife might require for her Christmas cakes and puddings, such as currants, sultanas, raisins, candied peel, figs, Valencia almonds, Tunis dates ... Nothing, it seemed, was unobtainable. The really diligent housewives would have made them by now, Ellen mused. (She had, several weeks ago.) Also, in ample time for the Christmas season, there would be a goodly supply of mince tarts and pork pies, turkeys, geese, ducks and chickens. Ellen had already placed her order for a twenty-pound turkey – or as near as he could get – with her local butcher.

She flicked over the page to yet more adverts, for restaurants, parties and dances. The opposite page, however, was devoted to what was becoming a regular feature of the paper; photographs of 'our gallant men', local lads who had answered their country's call to serve in the Army, Navy or Air Force. They were smiling broadly beneath their peaked or forage caps. As yet the war seemed to be little more than a game; although last week news had come through that Russia had attacked Finland. By and large, though, the general consensus of opinion was that nothing much was happening. A Mass Observation poll carried out by one of the national papers had revealed that nineteen per cent of the population thought that the war would carry on for at least three years, and one per cent pessimistically believed that it would last for ever or until 'Hitler dies of old age'. But the vast majority admitted that they didn't know, or staunchly went on trying to believe it would be 'over by Christmas'. Ellen was one who had hoped so; now, as Christmas approached, it seemed that such hopes were vain.

She carried on with her perusal of the newspaper. Modified street lighting had been approved for the Christmas period for every part of Britain except the south and south-east coast; but this year there was to be no civic Christmas tree in Blackpool's Talbot Square. The grimmest reminder that there really was a war on was a notice stating that provision was being made in the town for air-raid shelters for 5000 children; they had not yet decided what type, said Mr Harrison, the local Education Officer. Then they'd better get their skates on pretty sharpish, thought Ellen. She feared that when the war started in earnest it might very well take everyone by surprise. This 'bore war' was breeding complacency.

Still, 'sufficient for the day', she thought as she tucked the paper into the rack at the side of her chair. There was no point in meeting trouble before it arrived and she intended this Christmas to be a happy one. It might well be the last one they would share together as a family for quite some time. Who could tell? She knew that Ruby, as well as Pearl, had ideas about joining up, although Rachel strongly disapproved, at least as far as Ruby was concerned. She probably thought that her second daughter was not entirely to be trusted away from home.

Ellen leaned back and closed her eyes, enjoying a rare spell of solitude; Sally and George had gone to the pictures and the children were in bed. Plans for presents, family gatherings and festive food flitted contentedly through her mind. And this year, of course, there would be three extra little people as well as the Hobsons and Balderstones. Christmas with three children . . . How lovely that would be. It seemed a long time since her own children, or even her grandchildren were small; and, when all was said and done, Christmas was a time for children. Ellen smiled happily to herself; it was a good job she had ordered that big turkey.

As it turned out, however, there was only Gloria who was to be in Blackpool for the festive season. A letter arrived in mid-December from Mrs Cooper saying that she would be coming on Saturday, 23 December to take the children home for Christmas.

'Surely you're not surprised, are you, Mam?' asked Sally when the children were out of hearing. 'Of course they'll be spending Christmas with their mum and dad. It's only natural. As Mrs Cooper says, "Daddy" has got leave,' Sally grinned, 'and she wants them all to be together.'

'Yes, I suppose I should have expected it,' said Ellen, a little pensively. 'It's just that we've got used to them being here. They're part of the family now, aren't they, and I shall miss them. What about Gloria? Do you think she'll be going home as well? We haven't heard anything.'

'I shouldn't think so for one moment,' said Sally, crossing her fingers tightly. She was, in fact, dreading a similar letter coming from Gloria's mother or – more likely – her sister. 'You know as well as I do that her mother has never written to her once since she arrived, apart from that measly birthday card.'

'I was thinking of her sister, really,' said Ellen. 'I know her mother leaves a lot to be desired – at least we think so, although we've never met the woman – but that Monica seemed nice enough. Quite a genuine young woman, I thought, and she did seem to be interested in Gloria's welfare.'

' "Seemed" is the word, Mam,' said Sally. 'Oh yes, she seemed concerned enough . . . when she was here. So concerned that she hasn't bothered to get in touch with the child since. If you ask me it's a case of "out of sight, out of mind", with Monica O'Brien. She's only interested in Gloria when it suits her.'

'Don't be too hard on the lass, my dear,' said Ellen, her brown eyes a little anxious, as they always were when Sally touched on the subject of Gloria and her unsatisfactory family. 'It can't be easy for her, you know. She's got those two youngsters of her own and you can see what a handful they must be, although they were well behaved enough when they were here, I must admit. Overawed, probably, and tired with all that fresh air. I thought she managed them very well,' she added, nodding decidedly at Sally. 'And I daresay she's on her own now; she said her husband was joining up, didn't she? Don't be so quick to condemn her, love.' Ellen's tone was gentle, but firm. 'I expect she does her best, according to her own lights.'

'Yes, maybe,' replied Sally. 'I just don't want Gloria to be upset when she finds out that Wendy and Michael are going home for Christmas.' But Sally, deep down, felt that the child was not likely to be too upset by this news. Sally thought – or, more truthfully, hoped – that Gloria would be only too happy to spend Christmas with her new family.

Ellen was of the same opinion. 'I don't think Gloria will be too distressed,' she said. 'I daresay she'll be glad to have some time with Emmie when school finishes. They're getting quite pally, those two, aren't they?'

Gloria was not disappointed at all to be staying in Blackpool for Christmas. She felt a little sad on the Saturday when she said goodbye to Wendy and Michael who were going back to Salford with their mum, but she knew it was only a temporary parting; they were due to return in a week or so.

It had been a very exciting time both at school and at

128

home getting ready for Christmas, and the best – Christmas Day – was still to come. At school they had made endless coloured chains with gummed paper strips to festoon the walls, cards for members of their families decorated with snowmen and jolly fat robins, crackers using toilet roll centres (which didn't bang, but were still very nice to look at) and the girls had each made a needlecase out of Binca canvas and the boys a woven mat as a special present for their mums. Ellen and Sally had insisted that Gloria's should go to her mum in Salford and Gloria agreed that was only right; so the needlecase had been duly dispatched, tucked inside one of the snowmen cards. Gloria knew that her mam didn't do much sewing like Auntie Ellen and Auntie Sally did, but they assured her that she would love it and would be pleased that Gloria was thinking about her.

Gloria felt a little bit bothered that she didn't think about her mother more often. But she was so far away and Gloria knew she couldn't get over to Blackpool, what with their Rose and Lily and Vinnie to look after. Monica hadn't come again either since that day in October and that had been rather a disappointment; she had promised faithfully she would. A parcel had arrived, however, the other day with a few Christmas cards from members of her family, and Gloria knew that there were also two presents because she had seen Auntie Ellen quickly hide them away, 'not to be opened till Christmas Day'. So that was all right; they were still thinking about her.

It would have been nice if her mam and Monica – especially Monica – could have watched her in the school nativity play. Gloria had been the 'second innkeeper's wife' and Wendy an angel, and Auntie Ellen, who was in the audience, had declared it was the best play she had ever seen. There were not many evacuees left now in the school that Gloria attended; there were only six in her class, which was probably why she and Wendy had been given parts in the play. All the rest had gone back home to Liverpool or

Manchester. It seemed that it had all been a big panic about nothing. There were no bombs dropping on the big cities, as everyone had feared, and mothers were wanting their children back. Even Miss Butler, their teacher from Salford, had gone back home and the Salford children were incorporated quite easily in the classes with the local children. So they were now attending school full-time instead of part-time which didn't worry Gloria at all; she loved school.

It did worry her slightly at times, though, that many of her friends had gone ... and she was still here. Didn't her mother want her back home like the others did? But Gloria was not at all sure just what it was that was troubling her – the suspicion that her mother didn't seem to want her, or the thought of leaving Blackpool. That was a truly dreadful thought and one that Gloria always pushed to the back of her mind when it popped up. Most of the time, though, she didn't dwell on it all too much. She was far too busy and too happy.

It was turning out to be the happy Christmas that Ellen had anticipated, with all her family in accord, petty squabbles and minor clashes of personality set aside as they always were on this day of days. The gathering consisted of Rachel and Harry and their three girls; Sally and George, herself ... and Gloria. Ellen watched her now. The child was laughing merrily as she leaned across the table to pull a cracker with Emmie. Then she placed the flimsy paper hat on her head, beaming contentedly at them all. She was seated between Sally and George and, if one didn't know, one would suppose her to be their very own child, so well did they all get on together.

It was a long meal as they took their time over the turkey and all its trimmings, the plum pudding, and mince pies to complete the feast, washed down with the customary cup of tea. It was not a proper meal to Ellen unless it was rounded off with a cup of tea. Then they all leaned back in their chairs, at ease with one another, while Ellen switched on the wireless for the King's speech.

'A new year is at hand,' said King George in his hesitant tones. 'We cannot tell what it will bring . . .' But he urged them to step forward into the unknown, putting their hands into the hand of God. And Ellen felt, as she always did at this turning point of the year, slightly apprehensive at the thought of what 1940 might hold for them all. Joys and sorrows . . . there was sure to be a mixture of both as there always was; possibly more sorrow than joy for a lot of people if the warring nations didn't sort out their differences. There would be changes, many changes she feared, for the people here. Although she had never considered herself to be psychic, Ellen experienced now a presentiment of events to come – not all happy ones – as she looked round at the dear, dear faces of her family. But all she could do, all that any of them could do, was to step forward, as their King had encouraged them to do, in faith and with courage.

The first thing that happened before the New Year of 1940 got going was a letter from Mrs Cooper saying that Wendy and Michael would not be returning to Blackpool. She had decided to keep them with her in Salford and she would be coming in a few days' time, on her own, to collect the rest of their belongings. She thanked Mrs Hobson – both Mrs Hobsons – very courteously for all they had done for the children, but she hoped they would understand her action. The danger that had been anticipated had not materialised, she wrote, and children in their formative years needed to grow up in their own homes. Besides, many of the Salford evacuees had now returned and several of the schools were re-opening.

'The woman's lonely and that's the top and bottom of it,' said Ellen, tapping her finger on the neatly written page. 'I can't say I blame her. I know I couldn't have borne to be parted from my children. But I'm afraid she's making a big

131

mistake, Sal, don't you agree? All of them are, that have taken their kiddies back home again. I've a feeling this war is going to start with a vengeance before long . . . and when it does they'll be eating their words. I hope I'm wrong, but it seems to me to be very much a calm before the storm.'

'Yes, I fear you're right, Mam,' said Sally. 'But it's Mrs Cooper's decision and we have to respect it. At least Gloria's still with us,' she added, 'although I've a feeling she's going to be upset when she knows her friend isn't coming back. Shall I tell her, or will you?' Gloria had gone back upstairs to make her bed and tidy her room as she always did in a morning, and the three adults at the breakfast-table were mulling over the letter. Ellen had read its contents in silence before handing it to Sally, knowing full well that Gloria would not only be disappointed at the loss of her friend, but also puzzled as to why her own family had not made the same decision.

'I'll tell her, dear, shall I?' said Ellen. 'You and George will have to be getting off to work soon.'

The shops and factory had been closed for three days over the Christmas period and were due to re-open this morning, although Ellen guessed that the shops would not have many customers. There was always a slump following the Christmas rush and the weather had turned very cold. There was an icy wind blowing, a harbinger of snow, unless she was very much mistaken.

'Yes, I'll break the news to Gloria,' Ellen went on. 'She can help me with my baking this morning. She loves to do that and it will help to take her mind off things. I must make some more mince pies. I made two dozen before Christmas and, would you believe it, they've all gone.' Since she had handed over the reins of Hobson's to George and Harry, Ellen was finding she had far more time to spend on these homemaking tasks. She was discovering a fresh enjoyment in the jobs which formerly, because she was so busy, had sometimes seemed a chore.

'Gloria's not the only one who'll miss her pal,' said George pensively. 'We'll all miss 'em, won't we? Wendy was a nice little kid once she'd settled down. A bit prim and proper, but she was a nice little lass. And that Michael . . .' He shook his head, smiling a trifle sadly. 'He was a proper caution. We never did manage to go fishing, did we, him and me?'

'It's probably just as well, George,' said Ellen. 'I'd have been worried sick he was going to fall off the jetty. It's a big responsibility looking after kiddies, especially when they're somebody else's.'

'Somebody else's . . . yes,' said George reflectively. 'I'd have taken care of him, Mam. I wouldn't have let any harm come to little Michael. Still, it's too late now, isn't it?'

'Never mind, love. Gloria's still with us, isn't she?' said Sally for the second time.

'Oh yes, we've still got Gloria.' George smiled again, not sadly this time, in fact his eyes were glowing with pleasure. 'It would be hard to imagine the place without Gloria now, wouldn't it?'

Gloria, of the three evacuees, was the one who had, more so than the others, burrowed her way into all their hearts. The child had been here barely four months, thought Ellen, as she prepared the kitchen for her baking, but it seemed as though she had always been with them. She was so much a part of the family . . . and yet she had her own family back in Salford. However would the child cope when she had to return? And, possibly even more pertinently, how would Sally?

Gloria was disappointed to hear that her friend would not be coming back to Blackpool, but not as upset as Ellen had feared. She seemed more annoyed than distressed. 'But she never said goodbye to me!' She put down the fancy cutter that Ellen had given her to make her own little tarts and stared belligerently at Ellen. 'She was me best friend, that Wendy, and she's gone off back to Salford without even saying tara.'

'Now then, it's hardly her fault, is it, dear?' said Ellen. 'She didn't know her mum was going to keep her there, did she? And Michael,' she added, although Gloria didn't seem concerned about Michael.

'We've been friends ever since we was five, me and Wendy,' said Gloria, 'and now I won't never see her again.' She didn't look as though she was going to cry, though. Her mouth was set in a stubborn line as she picked up her pastry cutter and began, deliberately, to cut out some more shapes.

'Of course you'll see her again,' said Ellen gently.

'When?'

'Well, I don't know exactly when, dear, but you're sure to see Wendy again . . . sometime.'

'D'you mean when the war's over?' Gloria was looking intently at Ellen.

'Perhaps . . . I don't know. Maybe before then. None of us know, dear. When you go home again,' Ellen added falteringly. 'You'll see Wendy, won't you, when you go back home?'

'Back to Salford, d'you mean?'

'Yes, dear, I suppose so.' Ellen was feeling bewildered. She had little idea how best to answer the child.

'I don't want to go back to Salford, Auntie Ellen,' said Gloria in a small voice, turning back to her task. 'I want to stay here with you and Auntie Sally.'

It was the coldest January for half a century, so they were told on the newsreels and in the daily papers. Much of the weather news, however, was censored for security reasons, but news had filtered through that the River Thames had frozen over and the nightmare conditions of frozen pipes, snow-blocked roads and paralysed railways told their own story.

In Blackpool the snow was piled shoulder-high on the pavements and the schools were closed for a few days. When Gloria's school re-opened she found that even more of the evacuees had gone home; Wendy and Michael, of course, but several of the others as well. There were only four of the Salford children remaining in Gloria's class now; two boys, herself and a girl called Doreen Aspinall. She and Gloria had not been all that friendly when they lived in Salford, but since coming to Blackpool they had struck up more of a friendship, especially now as they were amongst the few that were left. Gloria thought that Doreen looked unhappy, and one playtime, as they stood together by the outside lavs waiting for the teacher to blow the whistle to summon them inside again, Doreen told her new friend just what was troubling her.

Ellen and Sally both knew that not all the householders who had taken evacuees had been as fortunate as themselves. They had had their problems at the outset, admittedly, with Wendy's homesickness, Michael's bed-wetting and Gloria's head lice, but these difficulties had been of short duration. Many people had fared far worse. Ellen frequently heard stories at her WVS meetings of unruly children who practically wrecked the homes of their landladies, children who refused to eat anything but chips or beans in tomato sauce, others whose toilet training was non-existent – making the tales of those who had no idea how to use a knife and fork pale into insignificance – and children who couldn't form a sentence without using a swearword. There had been so many complaints in the beginning that tribunals had been set up where billeting complaints could be discussed and, hopefully, sorted out.

But the problem was by no means one-sided. There were many evacuees who suffered at the hands of their hosts and their grievances were listened to and dealt with as well; always supposing that the children had the courage to speak up about what was happening. Ellen knew for a fact that many of the evacuees, especially the somewhat older ones, were being used in this seaside town as unpaid labour in the boarding houses; peeling potatoes, scrubbing floors, washing piles of dishes and pans – even emptying chamber pots. This was wrong, but not downright cruel as some of the so-called hosts were discovered to be. Sorry tales were told of children who had been ill treated, both mentally and physically. Some had been given meals of bread and dripping, or jam, whilst the family dined on chicken or roast beef. Others had been beaten or locked in dark cupboards because they had wet the bed. And there were many instances of parcels arriving from the children's homes, containing gifts of sweets or chocolates and toys which had been purloined by unscrupulous land-ladies.

'You never know, do you, what goes on behind closed doors?' Ellen remarked to Sally. 'Of course, some of these tales have lost nothing in the telling, I realise that. But I'm very much afraid that many of them are true enough.'

And there were some things that went on which were extremely difficult for the children to understand, let alone talk about . . .

'Auntie Sally,' said Gloria one evening in mid-January when Sally had gone into her bedroom to say goodnight. 'Can I tell you summat . . . I mean something?' The child's grey eyes were troubled and Sally at once sat down on the edge of the bed, ready to listen.

'Of course you can, dear. You know you can tell me anything. Come on, what is it? There's something worrying you, is there?'

Gloria nodded. 'Well, it's not really me what's worried. It's me friend, Doreen, at school. She sits next to me now Wendy's gone and she's been telling me summat – something – awful. It's this man, y'see, what she lives with . . . what he does to her.'

Sally felt her stomach begin to knot, already having an inkling of what she was about to hear. She decided to proceed cautiously, however. Some children had very vivid

136

imaginations. 'Are you sure she's speaking the truth, dear?' she asked warily. 'This Doreen – you're sure she's not making it up, whatever it is?'

'Oh no, Auntie Sally, she'd never do that. It isn't only her, y'see, it's her little sister an' all, their Susan. She's in Standard One – and this man's doing it to both of 'em. Susan told me about it 'cause Doreen said she had to tell me. He said – Mr Catchpole that is – that they hadn't to say nothing to nobody or he'd send them back home and they'd get bombed. But Doreen got so scared that she had to tell me. She started crying in the yard, y'see, and I asked her what was up.'

'And what did she tell you, dear?' asked Sally gently. 'Don't be frightened, there's nobody here but you and me. You tell me, then I'll see if there's anything we can do about it.'

'Well, he comes into their bedroom, Doreen and Susan's, and he kisses them, all sloppy. Doreen said she didn't like it, but it wasn't as bad as what he did after. He got in her bed and cuddled her, then he put his hand up her nightie and he . . .' Gloria knelt up in bed at this point and, cupping her hand round Sally's ear, she whispered the rest. 'I can't say it out loud, Auntie Sally,' she said, sitting down again. ''Cause it's wrong, isn't it?'

Catchpole . . . Sally frowned as a bell rang faintly at the back of her mind. It was rather an unusual name and one she had heard somewhere.

'So I wondered if they could come here and live with us, Doreen and Susan,' said Gloria now, looking pleadingly at Sally. 'We've got room, haven't we, now that Wendy and Michael have gone? Please, Auntie Sally . . . can they?'

'Oh dear.' Sally shook her head, quite nonplussed. 'You haven't said anything to them, have you, Gloria, about coming to live here?'

'No, 'course I haven't. I'd only just thought of it, actually. Can they, Auntie Sally?'

'I don't know, dear. I just . . . don't know.' Sally's head

was reeling. What on earth was she to do? 'Listen – how would it be if they were to come here for tea one day, your friends, Doreen and Susan? I could write a little note to the lady ... There *is* a lady as well, isn't there, besides this Mr Catchpole? There's a Mrs Catchpole?'

Gloria nodded. 'Yes, but he said they hadn't to tell his wife about ... you know.'

'Yes, I understand. Well, if I wrote to her, perhaps they could come for tea, and then ... we'll see. Now, you snuggle down and go to sleep, and don't worry any more about it. It'll be all right, darling, I promise. I'll try to sort it out.' Sally bent down and kissed the little girl's cheek, stroking her dark silky hair and tucking it back behind her ear.

Then she went downstairs more concerned than ever because she had just remembered who Mr Catchpole might be.

Chapter 11

Ellen had confirmed Sally's fears, that Mr Catchpole was a member of their Methodist church, a worthy man, seemingly, who served on the church council and several committees. His wife sang in the choir, which was really just a handful of mainly middle-aged people who led the singing. Ellen, who was more involved in church matters than Sally, knew both of them, not intimately, but well enough to pass the time of day. And she knew that they did have two little girls staying with them. They both attended the Sunday School and she had seen them sitting with Cyril Catchpole at morning service.

'We can't afford to waste any time, that's for sure,' said Ellen.

'No, indeed we can't,' replied Sally. 'It might still be going on, even at this moment, poor little mites.' She gave a shudder.

'Sally . . . he hasn't actually . . . ?' Ellen shook her head, looking embarrassed. 'This is very difficult to say. He hasn't actually . . . raped them, has he?'

'No, I don't think so, Mam. Just, you know . . .' Sally, too, was finding the subject very discomfiting. It wasn't something she had ever talked about with her mother-in-law, or with anyone for that matter. 'But it's bad enough.'

'Quite.' Ellen nodded. 'I'll deal with this if you like, Sally, seeing that I know the Catchpoles better than you do. I don't feel we should involve the police, or the billeting officers . . . or anybody in authority. It won't be easy, mind, but I'll do it. Now, let me see. I'll ask Mrs Catchpole – Edith, I think she's called – if her two little girls can come to tea with our Gloria. Then, if we can persuade them to tell us what they told Gloria, we can take it from there.'

'You won't tell her about her husband, this Edith Catchpole?' Sally sounded alarmed.

'No. I hope she won't need to know at all about what's been going on. Not a nice thing to find out about your husband, is it? Let's take it a step at a time, dear. To be quite honest, Sally, I'm just as confused as you are about the best way to handle it. We'll have to tread carefully, though, that goes without saying.'

Doreen and Susan Aspinall were timid little girls, nearly identical in appearance, with straight fair hair cut short in a fringe and rather prominent greenish eyes; wary, fearful-looking eyes. They certainly didn't have the same friendly, outgoing personality as Gloria, thought Ellen, but they were pleasant and well mannered and seemed very happy to have been invited out for tea. Ellen could well understand why they had said nothing about their predicament either to Mrs Catchpole or to anyone else, save Gloria. They would have been far too shy to talk about it; it was a wonder they had even discussed it with their friend. It was going to be difficult to persuade them to tell her, or Sally, mused Ellen, watching them tuck heartily, but not conversing much, into the egg and tomato sandwiches, jelly and blancmange and iced buns. She would wait until Sally came in from work, in about half an hour's time, and then perhaps they could be persuaded, tactfully, to open up.

Mrs Catchpole had seemed surprised, but quite pleased, when Ellen had proffered the invitation after the Sunday morning service. She approached the woman just as the choir was going back into the vestry. She was a forbidding-looking woman, tall and gaunt, with iron-grey hair, although Ellen guessed she could only be in her mid-forties, a rather hooked nose and black beady eyes which surveyed one inquisitively.

Surprisingly she smiled, though somewhat frostily. 'How kind of you, Mrs Hobson. Yes, I'll be glad to have them off my hands for a few hours. What I mean is, they don't often get invited anywhere. They're with me all the time and it does get rather tiresome. Not that they're any trouble – very quiet little creatures, they are – but I'm not used to having children about the place. To be quite honest . . .' she leaned forward, more confidingly '. . . I thought they'd have gone back home by now, but they didn't even go home for Christmas. Their mother's just had twin boys; she's been quite poorly, I believe, and their father's away in the Army, so it seems that we're stuck with them yet awhile. Two of yours have gone back, haven't they?' Her hawk-like eyes peered curiously into Ellen's.

'Yes, at Christmas, but we've still got Gloria. She's a grand little girl,' said Ellen, a shade defiantly. 'I'm glad she's made friends with your two.'

'Yes, of course.' Mrs Catchpole smiled vaguely. 'I didn't know they were friendly. They didn't tell me. They don't tell me very much at all.' Ellen was not surprised. Edith Catchpole was not the sort of woman to inspire confidence in a child. 'Where's your girl this morning – Gloria, did you say? She's not with you?'

'No, she's at home with George and Sally – my son and daughter-in-law, you know. She'll be at Sunday School this afternoon, but I think church once a day is quite enough for a little girl.'

'Our two come every Sunday morning. They sit with Cyril,' said Mrs Catchpole reprovingly. 'You can't start too young, I believe, instilling in them what's right and what's wrong. Not that we've ever had any children of our own,' she added.

Ellen had noticed the two little girls again this morning, sitting as quietly as the proverbial mice in one of the front pews with Cyril Catchpole, and her heart had missed a beat at the sight of them.

'Anyway, I'm much obliged to you, Mrs Hobson,' said Mrs Catchpole, bringing to a conclusion the longest conversation the two of them had ever had. 'They'll come home with your Gloria after school tomorrow then. And I'll send Cyril for them, shall I, at about seven o'clock? They go to bed quite early.'

'No, my son will see them safely home,' said Ellen hastily. 'Yes, about seven o'clock. Don't worry; we'll take good care of them.'

When Sally and George came in from work they decided they would dine later, as they often did, Ellen having had a midday meal with Gloria. George made himself scarce, as arranged, and Ellen went to wash up the tea-things whilst Sally settled down to play a game of Snakes and Ladders with the three girls. Doreen and Susan knew how to play, but Sally learned that it was the first time they had played that, or any game, since coming to live in Blackpool.

'What do you do, then?' she asked, smiling encouragingly at them. 'After you've had your tea, do you read books, or comics? Or listen to the wireless?'

Doreen shook her head. 'We don't have no comics. Mrs Catchpole says they're rubbish, and she doesn't let us listen to the wireless neither. We used to listen to *Children's Hour* at home,' she added wistfully. 'She lent us some books, what she had when she was a little girl, but they were dead boring and they smell all funny.'

'And we sew,' added Susan shyly.

'Oh yes, we sew.' Doreen nodded. 'Mrs Catchpole's making us do a sampler, both of us, like them she's got hung up on her walls. There's one over the mantelpiece.'

'Yes, it says *Trust in God*,' said Susan.

'And there's one in our bedroom,' Doreen went on.

'And what does that say?' asked Sally faintly.

142

'It says *Thou God Seest Me*,' said Doreen, pronouncing the words deliberately.

How very apt, thought Sally, wondering if Cyril Catchpole ever stopped to look at it.

'Doreen.' Sally leaned forward and took hold of the little girl's hand. 'Gloria's been telling me that you're rather worried about something, you and Susan. Something to do with . . . Mr Catchpole. Would you like to tell me about it, like you told Gloria?'

Doreen glanced warily at her sister and they both hung their heads. 'I don't like . . .' muttered Doreen.

'He said we hadn't to tell,' added Susan. Sally thought that she was probably the less inhibited of the two children, although they had both become more talkative over the game of Snakes and Ladders. 'He said we'd have to go home and then we'd get bombed if we told, didn't he, Doreen?'

'Well, that was rather naughty of him,' said Sally, 'to tell you that. For one thing, there aren't any bombs at the moment. You know that, don't you?'

'Can we go home then?' asked Susan. 'If there's no bombs . . .' She stared pleadingly at Sally.

'I shouldn't think so, dear,' replied Sally. 'Your mum's not been very well, has she? And she's got your new baby brothers to look after. That's exciting news, isn't it, Mummy having twins? Perhaps we might be able to arrange for you to go and see them for a day. Would you like that?'

Both little girls nodded eagerly. 'Can I go an' all, Auntie Sally?' Gloria chipped in. 'P'raps I could go and see our Monica . . . can I?'

'Perhaps. We'll have to see what we can do.' Oh dear, Sally was getting herself into deep water here. Besides, they were wandering away from the main issue. She turned back to Doreen. 'Don't worry that you'll get into trouble, dear. You won't, not at all. We just want to help you, Gloria's Auntie Ellen and I. Now, would you like to tell me . . . ?'

And so they did, both little girls whispering confidingly

into Sally's ear as Gloria had done. Sally was silent for a moment, her heart too full for words. It just showed that you couldn't tell what people were like below the surface. Mr Catchpole seemed such an upright and virtuous man, as well as being friendly, in a quiet way, and mild-mannered, a pillar of the church – and yet there was this . . . quirk. Sally hoped it was no more than that. She couldn't believe he was downright wicked. You could tell at a glance, of course, what sort of a woman his wife was. Equally virtuous and honest, but also rigid and unbending. Sally was quite sure that she had not ill treated the children, but neither had she understood them or even tried to. It probably wouldn't be very difficult to persuade her that it would be better for them to have a change of home. Sally and Ellen had already discussed this.

'So can they come and live—?' Gloria began, immediately clasping her hand to her mouth. 'Oh sorry, Auntie Sally! You said I hadn't to. Sorry.'

'It's all right, love.' Sally smiled at her. 'It doesn't matter now. Auntie Ellen and I have already talked about it.' She nodded confidingly at her. 'I think they could – if they would like to, that is.' She turned to the sisters. 'Doreen, Susan. If we can sort it out with Mrs Catchpole, would you like to come and live here, with Gloria?'

Such a change came over the two little girls' faces as they beamed delightedly at one another. It was Susan who spoke first. 'Ooh, that would be lovely,' she said. 'We'd like it more than anything, wouldn't we, Doreen?'

Ellen decided there was no time like the present and that she would broach the matter with Edith Catchpole the very next morning. She knew where the couple lived, in a semi-detached house in the area that was known as the Raikes Estate.

'What about Mr Catchpole?' asked Sally, when George had returned from taking the two little girls home and Gloria

144

was in bed. 'Are you going to tell him that you know?'

'I suppose I must,' said Ellen slowly, 'but it's going to be damned difficult.' She very rarely used a swearword, but this was one hell of a situation she was in. 'He's sure to put two and two together when the girls move . . . that's if his wife agrees with them coming here, and I think she will. I have to be in his company at church sometimes and I don't want there to be any embarrassment. Yes, I'll have to tell him what I've found out. And assure him that I won't tell his wife,' she added.

'Dirty old man!' muttered George. 'Serve him right, Mam, if you did tell her. And him on the bloomin' church council . . .'

'Going to church doesn't mean that we don't have any faults, George.' His mother glanced reprovingly at him. 'More's the pity. Yes, I'll go and have a word with him tomorrow, after I've seen his wife. He works at the library, I know that, so I'll try and see him there.'

Edith Catchpole looked suspiciously at Ellen when she first put forward her suggestion that the sisters could, perhaps, come and live with her and Sally and George.

'Why? Why should they come and live with you?' Her black eyes were a little hostile. 'They're perfectly all right with me and Cyril. We're doing our best for them. I don't see any reason . . . No, I don't think so.' She shook her head peremptorily and made as if to close the door. Ellen had not been invited into the house and, to her mind, it was the height of bad manners to leave a visitor standing on the doorstep.

She stood her ground although she was very unsure of how to proceed. To be too persuasive would arouse the woman's suspicions, and yet she couldn't give up too easily. Those poor little girls . . . Ellen smiled, confidingly, she hoped, as one woman to another.

'To be quite honest, it's Gloria I'm thinking about as much as anything. She's been so lonely since Wendy and

145

Michael went back home.' This wasn't strictly true, but a white lie didn't matter, not in circumstances like this. 'And when your two came to tea they all got on so well together. You should have seen them, laughing and having such fun.' Mrs Catchpole's lips moved fractionally in what Ellen thought was intended to be a smile. 'And you did imply, the other day,' Ellen went on, unabashed, 'that you were not really used to having children around . . . that you thought they might have gone home by now. I just thought we might be doing you a favour, Mrs Catchpole, taking them off your hands.' Ellen looked keenly at the woman as she repeated the words Edith Catchpole herself had spoken last Sunday. 'Of course, if you don't agree, then that's your decision. But we don't know how long this war is going to last, do we?'

The last sentence seemed to do the trick, as Ellen had hoped it might. There was a moment's silence, then, 'Come in a minute,' said Mrs Catchpole.

Ellen was not invited to sit down in the immaculate front room, but at least she had got over the threshold. Her eyes rapidly scanned the furniture, polished to such a gloss that you could see your face in it, the stiffly laundered chairback covers and the huge gilt-framed pictures (of Biblical scenes) which hung on the brown-papered walls of this icily cold room where not a thing was out of place. It was just as she had imagined it would be.

'I might be willing to fall in with your suggestion.' Edith Catchpole fingered her scrawny neck which protruded from the maroon, high-collared dress, a style dating from at least twenty years ago. 'But I'll have to see what Cyril says, of course. He seems to have become quite fond of the evacuees, I'm not sure why. Very timid, mousey little scraps, they are. Still . . .' She lifted her shoulders in a slight shrug. 'They seem to amuse him. The novelty, I suppose. As I told you, we never had any children. I can see, though, that it might be better for them to be with other children. Well, just one, isn't

146

it, your Gloria, especially as they've become friends. And the money you'll be paid will help, of course.' Mrs Catchpole gave a knowing nod, as though she was only too well aware of what might be Ellen's ulterior motive.

Ellen didn't bother to comment on such a ridiculous insinuation. As if the seven shillings and sixpence they were paid for each evacuee went anywhere near to the actual cost of looking after the children! The money didn't come into it at all with Ellen, but there might be no harm, maybe, in letting Mrs Catchpole think so if that was what she wanted to do. It would, at any rate, steer her away from Ellen's real reason for wanting the children.

'I'll talk it over with my hubby,' said Mrs Catchpole now, using the word Ellen particularly abhorred in speaking about one's spouse. She moved pointedly towards the door, signifying to Ellen that the interview was now at an end. 'And then I'll let you know. If Cyril agrees I'll arrange to let you have them as soon as possible,' she added, as though the children were parcels to be delivered.

Cyril will agree all right, thought Ellen, as she made her way along Church Street, heading towards the library. Because if he doesn't, his wife will be told of his misdemeanours. She hoped to intercept Mr Catchpole before he had his lunch-break. Her heart was in her mouth as she hurried up the stone steps of the library, but one part of her mission had been successfully concluded, at least.

Ellen stood back, unobtrusively, until he had finished stamping the books of three borrowers, then she stepped forward. 'Mr Catchpole, I wonder if we could have a word? This isn't library business, so we can't talk here. Is it time for your lunch-break?'

Mr Catchpole's mild blue eyes, behind his steel-rimmed spectacles, seemed only a little surprised. No doubt he thought it was some church matter or other. 'Yes of course, Mrs Hobson.' He glanced at his watch. 'Five minutes. I've brought some sandwiches, but I can eat them later. I'll see you outside in five minutes. Perhaps we could go and have a cup of tea somewhere?'

'I don't think that will be necessary.' Ellen's voice, to her ears, sounded more frigid than she had intended, so she added, 'Thank you all the same. I'll see you in a little while then.'

She stood shivering on the corner of Queen Street, but not entirely with the coldness of the day. She was beginning to regret the action she had embarked upon, but it was too late to turn back now.

'So, what can I do for you then, Mrs Hobson?' Cyril Catchpole was at her side. He was well protected from the cold with a red woollen scarf tucked inside his long – ridiculously long – tweed overcoat and a trilby hat covering his balding head. As he stood there rubbing his gloved hands together, peering intently at her, he seemed such an inoffensive, almost pathetic character, that Ellen could scarcely believe the stories she had heard about him.

'I've been to see your wife, Mr Catchpole,' she began. 'About your little girls, Doreen and Susan. As you know, they came to tea with us yesterday, and – well – the top and bottom of it is . . . we, that is my daughter-in-law, Sally, and I, we'd like them to come and live with us, instead of with you.'

'Why?' A wary look had come into the little man's eyes. 'I mean, they're quite happy with us. They're all right.'

'They are most certainly *not* all right, Mr Catchpole, and they are definitely not happy . . . and you know why, don't you? Just as you know why I want them to come and live with me.'

'Oh, dear God, no!' His already pale face blanched visibly as he cast terrified eyes upon Ellen. 'You haven't told her, have you – Edith? You said you'd been to see my wife. Edith *mustn't know.*'

'No, Mr Catchpole, I haven't told Edith,' replied Ellen, feeling, at least, that her worst suspicions had been vindicated. The little girls had been telling no less than the truth because what she was witnessing now was abject guilt . . . and fear. 'Nor will I tell her, if you agree to the little girls coming to live with us. She said, your wife, that you might not be very keen on the idea . . . but you're not going to raise any objections, are you?'

Mr Catchpole seemed to shrink right inside himself, as though he would like to completely disappear. 'We'd better go and have that cup of tea,' he said, his teeth beginning to chatter. 'And I'll explain—'

'No, I don't want a cup of tea,' said Ellen brusquely. 'But you're cold, and so am I. We'll walk round the block. Come on.' She stepped forward purposefully.

'The girls told you, then? Well, I suppose they must have done. I wouldn't hurt them, you know. I wouldn't do anything . . . really bad.' He shuffled along at her side, trying to keep up with Ellen's brisk stride. 'I . . . couldn't help myself somehow. I've always liked little girls. We never had any, you know, no children at all. And she's a hard woman, Mrs Hobson, my wife. She never wants to . . . hasn't wanted to for years. And, well, like I said, I couldn't help it. I wouldn't harm them . . .'

'You've harmed them a great deal, Mr Catchpole,' said Ellen, slowing her steps a little. 'And frightened them as well. And to tell them you'd send them back into danger if they told anyone . . . that was very wrong, wasn't it?'

'I wouldn't have. Of course I wouldn't,' he mumbled. 'Any more than I'd have hurt them. They're nice little lasses.'

'It wasn't myself that they told, as a matter of fact,' said Ellen. 'It was Gloria, their friend, because they had to tell somebody, they were so frightened. And she, Gloria, told my daughter-in-law. And so, you see . . .' She looked steadily at him. 'You will agree then? They can come and live with us?'

'I've no choice, have I? She mustn't know. She must never know.' He turned his watery blue eyes on her again. 'You won't tell Mr Prendergast, will you?' Mr Prendergast was the minister at the chapel. 'I couldn't lift my head up again if this was to get out, not at chapel.'

You should have thought of that before, thought Ellen, but she didn't say it. 'No, I won't tell another soul, not ever,' she replied, less severely, but she found she was unable to smile at him. 'Not if you keep your side of the bargain. And my advice to you would be to sort things out with your wife. Show her some . . . affection.'

'I can't. She's a hard woman,' he repeated. He shook his head sorrowfully. 'Not a scrap of feeling, not any more. You've no idea. I don't even want to . . . now, not with her.' And Ellen, conjuring up a picture of the rigidly corseted figure and the granite-hewn features of his wife, found that she couldn't entirely blame him.

'Have you never considered doing any warwork?' she asked, more tolerantly. 'I don't mean joining the forces.' He was above the age and she doubted, anyway, that he would be medically fit. 'My son's a Special Constable now, and my son-in-law's an ARP warden. And I know they're looking for recruits for the LDV – the Local Defence Volunteers. It might help to take your mind off . . . things.'

'I might. It's a good idea. Thank you, Mrs Hobson. And thank you for not saying anything. I shall miss them, little Doreen and Susan. I never wanted to frighten them, you know. I only wanted . . . well, it just got out of hand.'

Ellen looked at him impassively. 'It won't be mentioned between us, ever again. As far as I'm concerned, that's the end of the matter. Goodbye, Mr Catchpole.' She turned quickly and walked away in the other direction before he could say another word.

150

Chapter 12

Doreen and Susan Aspinall moved to King Street a couple of days later, Edith Catchpole having called round the following morning to tell Ellen that her 'hubby' was in full agreement with the suggestion.

The sisters settled down very well, Doreen sharing Gloria's bedroom, and Susan using the small room that had been Michael's. Ellen and Sally hadn't considered it would be fair to ask Gloria to move so that the sisters could be together. She had made the room so much her own. Emulating her grown-up friend and idol, Emmie, she had started a collection of little pottery animals, saved up for with her Saturday pennies and chosen with care from a pot stall in Abingdon Street market. She also had a few books, one or two that Emmie had given her and a couple she had bought from a second-hand stall with her own money. Somewhat tattered copies they were, of *Anne of Avonlea* and *What Katy Did Next*, but at least they were books and her very own. Sally, watching her elated face as she lovingly turned the pages, knew how much these first possessions she had ever owned meant to the child.

Doreen and Susan never spoke again of their experiences in the Catchpole household. They were, on the whole, uncommunicative little girls, but maybe that was because Sally couldn't help comparing them with Gloria, who was just the opposite. At all events, both Sally and Ellen were satisfied that the children were contented in their new surroundings, and that was all that mattered. Their mother had replied to Ellen's letter, thanking her for taking charge of the little girls and saying she would come over to see them as soon as she could manage it, but what with the twins and the bad weather, she was not sure when that would be.

'Auntie Sally,' said Gloria, one evening in early March, her head on one side and a tiny frown creasing her brow, her accustomed manner when she had something important to ask, 'd'you remember, you said we might go over to Salford, then Doreen and Susan could see their mam and their new twins . . . an' I could go and see our Monica? Well, when are we going?'

Oh dear, Gloria certainly knew how to pick her moments, thought Sally, with just the slightest tinge of irritation. Much as she loved the child she couldn't say that she was biddable and unassertive, in the way that Doreen and Susan were, or Wendy had been. The sisters had been quietly reading their comics and drinking their bedtime cocoa; now, at Gloria's question they were all ears, their greenish eyes fixed intently on Sally. And Gloria would want an answer, as she always did. There was no point in fobbing her off with vague promises of 'We'll see'. It wasn't that Sally hadn't meant what she said about the visit to Salford, but there never seemed to be much time to spare, with working at the shop and looking after three children at home, and the winter weather had been atrocious.

'Yes, I remember, dear,' Sally replied. 'And we will go – definitely.' She made a snap decision. 'We'll go next month, let's say the beginning of April. The worst of the weather should be over by then and it will be lighter in the evenings. And it will be your school holidays then, won't it? It wouldn't be a good idea to go when it's dark and cold, would it?' Although she knew that children never seemed to notice the hardships of winter, or the blackout restrictions, as much as the adults did. 'All right, Doreen . . . Susan? Shall we write to your mum and ask her when we can go? Would you like that? And we'll write to your mother as well, Gloria.'

The sisters looked at one another, then beamed and nodded their agreement. 'Mmm, yes please, Auntie Sally,' said Doreen quietly. 'That'd be lovely, wouldn't it, Susan?'

'Yipee!' said Gloria, bouncing up and down with delight. 'I'm dying to see our Monica again, an' our Len and Sam. It's years and years since I saw them.' It was, in fact, just over four months. 'It's funny she hasn't written, don't you think so, Auntie Sally? 'S funny our Monica hasn't written.'

Sally thought that 'funny' was not the word to describe it. In her view it was despicable, but she forbore to comment. Gloria hadn't mentioned seeing her mother, or her little brother and sisters, she noticed; it was just 'our Monica'.

They boarded a bus outside the station to take them to Salford. Gloria had forgotten how huge Victoria Station was, and how crowded and noisy – and dirty – was Manchester. Blackpool was a busy town, especially now, when it was swarming with RAF recruits, but not as much so as Manchester which seemed to be one heaving mass of people and vehicles. She had forgotten, too, a great deal about Salford, she thought as they alighted from the double-decker bus – a red one, not cream and green as they were in Blackpool – and started to walk through the narrow streets. The houses looked small and huddled closely together and everything looked so grey; the sky, the pavements, the buildings. The sky was grey not just because of the lack of sun – they had chosen a somewhat inclement day for their visit, but after all it was April, a month given to capricious moods – but because a pall of smoke hung over the city. Gloria took a deep sniff; the air smelled sooty and sour after the fresh invigorating seaside air she had grown accustomed to.

They passed the school that they had all attended, but it was deserted. Gloria knew that it had opened again because many of the evacuees had returned, but it was now the school holidays. Doreen and Susan excitedly led the way to their home which was in a little street tucked away behind the school. It was like all the other houses in the row, opening straight on to the street. Sally was pleased to see that the stone step was washed and 'donkey stoned' as were the window sills – northern women, by and large, took a pride in keeping their 'fronts' clean – and the lace curtains, though somewhat holey, were spotless.

There were a few children playing in the street, the girls skipping and the boys zooming around imitating enemy aircraft, which was a favourite game at the moment. One of the lads, a cheeky-faced youngster, stopped and stared at the little party in surprise.

'Hiya. Wotcher doin' 'ere?' He was addressing Doreen and Susan. 'You two – 'ave yer come back 'ome then?'

'No, we're only visiting,' replied Gloria, as the sisters seemed to have been struck dumb.

'Shurrup you, Gloria Mulligan,' said the boy. 'I weren't asking you. This ain't your street, anyroad.'

'Don't care,' said Gloria. She stuck her tongue out at the lad. 'Don't want to play in your rotten old street anyway. I live in Blackpool now.'

Sally, who hailed from Oldham, knew that there was an unwritten rule amongst children about playing in your own street and nobody else's, unless you had been specially invited. 'We're just here for the day,' she said now to the boy. She didn't believe in being offhand with children, as though their opinions didn't matter. 'We're going to see Mrs Aspinall now, and the twins. Come along, girls.'

The boy zoomed away and a little group of girls stopped skipping and stared interestedly at the newcomers. 'Come on, knock at the door,' said Sally to Doreen. 'It's your house, isn't it, so you knock.'

Doreen hung back. She seemed to have suddenly become shy, and it was Susan who stepped forward and raised the knocker. The door opened almost at once and there was no mistaking who this young woman was; she was the image of her daughters. Fair mousey hair escaping from its roll and prominent greenish eyes which lit up with delight at the sight of her two little girls. She enveloped them both in a hug and kissed them several times before she even glanced at Sally and Gloria. There were tears in her eyes which were spilling out and running down her cheeks, and Sally felt that her own eyes, too, were moist. Had she done the right thing, she wondered, in bringing them here? How would this young woman part with her children again when the visit of just a few hours was over?

'Oh, I'm sorry. How rude of me, leaving you standing there. But it's so exciting, isn't it?' Mrs Aspinall smiled at the two little girls, unable to refrain from touching them again, stroking their hair and then their cheeks as if to make sure they were really there. She held out her hand. 'Mrs Hobson, isn't it? The younger Mrs Hobson, of course. How d'you do, madam? I'm so pleased to meet you. And Gloria . . . Hello, dear. Nice to see you.'

'You know Gloria, do you?' asked Sally.

'Little Gloria Mulligan? Of course I know her. Her family live in the next street, don't they, love? Your mam'll be pleased to see you, won't she . . . and your sister. Anyway, come in and I'll make us a cup of tea, or are you wanting to get off to Mrs Mulligan's?' Mrs Aspinall added, as Sally glanced questioningly at Gloria. 'Silly me! Of course Gloria'll be wanting to see her mam, won't you, love?'

'No, 's all right,' replied Gloria. 'We'll go there in a bit. Can we go in, Auntie Sally?' She pulled at Sally's sleeve. 'I want to see the twins.'

They all followed Mrs Aspinall through the door which led directly into the living room. It was a welcoming sort of room with a huge fire blazing away behind a fireguard, and a clothes horse nearby on which were airing – inevitably – rows of sparkling white nappies, tiny vests and nightgowns. It was obvious that Doreen and Susan's mother was a house-proud woman because the room, though somewhat shabbily furnished, was extremely tidy and the surfaces of the furniture shone as though recently polished. The woman, no doubt, had been having a good clean and tidy-up in honour of her visitors, but Sally guessed that she was, at all times, one who liked to keep things nice.

The big black pram which stood by the sideboard seemed to dominate the modestly sized room. Mrs Aspinall pulled back the hood and turned down the blue blanket a little way. 'Come and have a peep at them,' she whispered, in a reverent sort of voice, her greenish eyes glowing with pride. 'But . . . shhh . . .' She put a finger to her lips. 'They're fast asleep, bless 'em. They've had their milk and now they'll sleep for a good hour or more – I hope!' she added, grinning at Sally.

Sally noticed the two empty feeding bottles on the table and gathered that the young woman was not feeding the twins herself. It would have been a lot to expect of her though; she was so slightly built, like both of the girls, that she looked as though a breath of wind might blow her over.

'Yes, there's our Mickey and our Mal,' said their mother, tenderly stroking each down-covered head. 'Michael and Malcolm, we've called them, Mrs Hobson,' she explained. 'Being twins, you see, we thought it was nice for them to have similar sort of names.'

Rather confusing, surely, thought Sally, as she leaned over the pram, especially when they get older and letters start arriving for them – love letters, maybe, or official communications – but it was none of her business. She felt the familiar pang, one she always experienced when she looked at other people's babies, as she gently touched each silken soft cheek. It was impossible to say that the twins looked like their mother or their sisters. They were just babies, but obviously healthy ones as their faintly mottled skins revealed, and bonny ones, too, with rounded cheeks and well-shaped heads. Their downy hair looked as though it might be fair when it grew, like their sisters', but there was very little of it at the moment.

'They're beautiful,' whispered Sally, very sincerely, although she felt a pang of sadness at the thought of bringing innocent little children into the world at such an awful time. God only knows what might be in store for them, or for any of us, thought Sally. She stood back. 'Come on, Doreen and Susan, and you, Gloria. Have a look at these lovely little boys. I bet you've never seen such tiny babies before, have you?' The twins were now about four months old, but still very small.

Three little heads, two fair and one dark, peered into the pram. 'I have,' said Gloria. 'I've seen little babies before, lots of 'em. Our Rose and Lily and our Vinnie. And Monica's two an' all, our Sam and Len. But they weren't as nice as these.' She shook her head in an old-fashioned way at Mrs Aspinall and Sally had to suppress a smile, a sad smile though, for the words were poignant. She knew that Gloria was not just being polite; she was speaking the truth as she saw it, as she always did. 'Not as clean neither,' she added. Mrs Aspinall cast an embarrassed look in Sally's direction, but neither of them spoke.

'They're very nice, Mum,' said Doreen, sounding rather disappointed. 'But it's not much good them being asleep, is it?' She jiggled at the pram handle. 'When are they going to wake up?'

Her mother restrained her. 'I've told you, dear; I'm glad of a bit of peace and quiet – you haven't heard how they can yell! They'll wake up before you go, don't worry, then you and Susan can hold them. Now, take your coats off and sit by the fire and I'll see to that cup of tea. You've had something to eat, haven't you? But I expect you can all manage a piece of cake. I've been baking specially.'

The four had eaten sandwiches that Ellen had prepared on the train, but they were glad of the warming drink and a piece of delicious sponge cake. Sally's admiration for little Mrs Aspinall grew, but she was still wondering how the young woman would be able to part from her girls again at the end of the visit. They were such a devoted little family and Doreen and Susan, now they had overcome their initial shyness, were chattering away twenty to the dozen, telling their mother about Blackpool and school and Sunday School, and how much they liked it at Auntie Ellen and Auntie Sally's house.

'We didn't like that Mrs Catchpole much, did we, Doreen?' said Susan. 'She made us sew and read dead boring books.'

'Mmm, and she smelled of mothballs,' said Doreen, wrinkling her nose. 'And she couldn't cook for toffee, not like Auntie Ellen can. D'you remember that awful meat pie, Susan? All that horrid thick gravy and gristly meat. Yuk!'

Sally and Mrs Aspinall exchanged understanding smiles. Sally was relieved that Mr Catchpole hadn't come into the conversation. He never did, the sisters having, apparently, put him right out of their minds. Sally had been afraid to warn them not to tell their mother about him, not wanting to revive memories that were best forgotten. 'I don't think she was very used to children,' Sally explained now. 'But they seem happy enough with us . . . and with Gloria.' She smiled at the little girl who was sitting there not saying a word, a very unusual state of affairs.

'I'm so glad they're happy,' said Mrs Aspinall. 'You've no idea what a relief it is to me. I haven't known what on earth I should do and that's a fact. So many kiddies from round here have come back, and it makes me feel so guilty leaving them with you. But I still think it's for the best, in spite of what the neighbours say. I've had to put up with some awful comments, I can tell you, Mrs Hobson. About having no time for them now I've got the twins,' she added in an aside. 'They don't say it to my face, of course, but it's come back to me and I've been very hurt. But it isn't true at all. I was quite poorly when the boys arrived, I must admit, and I don't know how I could have coped with four of them. I'm a lot stronger now and I could manage them well enough, but it's not going to be safe much longer, is it, Mrs Hobson, not now that he's moved into Norway. What do you think?' She turned anxious green eyes on Sally.

'I'm inclined to agree with you,' replied Sally carefully. She knew that the young woman was referring to Hitler, whose armies, only that week, had occupied Denmark and then neutral Norway. The British forces which had been sent to Norway had suffered heavy losses and, reading between the lines, it seemed that the land operations had been a complete shambles, although this was not stated directly. News bulletins, both in the papers and at the cinema, tended to veer towards a more optimistic view; but the more discerning drew their own conclusions.

'My husband feels that things are moving,' said Sally, 'and it may not be long before there's some action in France and Belgium. And that's only just across the Channel,' she added. 'Too close for comfort, I should think, if you live down there. Of course, we're safe enough up here, for the moment, but I think you're making a wise decision, Mrs Aspinall, leaving the girls where they are. We'll look after them, I can assure you, and you're very welcome to come over whenever you like. You could bring the pram on the train. Your sister did, didn't she, Gloria?' But Gloria seemed lost in her own thoughts. Sally looked anxiously at her for a moment, before turning back to Mrs Aspinall. 'What does your husband think about it?'

'Oh, Don's happy enough to leave it to me,' said Mrs Aspinall. 'But I know he'd want 'em to be safe, that's the main thing. He's in France, you know. I'm not sure just where and he can't say. They're not allowed to write about it – the letters get censored if they do – but we'll know soon enough, I don't doubt.'

'Yes, I'm sure we will,' agreed Sally, 'for better or worse. Anyway, we'd best be making a move. Come on, Gloria love, let's go and see your family.' She put on her coat and motioned to Gloria to do the same. The child seemed to be in a brown study, quieter than Sally had ever known her. 'I'll call for them at half-past five, shall I? That should give us plenty of time to catch the train.'

'I feel all funny, Auntie Sally,' Gloria confided as they walked along the street. 'It's ages since I saw me mam, and she's . . . well, she's not much like Doreen and Susan's mam, y'know.'

'I wouldn't expect her to be, dear,' said Sally cheerfully. 'Why should she be? We're all different, aren't we? You know what Auntie Ellen is always saying, "It wouldn't do for us all to be alike." '

'But she's not.' The child shook her head perplexedly. 'She's not a bit like that. You'll see.'

'All right, dear.' Sally took hold of Gloria's hand and squeezed it tight. 'You just show me where your home is. And don't worry. Everything's going to be fine.'

The house where the Mulligan family lived was in the next street, one that was almost identical to the street where the Aspinalls lived. Small red-brick terraced houses, formerly homes solely for the mill-workers, Sally guessed, with no gardens, but mostly with well-scrubbed front steps and window sills. Daisy Mulligan's house, Sally noticed at once, with a sinking feeling in her stomach, stood out from its neighbours because of its rundown appearance. Here, the stone steps and ledges were not washed or 'donkey-stoned', the lace curtains which had once been cream were now a dingy grey, hanging in tatters against the dirty windows, and the paint was peeling off the front door. It faced the afternoon sun, admittedly, but was blistered and cracked and couldn't have seen a coat of paint for years.

'We're here,' said Gloria in a small voice. She smiled faintly, then lifted the tarnished knocker and banged it three times, somewhat timidly, Sally felt.

Daisy Mulligan was pretty much as Sally had anticipated, only more so. She had expected the woman to be careworn, but not, perhaps, quite so slovenly or so old-looking or so fat and blowsy. She could only be in her mid-forties, just a few years older than Sally, but she looked nearer sixty than fifty. Her iron-grey hair was roughly skewered in a roll around her florid face, a floral – very stained – overall covered her drooping bosom, and her feet were encased in down-at-heel carpet slippers. Sally couldn't help noticing, with a pang of sympathy, the unsightly bulges beneath the woman's lisle stockings. She obviously suffered from varicose veins and Sally told herself, there and then, not to be too critical. This woman had had a hard life. Compared with Daisy Mulligan Sally didn't know she was born. The contrast, however, with neat and tidy little Mrs Aspinall, couldn't be more apparent, and Sally knew exactly what had been bothering Gloria.

But she was the child's mother when all was said and done and, to do the woman credit, she smiled and drew Gloria to her in a brief embrace.

'Hello, Mam,' said Gloria quietly. 'This is me Auntie Sally.'

'How d'yer do? Pleased to meetcher.' Mrs Mulligan held out a red, roughened hand which Sally took with a show of eagerness.

'And I'm very pleased to meet you, Mrs Mulligan,' she said warmly. 'Gloria's told us such a lot about you.' A white lie was permissible, surely? 'And she's been looking forward to seeing you all again.'

The woman's grey eyes – very much like Gloria's, and like Monica's, too; the three of them, despite the obvious differences had a definite family resemblance – looked shrewdly at Sally, somewhat critically, too, Sally felt. She was very much aware of her 'best' coat with its fur trimming and she wondered if the tiny red hat she was wearing, tilted over her forehead, might be the tiniest bit too 'chic'.

Mrs Mulligan nodded curtly. 'Aye, well, we've been looking forward to seeing her an' all. Bill's at work, of course, and I expect you'll be gone before 'e gets 'ome. And the lads, our Frankie and Arthur, you won't be seeing them. But

161

Rose and Lily are here, and our Vinnie. You'd best come in.'

Sally smiled encouragingly at Gloria and they followed Daisy into the living room.

An odd smell permeated the air, comprising of stale food, sweat, damp clothes drying and, overlying all the other smells, an unmistakable one of urine. A red-cheeked baby – that must be 'our Vinnie', Sally guessed, a child about one year old – was sitting on the rag hearthrug together with 'our Rose and Lily', two little girls with ginger hair and pale stolid faces that stared uncomprehendingly at the newcomers. The baby, however, grinned widely on seeing them, revealing two tiny teeth, and his blue eyes lit up with interest. He had a bonny face and was far more like Gloria than the other two, but it was a pity his mother hadn't bothered to wipe his mouth after his dinner or to remove his gravy-stained bib.

'Look at him laughing, Auntie Sally,' cried Gloria in delight, kneeling on the rug amidst the jumble of wooden bricks and tin cars. 'He remembers me, don't you, Vinnie?' She seized hold of his hands and drew her face closer to his. 'Are you pleased to see Gloria, then?'

Sally didn't imagine that the child could really remember Gloria. He was no doubt pleased at a diversion, being far more animated than his doltish-looking sisters.

'Hello, Rose . . . Hello, Lily.' Gloria was trying hard with the other two. 'You remember me, don't you? It's Gloria.' They both stared at her impassively, then one nodded without much interest while the other one turned back to her game of tower building.

'How the hell d'you expect 'em to remember you?' said Daisy Mulligan. 'Don't talk so daft. We haven't seen hair nor hide of you for six months and more.' And whose fault is that, thought Sally, bristling inwardly at the overt tactlessness of the woman. 'Anyroad, you're 'ere now and you'll be ready for a cup of tea, I daresay. Sit yerself down, Miss . . . no, Mrs 'Obson, i'n't it?' Daisy hurriedly removed a pile of papers and comics from the seat of a sagging armchair and Sally, quite literally, sank into its depths. The springs had gone and her knees nearly touched her chin.

'Go and talk to your mum,' she said, smiling encouragingly at Gloria. 'Go on . . . she'll be wanting to hear all your news.' Gloria cast her an anxious glance before following Daisy into the kitchen.

Sally looked around. The dampish smell was coming from a row of nappies drying on a clothes horse near a sulky fire, not pristine white ones, however, as Mrs Aspinall's had been, but threadbare cloths of a greyish hue, some badly stained. Sally shuddered, her eyes taking in the cracked linoleum, the peeling wallpaper with patches of damp round the window, the huge sideboard piled high with the conglomeration of everyday living – clothes waiting to be ironed, unwashed cups and saucers, babies' bottles, a cracked pottery jug and a tarnished tea caddy and, in the middle of the mêlée, a statuette of the Virgin Mary (Gloria had told her about that) – and the table spread, unbelievably, with newspaper, on which the debris of the midday meal still remained. As her eyes tried to take in all this incredible squalor, a cockroach ran across the lino near the door, disappearing into a crack in the skirting board. It took Sally all her time not to jump up and yell.

Poor Gloria. Poor little girl. Sally was understanding now, more than ever, what it must have been like for the child to leave this pigsty – there was no other word for it – of a house and come to live in Blackpool. And yet it was the child's home. It was the place to which, eventually, she would have to return. Sally tried to make herself accept this, but the reality was too awful to contemplate. A feeling of despair began to overwhelm her. Poor Gloria. Whatever could she do?

Gloria seemed slightly more animated when she returned with her mother, carrying a plate of biscuits, Daisy following with a tin tray holding cups and saucers and a brown earthenware teapot. Sally had heard the rise and fall of voices but, lost in her own thoughts, had not been listening to the conversation. At all events, it would have been wrong to eavesdrop.

'Seems she's been 'aving a rare old time,' said Daisy, handing a cup of strong, dark brown tea to Sally before sitting down at the table and drawing a packet of cigarettes from her overall pocket. She held it out to Sally, withdrawing it quickly as Sally shook her head. Daisy lit a cigarette and inhaled deeply. 'Aye, it sounds as though Blackpool's one long bloomin' 'oliday. Goin' on t'sands, and goin' to t'pictures. And to cap it all, a bloomin' rock factory! Some folks don't know they're born, do they?' She grinned at Gloria, a friendly enough grin, Sally had to admit, and she noticed that one of the woman's front teeth was missing. Just decayed, wondered Sally, or was her husband too handy with his fists?

'It's not all play, Mrs Mulligan,' said Sally. She took a sip of the tea. 'Haven't you told your mum about school and how much you enjoy it? And about Doreen and Susan? And Emmie? You've made friends with Emmie, haven't you, love? That's my niece,' explained Sally. 'She's a few years older than Gloria, but you've become real good friends, haven't you, dear?'

Gloria nodded, seemingly tongue-tied again.

'Aye, well, it sounds to me as though she'll never want to come back 'ome,' said Daisy. There was a moment's silence before she cast a suspicious glance in Sally's direction. ''Ere, that's not why you've come, is it? To bring 'er back, or to tell us you want shut of 'er?'

Sally was horrified. Want shut of her, indeed! 'Of course not,' she replied, trying not to sound too indignant. 'We're just here on a visit. I know you can't get to Blackpool, Mrs Mulligan, with the children and everything, so we thought we'd come to see you. And Doreen and Susan wanted to see their new twins, so . . . here we are.' She smiled brightly. 'Oh, I mustn't forget. We've brought something for the children, haven't we, Gloria?' She reached into her bag and took out six sticks of rock, three pink (peppermint) and three yellow (pineapple). 'Some for now and some for later. That is, if it's all right for them to have it now? It might be too much for the baby, but he can perhaps have a little suck of it. We usually chop it into small pieces, don't we, Gloria? Of course we don't let her eat too much, Mrs Mulligan,' Sally went on to explain. 'Just a bit at a time, when she's finished her tea. Too much might spoil her teeth.'

'Oh, I ne'er worry about all that,' said Daisy. 'It's there to be enjoyed, i'n't it? 'Ere, what d'yer say, kids? Say thank you to this kind lady.'

'Fank you. Ta,' muttered Rose and Lily before pulling back the waxed paper and beginning to suck furiously. Likewise, baby Vinnie, and soon his mouth and chin and hands were a bright pink gooey mess. His mother made no move to wipe him.

'We've got some for Monica's boys as well, haven't we, Auntie Sally?' said Gloria. 'She knows we're coming, doesn't she, Mam? We can go and see her, can't we?'

'Oh aye, she's expecting you,' said Daisy, tapping a pile of ash into her saucer. 'She's gorra surprise for yer.'

'Has she? What is it?'

'Oh, I'll let 'er tell yer,' said Daisy. 'Well, she won't need to tell yer. You'll know as soon as you set eyes on her.'

Sally realised what Daisy was hinting at, which was probably the reason that Monica O'Brien had not been over to see her little sister. Changing the subject, Sally turned to Daisy. 'You're willing to let Gloria stay with us a while longer, then, Mrs Mulligan? I know a lot of the children have come home, but Mrs Aspinall was just saying to me that she thought it might be better to leave them where they are. We never know when things may . . . change, and you want her to be safe, don't you?'

'Oh aye, so long as she's 'appy then that's all right with me,' said Daisy carelessly. 'I've got me work cut out with 'er

165

dad and the lads and this tribe 'ere. I reckon she's not done too badly for 'erself, going to Blackpool. Proper swankpot in that dress, ain't yer?' She nodded eloquently in Gloria's direction. 'Talking real posh an' all, ain't she?'

'We're doing our best,' said Sally quietly.

The two women chatted for a little whilst Gloria played on the rug with her baby brother and sisters. Daisy spoke of her husband and his job on the bins, her son Frankie, who was a telegraph boy, and Bill's son, Arthur, a grocer's assistant. Sally gathered that there was, in reality, a fair amount of money coming into the house, and it sounded as though Bill did very well with his spoils from the dustbin round. She came to the conclusion that Daisy Mulligan was not all that poor and unable to make ends meet, as she had assumed, but just feckless. Mrs Aspinall must be finding it something of a struggle with her husband away and two babies to care for, but her home was spotless. Sally tried to tell Daisy about her own family, about Ellen, George, Rachel and Harry and the girls, but the woman didn't seem very interested.

In about half an hour conversation seemed to wane and Sally glanced in Gloria's direction.

'Aye, off you go,' said Daisy. 'Go and see our Monica. She'll be waiting for you.'

'I wonder if I could just use your toilet?' asked Sally. Needs must, unfortunately.

'Aye, help yerself,' said Daisy, rising laboriously to her feet. She opened the kitchen door. 'It's at th' end o' t'yard. You'd best go and spend a penny an' all, hadn't you, Gloria, when your . . . your auntie's been?'

'Auntie Sally's got a bathroom upstairs,' Sally heard Gloria saying as she went through the kitchen. 'We don't need to use potties an' all that.'

'Oh well, it's all right for some folk,' was the last remark Sally heard as she stepped out into the yard. She did hope that Gloria would not go on too much about the 'posh house' where she was now living, but somehow she didn't think that the child would do so. There were times when Gloria seemed to have a wisdom beyond her years.

The 'lav' was a bit smelly, with squares of newspaper hanging on a nail, but reasonably clean and at least there was a chain to pull. Sally had half feared an earth closet, but this one was like the one they had had at her childhood home in Oldham. Not too bad at all, considering. She quickly swilled her hands under the tap in the kitchen and wiped them on a grubby striped towel that hung nearby. Gloria had already put on her coat and pixie hood and she went off down the yard while Sally put on her own coat.

'Thank you for making me so welcome,' she said to Daisy. After all, what else could she say and she supposed the woman had done her best. 'And don't forget, if you feel like a visit to Blackpool, we'll be very pleased to see you, and the children.'

'Aye well, pigs might fly,' said Daisy sniffing, 'but still, ta very much, Mrs 'Obson. So long as Gloria's being looked after, that's all that matters.' She gave the child a quick hug and a peck on the cheek when she came back into the house. 'Righty-ho then, off yer go, and we'll see yer when we see yer.'

'Tara, Mam. Tara, you lot.' Gloria wiggled her fingers at the trio of children.

'Tara, Gloria,' said the two little girls, who seemed by now to have realised who she was, and the baby grinned again. He was a pleasant, jolly little lad, thought Sally, hoping he would manage to survive in such an inadequate household.

Monica O'Brien's home, a few minutes' walk away, was marginally tidier and cleaner than her mother's. Sally guessed that at least the young woman had made some effort to make the place look ship-shape. And there was no doubt that she was delighted to see her little sister again. Her arms went round the child and her grey eyes were moist as she held her close in an affectionate embrace; as close as she could

167

because it was obvious at a glance that Monica was some six or seven months' pregnant.

'You're having a baby, Monica,' said Gloria when the young woman released her. 'An' I never knew.'

'Ah well, we don't tell you everything, little 'un,' said Monica, tapping her playfully on the nose. 'Anyroad, you know now, don't you? Come on in.' She grinned at Sally. 'Nice to see you again. It's 'cause of this that I haven't been over.' She patted the bulge of her stomach. 'I were real bad at first, much worse than I were with the others.' But you could have written, thought Sally.

All the same, she listened sympathetically as they sat in Monica's quite comfortable living room – at least there was a nice warm fire – and the young woman recounted tales of her morning sickness and her swollen ankles and how the other two had been playing her up something awful. It was ironic, thought Sally, how some women seemed able to conceive so easily, 'at the drop of a hat', as Monica would say, whereas she, Sally, who had so desperately wanted a child had never been in that fortunate state. Nor would she want to be now, at forty years of age . . . but life wasn't always entirely fair.

They stayed for a few hours, far longer than they had stayed at Daisy's, and Monica made them quite a tasty meal of Spam and chips followed by tinned peaches and mock cream. Some food was now on ration, but Monica explained that this was a tin she had been saving for a special occasion. Sally felt very gratified at this remark and found herself warming again to Monica. This young woman, she felt, was someone whom she could trust to see to Gloria's welfare, when the time came. But she hastily brushed such a thought away.

Sam and Len seemed to remember Gloria, and Sally, too, from their visit to Blackpool, and were on their best behaviour. Sally was glad to see that Monica didn't let them have the rock until they had finished their tea, and then only

168

a small amount of it, the rest to be kept for another time.

'How's she doin' then?' asked Monica, grinning companionably at her sister. 'Not giving you no trouble, is she? She's been telling me all about her friend, Emmie, and I believe you've got the Aspinall kids now, instead of Mrs Snooty Cooper's two? I didn't think they'd stay long, somehow. Behaving herself, is she, our Gloria?'

'She is indeed. It's a very great joy for us to have her,' said Sally, 'for me and my husband, and my mother-in-law. I can't tell you how much difference she's made to us. Thank you for letting her stay,' she added quietly. 'So many of the children have come back but, as I was saying to your mother, I think you've done the right thing.'

A sorrowful expression flitted across Monica's face, momentarily, as she looked at Sally. Then she shrugged. 'It's Mam's decision, not mine. It has to be – and she thinks she'll be safer where she is. Happen she's right. It can't go on like this much longer, can it, this bloomin' war? It's as though we're on the edge of a bloody volcano. Something's got to happen soon, hasn't it? My husband Gerry's over there, in France; God knows when I'll see him again. Not before this arrives, I don't suppose.' She patted her bulge again.

'When is the baby due?' asked Sally, feeling very sorry for her, as she had for Mrs Aspinall. Two young women, both more or less in the same position. Different personalities with different priorities, maybe, but they both must be worried sick about their husbands. Sally guessed that Monica's nonchalant attitude towards her own spouse covered quite a wealth of caring.

'End of June or thereabouts,' replied Monica. 'I'd 'ave come over to see our kid, honest, if it hadn't been for this.'

'Don't worry,' said Sally, as they took their leave of her and the boys. 'If you can't come to see us, then we'll come to see you, won't we, Gloria?'

Monica hugged and kissed the little girl, but in a jocular rather than an overly affectionate manner. 'Be seein' yer, kid. Off you go and enjoy them Blackpool breezes.'

'Tara, Monica. Tara, you two – see yer soon.' Gloria didn't seem at all upset to be parting from them and was very chatty as they walked along to collect Doreen and Susan. 'Just fancy, Auntie Sally, our Monica having another baby. That'll be another nephew for me, won't it, or a niece if it's a girl? I hope it's a girl this time. I think Monica 'ud like a girl . . .'

Mrs Aspinall was being very brave, as were the two little girls. Sally had half expected that the woman might change her mind and decide to keep her daughters with her, but common sense prevailed. They parted without any tears and Mrs Aspinall promised to come over and see them before very long.

Doreen and Susan were quiet on the way back, holding hands as if for moral support of one another. Gloria seemed subdued, too, although Sally guessed that she was tired, more than contemplative, as she watched the little girl staring out of the carriage window into the unrelieved darkness. Her eyes closed as the rhythmic motion of the train sent her into a doze, and Sally glanced at her affectionately, resisting an urge to reach out and stroke the gently rounded cheek of the child who had come to mean so much to her.

Instead, she grinned at Doreen and Susan, sitting opposite her. 'Old sleepy-head, isn't she? Now, you two, watch and see if you can spot Blackpool Tower. It's dark, but you might just be able to make it out.'

'Isn't it nice to be home again, Auntie Sally?' said Gloria as they turned in at the gate on King Street.

Sally's heart missed a beat as she answered the child. 'Yes, dear. Very nice.' Blackpool was well and truly 'home' to Gloria now . . . but for how long?

Chapter 13

Food rationing had been brought into force in January, covering at first only bacon, ham, sugar and butter. The news, for most people, was reassuring rather than alarming, meaning, as it did, that there would be fair shares for all. For those involved in the sweet-manufacturing business, however, the news was not good. The Food Ministry had announced that sweet-makers were to be allotted only seventy per cent of their peacetime quota. The local newspaper predicted, somewhat gloomily, that there would be far less rock on sale in Blackpool during the summer season of 1940 and it would be double the price.

'Job's comforters they are, and no mistake,' George remarked to Harry. The two men were now sharing the responsibility of Hobson's quite amicably, with only the occasional slight difference of opinion, whilst Ellen was enjoying her semi-retirement. 'We'll see how things go, won't we, before we consider raising the price, to that extent at any rate. Double the price, indeed! We don't want to put ourselves out of business.'

'We must be realistic, though,' Harry had replied. 'You know as well as I do that the price of sugar has almost doubled, and the waxed wrapping paper's dearer as well, so the customers are going to have to pay more, it stands to reason.'

'Mmm, maybe,' George conceded, though grudgingly. He wasn't entirely convinced. But when in May the amount of sugar available dropped to sixty per cent of the previous year's quota there was no alternative but to make a substantial increase in the selling price of the rock and other confectionery.

It made very little difference to the buying public. The visitors who were still flocking to Blackpool, though not in quite such large numbers, in the spring and early summer of 1940 seemed only too willing to pay the going price for their rock. Hobson's, along with other manufacturers, found that demand for the product was exceeding supply, and they were unable to make as much rock as they knew they could sell. With the workforce, made up largely of women, working at full pressure, they were producing a week's supply in only a few days . . . and selling it just as quickly.

'You were right,' George admitted to his brother-in-law. 'We had to put the price up or else we'd have been in Queer Street. And the visitors don't seem to have noticed either. Sally says they're buying sticks of rock as though there's no tomorrow. I suppose it's a case of "Eat, drink and be merry . . .".' He didn't finish the quotation, suddenly aware of how prophetic the last few words might be: . . . *for tomorrow we die.*

Ellen, more concerned with the running of her household these days than she was with the organisation of Hobson's, was finding that sweet manufacturers were not the only ones affected by the sugar shortage. When time permitted she had always liked to make her own marmalade, considering it far superior to the shop-bought varieties. Housewives wanting to make marmalade now had to obtain permits from the local Food Office entitling them to sugar, provided they had bought the required amount of Seville oranges and had a receipt to prove the fact! Three pounds of sugar were allowed for every pound of oranges bought, there being a limit of one pound of oranges to each person in the household. Ration books had to be produced to show how many people were living in the house. As there were six in Ellen's household she was allowed six pounds of oranges – eighteen pounds of sugar! Enough

172

to keep them in marmalade for the next year and more, she thought as she donned her apron and made ready her jam pan and sterilised jars. It seemed to her that every aspect of life, both at a national and a personal level, was regimented these days, even jam-making.

Very soon the war news became so grim that trivial matters like the making of marmalade, and even the production of rock, paled into insignificance. On 10 May the Germans burst into Holland, Belgium and France, and Neville Chamberlain, a sad and broken man, was removed from office. Winston Churchill with his promise to the nation of nothing but 'blood, tears, toil and sweat' became Prime Minister.

'For want of a better alternative, if you ask me,' George remarked. He had tried, in the beginning, to go along with Chamberlain's doctrine of appeasement, remembering only too well the horrors of the Great War; although Chamberlain's declaration, only recently, that 'Hitler has missed the bus', was seen now to prove how deluded he was and how out of touch with the reality of the situation. 'They're saying the King would have liked Lord Halifax to take over, but the Labour lot won't go along with that.'

'No, indeed,' said Harry. 'I should think not. He was a man of Munich, wasn't he?' Unlike his brother-in-law, Harry had never believed that Germany could be made to toe the line. Now, with Churchill at the helm, they might begin to see some action. Maybe now, he, Harry, would have some more vitally important work to do in his job as ARP warden, apart from parading the darkened streets with his cry of, 'Put that light out!' – a catchphrase which was rapidly becoming a target for ridicule. 'I think Churchill's the right man for the job,' he added. 'The only man in my opinion.'

The news went from bad to worse with the fall of Holland, then of Belgium, followed by the evacuation of the Allied troops from the beaches of Dunkirk. The adults in the Hobson household listened to the news bulletins and read the newspapers with feelings of anxiety and trepidation. They said very little to the children, not knowing how much the three of them realised what was going on or what they understood about it all. Doreen and Susan's father was over there; so was Gerry, Gloria's brother-in-law, but they were never mentioned. Then, at the beginning of June, a letter came from Mrs Aspinall to say that her husband was safe and had come home for a week's leave, followed very soon by a letter from Monica to say that Gerry, likewise, had escaped unharmed. Gloria had seemed unaccountably pleased at this news and Sally assumed it was because that young fellow had been one of the few, in that far from perfect family, who had been kind to her. But Monica also said in her letter that Mr Cooper, Wendy and Michael's father, had been reported missing, believed dead.

'Poor "Daddy",' said Sally, remembering how the woman had spoken of her husband. 'And poor Mrs Cooper, too, and Wendy and Michael. She was trying to be so brave about it all that time she came here. What a tragedy it is.' Sally's heart went out to her, as it did to all the women who were in similar circumstances. And she thanked God again, though not without a feeling of guilt, that her own husband was safe at home with her and quite likely to remain so. Even his part-time job as a Special Constable was not taking George into any real danger.

There wasn't much danger in Blackpool. They were still isolated, it seemed, from the perils of war up here in the north of England. The town was swarming with RAF recruits, Wellington bombers were being made at the Vickers-Armstrong factory at Squire's Gate and in the top storeys of Talbot Road bus station, which was an annexe to the main factory. But apart from that, life was going on pretty much as usual. In a spirit of bravado, Hobson's, along with other manufacturers, were now producing rock with the Union Jack running through it and this was an immediate success with both residents and visitors. People were not only working

174

hard, but were endeavouring to play hard as well. The dance halls had never been busier, the ballrooms of the Winter Gardens, the Tower and the Palace packed nightly with local girls and uniformed men, not only the British airmen but, after Dunkirk, their comrades from Poland, France, Scandinavia and Holland.

And the cinemas were doing a roaring trade. It was soon after the news had arrived that Doreen and Susan's father was safe, and Gerry, too, that Sally decided to take the girls to see the film *Pinocchio*. It was showing at the Princess cinema and they went to an early Saturday evening performance. It would be a pleasant diversion from the dreadful war news, Sally thought, and obviously many more people were of the same opinion because the cinema was packed.

They watched the usual newsreel, coated, as always, with an optimistic gloss. Cheerfully grinning soldiers, Cockneys, the ones that were interviewed, told how having been released from the 'jaws of hell' they would soon be ready to go back and ' 'ave another bash at 'Itler'. The 'miracle of Dunkirk', as it was being called, was the main story, but there was also the news, suitably expurgated, that Italy had now declared war on Britain and France.

There was much of the child, still, in Sally. She had retained, over the years, a great deal of her youthful optimism and sense of wonder, but she hadn't expected to be quite so captivated by the story of the little wooden puppet who wanted to be a real live boy. She was just as entranced as the three girls were by the catchy songs, the heart-stopping adventures that befell Pinocchio, and Walt Disney's superb characterisation of the aging wood-carver, Gepetto, and his animal companions, Cleo, a charmingly glamorous goldfish, and the wily cat, Figaro.

The songs were constantly being heard on the wireless at the moment and as they walked home along Talbot Road all three children were singing Jiminy Cricket's song. Gloria, as might be expected, was leading the chorus, 'Give a little whistle', with the other two joining in with the 'Whoo whoos' as best they could.

'Wasn't it lovely, Auntie Sally!' cried Gloria, grabbing hold of Sally's arm. 'What did you like best? What was your favourite bit?'

'Oh, I don't know,' said Sally. 'It was all so good. I think I liked the part where Pinocchio's nose grew and grew because he wasn't telling the truth. That was funny, wasn't it?'

'I liked the fox and the cat,' said Doreen. 'Weren't they awful, Auntie Sally?'

'An' I liked all those pretty fishes,' said Susan. 'You know, when Pinocchio was in the sea, and Gepetto was looking for him.'

'D'you know what I liked best?' Gloria stood still for a moment, causing the others to pause, too, to hear what she was saying. 'I liked that blue fairy, and the star, and the part where Pinocchio was making a wish. "When you wish upon a star," ' she started to sing, almost under her breath, before setting off walking again.

'Yes, that's a lovely part, isn't it?' agreed Sally. 'I liked that, as well.' She had thought that the exuberant, outgoing Gloria might have opted for a more exciting part of the film for her 'favourite bit', but the child was surprisingly sentimental and reflective at times.

'D'you think there'll be any stars tonight?' asked Gloria now. She peered up into the summer sky. ' 'Tisn't even dark yet.' It was a glorious June evening, less than a couple of weeks away from the longest day, and with Double British Summer Time it was not likely to go really dark much before midnight.

'There may be some stars later, when you're tucked up in bed,' replied Sally. 'Don't be wanting it to go dark, Gloria. It's nice not to have to bother with the blackout curtains, isn't it? And not to have to take my torch when we go out.'

176

'Why d'you want there to be stars?' asked Doreen. 'D'you want to make a wish, like Pinocchio did?'

'I might.' Gloria shrugged evasively.

'What yer gonna wish for then?' asked Susan. 'I'd wish I could have a pretty dress, like that fairy wore.'

'Don't be so daft!' scoffed her sister. 'Fancy wishing for a soppy thing like that. You should wish that the war 'ud be over, shouldn't she, Auntie Sally?' Doreen turned to Sally, looking up at her a trifle self-righteously.

'Well . . . yes, dear,' replied Sally. 'We all wish that.'

'And I'd've wished that our dad 'ud come back safe from France,' Doreen went on. 'But he has, hasn't he? So that's all right,' she added prosaically. 'I don't need to wish for that any more.' The plight of the British troops, especially the ones known to them, had probably been on the children's minds more than she realised, thought Sally. 'So, I don't know what I'd wish for, not really.' Doreen turned to Gloria. 'Come on, Glor, tell us your wish.'

'No, I can't.' Gloria shook her head. 'You haven't to tell wishes or it stops 'em from coming true. D'you remember, Auntie Sally, at my birthday party, that's what we said then, didn't we? That you hadn't got to tell.' Sally nodded; she remembered. 'You weren't there,' Gloria said to Doreen and Susan. 'You were still with that Mrs Catchpole. But I wished for summat . . . something . . . then, and that's what I'd wish for again.'

'Didn't it come true then?' asked Doreen. 'It can't have done, or you wouldn't be wishing for it again. I think that's daft.'

'Well, it did then, so there!' Gloria stuck her tongue out at her friend. 'Shows how much you know, Clever-Clogs! I just want it to go on coming true, that's all.'

'Well, I still think it's daft. I bet it's a dead stupid wish.'

'Shurrup, you! You don't know what you're talking about, Doreen Aspinall!'

'And that's quite enough, Gloria!' said Sally firmly.

'We've heard enough about wishes for one night, thank you very much.' An aggressive streak was still apparent in the little girl sometimes, when she got over-excited or cross. 'I'll tell you what *I* wish. I wish you were all in bed. I'm getting fed up with all this arguing. I shan't take you to the pictures again if this is how you're going to behave.'

But Sally was smiling to herself, and Gloria, glancing up at her, knew that she was.

'We didn't mean it, Auntie Sally, did we, Doreen?' she said in a small voice. 'We can stay up, can't we, and listen to *Band Waggon*?'

'We'll see,' said Sally, but her secretive little smile indicated to Gloria that the girls would get round her. They usually did.

Gloria crept out of bed and tiptoed across the dark room. Doreen was fast asleep, breathing heavily, as she had been for the last hour and more, but Gloria had been willing herself to keep awake. She pushed back the pink curtains, grey, now, in the darkness, then the blackout blinds. She moved them only a few inches, not wanting the swish of the curtain rings on the rail to waken her friend. But there was space enough for her to see and she peered out into the night. The moon was shining over the rooftops opposite and . . . yes . . . there was just a sprinkling of stars. One, to Gloria's eager eyes – or it might just have been her fancy – seemed brighter than all the others and she fixed her sights on it. She half closed her eyes, seeing, in imagination, the star coming closer and closer to her, just as it had in the film. And the blue fairy, too, was there, telling her to make a wish. Gloria could see her, in her mind's eye, as clearly as anything. And, just like Pinocchio had done, Gloria made her wish.

Closing her eyes tightly, she wished. She even whispered it out loud. No, not loudly, just the faintest sibilant sound in the quiet stillness of the night. '*I wish . . . I wish that I could stay here, with Auntie Sally . . . for ever and ever.*'

On 14 June, German troops marched through the city of Paris and France asked for an armistice with Germany. Britain now stood alone.

'Let us brace ourselves to our duty and so bear ourselves,' said Churchill, the next day, to the House of Commons, 'that if the British Commonwealth and Empire last for a thousand years, men will still say, "This was their finest hour." '

The Channel Islands were occupied on 1 July, and many people felt, though were loth to express their feelings out loud – that would be 'defeatist talk' – that the invasion of southern England would follow very soon. Augmenting the troops of the British Army, who were now, by and large, stationed in the south of England, in readiness for attack, were the Local Defence Volunteers, men aged between seventeen and sixty-five – though mainly from the younger and older age groups – who had come forward to train, unpaid, in their spare time.

'I think we're doing just as important a job as they are,' Harry remarked to George, after watching a group of LDV parading in their makeshift uniforms, with rubber truncheons and broom handles, in the absence, as yet, of real weapons. 'Although I must admit I get a bit fed up of being the butt of feeble jokes. If one more small boy yells at me, "Hey mister, put that light out!" I feel I won't be responsible for my actions, I can tell you! But at least I've learned how to use a stirrup pump, and I can find my way round inky-black buildings better than any cat burglar.'

'Yes, a lot of your work seems to overlap with the courses we're doing,' replied George, who was training as a Special Constable, 'like First Aid and fire-fighting and anti-gas precautions. It's all very well though, Harry, but I can't help feeling that we're only playing at it. It's not for real.'

'Don't speak too soon, mate. Our day will come, you mark my words.'

'What? Here, in Blackpool?'

'I shouldn't be surprised,' said Harry. 'In fact, I'd be more surprised if it *didn't* happen, sooner or later. Not a word to the ladies, of course. We don't want to put the wind up them.'

'No, of course not,' agreed George. The two men often had these confidential little talks, away from the women of the family. They were enjoying an 'off-duty' drink at the Raikes Hotel, a quiet pub not far from both their homes. Only a half of bitter for George, however; he knew where to draw the line now. Their talk these days seemed to be concerned more with their voluntary warwork than their paid occupation at the rock factory. 'What d'you mean, though?' George went on. 'It's the south of England that's going to cop it, surely, if there's an invasion.' He spoke the word in a whisper, looking round uneasily to make sure that no one was listening. They were constantly being warned that 'Careless Talk Costs Lives', but their table in the corner seemed to be out of earshot.

'I'm not thinking so much of invasion as an air attack,' said Harry in a low voice. 'Just think about it. We've got a massive aircraft factory at Squire's Gate, and another one over the bus station. To say nothing of the thousands of airmen training here, at the biggest training ground in the country, I shouldn't wonder. We're a sitting target in Blackpool, if you ask me.'

George felt more than a slight tremor of unease. 'But they sent the evacuees here! I know most of them have gone back now, but surely they wouldn't have sent them here if they'd thought there was any real danger.'

'You'd think not,' agreed Harry, 'but they don't know all the answers. Any more than I do,' he added. 'I might be wrong. Let's hope I am. Cheers, mate.' He lifted his pint glass. 'Let's try and look on the bright side, eh? And, like I said, not a word to the ladies. Our Pearl's applied for the Land Army, did I tell you? And Ruby's thinking of going to work at the aircraft factory. She feels she's wasting her time serving in the shop when there's more vital work to be done. I must say, I admire her spirit.'

'They're not having all our saucepans,' Ellen remarked to Sally at the beginning of July. There had been an appeal from Lord Beaverbrook, the newly appointed Minister for Aircraft Production, to the women of Great Britain, to give everything made of aluminium they could possibly spare to be made into aircraft. 'I'm as patriotic as the next person, I hope, but enough's enough. They can have these three and like it.' She had put to one side three oddments that had seen better days. Then Ellen pursed her lips thoughtfully. Perhaps she wasn't being sacrificial enough. After all, she would hardly miss these battered old things.

'And this one.' She reached up to the shelf and took down the medium-sized one of a set of three pans, all in fairly good condition. 'And that's the lot. I've got to hang on to my frying pan, and milk pan, and jam pan. For heaven's sake, they've already taken our garden railings.'

'And our gate,' added Sally, smiling. She hadn't smiled that evening, however, on coming home and finding, for the third time, a pile of dog muck near the front step. The stray dogs of the neighbourhood now had free access to the garden areas. 'Never mind, Mam. I suppose it's all in a good cause.'

That was what they were constantly telling themselves, and one another, these days, mused Ellen. And, should they forget, there were always the posters, on walls, hoardings, buses and buildings, all over the place, to remind them. Ellen had counted thirty different posters the other day as she was walking through Blackpool. There would have been more, but at that stage she had given up counting, having stopped at the window of Sally Mae's dress shop to look at a very nice two-piece suit.

'*We want your kitchen waste!*' proclaimed a pig with a jolly grin, standing near to a bin marked *Pig Swill*. And there was 'Doctor Carrot, the Children's Best Friend', prancing along with his little black bag; and Potato Pete, declaring '*I'm an energy food!*' as he leapt into a shopping basket.

'*Let us go forward together*,' urged Winston Churchill, from another eye-catching poster. '*Don't do it, Mother. Leave the children where they are*,' another implored (whilst a shadowy figure of Hitler, in the background, argued '*Take them back*.') This was an example of a poster that hadn't had the desired effect. On the whole, though, the posters were persuasive and the humorous note they conveyed was more effective than straightforward propaganda would have been. You were exhorted to join the ATS, to register for Civil Defence, to carry your gas mask, to come into the factories, to refrain from careless talk . . . and to join the Women's Land Army. A picture of a rosy-cheeked, fair-haired girl wielding a pitchfork reminded Ellen that her beloved eldest granddaughter had already applied to do just that.

'I've got something to tell you, Gloria.' Emmie's face as she let her young friend into the house held a secretive look. 'Come upstairs, and then Mum won't hear us.'

But Rachel had already popped her head out of the living-room door on hearing voices in the hall. 'Hello, Gloria dear.' She smiled brightly, rather too brightly, Gloria couldn't help thinking. She knew that Rachel didn't entirely approve of the friendship that had developed between her youngest daughter and her mother's evacuee. 'What are you two whispering about? Is it something I shouldn't hear, eh?' She was still smiling, but she raised her eyebrows and there was an edge to her voice.

'No, Mum. 'Course not. Why should it be?' Emmie gave an evasive shake of her head. 'Gloria's just come round to borrow some books. I told you she was coming.'

'So you did, dear. I must have forgotten. Are you staying for tea, Gloria, or will my . . . your Auntie Ellen be expecting you back?'

'Yes, I expect she will,' Gloria replied. 'Thank you,' she added, although she realised there was nothing, really, to thank Rachel for. It hadn't been a proper invitation to stay for tea, rather a hint that she wasn't exactly welcome. And she still couldn't bring herself to call Emmie's mother anything. Certainly not 'Auntie Rachel' – she hadn't been invited to do so, anyway – and 'Mrs Balderstone' was such a mouthful. Gloria liked the rest of the family very much. Ruby was terrific fun, although it made Gloria gasp the way she answered her mother back sometimes; Gloria didn't blame her, though. And their dad, Harry, was quite nice as well, like Pearl. And Emmie, of course, was her special friend. But she had never taken to Rachel and she suspected the feeling was mutual.

'Very well then. Don't keep Gloria too long, will you, Emerald? My mother gets the tea ready early, I know, for the evac ... for Gloria and the other two. And you've your homework to do, don't forget.'

'Not now I haven't, Mum.' Emmie sounded a trifle exasperated. 'School Cert's finished. They're not giving us any homework now. There's no point, is there?'

'I'd say there was quite a lot of point. They shouldn't let you slacken off, or else it's going to be all the harder when you go into the Sixth Form. Still, I suppose the teachers think they know best.' Her tone conveyed that they didn't know nearly as well as Rachel Balderstone.

Emmie pulled her mouth down in a grimace at her mother's retreating back before leading the way upstairs. She pushed open the door of her little room and flung herself on to the bed. 'Honestly! That's all I ever hear. "You must work hard. You must do your homework." And, "Our Emerald's very clever, you know." ' Emmie was putting on a posh-sort of voice, like her mother's; Rachel, of all the family, was the one with the least 'northern' accent. ' "Our Emerald's going into the Sixth Form, you know. Her daddy and I are hoping she'll go to university." Well, I'm telling you, kid.' Emmie lowered her voice. 'I'm not!'

Gloria stared at her in surprise. She had never heard her friend speak so forcefully. Emmie was usually such a placid sort of girl. 'What d'you mean? You're not what – going to university? Well, that's ages off yet, i'n't it? You can't go till you're eighteen, can you?'

Gloria had always liked to hear Emmie talking about school. It was usually the older girl's main topic of conversation; about the set books they were reading for School Cert; the topics being studied in history (the Causes of the French Revolution, and the Napoleonic Wars); the conjugation of French verbs and the intricacies of Algebra and Geometry – things Gloria had never even heard of before, but it all sounded so grown-up and fascinating and she lapped it all up. Gloria loved her Junior School and she hoped that one day she might go to the Grammar School that Emmie attended – if she was still in Blackpool, of course. (But she had made her special wish so she probably would be.) Gloria knew that Emmie was really something of a 'blue-stocking' – not all girls were as keen on their studies as she was – and that her friend was, in some ways, a little bit young for her age, whilst she, Gloria, was rather grown-up. And so the seven years between them seemed much, much less and they got on very well. They were turning out to be 'kindred spirits' as Gloria had hoped they would. And now Emmie seemed to be saying she'd had enough of all this book-learning.

'What d'you mean?' Gloria asked again. 'Have you got fed up with all yer schoolwork then?'

Emmie sighed. 'I don't know, maybe I have. But I wasn't just talking about university. I don't want to go there. I never have really, but it's no use trying to tell Mum and Dad that, especially Mum; she just won't listen. I mean the Sixth Form. I don't want to go into the Sixth Form. I want to leave school now and get a job, but I daren't let Mum know. She'll have kittens . . . she'll go up the bloomin' wall. I'm dead scared of telling her, Gloria.'

'Is that what you wanted to talk to me about?' Gloria knelt up on her haunches, staring intently at her friend. She

184

had taken up her usual seat on a cushion at the side of the bookcase on entering the room.

Emmie nodded. 'Yes. I haven't told anybody else yet, only one of my friends at school. She's leaving anyway, because her parents can't afford for her to stay on. She's going to try and get an office job.'

'And is that what you want to do, work in an office?'

Emmie wrinkled her nose. 'Not really, but I suppose I'll have to, for the time being. I want to be a nurse, you see.' She stared back earnestly at Gloria, her hazel eyes glowing greenly as they did when she got excited. 'I've been thinking about it for ages, but I've never said anything, certainly not to Mum. She wouldn't like it.'

'Why not? I should think it's a real good thing to be, a nurse. You know, looking after sick people; not selfish or anything.' Gloria didn't quite know the words to express what she meant.

'Noble, you mean? A worthy sort of job? Yes, nursing's all that, I daresay, but Mum wouldn't look at it like that, would she? She's pernickety, is Mum. She'd think about the blood and the mess and all that. She'd think it wasn't "quite nice". Anyway . . .' Emmie plumped up the pillow on her bed and leaned against it. 'I can't train to be a nurse till I'm eighteen, I know that. And I don't see any point in wasting two years in the Sixth Form if I'm not going on to university, so I want to leave now. I'll have to tell them at school soon, and I'll have to tell Mum. I'm dreading it, Gloria, honest. But I know it's something I've got to do. There's a war on and everybody's doing something, except me. Dad and Uncle George are helping, and our Pearl's waiting to go in the Land Army, and Ruby's at the Vickers-Armstrong factory. She's been there a fortnight. That's what I'd like to do, really, help to make aeroplanes, but I know Mum wouldn't let me do that. She'd do her nut.'

'Why? If your Ruby's there . . .'

'Ah well, Ruby's different from me, isn't she? Our Ruby's

always done what she flippin' well likes. But they wouldn't let me do it, that's for sure. Mum says that Ruby's getting in with "the wrong sort of girl" working at that factory.' Emmie giggled. 'There was no end of a row the other night, I can tell you. Mum and Dad caught Ruby with an RAF lad in the back entry, just round the corner. I don't think he'd have said anything if he'd been on his own – Dad, I mean; he's all right, is Dad – but he and Mum were together, coming back from the pictures. And there was our Ruby with this lad.'

'What were they doing?' Gloria's eyes were as big as saucers.

'Well, kissing and that, weren't they? Anyway, Mum made her stay in for two nights and she says she's got to be in by ten o'clock from now on. Don't suppose it'll last very long though. Our Ruby usually gets her own way. She's out dancing nearly every night now, at the Winter Gardens or the Tower. To hear her talk, she can get any lad she wants.'

'Can she? Yes, I 'spect she can.' Gloria nodded. 'She's real pretty, your Ruby, isn't she? 'Course, you are as well, Emmie,' she added loyally. 'You've got lovely green eyes. I wish I had eyes like that. Haven't you got a boyfriend, Emmie?'

'No, of course I haven't.' Emmie laughed. 'I've never had time, have I? Nose to the grindstone, that's me. But not for much longer.' She looked appealingly at her young friend. 'Think about me, Gloria, won't you, when I have to tell Mum? Keep your fingers crossed for me.' She held up two fingers tightly entwined. 'Anyway, come on, you'd better choose your books, hadn't you, or Mum'll be up telling us to get a move on.'

Gloria hastily chose another Mary Poppins book and an Arthur Ransome story. She was never likely to go to sea in a little boat, as these intrepid children did, but they were good exciting stories. Emmie walked with her as far as Whitegate Drive and saw her safely across the busy road.

'Wish me luck,' said her friend again. 'I'm going to tell her tonight. I know I've got to.'

'Don't worry,' said Gloria, grinning cheerfully. 'She won't kill you, will she?'

Which was little consolation to Emmie. No, of course her mother wouldn't kill her. She knew that her mother only wanted 'the best' for her, but Rachel's idea of the best and Emmie's were two very different things. Rachel was used to getting her own way and she didn't like it when someone was seen to get the better of her.

Emmie chose a time in the early evening when her father was there to give her moral support; although she wasn't sure whether Dad would support her or not. At all events, he could be trusted to behave rationally, which was more than could be said for her mother. Rachel reacted just as Emmie had feared she would.

'Leave school? Now? You'll do no such thing, my girl. You'll go into the Sixth Form, like your dad and I have always planned. Then you'll go to university. You're a very clever girl and—'

'Hold on a minute, Mum. Let me finish.' Emmie went on to explain that she wanted to train for nursing. There was no point in any further schooling; she might as well get a job, then she could feel she was doing something useful.

Nursing! Rachel threw scorn on the very idea. It was the first she had heard of it; Emmie had never mentioned it before, and what made her think she'd be any good at it? She wasn't strong enough, or tough enough. She'd faint the first time she saw a drop of blood; she wouldn't have the patience . . .

Emmie knew that her mother was only listing what her own objections would be to the concept of nursing and, of course, everyone had to agree with Rachel, or else . . .

'I know all these things, Mum,' said Emmie, determined to stick to her guns, 'and I've decided it's what I want to do. And I'm going to do it. When I'm eighteen. And till then I'm going to get a job, and you can't stop me.' In her effort to get her point over she was speaking more loudly than she intended.

'Don't you shout at me like that, young lady.' Rachel sat bolt upright in her chair, her fists clasping tightly into balls. 'You'll do as you're told. And we *can* stop you. Oh yes, we can, and we will. You're only sixteen and—'

'Steady on, Rachel,' said Harry. It was almost the first time he had spoken, although he had been nodding, encouragingly, Emmie felt, while she told of her plans. 'The lass does have a point, you know. It's no use us forcing her to go back to school if she's really set her mind on leaving.' He turned to Emmie. 'Are you sure though, love? It isn't just that you're feeling tired? You've been working hard at school so you're bound to feel you've had enough of it, for the moment.'

'No, Dad, I'm sure. It's what I really want to do.'

'Well, you're not doing it!' Rachel was still determined to get her own way. 'Don't be ridiculous, Harry, taking her side like that. Can't you see it's only a whim? She'll soon change her mind.'

'Oh no I won't! I'm going to be a nurse, and you can't stop me. If you try, I shall go and live with my gran.' Emmie was surprising even herself by her outburst. She was usually pretty level-headed, but Mum was making her see red. 'Gran'll understand. She won't try to—'

'How dare you? You cheeky young madam!' Rachel bounded from her chair and dashed across the room, her hand upraised . . . until her husband stopped her. Neither of them had ever hit any of the girls.

'Stop it, Rachel. This is all getting out of proportion. Sit down.' Harry got hold of her arms and propelled her back across the room and pushed her into the armchair. 'Now, calm down. And you too, Emmie.' Harry looked at her reprovingly. 'There's no need to be cheeky. We can sort this out. And of course you can't go and live with your gran. Don't be silly. This is your home and—'

'Live with your gran, indeed! I've never heard such nonsense.' Rachel still sounded angry, but Emmie could see, also, that her mother was close to tears and she began to feel sorry. It was the first time that she, Emmie, had ever been the cause of a row like this, although there had been many a one between Ruby and her mother. 'There's no room for you there anyway, is there?' Rachel's tone was peevish now. 'My mother's too busy with her waifs and strays. What makes you think she'd want to be bothered with you? It's all Gloria now, and those other two she's taken on. That kid that was here today . . .' Rachel stopped, looking at Emmie accusingly. 'Is that what you were whispering about, you and that evacuee girl? I bet you went and told her, didn't you, about this nursing carry-on, before you could tell me, your own mother.'

'I've talked to her, yes,' replied Emmie evenly. 'And don't call her "that evacuee", Mum. She's got a name. I enjoy talking to Gloria. She likes to listen to me and I don't think anyone's ever talked to her much before. I know she's a lot younger than me, and I know you don't like me being friendly with her, but I felt sorry for her at first, and now . . . well, I like her and I want to make her feel that somebody cares about her.'

'And that's quite right, too,' said Harry. 'You're a very thoughtful girl.' He sighed. 'But we're not really discussing Gloria, are we? It's you – and what we're going to do with you.' Emmie was pleased to see that her dad was smiling at her, shaking his head in a rueful manner. 'What *are* we going to do with you, eh? Have you thought about what sort of a job you want to do, until you're eighteen?'

'An office job, I suppose, Dad,' said Emmie quietly. There was an exasperated 'tut' from Rachel.

'What about *my* job, Emmie? Would you like to take that over?' Pearl had been sitting quietly in the corner, ostensibly reading a magazine. Nobody had taken any notice of her so it was the first time she had spoken.

'No, of course she wouldn't!' snapped Rachel. 'What a silly idea! Emerald doesn't know the first thing about typing and book-keeping. And anyway, you're still there. They may not call you up for ages. Besides, I never wanted Emmie—'

'No, you never wanted me to have anything to do with the rock factory, did you, Mum? You've told me that many a time – hinted at it, anyway. Well, I think it's a jolly good idea. Thanks, Pearl.' Emmie nodded towards her sister. The fact that her mother didn't want her to do it was making her even keener on the idea. 'And I can learn to type and look after the books, can't I? You're always saying how clever I am. It should be dead easy for someone as brainy as me! And if the rock factory's good enough for everybody else – for Dad and Gran and Uncle Harry, even for you, Mum – then it's good enough for me.'

'That'll do, Emmie.' Her father's warning frown and surreptitious glance in her mother's direction made Emmie realise she had gone far enough. Rachel was sitting motionless, staring down at her hands which were twisting her lace handkerchief round and round. Her shoulders slumped as though she knew she was defeated.

'Sorry, Mum,' said Emmie quietly. 'I didn't mean to be rude, but I can't go back to school. There's a war on, and I want to do something useful. I think Pearl's job would be a good idea for now, don't you?'

Rachel's eyes as she looked across at her daughter were apathetic rather than hostile, but Emmie knew that she had won. 'I suppose so,' said Rachel. 'You please yourself. I'm quite used to people in this house pleasing themselves. My opinions don't matter . . .'

Emmie knew that all the family might suffer for a while from her mother's martyrdom, but they would survive.

Chapter 14

Harry had just finished his patrol on the night of Thursday, 12 September, and had turned into Church Street ready to walk the last half-mile or so to his home. Then he heard it – a plane almost directly overhead, flying quite low by the sound of it. He looked up; the note of the engine was different, somehow, and yet there had been no siren so it must be 'one of ours'. As he watched, the plane swooped lower.

'My God!' said Harry out loud. 'It's a Jerry. It's a bloody Jerry.' Before he had time to draw breath he heard the screaming sound of a bomb falling. It was almost the first one he had heard; Blackpool had escaped the bombing raids so far, apart from two bombs that had fallen, a couple of weeks before, on North Shore Golf Course. But the sound was unmistakable. The ground shook and the ear-splitting din seemed to tear him apart. He stood stock still, putting his hands over his head in a moment of blind panic; then, as more explosions followed, he began to run in the direction of the sound, along Abingdon Street, up Talbot Road towards North Station. That's where it must be; the bloody Germans were bombing North Station . . . or the factory.

Oh God, no – not the factory! Ruby was there, wasn't she? He panicked for a moment before remembering that his daughter was on early shift this week. She was safe at home in bed. His wife and all his daughters were – no, not all his daughters; Pearl was in the Land Army now. They would be awake now, no doubt, perhaps making for the safety of the Anderson shelter.

He hesitated for a moment, just a brief moment, as he thought of his family – he should be there, with them, during this first air raid on the town – but he knew that he was needed elsewhere. This was what he had been training for, all those evenings of fire drill and First Aid. And now it was for real. He knew he could trust his wife to behave sensibly when it came to the crunch. Rachel wasn't without guts when put to the test, although she did like to play at being a martyr sometimes. She was still acting up about Emmie working at Hobson's, although the girl was making a damned good job of it from what he could see.

Oh, what the hell did it matter? He paused for a moment to ease the stitch in his side and to rid his head of these jumbled incoherent thoughts. Only natural, though, that he should think of his family at such a time, but he had a more important job to do. His breath was coming in short pants and his chest was aching a little – he wasn't quite as fit for his forty-two years as he had thought – but he took a few more deep breaths and started running again.

When he reached the junction with Dickson Road he could see, to his relief, that it was not the factory that had been hit. The bus station, the upper floors of which contained the aircraft factory, seemed to be all in one piece. But it was somewhere near, that was certain. This part of Talbot Road was littered with broken glass, shattered paving stones and red Accrington bricks, the sort that were used in the construction of nearly all the Blackpool houses. Which meant that some poor blighters nearby had lost their homes. And there was a strong smell of gas; one of the mains must have been shattered.

'Where is it?' he asked a couple of airmen who were running in the same direction. 'Where's it landed?'

'Just round the next corner, we think – Seed Street.'

It was, indeed, Seed Street where the incendiary bomb had landed, along with several high explosives. Already, only a few minutes after the first impact, members of the Civil

Defence services were there at the scene. Harry noticed several of his fellow ARP wardens as well as policemen, Local Defence Volunteers – the Home Guard, as they were now being called – and more than a few of the RAF lads who were billeted throughout Blackpool, many of them in the nearby boarding-house area. But they were still waiting for the fire brigade, and it couldn't come a moment too soon, thought Harry as he gazed, horror-struck, at the scene of devastation that confronted him.

Where, only a few moments before, had stood a street of small terraced houses, there was now a blazing, reeking inferno, the flames of which were illuminating the dirt-streaked and sweating faces of the rescuers. The rescue work had started in the homes on the fringe of the blast, but the main work couldn't begin until the fire, gaining momentum with every second, was extinguished. Beneath that burning rubble there must be people, children maybe? Harry wouldn't let his mind form the thought that there might be . . . bodies. Bodies meant that the people were dead, and they mustn't be, they mustn't be. Thinking, fleetingly, of his own wife and two of his daughters in the safety – he hoped – of their home he began to tug, with his bare hands, at the piles of bricks and splintered wood and plaster.

'Here y'are, mate. Use this.' The man next to him, a Home Guard fellow, handed him a pickaxe and they worked together in silence, endeavouring to clear some sort of a pathway through the rubble.

The clang of the fire engine soon drowned out all other sounds, and fervent cries of 'Thank God!' echoed through the crowds of helpers as they stood aside to let the firemen do their work. Strangely enough there seemed to be very little blind panic, although there was confusion as the various groups tried to sort out how they could best help in this, their first real test. There was anger, though. Harry heard several complaints shouted from behind shattered windows.

'Why didn't the bloody siren go off? Fine how d'you do,

i'n't it, when we're bombed to blazes and there ain't no warning?' a pyjama-clad man was yelling from a nearby window.

Harry doubted that a warning would have made any difference. As he had seen for himself, the approach of the enemy aircraft – one lone aeroplane – had been so quick and so sudden that there would have been little time to take shelter. He knew, from his Civil Defence training, that there was controversy as to whether the public should be warned about lone aircraft. The fellow who was complaining would do better to get his clothes on and come and help . . . and to thank God he was still alive. Harry soon realised that his thoughts – unspoken – had been too hasty, as the man followed his grousing with the words, 'I'll come down and give you a hand. I'll just get me trousers on.'

'Why the hell didn't they turn those blasted lights out?' called another irate voice from further down the street. 'There's supposed to be a ruddy blackout, isn't there, and yet there's lights burning over yonder night after flippin' night. That's why we've copped it, I tell yer, 'cause of them blasted lights. I'm going to complain. I'm going to tell the Council . . .'

Harry assumed that the fellow was referring to the lights at North Station. He had heard them mentioned before in his duties as air-raid warden, but the station couldn't function without some sort of subdued lighting. It must have been light enough, though, for the bomber to see and drop his load. A great pity it was in a built-up area, but then stations usually were.

Harry kept on digging and was relieved to see, as he worked, that many people were being rescued. Little children, clad in pyjamas and nightgowns, some crying piteously, others climbing dumbly over piles of wreckage, were being succoured by neighbours and gradually reunited with their anguished parents. For the most part. One little girl near to Harry was sobbing bitterly.

'Over there . . . over there . . .' she kept on crying. 'Me mam's in there. Go and get her. I want me mam!' A woman in a WVS uniform had her arms round her.

'Hush, dear, shhh. Look, they're digging over there. They'll soon find your mummy.' The woman exchanged an agonised glance with Harry which said, all too clearly, 'Please God, let them find her!'

The child was pointing to a house at the edge of the crater which seemed to be more or less intact, apart from a side wall which had been ripped away revealing a staircase and a bedroom. Part of the roof had gone, but the room seemed to be all in one piece. The large bed standing in the middle of the room looked as though it hadn't been slept in; the paisley patterned counterpane was undisturbed. Maybe the woman, the little girl's mother, had not gone to bed when the bomb fell. Perhaps she was still downstairs in the middle of all that unbelievable chaos. The lower rooms and what they contained – of either furnishings or people – couldn't be seen through the mountainous piles of rubble.

Harry turned to smile at the child. He liked little girls. He had three of his own. 'Where was your mam, love?' he asked. 'Do you know? Had she gone to bed, or—'

'No, she was in t'back kitchen,' sobbed the child. 'I couldn't get to sleep, an' I came down an' she said she'd go and make me a cup of cocoa. So I stayed in t'kitchen, an' then there was this big bang an' the wall fell down an' I couldn't find me mam. She's still in t'back kitchen . . .'

Harry remembered from his own childhood – and in Rachel's, too, he guessed, though she had forgotten all that since she went 'up in the world' – that the 'kitchen' was the place where one lived, otherwise the living room, whilst the 'back kitchen' was the place where the cooking was done. The back kitchen in this house was at the back, as the name denoted, behind all that debris; the bricks, mortar, splintered woodwork and shattered glass, through which the rescuers were endeavouring to clear a pathway. It would be a miracle

195

if anyone was still alive in there. It was a miracle that this little girl had managed to get out.

'Is there anyone else there, dear,' asked the WVS woman, 'as well as you and your mummy? Have you any brothers or sisters?'

'No, there's only me and me mam,' replied the child. 'Me dad's in the Army and our Freda don't live with us any more.' She sipped at the cup of tea the woman had given her, seemingly somewhat calmer now; but just then a couple of stretcher-bearers went past, carrying a woman who was moaning piteously, blood streaming from a wound on her temple. The child's composure left her. She grabbed at Harry's arm as the half-full cup of tea fell to the ground unheeded. 'Get her out, mister. Please . . . go and get me mam.'

Harry, who had seen such horrors as he thought he would never forget in the trenches, felt his heart moved to pity at the sight of this little girl. Such a pretty little thing she was. Her fair hair and brown eyes reminded him of his eldest girl, Pearl; she had had that same air of fragility when she was younger.

'Of course I will. Right now.' He patted the child on the shoulder as he exchanged a grim smile with the WVS woman. 'I'll be as well over there, on that side of the street. There's enough of them here. Makes no odds anyway, does it?' He gave a slight shrug, then motioned his head towards the child. 'Can't you take her away somewhere? She shouldn't be watching.'

'Yes, that's what we're doing, or trying to,' said the woman. 'Finding all the children. We've got a place at the end of the street, one of the houses that's escaped the blast. We'll take care of them in there until . . .' She didn't finish the sentence. Until . . . what? Many of the children would have no homes to return to. Some of them might not have any parents. 'Come along, dear,' she said, taking hold of the little girl's hand. 'What's your name? I don't think you told me.'

'Beryl,' said the little girl.

'Very well then, Beryl. We'll go and see if we can find some of your friends, and this nice kind man will go and look for your mummy.'

'I will that.' Harry winked at the little girl. 'Leave it to me, Beryl,' he said, with far more confidence than he was feeling. 'I'll soon find your mum.'

At least he felt that he was doing something more useful if he was searching for a particular person, Harry thought, as he picked his way through the debris. There was a huge crater, some fifty feet wide, completely filling the narrow street, hindering communication between one side and the other. The heart of the fire had been more or less extinguished now, thanks to the efforts of the fire brigade, but here and there there were still small spurts of flame stabbing into the darkness, and the beams of flashing torches and flares from hurricane lamps. The scene of horror and destruction assailed all the senses. The stench of gas was the over-riding smell, masking even that of the burning rubble, the smoke from which was making Harry's eyes smart and clogging his throat. And all around, as a background to the mayhem, were the sounds of picks and shovels, the clang of ambulances and, occasionally, the tormented cry of a little child.

'Hello there,' said a terse voice at Harry's side. 'Bad do, isn't it?' There was George, a splendid figure in his Special Constable's uniform, although his face was streaked with grime and the shoulders of his jacket were liberally sprinkled with grey dust and particles of cement. 'I couldn't help remembering what you were saying a while back, Harry – you know, about Blackpool copping it sooner or later. D'you think this is it, then? D'you think it might be the start of a whole lot more?'

'I dunno. Who can tell?' replied Harry grimly. 'But if this is the damage that one bomb can do, then God help the poor blighters in Liverpool and Manchester.' There were other cities further afield, of course, notably Plymouth, Portsmouth and London who were suffering in what they were calling the Blitz, but Harry was thinking primarily of the ones nearer home. The evacuees that had been sent to Blackpool at the start of the war had been mainly from the Liverpool and Manchester areas; and now, ironically – because of the slow start, the 'bore war' – most of them were back home again in the thick of it.

'We'll just have to take a day at a time,' Harry continued, 'and do what we can to help. At least we're doing something useful now, not just fooling around with buckets of water and stirrup pumps. Remember what you said, George? We were just playing at it. Well, it's for real now, sure enough. There's a woman in there, trapped in her kitchen, and I've promised her little lass I'll try and get her out. There'll be others as well, scores of 'em, I shouldn't wonder, but it's her I'm thinking about, and her kiddie. Bonny little lass she is, George, just like our Pearl when she was a nipper. Crying for her mam, poor lass. I don't know how I kept from blubbing myself, I can tell you. Daft, aren't I? After all I've seen in the last lot . . . and you too, mate.'

George shuddered. 'Aye, don't remind me. But that was twenty years ago . . . and this is now. Come on, what're we waiting for? Let's find her.'

Harry was impressed at the way George, in his role as Special Constable, took charge of the little group of men who were digging in that part of the street. Not only was George an acting policeman, but he was a powerfully built chap whose height of six feet and broad shoulders helped to inspire confidence in the others. It hadn't always been so, Harry found himself reminiscing. There had been times when he, Harry, had been the one with the initiative and 'get up and go'. But he would take his hat off to his brother-in-law now. He was obviously making a first-rate job of this voluntary warwork he had undertaken, and all credit to him.

It was some twenty minutes or so before they had cleared sufficient of a pathway to enable them to see into the kitchen at the back of the house. George had been the undoubted leader, heaving away at piles of bricks and obstructions that the other men, less strongly built, were unable to budge. They had seen a couple of stretchers being carried out from neighbouring houses – obviously dead bodies because the poor blighters' faces had been covered over – which made them even more determined to get this woman out alive, if possible.

In some places there were beams that had to be moved, very carefully, or else the whole wall or ceiling which they were holding up might collapse. So it was in the kitchen at the back of this house. Through the pathway they had cleared they could see a woman, unconscious – please God that was all she was, breathed Harry – lying near to a gas stove. Pots and pans and cooking utensils, as well as bricks and cement, littered the floor, but the space around her was fairly clear, apart from a beam which was obstructing the area in front of her, a beam which would have to be moved before she could be got out. Unfortunately it was holding part of the ceiling in position.

It was George who was the first to step over the wreckage into the kitchen area. It was George who tugged, cautiously but firmly – it had to be moved – at the protruding beam. And it was George who was underneath when the beam gave way bringing down the ceiling and the floorboards of the room above.

Sally and Ellen were not in bed when Harry knocked at their door in the early hours of Friday, 13 September. Friday the thirteenth, Sally was to think later, although she had never been superstitious. They had been wakened by the sound of the bomb falling, as they were sure most of the folk in Blackpool must have been. Two hours later they were still up, still drinking tea, having decided that now they might as well wait until George came home. Neither of them felt they would sleep until they knew George was safe. He had been out all evening on his police duties and now, no doubt, had become involved in the rescue work, wherever the bomb had fallen.

'It's a bomb, isn't it, Auntie Sally?' Gloria had been sitting up in bed, her eyes wide, as much with excitement as with fear, when Sally dashed into the girls' room. Doreen, too, was awake, and Susan in her smaller room. They all hastily donned their slippers and dressing gowns and sheltered under the stairs with Ellen and Sally in case there should be any more explosions. There was no room in their back garden – which was no more than a yard, really – for an Anderson shelter, and they had been informed that the 'glory hole' under the stairs was the safest place in the house.

'Yes, dear, I'm afraid it's a bomb,' said Sally. There was no point in dissembling. 'But we've been very lucky in Blackpool, haven't we, so far? I shouldn't think it'll happen again.' But she didn't know. How could any of them know?

'It's happening in Manchester, though, isn't it, Auntie Sally? And in Salford.' Doreen, in the darkness of the cupboard, clutched at Sally's arm. 'D'you think our mam'll be all right? And the twins?'

'Yes, of course they will, dear. It's the factories they're bombing, isn't it, where they make aeroplanes and weapons and things like that. And shipyards. Not people in ordinary houses, like your mum.' But Sally knew that it was only a half-truth, or a half-lie, depending on which way you looked at it.

She had tried to convince herself, many times, that surely the Germans didn't want to drop bombs on ordinary folk, the civilian population, any more than our own RAF lads did. But even the most carefully aimed bombs must sometimes fall short of their intended targets. She knew she had to console the children, though, as best she could. It was the first time that any of them had mentioned the bombing raids, although they must have known about them from reports in

200

the newspapers, until now, when they were experiencing it for themselves.

'And our Monica and the boys and the new baby – d'you think they'll be all right?' asked Gloria. 'And me mam,' she added, as though it were an afterthought.

'Let's hope so, dear,' said Sally, suppressing a sigh. 'We'll just have to say our prayers, won't we, extra specially hard, and ask God to keep them safe.'

Another incongruity, she thought privately. What a lot we are expecting of the Almighty, to sort this lot out. No doubt thousands of Germans were praying to Him for the selfsame thing, the safety of their loved ones. And yet what else could one do? You had to keep on praying, and trusting, and believing it would all be over one day.

'I think the air raid's over now,' said Ellen gently. 'There haven't been any bangs for quite a while. Let's get out of here, shall we, and go and make a cup of tea? And I'm sure the girls would like some cocoa, wouldn't you, before you go back to bed?'

'Auntie Sally,' said Gloria, when they were all sipping their hot drinks, warming themselves at the rekindled embers of the fire. Ellen had banked it down with slack before going to bed; now she had given it a vigorous poke to revive the flames. 'Auntie Sally . . .' The child's voice held the questioning tone that Sally had come to know so well. 'When am I going to see our new baby?'

Sally noted the possessive pronoun, but she told herself it was only natural that Gloria should want to see her sister's child, her own little niece. Unfortunately she didn't see how they could manage it, not yet awhile. Monica had given birth to a girl, christened Kathleen Theresa, at the beginning of July, and Gloria had been pestering, intermittently, ever since about when she was going to see the new arrival.

'We can't go at the moment,' said Sally. 'You're at school, aren't you, and the trains are so crowded at weekends. Besides, you know what they keep saying now, don't you,

201

dear? "Is your journey really necessary?" You've seen it on the posters, haven't you? They want to keep the trains free, as much as they can, for all the soldiers and sailors and airmen that are travelling about. We can't go gadding about enjoying ourselves when there's a war on.' She looked at the child's pensive face and relented a little. 'We will go sometime. Perhaps nearer Christmas, mmm? You could save up your pocket money and buy something for the new baby, couldn't you? That'd be nice. I can't promise exactly when though. You do understand that, don't you, Gloria?'

'Yes.' The child nodded stoically. 'I understand. "Don't yer know there's a war on?" ' she said, giving a grin as she mimicked the phrase she had heard so often on the grown-ups' lips. ' 'S what they keep on telling us, isn't it?'

'I'm afraid so, dear,' smiled Sally. 'Now, I think it's "up the wooden hill" again for you three now, or you'll never be up for school in the morning. Come on, let's be having you.'

It was about an hour later that the knock came at the door. Sally and Ellen had conversed very little, but such was their empathy that each knew the other would not want to go back to bed until George was home.

'That'll be George,' said Sally, a smile lighting up her face. She put down the sock she was knitting (for Pearl, to keep her feet warm in the cold Yorkshire winter) – she had had to keep her hands occupied while she was waiting – and sprang to her feet. 'I'll go and let him in, Mam. He must have forgotten his key. It'd be all the same if we'd been tucked up in bed, wouldn't it, the silly chump!'

'Mind the blackout,' called out Ellen. 'Don't put the hall light on.'

But the dark-clothed figure standing there in the gloom was not George, but Harry. His face was unsmiling.

'Sally, I've been with George,' he began. 'He was helping with the rescue work – we both were – Seed Street, it was, where the bomb fell, but . . .'

'Where is he then? Where's George?' Alarm was mounting

202

in Sally as she watched Harry's grim face.

Then Ellen appeared. 'What is it? Harry, what are you doing here? Come in, don't stand there on the doorstep.' She ushered him into the hall. 'Where's George?'

'Go in there, Mam. And you, Sally.' He put his arm round her, guiding her back into the living room. 'I'm afraid there's been an accident. George and I, we were helping with the rescue work . . . and a wall collapsed. George was underneath.'

'Are you trying to tell us that George is . . . ?' It was Ellen who was speaking, slowly and deliberately.

'No.' Harry let out a deep sigh. 'He's not dead. But he is badly injured, I'm afraid. We managed to get him out, God knows how, and the woman who was in the house as well. He was so brave, Mam. I've never seen him so determined.'

'And where is he now? Where's my husband?' Sally felt numb. It all seemed so terribly unreal.

'Is he going to be all right?' Ellen's voice was the merest whisper.

'Let's hope so, Mam. He was unconscious, but alive, thank God. That's all I can say. He's in Victoria Hospital, with a lot more of the casualties. There were so many.'

But Sally was concerned, at that moment, only for her husband. 'I must go to him,' she babbled. 'I'll have to walk, but it's not far. Along Church Street, up Newton Drive—'

'Sally, you can't.' Harry took hold of her arm. 'Not at this time of night. It's a couple of miles and more. Be sensible, love. We'll go and see him in the morning. By then they might know something. I'll run you there, you and Mam.' Harry had bought a small Ford car, his first, just before the war started, but didn't use it much now in an effort to save petrol. 'I think we could use the motor in an emergency like this, don't you?' He gave a weak smile.

Ellen buried her face in her hands, suddenly overcome. 'Please God, let him be all right,' the other two could hear her murmuring, before she lifted a tormented face to them.

'He came safely through the last lot . . . just. Don't say he's going to be taken now, when he's not even in it.'

'Steady on, Mam.' Harry quickly went and knelt at the floor by her side, putting his arms round her. 'He's a fighter, is George. You should have seen him tonight, battling to save those people. You'd have been proud of him. He'll pull through, you'll see.'

'Yes, yes, he will. He must.' Sally could see from the earnest appeal in Ellen's deep brown eyes that her mother-in-law was willing George to be all right. She added her own unspoken prayer. *Please God, bring him through this.*

'Thanks very much, Harry,' she said. 'Thanks for letting us know. You'd better be getting back to Rachel now, hadn't you? She'll be worried, like we were.'

'Rachel'll cope,' said Harry impassively. 'At the moment it's you I'm concerned about, and George. Still, as you say, I'd best get home. See you in the morning – later this morning, I mean.' It was already well into the early hours of the next day. 'I don't know about visiting times at Victoria, but I expect they'll let us see him for a few minutes. I'll come about nine. Try and get some sleep now, Mam, and you, Sally.' He kissed both of them, then he was gone.

'Oh, Sally . . .' 'Oh, Mam . . .' they cried together as they wrapped their arms round one another.

They were unable to see George, however, because when they arrived at the hospital he had just been taken down to the theatre. The sister on the ward took them into her room and explained the situation to them quite dispassionately. She told them that Mr Hobson had regained consciousness last night for long enough to give his permission for them to operate. Not that they would have had any choice, she explained, as his right leg was very badly crushed and would have to be amputated just below the knee.

'Oh no! No, don't say that! That's terrible!' Sally gave an

involuntary cry, but both Ellen and Harry seemed to accept the news more resignedly.

'And . . . you say he knew?' asked Ellen. 'He understands what is happening?'

'We think so, yes,' replied the sister. 'But, as I said, it had to be done. You'll be able to see him later today for a little while. Come back this afternoon, towards tea-time. He should be coming round by then.'

Her manner was efficient, to the point of being abrupt, but Sally supposed it had to be so. Nurses couldn't afford to get emotionally involved with patients and their families. All the same, she would have been glad of a touch more sympathy. It was such shocking news. She was silent for a while on the journey home, too stunned to converse.

'At least he's alive,' Ellen kept saying. 'He's still with us. And he's going to be all right. He has no more injuries, that sister said. Nothing internal and no head injuries. Only his leg.'

'Only his leg!' echoed Sally. 'How can you say that, Mam? My George . . . with a wooden leg. Oh Mam, I don't think I can bear it!'

'Come along, dear. Don't be silly.' Ellen, in the back seat of the car, took hold of her daughter-in-law's hands, rubbing them gently between her own. 'We've got to be brave for George's sake, haven't we? Anyway, I don't think they have wooden legs nowadays, do they? They can make all sorts of clever things. And . . . don't you see?' Her brown eyes were gazing intently into Sally's. 'It means he'll be out of it from now on. There'll be no question of him joining up now.'

'Joining up?' Sally stared at her. 'But he wouldn't have—'

'Oh, don't you be too sure, dear.' Ellen patted her hand. 'I've a feeling that the Special Constable business wouldn't have been enough for our George. Sooner or later he'd have gone back into the Army. Don't you think so, Harry?'

'Yes, Mother-in-law; I think you may well be right,' replied Harry, keeping his eyes on the road.

Sally was pensive. Yes, she supposed that what Ellen was saying was true enough. She, herself, had noticed signs of restlessness in George, though she had tried to ignore them, not wanting to face up to the fact that he might join up. 'In that case,' she said slowly, 'I suppose we must be thankful.'

Chapter 15

BUCKINGHAM PALACE BOMBED. THEIR MAJESTIES UNHARMED proclaimed the headlines in the *Blackpool Evening Gazette* on Friday, 13 September, 1940.

'So what?' said Sally, a trifle bitterly. 'They've got plenty more houses, haven't they? There's Windsor Castle and Sandringham, and goodness knows what else. Not like those poor folk on Seed Street who've lost everything they possess.'

They had just returned from visiting George in hospital. He was just coming round from the anaesthetic and had been unable to do much more than smile weakly at them, murmuring that it was good to see them and that he was all right . . . then he had drifted back to sleep again. The enormity of what had happened had hit Sally afresh. It was some consolation, she was forced to admit, that George's injuries would prevent him from rejoining the Army, but that didn't take away the fact that her husband had lost a limb. And she was sure it would be no comfort to George to know that he was now prevented from giving further of his energy to bring this wretched war to a close. Maybe she and Ellen were being selfish in looking at things this way. You could hardly blame Ellen though. George was her son – still her little boy, Sally supposed – and the last war had brought its fair share of grief to Ellen. Sally had little sympathy to spare at the moment for the Royal Family. To her mind there were far more important considerations.

Ellen looked at her in some surprise. 'That's not like you, Sal. I thought you were an ardent Royalist, like me.'

'So I am, Mam, usually. But it's all relative, isn't it? You've got to get things into perspective. They're not suffering like thousands of other poor Londoners, are they? Or like the folk in Seed Street?'

'No, I suppose not, dear.' Ellen sighed. 'But listen to what it says here. "I'm glad we've been bombed," said the Queen. "It makes me feel I can look the East End in the face." So it sounds as though she's feeling a bit guilty, you see, about the inequality of things. And they have decided to stick it out here instead of going abroad to somewhere safe. You've got to admire them for that. The Queen wouldn't let the Princesses go without her, and she has to stay where the King is, in London. He's got a lot of responsibility, poor man . . . and it should never have been his in the first place.'

'All right, Mam. You've convinced me.' Sally gave a weak smile. 'The King and Churchill seem to be putting their backs into it, I've got to agree. But you can't blame me for being more concerned about our own affairs. Oh, I wonder how long George will be in,' she fretted. 'They didn't say, did they?'

'I don't suppose they know, dear. They'll not keep him any longer than necessary, you can be sure – they'll need the beds. Let's hope there won't be any more air-raid casualties though. I wonder if last night's raid was just a flash in the pan? Or will there be more . . .'

'Who can say, Mam? We must just be thankful that things are no worse. It was good news, wasn't it, that that woman was all right? You know, the one who was trapped in the kitchen, the little girl's mother that Harry was so concerned about. She escaped with only a broken arm, so I suppose she was very lucky.'

'Yes, dear, so she was.' Ellen was perusing the newspaper. 'Funny way they have of reporting the facts, Sally. Listen to what it says here. "There were several casualties, some fatal, in an air raid on a north-west coast town last night . . ." North-west coast town! Everybody knows jolly well they mean

208

Blackpool, so why don't they say so?'

'Security, I daresay, Mam. You know, in case any German spies look at the paper. They keep telling us, don't they, "Careless talk costs lives." '

'Huh! Lot of nonsense, if you ask me,' retorted Ellen. 'Surely the Germans know where they've dropped their bloomin' bombs, so what's the harm in saying so? Still, ours is not to reason why . . . And listen to this: "The demolition squad did splendid work and there were several remarkable rescues." That's our George.' She gave a watery smile, tears misting her eyes. 'We should be very proud of him, Sally.'

'And Harry, too,' replied Sally. 'Don't forget him – he was the one who helped to get George out. He's been grumbling about wasting his time as an air-raid warden. Now perhaps he'll realise it was all worthwhile.'

But Harry was not entirely convinced about the importance of his warwork. His prediction that Blackpool would 'cop it' sooner or later proved to be pessimistic. Why Blackpool was to escape the full fury of the Blitz no one really knew, although there were a few wry comments bandied around in 'hush hush' tones that maybe Hitler had the resort earmarked as a recreation centre for his troops once he had conquered Britain. There were a few more isolated bombing incidents that year, but nothing of great consequence; one in September and two in October, all in the South Shore area. And then . . . nothing.

Harry agreed that 'an ounce of practice is worth a ton of theory', as a leading article in the *Blackpool Gazette* had stated, soon after the air raid. The actual experience of bombs falling, and their effect, had taught everyone far more quickly than any amount of lectures and 'messing about' had done. Still, Harry felt that he could do more, much more. His eldest daughter was in the Land Army, his middle daughter was working at the aircraft factory and his youngest one had left school in a patriotic attempt to 'do her bit'. And his brother-in-law, poor old George who would never harm a fly, had lost his leg in a rescue attempt. Harry felt quite sure that George would have joined up again before long. Now he was unable to do so ... but he, Harry, could. And he would. Never mind what Rachel might say about letting the younger men do it, Harry knew where his duty lay. In November he volunteered to serve with his former regiment, the Loyals, and a few weeks before Christmas he was sent to the south of England ... in preparation for the expected invasion.

Rachel, in fact, said very little about her husband enlisting. She had noticed his unrest and his desire to do more and she realised that what must be, must be. She was really quite proud of her family and the sacrifices they were making for the war effort, although she found it hard to tell them so. But were they actually sacrificing all that much, she sometimes wondered. It seemed to her that her daughters were having a whale of a time. Pearl, admittedly, had given up a nice comfortable well-paid office job to join the Land Army, but her letters home were full of her new life – the friends she had made, the beauty of the Yorkshire countryside, and the many and varied jobs she was doing on the farm. Come the winter, though, Rachel guessed that she might not be so enthusiastic; Yorkshire winters could be grim. She hoped Pearl would be home for Christmas. Rachel missed her eldest daughter very much. She had always been such an amenable, pleasant girl. Rachel couldn't remember them ever having exchanged a cross word, nothing to speak of, at any rate.

As for Ruby, she was having a rare old time at that factory. She, too, was full of her new-found friends – some of them rather 'common', Rachel suspected – and *Workers' Playtime* and lunch-time concerts. And she was out nearly every night, dancing or off at the pictures. Precious little sacrificing Ruby was doing! Still, Rachel was glad she hadn't joined the ATS or the WRNS. At least if the girl stayed in Blackpool she could keep an eye on her. Or half an eye . . . you never knew what Ruby might do next.

Emmie had settled into the job at Hobson's very well, but that was only to be expected. She was a clever girl, far too clever to be working in a rock factory or even the office of one. She had left school with an outstanding School Certificate – five distinctions and four credits. What a waste! Rachel felt that she, rather than her daughter, was the one who had made the biggest sacrifice here. She had had such hopes and dreams for her youngest girl, and the silly lass had gone and thrown it all away. But Rachel still hoped that the idea of nursing might pall before Emmie was eighteen. She had joined the St John's Ambulance Brigade and she was very quiet about what she was doing there. Maybe messing around with bandages and broken limbs was not so alluring as Emmie had thought? Rachel couldn't help but hope so. Maybe, once the war was over, she might reconsider and take up her studies again. It would be nice to have a daughter who was a teacher, or a barrister – or even a Member of Parliament!

'Here, hold still a minute while I wrap this end round. How the heck can I bandage your arm when you keep on jiggling it up and down? Oh hell, it's all come undone again!'

Emmie and her partner at the St John's Ambulance class, Davey Clarkson, burst out laughing as the roll of bandage fell to the floor and unravelled itself. 'Shhh! We'll be in trouble if we act silly,' Emmie admonished him as she stooped to retrieve the bandage. 'Come on, let's try again. It must be easy when you know how, and we're not going to let the others beat us, are we? Look how well they're doing. Now, don't you dare move or I'll brain you! There . . . that's better. Whew!' Emmie gave a sigh of relief, then a satisfied smile as she surveyed her handiwork.

'Well done,' said the nurse in charge when she examined Emmie's effort.

Emmie and Davey grinned at one another and Emmie thought again what a good team they were. She was pleased she had found someone as easygoing and friendly as Davey to work with. She had known him at Junior School although Davey, being a year older, had been in the class above her, and she couldn't remember having seen him since then. She had recognised him almost immediately though, when he had spoken to her at her first meeting of the St John's Ambulance Brigade.

'Hello there. Emmie Balderstone, isn't it?'

It had taken only a few seconds for her to recognise the ginger-haired, freckle-faced lad who was smiling at her so amiably. 'Good gracious, it's David Clarkson, isn't it? I haven't seen you since you were eleven! And you haven't changed a bit.'

'I've grown a bit, I hope.' He grinned ruefully, and Emmie remembered he had always been of a short, but stocky, build. 'Titch', they had called him, because he was the smallest boy in the class. 'I'm out of short trousers now! And I'm Davey now, not David. You look just the same as well, Emmie. Emerald, isn't it, your proper name? I remember your green eyes . . . and you used to wear a bright green hair ribbon, didn't you?'

'Yes.' Emmie smiled, a little shyly. 'Fancy you remembering that. Yes, my mum used to have a thing about dressing me in green when I was a kid . . . and our Ruby in red. Daft idea!'

She gave a nervous laugh, but soon realised there was no need to be shy or nervous with Davey Clarkson. He was really nice, and from that moment they had got along famously. By mutual agreement they sat together at lectures, were partners in practical work, and after the cup of tea and biscuit which ended each meeting, Davey had fallen into the habit of walking home with her. It wasn't very far, the classes being held in the hall of the Junior School they had both attended.

Davey lived in the other direction, in a street of small

terraced houses off Central Drive. Emmie always insisted he left her at the end of her road as he had quite a long way to walk home afterwards. At least, she tried to convince herself that this was the reason for not letting him come any further. Deep down, she knew it was because she didn't want her mother to set eyes on him. Rachel most definitely wouldn't approve of her daughter being friendly with a lad who was . . . a window-cleaner!

On leaving school at fourteen, Davey had started helping his father with the window round; until that time Mr Clarkson had done the job single-handed. Now, with his father in the Army, Davey was in charge, assisted by a young lad who had just left school. Over the years they had built up a good business, Davey told Emmie, with some pride. They held the contract for many of the big hotels, boarding houses and shops in central Blackpool, and that, he assured her, was not to be sneezed at.

Emmie considered that a window-cleaning round was just as respectable a way of earning a living as, say, working in a rock factory, but she knew her mother wouldn't see it like that. If he had been an accountant, or a librarian, or an insurance agent, Emmie mused, she might have told her mother about him. There were occasions when Emmie didn't like herself very much. Her mother's snobbery and petty-mindedness seemed, at times, to affect her own judgment and way of thinking. Emmie often wished she had the same devil-may-care attitude as her sister, Ruby.

'Go on, Ruby, why don't yer? You'll be tons better than that dreary girl they had singing for us last week, won't she, Brenda?'

'I'll say!' Brenda giggled. 'She sounded like a dying duck in a thunderstorm! God knows where they found her, or some of the other acts they seem to think'll entertain us. Yes, I reckon we can put on a show just as good as ENSA.'

'Better,' added Greta.

'Yeah, better, why not?' Brenda nodded. 'And seeing that our Ruby's the only one as can sing in tune . . .'

'And the best-looking,' put in Greta.

'Give over, you'll make 'er 'ead so big she won't be able to get 'er 'at on.' Brenda grinned, then she turned to Ruby. 'You'll do it, though, won't you, kid? You'll give us a song . . . or two or three. That weary girl sang about four. I thought she was never goin' to shurrup. What'll you sing, duck? What about *We'll Meet Again*? Or *It's A Lovely Day Tomorrow*? Or *Yours*? "Yours till the stars lose their glory . . ." ' Brenda began to sing in a very high, very off-key voice.

'Oh, for Gawd's sake, pack it in!' Greta put her fingers in her ears. 'You'll make it rain. You're no bloody Vera Lynn, are you, Bren? Nobody'd ask you to entertain us, that's for sure! Right, Ruby, can we put your name down?'

'Hey, hold on. I haven't said I'll do it yet. I don't want to make a fool of meself.' Nevertheless Ruby was delighted and flattered to have been asked. The workers at the aircraft factory had decided to put on their own lunch-time concert, considering it would be equally as good as the ENSA groups they sometimes had to entertain them; third-rate singers and comedians for the most part, the ones not considered quite good enough to entertain the men and women in the armed services. They, of course, were entitled to the very best.

Music played an important role in keeping up the spirits of the workers on the factory floor. Nevertheless, the BBC, in their wisdom, had decided to ration *Music While You Work*. The warworkers responded, in many cases, by making their own music, in addition to the radio broadcasts. At the Blackpool factory one girl had brought her own wind-up gramophone and a pile of records, and had been given permission to play them over the loudspeakers. The best tunes were the ones that could be sung along to, which was how her fellow workers came to realise that Ruby Balderstone had a better than average singing voice. And, in spite of her protestations, they knew that she was not afraid of making a fool of herself. She wouldn't do so anyway. Her curly black hair – usually tucked away beneath a turban – and her bright blue eyes, to say nothing of her curvaceous figure, would captivate her audience even if her voice was only mediocre.

Ruby had never been so happy as she was working at the factory. At first the noise and bustle of the factory floor had come as a shock to her, but she had soon adapted to her new way of life. She had made a lot of new friends. Ruby had never found it difficult to get along with people, but the workforce here was certainly a mixture, drawn from all walks of life. There were former shop assistants, like Ruby herself, housewives, secretaries, even the wives of solicitors and doctors, some of whom had hardly soiled their lily-white hands before, let alone gone out to work. But a camaraderie seemed to prevail amongst all of them, from those out of the 'top drawer' to those who were most certainly not.

Ruby didn't enjoy the actual work very much, but she told herself that it had to be endured; she was doing her bit for her country and that was all that mattered. One of the worst jobs, the one to which Ruby had been assigned at the moment, was stitching canvas covers for the aircraft. The curved needles tore at the women's fingers and the waxed thread, pulling through the coarse fabric, cut deep into their hands. Ruby often looked despairingly at her roughened, chapped and reddened hands which once, fingernails tipped with bright red varnish, had been a source of pride with her. Still, it was all in a good cause, she told herself as she rubbed Vaseline into the cracks and re-applied the varnish to her splintering nails in readiness for another evening at the Winter Gardens. She just needed to run a comb through her curls, then she would be ready. Many of the girls wore their dinky curlers all day, hidden beneath their turbans or snoods, but Ruby with her naturally wavy hair had no need to do so.

There were very few young, eligible men at the factory (they were all in the forces); only middle-aged ones were left or those who were proclaimed medically unfit. But Ruby made up for this with the RAF lads whom she met nightly at the dance halls. She couldn't count the number of dates she had had – some just for one night, others lasting for a couple of weeks or more – since the RAF came to Blackpool. But so far she hadn't met anyone who, as the song put it, started a flame in her heart.

Ruby had been nervous, very much so, when she stepped up on to the impromptu stage erected at the end of the factory floor, but the encouraging grins of her workmates had given her the confidence she needed; and once she started singing all her tension had eased away and she had enjoyed every minute of it. Ruby lapped up their compliments now. She was not impervious to flattery – which girl was? – but she had the sense to know it for what it was: over-fulsome praise for an attractive lass who was doing her bit to relieve the monotony of this endless war. Ruby, if they only knew it, intended to do far more towards the war effort. She would be nineteen next year and that was when she was going to join the WAAFs. She hadn't told anyone yet – certainly not her mother, who would probably hit the roof – but that was what she was determined to do.

Pearl's Land Army uniform, consisting of khaki corduroy breeches, green jersey and tie, cream Aertex shirt, fawn overcoat, strong walking shoes, boots with studs and steel heelplates ... and the hat, had arrived in the post in mid-August, a few days before she was due to leave for her training in Yorkshire. It caused a great deal of hilarity with her sisters as she tried it on in front of the full-length mirror in her bedroom. Especially the hat! She hadn't known the best way to wear it; at the back of the head, plonked straight on the crown, or at a jaunty sideways angle. Now, after she had completed her six-weeks' training and had been sent to her first live-in farm, Pearl knew to wear the hat as little as possible. It was impractical for work as it kept falling off, so the girls only wore their hats when they went out on infrequent jaunts to the nearest town, or in the evening on their way to a village 'hop'.

The hostel where Pearl had lived for the first six weeks was in North Yorkshire, quite near to the town of Malton. The spartan living conditions – bare wooden floors, iron bedsteads and lumpy mattresses, oil stoves and draughty windows – had come as a shock to her even though she should have known what to expect; and she certainly didn't let on to the folks at home that anything was less than hunky-dory. They would only worry, especially Gran, and they had enough worries already, what with Uncle George's accident, and looking after the evacuees, and trying to carry on as near to normal at the rock factory with ever-decreasing supplies.

Besides, it wasn't too bad when you got used to it, and Pearl knew that that was what she jolly well had to do. The local farmers, understandably, were reluctant at first to accept the girls from the hostel to work on their farms. But they soon realised that the majority of them, even the city girls, were capable of hoeing, hedging, nettle cutting, mucking out and milking, all of which Pearl had learned to do, after a fashion, during her initial training.

Pearl was glad she had learned to ride a bike because that was the usual form of transport for the Land Army girls. It was a case of the early bird catching the worm. There were plenty of bikes, enough for everyone, but only half of them were roadworthy. The others had faulty brakes, no lights, chains hanging off . . . The girls gobbled their breakfasts, usually quite a decent fry-up, to bag the best machines.

Cycling to the dance in Malton on a Saturday night was hilarious, travelling along the dark country lanes (pitch black at the best of times, even before the blackout) in a long crocodile with a bike with a light at the front, and one with a light at the back.

In her first post after training, Pearl was to find that living

217

in a farmhouse with the farmer and his wife was not nearly so much fun as sharing a hostel with lots of other women. It was more peaceful, but not so convivial. She was looking forward to her few days at home at Christmas.

Emmie had decided she was not being entirely honest in her dealings with Davey and it was time she came clean with her mother. She was going to invite him for tea on Boxing Day and her mother could like it or lump it. They would all be at her gran's on Christmas Day and Davey would be with his own family, so Boxing Day was an ideal time.

Rachel had raised her eyebrows when Emmie had broached the subject, but if she had been surprised at this talk of a friend (a male friend) of Emmie's whom she hadn't heard about before, she didn't show it overmuch. 'Yes, dear, of course,' she said. 'Your friends are always welcome here. You know that.'

Surprisingly she hadn't asked any questions, but Emmie knew that her mum was preoccupied these days with both Pearl and her father away and Ruby out nearly every night, up to goodness knows what. And she was concerned, too, about Uncle George, trying to get used to his new leg, and Gran, who had gone back to her former job, supervising the factory and shops. She had had to, with Uncle George out of action and Dad in the Army.

Dad was home for Christmas though, on a forty-eight hour pass, and so was Pearl. They were all there for Boxing Day tea although Emmie was the only one who had invited a visitor. Rachel, in her twinset and pearls, was quite the lady of the manor as she always was when there was 'company'. In spite of rationing there was a more than ample spread on the damask cloth covering the table. Cold turkey (provided by Gran who had bought, as usual, a bird almost as big as an elephant!) with pickled onions and sliced beetroot. Emmie noticed that Pearl had pushed the glass dish of beetroot away with a shudder. Memories of muddy fields and beet-pulling, perhaps? There was sherry trifle, mince pies, maids of honour, chocolate biscuits and Christmas cake. Emmie knew that Rachel had been 'hoarding' a bit at a time for several months.

Emmie was waiting for it . . . and it came, as she knew it would.

'And what do you do, Davey?' asked Rachel, smiling graciously. 'Emmie has told us you met at the St John's Ambulance Brigade, but what is your job? What do you do for a living?'

'Me? I'm a window-cleaner,' replied Davey openly. His somewhat surprised glance at Emmie, a second later, seemed to say, Didn't they know? But Emmie, tucking into her trifle, didn't hold his glance and decided to let them get on with it. She noticed her mother's smile flicker for a moment and her eyes, narrowing slightly, turned fleetingly on Emmie, but Rachel was too polite to say anything there and then. She didn't have time to answer before Davey continued.

'That's to say, for the moment. It was my father's business and, though I say it myself, we've come on by leaps and bounds recently. But I'm not sure what's going to happen in the future. I'll be eighteen soon, you see, and I'll be joining the RAF.'

Rachel's relief was palpable; she obviously had not considered that he might well do his training right here, in Blackpool, and she continued to smile charmingly as she replied, 'Yes, of course you will. You young men all have to do your bit, don't you? Have you applied, Davey, or will you wait till they call you up?'

'No, I won't wait for call-up, Mrs Balderstone,' replied Davey. 'I'll go as soon as I can, but I promised my mum I'd wait till I was eighteen, with Dad being away, you see.'

'Then that makes two of us,' said Ruby suddenly. ' 'Cause that's what I'm going to do as well.'

Everyone looked at her in surprise, but it was Rachel who spoke. 'Do what, Ruby? What on earth are you talking about?'

'Join the RAF, like Davey. Well, the WAAFs I mean, of course, not the RAF. That's what I'm going to do, when I'm nineteen – next July,' she added with a bold look at her mother, as though Rachel didn't already know that fact.

Rachel's mouth dropped open and she was too dumbfounded to speak – for the moment, at least, but Emmie knew that her mother would soon find her tongue and that when Davey had gone she would have plenty to say. But her mother would now have something else to think about, besides Davey's lack of a suitable career.

Chapter 16

'It sometimes helps if you sing to 'em, especially that one.'
Pearl looked up from her task of milking Primrose, one of
the least friendly of the herd of cows, as Ralph, the farmer's
son, came into the shippon. He was grinning cheerfully, as
he often did, and Pearl thought again how very nice he was.
He had been so kind to her and Millie since their arrival at
'Greengates' in Wensleydale a few days ago, helping them
to settle into the new surroundings of their second farm.

'What?' Pearl smiled at Ralph, a trifle unsurely at first.
'Sing to her, you said? She'll calm down, do you think, if I
give her a song?' She burst out laughing at the absurdity of
the situation. 'You haven't heard me sing! She'll be more
likely to take to her heels and run, I can tell you.'

'You couldn't be as bad as me,' said Ralph, placing a hand
on Primrose's flank. At once her tail stopped twitching. (She
can tell an expert from a novice, thought Pearl.) 'I've a voice
like a corncrake,' Ralph continued, 'but it seems to soothe
'em. You try it.' He glanced in the bucket at Pearl's feet.
'Anyroad, you don't seem to be doing too badly. You're OK
with this lot, are you, at this side? I'll go and see how your
friend's coping.'

Pearl was sure that Millie would be coping admirably.
She was a country girl, born and bred, not actually from a
farm, but she had been brought up in a Cotswold village
surrounded by animals. Cows, sheep, horses, goats; there
seemed to be very little that Millie didn't know about them
and she tackled everything with a will. Pearl was glad they

had been put together. They had met on the training course, and Pearl had liked Millie and admired her competence. She was glad of her companionship and, it must be admitted, her help at times. Although Pearl was determined to cope, whenever she could, single-handed, and she would win the battle with these blasted cows if she died in the attempt!

Sing to Primrose, eh? It might not be such a bad idea. She glanced across to the other side where Ralph was now chatting amiably with Millie. They didn't seem to be taking any notice of her – so she decided to give it a try. What should she sing? Something soothing . . . After another surreptitious glance over the row of stalls she began. 'Somewhere over the rainbow, Way up high . . .' she crooned to Primrose, and the cow lowed at her in response.

For the first time in several months, Pearl felt happy and contented. The farmer and his wife, Mr and Mrs Butterfield, and their son Ralph, were amiable folk, kind and generous-natured, and their welcome of the two girls, Pearl and Millie, couldn't have been warmer. Wensleydale itself was beautiful, a wide vale with gently wooded slopes, cascading waterfalls and olde-worlde greystone villages. Spring 1941 was on its way, slowly but surely, and Pearl was looking forward to exploring the hidden places of this lovely part of the country with Millie. And maybe with Ralph, too . . .

The farmer's son had taken the two girls for a drink at the village pub soon after their arrival and had escorted them to a village 'hop', dancing with each of them in turn. Pearl couldn't help but admire the ease with which Millie chattered to him and the relaxed, comfortable relationship the two of them seemed to enjoy. Not that they made her feel like a gooseberry or anything like that; not a bit of it. But she had never found it easy to talk to men, not like her sister, Ruby, was able to do. Ralph, however, was one of the most amiable fellows she had ever met and Pearl hoped that she might get to know him a little better.

'Davey's gone then, has he?' asked Gloria, plonking herself down on Emmie's pink eiderdown. 'He's joined the RAF?'

'Yes, last week,' replied Emmie. 'He's down in East Anglia, doing his training.'

'I bet you wish he could have stayed here in Blackpool, don't you?' Gloria looked coyly at the older girl. 'I wonder why they didn't let him stay here? There are lots of RAF billets in Blackpool, aren't there?'

'Yes, but maybe they thought it was better if he did his training somewhere else,' replied Emmie. 'I don't know. It would have been nice if he'd stayed here, I suppose, but it doesn't really matter.'

'Doesn't it?' Gloria stared at the older girl in surprise. 'He's your boyfriend, isn't he? I thought you'd've been dead upset.'

'Not exactly a boyfriend, Gloria. Just . . . a friend.'

'But I thought he was your boyfriend,' Gloria persisted. She frowned a little before blurting out, 'Didn't he kiss you or anything?'

Emmie smiled. She wasn't sure if Gloria knew what she meant by 'or anything'. At all events there hadn't been any 'or anything' with Davey Clarkson, although he had kissed her once or twice before he went away. Emmie felt herself blushing at the thought of it, especially as Gloria was staring at her so searchingly.

'Mind your own business!' she said, laughing at the little girl.

'I can tell he kissed you,' said Gloria, ' 'cause you've gone all red.'

'Oh, only when he said goodbye.' Emmie tried to shrug it off. 'You always kiss your friends, don't you, when you say cheerio, and I've told you, Gloria, that's what Davey is – just a friend.'

'Well, I thought he was dead nice,' said Gloria loyally. 'If I was you I'd've fallen in love with him. He was real kind to me and he made me laugh. I think he looks a bit like Mickey Rooney,' she added.

Emmie burst out laughing. 'Good grief! Is that supposed to be a compliment?'

' 'Course it is. I like Mickey Rooney, an' I like your Davey. What's he doing anyroad, in the RAF? Is he flying aeroplanes?'

'I shouldn't think so,' replied Emmie. 'Not yet awhile, at any rate – if ever. No, they train them to find out what they're best suited for. A lot of them end up as ground crew, servicing the aeroplanes and that sort of thing, not flying.'

'Oh.' Gloria sounded rather disappointed. 'I thought he'd've been flying over Germany, dropping bombs.'

'No, he's gone in as an AC2, that's the lowest rank,' Emmie explained. 'You have to be a Sergeant at least before they let you pilot a plane. Most of the pilots are officers, I believe, but there are bomb-aimers and gunners and navigators and all that. We'll just have to wait and see what Davey ends up doing.' Emmie couldn't help hoping that Davey might never be a flier, glamorous though it might seem. She was very fond of him and wanted him to be safe.

'Anyway, let's change the subject,' said Emmie now. 'What about you? Gran says your sister came over last week to bring her new baby to see you. What's she like? I bet she's lovely, isn't she?'

Gloria's eyes shone. 'Yes, she is. She's real pretty, our Kathleen. She's not really a new baby now, though. She's eight months old, but it's the first time I've seen her.' Emmie knew that her Aunt Sally had intended taking Gloria over to Salford, but when the bombing raids had started on Manchester she had decided that it wasn't a very good idea; and so they had had to wait for Monica to make the journey.

'She's going to be beautiful,' Gloria breathed. 'Not like our Rose and Lily. They look like me dad, I mean Bill. But then she wouldn't look like Rose and Lily, would she? They're only her half-aunts ...' She shook her head impatiently. 'Oh, I dunno. It's all dead complicated. Anyroad, like I was saying, she's real pretty, and our Monica says she thinks she looks like me.' Gloria beamed proudly before adding, 'Not that I'm saying I'm pretty or owt – I mean anything – but she's got dark hair and grey eyes like I have. And she was sitting up in her pram, smiling and laughing all the time. I think she knows me already.'

'Well, if she turns out to be anything like you then she'll be a grand little girl,' said Emmie, smiling at her. 'Did your Sam and Len come as well? Gran didn't say.'

'No, only the baby,' said Gloria. 'Monica left the other two with me mam. D'you know, I haven't seen me mam for nearly a year,' she added, as though the thought had only just occurred to her. 'But Monica says I'm better off here with your gran and Auntie Sally 'cause they're still having bombing raids in Manchester. Not acksherly so much in Salford, but it's only just down the road so me mam says I've got to stop here. I'm glad.' A brilliant smile lit up her face. 'I like it here. I don't ever want to go back there.' The glow that had transformed her features seemed to fade a little.

Emmie spoke quickly. 'And Doreen and Susan are staying here a bit longer, aren't they? Gran says their mum came over with the twins.'

'Yes, just before our Monica came. It's all coming and going in wartime, isn't it, Emmie?' Gloria shook her head in an old-fashioned way. 'That's what Auntie Sally says. Your Ruby's gone now, hasn't she, as well as your Pearl? And yer dad. So there's only you at home with yer mum, isn't there?'

Emmie cast her eyes heavenwards. 'You can say that again! Yes, only me and Mum. She's thinking of having a couple of civil servants to stay with us while we've a spare room. Women, of course.' Emmie gave a giggle. 'She won't have any RAF lads in case they try to get off with me. She hasn't actually said so, but I can read Mum like a book . . . And talking of books, you'd better get a move on and choose yours, hadn't you? Gran'll be wondering where you are.

Come on, hurry up, and then I'll walk up to the main road with you . . .'

Ruby had joined the WAAFs in the March of 1941, a few months before she was nineteen. Rachel had been forced to come to the conclusion, eventually, that she might as well give in with a good grace. She would get no peace if she didn't. Ruby was always so set on getting her own way and it was often easier to let her do so rather than argue. Besides, another urgent appeal had gone out to the women of the nation to volunteer for warwork. Conscription for women was not yet in operation, but the general feeling was that it would be before very long. Ruby was already doing her bit at the factory, as Rachel had reminded her, but she obviously felt that that was not enough. Rachel would have been surprised if she had known how desperately unhappy and homesick Ruby was during those first few months of training. Ruby was surprised, too. She hadn't expected to miss her home and her family quite so much. She had got used to her dad and Pearl being away, and living at home with her mother and younger sister had been getting on her nerves more than a little. Mum did fuss so, although she had been better since Emmie's boyfriend had joined up and her youngest chick was safe from marauding male hands once again. So it had come as a shock to Ruby to realise that the scalding tears that oozed from under her eyelids, despite her attempts to quell them, into her lumpy pillow in the dead of night were really tears of homesickness. And that it was Mum that she was missing more than anyone else. Ruby had never been away from home before on her own and what she had been looking forward to as unlimited freedom was turning out to be anything but that. It was mainly regimentation – and Ruby had never liked being told what to do – plus periods of boredom and this awful nagging longing to be back home with the people she was now realising she loved.

Her initial training was at a camp near Harrogate. Ruby,

naively, had envisaged herself as a possible radio operator, guiding the brave young pilots back to base, or being involved in secret Intelligence work. At the very least she had thought she might be trained as a mechanic or a welder or a carpenter, essentially male jobs which they were now training women to do in order to release the men for combatant duties. The reality was very different. Ruby was informed that as a former shop assistant the only options available to her were as equipment assistant, dealing with the supplying of uniforms, or as a domestic worker, employed in the mess or the cook-house. They had appeared to take little notice of the fact that Ruby had worked in the aircraft factory for over a year; and so she had opted for the first alternative. She had never had anything to do with cooking or cleaning – Mum had done all that – and with her experience as a shop assistant, doling out equipment should be a piece of cake. And in this job she was sure to come into contact with lots of dishy flying officers . . .

In point of fact the air crew took very little notice of Ruby, though she knew she looked attractive in her uniform; buttons and buckle brightly polished, the Air Force blue enhancing the blue of her eyes and her hair curling prettily beneath her peaked cap. Not that she wore her cap in the store, of course, but her hair had always been her crowning glory, or one of them, because Ruby was not unaware of her many charms. Why then did these arrogant males act as though she was merely another piece of equipment? She had met scores of RAF lads in Blackpool and they had fallen over themselves in admiration for her. But they had been recruits, she reminded herself, AC1s or AC2s – AC Plonks or 'erks', as she now knew they were known – whereas she had been a civilian. And that made all the difference.

'They think they're God almighty, some of these air-crew bods,' one of her colleagues remarked to her, as a particularly supercilious officer walked off with his supplies without so much as a thank you or even a nod. 'Can't get used to having us women around, that's the trouble. Some of 'em are long-serving officers, you see, and it's been an all-men's world for too long. The ones who've joined up since the war started aren't so bad, at least, those who don't regard us as empty-headed popsies good for nothing else but a bit of "you know what". Cheer up, luv, you'll soon get used to it,' the girl added, giving Ruby a friendly poke in the ribs, and Ruby tried to give an answering smile.

'Feeling a bit homesick, aren't you? I can tell.' The girl nodded sagely. 'I was just the same when I first came here, but you've just got to grin and bear it. And it's not all bad, surely? There's a dance tonight at the Sergeants' mess. Are you going?'

Ruby agreed that she probably would and cheered up somewhat at the thought. She had always loved dancing at home, at the Tower or the Winter Gardens; but here, of course, it was vastly different. There was none of the glamour and the glitter, and the wind-up gramophone couldn't compare with the superb dance bands or Reginald Dixon at the Wurlitzer! You've been spoiled, Ruby, my girl, she tried to tell herself. And she knew it was not only with the sophisticated pleasures of her home town, but by her mum, waiting on her hand and foot. Ruby, deep down, was a realist and she was well aware that her inability to settle down to service life was chiefly her own fault. She was just beginning to realise what a sheltered existence she had led compared with some of the other girls. And, strangely enough, Ruby, usually so lively and popular, had not yet made any close friends, of either sex.

But whatever grumbles she had, Ruby, like Pearl, wouldn't dream of divulging them in her letters home, to Mum, Gran or Auntie Sally. They must be led to believe that everything was just fine, or 'wizard', as they said in the RAF.

Perhaps things would improve next week, when several of them were being transferred to an airfield near Norwich. At least it would be a change – what was it Gran was always

228

saying? A change is as good as a rest – and Norwich was a city that Ruby had not yet seen. She willed herself to look forward to it.

It was an evening in mid-March and Pearl and Millie were getting ready to go for a drink at the local pub, with Ralph, as usual. Watching what she thought was a budding romance between Millie and Ralph, Pearl had quickly come to the conclusion that it was only a casual friendship – a fact borne out by Millie's disclosure of a boyfriend, Jim, a Corporal in the Army, stationed down South.

'You and me, we get on really well, don't we?' said Millie comfortably, dabbing at her lipstick. 'And you like it here, don't you? I can tell you do.'

'I love it,' said Pearl simply. 'I'm so glad I joined the Land Army. I should've thought that you'd seen enough of the countryside, though. Did you never consider going in the ATS or joining the WAAFs?'

'Not really,' admitted Millie. 'This is a job I knew I could do well, and it's what Mum and Dad wanted me to do. And my boyfriend, Jim. He's rather possessive, is my Jim, and he felt I'd be safer in the WLA, with only sheep and beets for company rather than rampant servicemen, so I gave way to pressure. Willingly, I must add. I usually take the safe option . . . I do admire you, Pearl, choosing this job when you don't look like the type at all. Sorry, luv, but you don't. And yet you're a real gutsy lass, aren't you, in spite of looking like a piece of Dresden china?'

Pearl smiled and nodded slowly. 'I'm discovering I'm tougher than I thought I was, certainly. If only I could master milking those blasted cows!'

'Oh, don't worry, you will,' replied Millie cheerfully. 'Let me tell you something else. You'll have Ralph all to yourself this weekend, so he can give you a few lessons.' Her eyes twinkled. 'I'm off home for a few days. Jim's got embarkation leave. We think he must be going to Egypt, the desert campaign, you know, but we're not really sure. It's all frightfully "hush hush". Anyway, like I say, you'll be able to get to know Ralph a lot better, won't you?'

'What makes you think I want to?' said Pearl, but she was smiling. She couldn't help it.

'Oh . . . intuition.' Millie tapped her forehead. 'You'll get on well, you and Ralph, once I'm out of the way. Sorry I rabbit on so much. I just can't help it. My mum says I was inoculated with a gramophone needle. You're both quiet and thoughtful, you and Ralph, and both so *nice*. Yes, I think you'll get on like a house on fire.'

The village pub was one of the homeliest places Pearl had ever known. It didn't seem like a pub at all, at least not like the pubs she had seen in Blackpool; seen from the outside, that was, or glimpsed through an open door, because Pearl, before she joined the Land Army, had never set foot inside one. It was unheard of for well-brought up girls like Pearl to go into pubs unless they were accompanied by a man, and she had had very few boyfriends. What is more, in her Methodist background, drinking was frowned upon.

But here, the 'snug' room, with its wheel-backed chairs and low oak-beamed ceiling, looked very like the kitchen at 'Greengates'. Tonight, having Ralph to herself, Pearl was appreciating its warmth and friendliness even more than usual. There were a few local farmers standing at the bar and mainly younger folk seated round the tables; one or two Land Girls whom Pearl recognised and a few soldiers and airmen. Most of the younger men were in uniform.

'We'll go out tomorrow night, shall we, just you and me?' Ralph had asked her, somewhat shyly, after Millie had departed on the Friday afternoon.

'Yes, that would be nice,' she had replied, a trifle primly. 'Thank you.'

He leaned across the table now and took hold of her hand, his deep-set grey eyes looking earnestly into her own. 'I feel real bad, you know, Pearl, not being in uniform.' He glanced down at his grey flannel trousers and casual blue jumper. 'The folk round here know me and understand, but I can just imagine what's going through the minds of some of the young soldiers and airmen.'

'But farming's a reserved occupation, isn't it?' said Pearl. 'I know they've called up a lot of the farm-hands, but you're the farmer's son and your father depends on you, doesn't he?'

'Look – I'd have gone if I could.' Pearl raised her eyebrows enquiringly. It was the first time she had heard Ralph mention the subject. 'Yes, I did volunteer, as a matter of fact, for the Army, but I was turned down flat. So that was that. I know where I stand now so I'm just getting on with the farming job and trying to make the best of it. It's not easy, though, when I see young chaps like that.' He motioned towards the bar where there stood a couple of RAF Sergeants who looked no more than twenty or so, several years younger than Ralph, at any rate. 'And I know that they're risking life and limb while I'm on a cushy number.'

'Not necessarily,' said Pearl evenly. 'They're most likely ground crew, not in much danger at all.' She was thinking that Ralph should thank his lucky stars he was safe. She knew that she would be thankful if Ralph were her brother, or her young man . . . She glanced up at him now. 'Why did they turn you down anyway?'

'Rheumatic fever,' replied Ralph. 'I had it when I was a child and it's left me with a lung that's less than perfect. And, as well as that, my eyesight's none too good. To add insult to injury I've got flat feet! Not much hope for me, is there?' Ralph cleared his throat apologetically. 'I hope you don't mind me saying so, but when you first arrived I thought you looked like one of them china shepherdesses. I was a bit worried about you, to be quite honest – I wondered how you'd cope – but I know different now. I reckon you'll do. You're a plucky lass and not half as fragile as you look. And you're happy with us, aren't you?'

'Very, thank you.' Their glances held for a few moments, before Ralph turned round at the entry of Mrs Hawthorne, the publican's wife.

'Good – here comes supper. You can manage some, can't you, Pearl? It'll help you to get your strength up.'

Supper consisted of crusty home-made bread rolls between which were sandwiched thick slices of roast pork, followed by deep apple pie flavoured with cloves. Pearl could feel her mouth watering and her taste buds tingling at the first whiff of the pork and the apple.

'We killed one of our pigs this week,' said Mrs Hawthorne, very matter-of-fact, as she placed the steaming dishes in front of them.

This remark, which would at one time have unnerved Pearl more than a little, didn't trouble her overmuch now. When she first joined the WLA she had, of necessity, passed through the sentimental phase and learned to regard the animals in her care in a more detached manner, not as pets, which they certainly were not.

Tucking into food like this it was hard to believe there was a war on. Pearl had already eaten a hearty farmhouse tea – crusty bread with crumbly Wensleydale cheese and slices of rich dark fruit cake – but she was unable to resist the bounty in front of her. She rose from the table feeling so full she could hardly move. It was a good job they had walked the mile or so from the farm and not cycled; she doubted if she would have been able to mount the machine! Besides, after two glasses of shandy, even well diluted with lemonade, she felt that she was on a different planet. It wasn't an unpleasant feeling though, and Pearl fell asleep surrounded by happy comfortable thoughts of what the morrow might bring.

As the seasons passed from 'lambing-time' to what the farmers called 'cuckoo-time', then 'hay-time', then 'back end', Pearl spent more and more time with Ralph, exploring the glories of his native Wensleydale. They went further afield, as well, to Richmond, to Swaledale and the Buttertubs Pass and Hawes. And during all this period Pearl waited, almost willing herself to fall in love with Ralph. But it didn't happen. She knew that she liked him a lot; more than that, she was very fond of him. In the books she had borrowed from Boot's Lending Library, back home in Blackpool, she had read of starry-eyed young heroines. Bells had chimed when they were kissed, and like that song they were always playing on the wireless, a nightingale sang in Berkeley Square! But nothing like that had happened to Pearl.

Millie, trying to be tactful, did not often accompany the pair on their weekend jaunts around the countryside.

'There's no need to leave us on our own,' Pearl insisted. 'There's nothing going on between us, honestly.'

'Well, he's crazy about you,' said Millie, a trifle crossly. 'Anybody with any sense can see that. And it's not fair of you to have the poor fellow dangling on a string.'

'I'm not, truly I'm not. At least I don't mean to. Oh, Millie, leave me alone, can't you? I just don't know how I feel, and that's the truth.'

Pearl knew that Ralph was quite keen on her. He had kissed her several times and she had sensed that, with a little encouragement from her, his kisses could become more amorous . . . and that might lead to things getting out of hand. Pearl wasn't ready for that sort of commitment, not yet, and so she had given him little encouragement. He seemed surprised, especially when, one day as summer was drawing to a close, he asked her to marry him, and she refused.

They had cycled one Sunday afternoon to Jervaulx Abbey, a once great Cistercian monastery, founded in the twelfth century and then dissolved by Henry VIII and allowed to fall into ruin. The place was deserted as they parked their bicycles in the narrow lane outside. Summer was at its height and, for once, there was no mistaking the season. Rowan berries, red as blood, glowed amidst the profusion of green, but here and there the odd leaf was tinged with brown or yellow and the near hills were already carpeted with purple heather. Autumn would soon be here.

Pearl was moved by the tranquillity of the surroundings, as though the spirits of long-dead monks had, over the centuries, imbued the place with their lingering presence. It was wellnigh impossible to believe that in various airfields, not many miles to the south and east, air crews were preparing for their nightly bombing raids over Germany, or that enemy planes might in a few hours be flying up the Humber estuary for another attack upon Kingston-upon-Hull.

She said as much to Ralph. But Ralph had other things on his mind. He drew her into his arms in the shade of the ruined cloisters; and when he kissed her she responded a shade more fervently than she had previously done. 'Will you marry me, Pearl?' he asked softly. But Pearl shook her head.

'You're saying no?' Ralph held her away from him at arms' length, gently, but firmly, grasping her shoulders. 'But why? You know I love you.' It was, in truth, the first time he had said so and Pearl was surprised to hear him say it now. 'We get on well together, don't we? And you like living in Yorkshire? Pearl . . . why, why are you refusing me?'

'I don't know,' Pearl said sincerely. 'I'm very fond of you and yes, we do get on well. And of course I *do* like living here. But I'm not sure that I want to marry you. We haven't known one another all that long.'

'Six months, Pearl. That's quite long enough for me to know that I want you to be my wife.'

'It's not long compared with a lifetime, Ralph. Let's just leave things as they are . . . please. There's a war on. You can't think straight in wartime.'

'I can.' And Pearl could tell by the earnest look in his grey eyes that Ralph was, indeed, thinking straight. He was sure he wanted to marry her. She knew that he was a level-headed man, not likely to be swept off his feet in a sudden romantic attachment as so many couples were at the moment. 'I know what I want, and I want to marry you, Pearl. But if you say no . . . Well then – we know where we are, don't we?'

Pearl was level-headed, too, and it was because of this she knew it wouldn't be right to accept Ralph's proposal.

'I'm sorry, Ralph,' was all she could say now. 'But we can still be friends, can't we? I shouldn't like us . . . not to be friends.'

'Of course,' he replied easily. But there was a look of puzzlement – hurt, almost – in his eyes. The sun passed behind a dark cloud and for a moment the brightness had gone from the day. Pearl knew that Ralph was a proud man and that he wouldn't ask her again.

Chapter 17

'It says here that they'll soon be extending conscription to include all men from eighteen to fifty-one,' George mumbled, his head as usual deep in the pages of the morning paper. 'What d'you think about that, eh? I'd've been called up, you see, if it hadn't been for this bloody thing.'

He put the paper down in a sharp movement, slapping at his trouser leg which hid the aluminium false limb. Sally knew from his use of the swearword that the bitter feelings that often engulfed him were surfacing again. She also knew that it would be tactless to say what was really in her mind: that he should count his blessings. He had escaped with his life and, because of his lost leg, he would escape the rest of the war. Hadn't he often told her how, in the 'last lot', some soldiers had even gone so far as to inflict such a wound on themselves – a 'blighty' – in order to escape the conflict? But George didn't want to escape, she knew that, and he didn't consider his artificial leg to be much of a blessing.

Sally tried to answer him patiently. 'Yes, maybe you might have been called up, eventually. We don't know. But it isn't as if you're sitting there doing nothing, is it? Nobody could have tried harder than you did with that leg.' That was true; he had persevered, in spite of the obvious pain that his stump caused him, and now he was able to walk a fair distance, although he still used a stick. 'And you're doing a useful job of work.'

'What! Serving in a bloody toffee shop?'

She ignored the remark, going on to talk about other

members of the family to take his mind off himself. 'Yes, you may well be right about the call-up. I daresay they might have called Harry up by now if he hadn't already volunteered.' Harry was still stationed at a camp in the south of England. 'I must say that family are doing their share, what with Pearl in the Land Army and Ruby in the WAAFs.'

Sally smiled fondly as she thought about Ruby, her favourite of her three nieces. 'She seems much happier, our Ruby, since she was posted to that camp near Norwich. She never said very much, mind, but I could tell she wasn't any too happy in Harrogate.'

She glanced across at George, but he no longer seemed to be listening. He had returned to his perusal of the *Daily Express*. When he had finished that he would turn to the *Evening Gazette* for the local news. It was his favourite occupation now, keeping abreast of the war news. From time to time he would read out bits to Sally, knowing that she didn't always have the time to read the papers from cover to cover as he did.

'Rudolf Hess is here,' he had told her in May. 'Well, not here of course – in Scotland. He landed by parachute, it says.' The German Nazi leader had made a secret flight to Scotland in order to negotiate a peace settlement with Britain – unsuccessfully, it turned out. In the same week he told her that the House of Commons had been hit in a night air raid and, later that month, in a more optimistic mood, that the German battleship, *Bismarck*, had been sunk in the North Atlantic.

And, 'Poor old Malta's copping it again,' he frequently reported. And General Rommel, the 'Desert Fox', was making alarming advances in the Egyptian desert.

It seemed as though the war had been going on for ever although it was not yet two years old. On the Home Front the outlook was bleak and Sally, in spite of her anxiety for what was going on overseas, admitted that this aspect of the war affected her most. Food shortages were really stringent now.

There was not a banana or orange or lemon to be had for love nor money; jam, marmalade and lemon cheese were rationed (although Ellen still tried to make her own, in spite of being back at work); 'points rationing' had been extended to most groceries, and to crown it all clothes rationing had now been introduced.

Women's magazines were full of hints on how to 'make do and mend'; dressing up an old costume or frock by adding a new collar and cuffs in a contrasing material, or painting the buttons different colours with nail varnish; unravelling jumpers and using the best of the wool to create a new garment; and making use of old blankets, bedspreads and curtains for dresses and skirts. Sally had seen a photograph in a newspaper last week of a woman wearing a coat made from a candlewick bedspread, a novel idea and very smart, too, although it was obvious it had come off a bed. It had given Sally an idea. She had unearthed two such old bed-spreads that had been shoved away in a cupboard, one pink and one blue, and she was at present busy making dressing gowns for the three young girls. One pink, one blue, and the third would have to be a combination of the two colours; blue, with pockets, facings and sleeves of pink, she thought. And it would no doubt be Gloria who would choose to wear this unique garment.

The three girls, in the summer of 1941, were still in Blackpool. Air raids continued to harass the major cities, but less frequently as Hitler had now switched his bombers to the Eastern Front and the invasion of Russia. Sally felt sure that Mrs Aspinall would soon decide to have Doreen and Susan back home again. She had been over to see them on a few occasions with the twin boys, and each time it was obviously more and more difficult for the little family to say goodbye. Sally knew she would miss them, but not with the heartrending ache she would experience were Gloria to leave. However, it had been just as she expected; Mrs Mulligan had never been over to see the child and Monica had paid only one visit since her baby was born. Gloria was mentioning her sister less and less these days, and Sally had lulled herself into a false state of security with regard to the little girl, pretending she would be here for ever. In her more rational moments she knew that this was not so – Gloria's home was in Salford and neither of them should be tempted to forget it – but for the sake of stability in the child's life she had to act as though Gloria were here to stay.

Gloria was already talking about the scholarship exam she would take, along with the local children, in the next school year, and about the Grammar School she would go to – the one Emmie had left last year – when she passed. There was never any doubt in Gloria's mind that she might not pass, neither was there in Sally's – she was a bright and clever child – but for how long would she be able to attend the Grammar School should she be given a place there? This was a question Sally hardly dared ask herself.

'I don't see why I couldn't have joined up, even with this.' George's words broke into Sally's thoughts. She glanced up from her knitting to see her husband stretching his leg stiffly out in front of him, a belligerent expression on his face that she knew only too well. 'It didn't stop that Douglas Bader chap, did it? And he's got no legs. Shooting Jerries down right, left and centre, he is.'

'He was in the RAF long before the war started,' Sally remarked patiently. 'He's an officer.'

'What difference does that make? He's doing his bit, isn't he, which is a damn sight more than I'm doing. He's a brave chap if ever there was one.'

'If you ask me I'd call him foolhardy,' replied Sally. 'And I'm sure his poor wife must think so too. Oh, come on, George.' She smiled at him sympathetically. 'I know how you must feel. But you did your share in the last war – you've often said so yourself – and in this one as well, before your accident.'

'I know, I know. It's just that I get so frustrated. I'll have to try and settle myself, but for heaven's sake don't keep telling me I'm doing a useful job when I know damn well I'm not.'

'All right, I won't then.' Sally grinned wryly, although she really did consider that making and selling sweets was quite important, as a morale booster, in these dark days.

'Mam's working harder than I am,' George went on, 'back in her old job of supervising. And to think she said she was retiring; we might have known she never would. She's doing too much though, Sal, what with that and her WVS work.' That was where Ellen was this evening as she was several times a week, either at a meeting or engaged on some task for the WVS.

'I know, but you try telling her,' agreed Sally. 'Mam has to feel she's being useful or she'd go under. I knew she wouldn't settle to being a housewife again after being involved in the business for so long.'

There had been some moving around of jobs at Hobson's, but the key positions were still held mainly by members of the family. George and Sally had more or less swapped jobs, hence George's complaint that all he was fit for was serving in a 'bloody toffee shop'. It hadn't been practical, in view of his injury, for him to continue in his supervisory role, visiting – on foot, as he had done – the shops, factory and various outlets. Sally and Ellen, between them, now did this job. In addition Ellen worked at her chocolate-making – a somewhat modified selection now, because of the shortage of luxury ingredients – from her own kitchen, as she had always done; whilst Sally had undertaken the promotion of Hobson's goods in the sweet shops around Blackpool and the Fylde. They no longer employed a commercial traveller for orders further afield, but the standing orders from places such as Scarborough, Llandudno and Rhyl, to name but a few, still held good. Hobson's Rock – The Only Choice – was still going strong in spite of the war.

One big difference was that George and Sally now owned

a car, a small Ford – something which, until now, they had insisted they did not need. Following George's injury, however, it had become imperative and it was Sally, perforce, who was the one who had learned to drive. This didn't go down too well with her husband, but he vowed that he, too, would take to the wheel just as soon as he could make his dratted leg behave in the way he wanted it to. Sally now dropped George off at the Dickson Road shop each morning where, like it or not, he was the manager, before going on to make her various calls. Petrol was strictly rationed, but the allowance was ample for their needs as the journeys were short and they never used the car for pleasure. Ellen could very rarely be persuaded to get inside, let alone learn to drive it, as Sally tried to tell her she should do. Ellen had never entirely forgotten Ben's tragic death at the wheel of his car and vowed that shanks's pony was good enough for her and always would be.

In the summer season of 1941 it seemed that rock was Blackpool's number one queue attraction. People had learned to queue in an orderly fashion for everything; for trains, buses and toilets, for beer and cigarettes, for the very limited supplies of oranges or tomatoes, lipsticks or hairgrips. And the visitors, who had more time than most, seemed to enjoy spending a goodly amount of it queuing (to the annoyance of the residents who often found that the supplies of tinned fruit, say, or soft toilet paper, had been snapped up by grasping holidaymakers!). But the biggest queues in the town were for rock. Sally, visiting the Dickson Road shop or the one in Bank Hey Street where Rachel was in charge, often found a queue, three or four deep, snaking for a good twenty yards along the street. Families were using their monthly sweet ration on as many sticks as the coupons would allow to take home for friends and family, or for themselves. Production, of necessity, was somewhat restricted, but a wide range of fruit flavours was still available as well as the traditional – and all-time favourite – bright pink peppermint rock.

'There's a queue, y'know. Get to t'back of it! Ne'er mind pushing in. We've bin 'ere a good half hour and more, I'll 'ave you know.'

Sally smiled as sweetly as she was able at the irate woman. 'I work here, love,' she said, marching into her husband's domain. Will we always have to queue, she wondered, even when the war is over?

'You're telling me you want to *marry* this young man?' Rachel gasped. 'Good gracious, Ruby, you've only just met him. What on earth are you thinking about? No, definitely not! It's out of the question. You're only nineteen . . . What a silly idea!'

Ruby might have guessed what her mother's reaction would be. When did Rachel ever agree to anything without making a great big fuss about it at first? But Ruby also knew that her mother often gave way, eventually, when she had had her say, like she had been forced to do about Emmie leaving school and about her, Ruby, joining the WAAFs.

Martin Ingram, the love of Ruby's short life, had been unable to come to Blackpool with her this weekend in mid-November; as a rear-gunner on a bomber crew he was flying, so she had come on her own. During their whirlwind courtship, she had met Martin's parents and liked them and she felt they liked her, too; Mrs Ingram, a motherly person who had made her more than welcome, and Mr Ingram, an older version of Martin with whom he shared his garage business, or had done in peacetime. They had seemed to accept the fact that the couple wanted to marry very quickly. After all, why not? It was wartime; so many young couples were tying the knot, trying to make the most of their time together, long or short . . . These thoughts were not spoken, but they hung in the air.

'I don't see why we can't,' said Ruby, trying not to sound petulant. She had grown up quite a lot recently and wanted her mother to see that she had. 'We love one another, and

242

lots of couples are getting married. Can't you understand? We want to be together.'

'Ruby, please don't tell me what other people are doing. If you ask me they're just plain stupid. These wartime marriages . . . they'll come to grief. The people who do it hardly know one another. And you don't know this Martin, not properly.'

And so it had gone on; Rachel could not be dissuaded. Ruby knew that she could go ahead and marry him anyway; she was under-age, admittedly, but felt sure there would be some way round it – a special licence or something – but she wanted her parents' blessing. Dad was away, but she knew he would never seriously go against her mother's wishes. Rachel was the one who had to be convinced. But Ruby's pleas fell on deaf ears.

'You will have to wait till the end of the war,' was Rachel's uncompromising statement. 'By then you'll probably be old enough to do as you like. But you'll no doubt find you've changed your mind by then, you take it from me.'

'What!' Ruby was horrified. 'The end of the war? We could be waiting for ever. You're being very unreasonable, Mum.'

'Wait until you're twenty-one then,' said Rachel, relenting a little. 'That's a year and a half, and it may very well be the end of the war by then, for all we know. Anyway, you haven't even got a ring yet. Oh, come on, love . . .' Her voice softened and Ruby noticed that her mother's eyes were a tiny bit moist. 'Marriage is for a long time, you know. You have to be sure.'

At least she agreed to meet Martin at Christmas-time, if both of them could get leave.

'I can't help feeling you're being a bit hard on the lass,' said Ellen when Rachel came to tell her the tale. Ruby, who had now gone back to camp, had already been to see her gran and Aunt Sally, and they could both tell that Rachel's ultimatum had upset the girl. She was a young woman in love, that was obvious, and with her newfound happiness there seemed to have developed a new maturity.

'Our Ruby's grown up quite a lot,' Ellen went on, 'and I'm sure she knows what she's doing. Don't alienate her, Rachel love. You may regret it.' But Ellen spoke guardedly, knowing how quickly her daughter could fly off the handle. There was just the faintest gleam in her eyes as she continued, 'Don't I remember a certain young lady – she could only have been nineteen or so – wanting to marry her young man? Getting engaged without telling anyone . . .'

'I was twenty-one when I married Harry,' retorted Rachel with dignity. 'We were courting for ages.'

'Because he was in France,' replied Ellen. 'If he'd been here I've no doubt you'd have been as anxious as Ruby is to get married quickly. Surely you can't have forgotten how you felt, love?'

'No, of course I haven't,' said Rachel, a trifle irritably. 'But she's had so many boyfriends. How can she be sure that this Martin is the right one for her?'

Ellen smiled. 'I seem to remember saying the same thing about you . . . and weren't you sure?'

'Yes, I was,' said Rachel slowly. 'Well, I've told her we'll meet him at Christmas. Harry will be home then, I hope, and Pearl, maybe. Then . . . we'll see.'

Rachel's final decision – and Harry's, after his wife had persuaded him – was that the young couple could marry after Ruby was turned twenty, that would be in the July of 1942.

'It's not so long, darling,' Martin consoled her as they strolled along the lower promenade, arms entwined tightly around one another, late on Boxing Day afternoon. The sun was setting, a fiery red ball, over the dark grey sea, and the hills of Barrow, far to the north, were clearly visible as they always were on a cold, bright day such as this. Very soon they would be catching a train back to their camp in East Anglia, having spent their forty-eight-hour leave at Ruby's home. Martin's parents hadn't minded as they saw a lot of their son with him being stationed so near. 'It'll soon pass, you'll see. And it isn't as if we're being separated, is it? We're at the same camp; we can see one another nearly all the time.'

'Yes, I suppose so . . .' Ruby was only half convinced. She did so want to belong to Martin, in the fullest sense, and soon, too, but at the same time she didn't want to go too much against her parents' wishes. It was Martin who had warned her not to argue with them.

'I can see that sparks fly quite often between you and your mother, don't they?' he had said. 'Two of a kind, aren't you, love? Don't let's cause any trouble, Ruby, not about this. It's too important. Your mum seems to like me, doesn't she? And I want her to go on liking me.

'I like your sisters, as well as your parents,' said Martin that winter afternoon. 'And your gran and Aunt Sally and Uncle George. To tell you the truth, I'm highly delighted with the whole family.' They stood still for a moment while he kissed her. 'So different, though, aren't you, the three of you, you and Pearl and Emmie? They're both much quieter than you, of course.' He gave her a friendly poke in the ribs. 'Do you think they'll be bridesmaids, along with the three little girls who live with your Aunt Sally?'

'I hope so,' Ruby replied dreamily. She was picturing herself floating down the aisle in a billowing and glamorous wedding gown made of parachute silk . . .

'I wish it had worked out for you with that Ralph chap, love,' said Ruby, jumping into bed and pulling the covers up to her chin. The two sisters were sharing their old bedroom during the Christmas holiday in Blackpool, as they had done before they both joined up, whilst Emmie had volunteered to sleep on the sofa downstairs, vacating her small room for their guest, Martin. 'I'm so happy and I want you to be happy, too. I'd be happier, though, if I could marry Martin straight away.

245

Mum's a spoilsport, making us wait. Anyway, enough said about that.'

'It must be the first time you haven't got your own way,' said Pearl, with a twinkle in her eye.

'Ha ha, very funny. Goodnight, Pearl. Sweet dreams. Dream about old Ralphie, why don't you?'

Pearl gave a snort and reflected, as she lay awake for a while in the quiet darkness, that it hadn't taken long for 'old Ralphie' to console himself. He had started seeing one of his ex-girlfriends again. Nora, she was called, from a nearby farm. Pearl had, in fact, felt more than a little peeved when she had heard that Ralph had resumed his friendship with Nora, though she couldn't have explained why.

Ruby stood at the end of the runway counting the planes in. Always she vowed that she wouldn't do it, not this time, but invariably she did. Eleven planes had gone out last night and as she watched them return – six, seven, eight, nine – all landing safely, she knew, with a feeling of foreboding, that Martin's plane was going to be the last to arrive. It was ironic that on this, the last op of the tour, there should be this heart-stopping fear that this time he was not going to make it. No! She wouldn't even let herself entertain that thought. Of course he would make it, as he had always done before.

It was only six weeks to their wedding and they would be six gloriously carefree weeks, unspoilt by the thought that tonight Martin might be flying. He was to have a few days' leave at his parents' home, then her fiancé was taking up a post as an instructor.

The tenth plane was coming now. Ruby anxiously scanned the fuselage for the familiar numbers and the photo of Betty Grable. She sighed again as the aircraft drew nearer. No, it wasn't Martin's plane. This one sported Rita Hayworth. It was as she feared; he was going to be last. Sod's law was operating this morning, sure enough, just when she wanted everything to be hunky-dory.

And it was time that she was turning in for work. She had told Avril she wouldn't be long; now she knew she would have to step on it to get there in time. She gazed once more towards the horizon where the blue sky – what a glorious blue it was this morning – met a copse of trees, then she let out a long deep sigh and turned away. At least she would be able to see the last plane arriving – as it surely would; it must! – from the store-room window.

It was impossible to concentrate. Ruby found that her hands were trembling as she picked up first one box, then another, not aware of what she was doing, her eyes constantly straying to the window. No, I won't keep looking, she told herself. I'm not going to look again for five whole minutes.

Then she heard the unmistakable drone of an approaching aircraft, and this time she ran to the window for it sounded as though the engine was in trouble. Hardly able to breathe, let alone speak, she watched in slowly mounting horror as the plane limped home. Avril stood at her side, clinging to her arm, as silent as her friend. Yes, it was Martin's plane sure enough; there was Betty Grable on the undercarriage, flashing her gorgeous legs and smiling seductively over her shoulder. Ruby stood rooted to the spot as the plane lurched and dipped and cartwheeled. It was trying to find the runway, but it was wildly out of control. It was heading towards their hut, losing height with every second. It was falling, dropping out of the sky like an avalanche. Ruby and Avril had no time to get out of the way. They flung themselves to the ground as the plane landed on top of the Quartermaster's Stores, ripping the flimsy Nissen hut to shreds.

Rachel stared at the telegram in her hand, unable to comprehend the stark black words that faced her. REGRET TO INFORM YOU . . . CORPORAL RUBY BALDERSTONE . . . KILLED ON ACTIVE SERVICE. It just wasn't possible. Ruby was only a WAAF, for God's sake, not a fighter pilot. She worked in the store room; she wasn't flying a plane. How could she have been killed?

There must be some mistake. Tears stemmed by her total disbelief, Rachel managed to get to the phone to summon her mother and Sally. It was Wednesday afternoon, half-day closing, and they were both at home.

'Come quickly,' she gasped. 'Please, Mum. I've had some awful news about Ruby. I don't believe it . . . it *can't* be true. But please come, for God's sake, Mum. Please help me.'

Ellen and Sally, and George, too, were with her in less than quarter of an hour. It was George who coped with the situation. He would ring the airfield and find out, he assured Rachel. His grim face as he came back into the room told them all they needed to know. So it *was* true. He broke the news to them just as it had been relayed to him; a plane had crash-landed on to the store room and three WAAFs who were working there had been killed instantly, along with four members of the crew.

'It's my fault, it's all my fault,' sobbed Rachel as her mother and sister-in-law, distraught themselves, but trying bravely to bear up for Rachel's sake, tried to offer her some comfort. 'Ruby always used to get her own way with me, and this time she didn't. I said they had to wait. If I hadn't made them wait, Ruby and Martin, it would never have happened. They'd have been married now, safe and away from it all.'

'No, Rachel, no. That doesn't make sense,' said Sally. She took hold of both of Rachel's hands, trying to stop the trembling, whilst Ellen, in the kitchen, made the inevitable cup of tea. Sally herself could hardly speak for the lump in her throat and the tears that were flowing down her cheeks, but she had to help Rachel if she could. Rachel had lost a daughter, whereas she, Sally, had lost only a niece. A much-loved one, though. Oh yes; Ruby had been like a daughter to her and she was sure that Rachel's grief could not surpass her own.

'Hush, love . . . hush,' she murmured, putting both arms around Rachel and rocking her, although she knew it was necessary for the tears to flow unrestrainedly, and for Rachel to rail against Fate or whatever it was, or against herself if she must. Just as Sally knew she would have to let her own grief overflow, later, when she was on her own. 'It wasn't your fault at all. You mustn't even think it.'

'Martin!' Rachel's sobs ceased for a moment as she stared at Sally. 'We don't know what has happened to Martin, do we? Do you suppose it was his plane that . . . ?'

Sally was silent for a moment, shocked beyond belief. Slowly she shook her head. 'I shouldn't think so, love. It would be too much of a coincidence if it were Martin's plane. Too awful if they were both . . .'

'But we'll have to find out.' Rachel seized hold of Sally's hand, almost making her wince with the intensity of her grip. 'I've got to know what has happened to Martin.'

George intercepted Sally's anguished look and nodded gravely. 'I'll phone,' he mouthed, disappearing into the hall once again. It was a while before he reappeared, as a long-distance call to Norfolk took a while to negotiate. The three women tried to occupy themselves with the ritual of tea drinking, each lost in their own thoughts. Three anxious faces searched George's grim one as he re-entered the room. Sally found herself still praying that there might have been some mistake, that it was all a ghastly nightmare.

'It *was* Martin's plane,' said George heavily. 'They told me that Flying Officer Banks had been killed and three members of his crew. Martin wasn't one of them. He's badly injured, but he's not dead. I had to tell them who I was, that we wanted to know because of Ruby being his fiancée.' His voice broke.

'At least I suppose we must be thankful that Martin's alive,' said Rachel in a dead sort of voice. 'He's a nice lad, and he loved our Ruby so much. I wouldn't want to think he'd been killed. Not both of them.'

But Sally couldn't help but wonder if it might have been better. How was that poor young man going to bear it when he found out what had happened?

Sally had just returned home when the door was suddenly flung open and there stood Gloria, back from school. She was on her own; the other two evacuees, Doreen and Susan, had gone back home to Salford, as Sally had anticipated. The little girl looked in puzzlement at Sally's sad face. 'What's up, Auntie Sally?' she asked.

Sally rose to her feet, ushering the child out of the room, 'Let's go upstairs, love,' she said, 'and I'll tell you. We've had some very bad news . . .'

Gloria listened in silence, her grey eyes filling up with tears. 'Poor Ruby,' she said. 'That's awful. I did like Ruby. She was such a lot of fun, wasn't she, Auntie Sally?'

Sally nodded abjectly. Yes, there wasn't a girl anywhere who had been more fun-loving than Ruby, although she had been somewhat quieter of late. Gloria edged nearer to her as they sat on the bed, putting her arm round her as though she, Sally, were the child.

'Don't cry, Auntie Sally,' she said. 'I'm here now, aren't I? And I do love you, Auntie Sally.'

Sally held her close. There was only one good thing to come out of this accursed war as far as she could see; this lovely child who had been put into her care. She prayed that Gloria would be with her for ever.

Chapter 18

Emmie was finding her work at Victoria Hospital interesting, but hardly as life-and-death essential as she had thought a nurse's work might be. At the moment she was on the children's ward, coping mainly with youngsters who were in for the removal of tonsils and adenoids or other minor surgery, dealing with bedpans and baths and taking of temperatures and running messages. As the very junior nurse she seemed to be the general dogsbody.

In the beginning, when she had first startled her family with her announcement that she was going to be a nurse, Emmie had anticipated looking after wounded servicemen or victims of air raids, dealing with broken limbs and severe burns, the casualties of a country at war. It was to be her warwork, she had declared patriotically, her way of 'doing her bit'.

The reality was that there were no longer any air raids in Blackpool. After 1940, when her Uncle George had lost his leg, it had all gone very quiet in the town. War injuries were more likely to be sustained by those who had walked into lamp-posts or had had minor car accidents in the blackout. Neither did the RAF recruits run into much danger in Blackpool; that came later when they had done their training and moved on to the airfields proper.

For all of which Emmie supposed she should be thankful. No one but a fool would want the air raids to start again here. She consoled herself that working at the hospital, however mundane, must be more valuable than doing the accounts at the rock factory, and it was helping to take her mind off the tragedy of Ruby's death.

Since Davey joined the RAF she hadn't been out much at all. He still wrote to her. She was relieved to learn that he was training as a ground mechanic, seeing to the maintenance of the aircraft and would not, therefore, be flying. At least he was safe, as safe as it was possible to be; look what had happened to poor Ruby...

'Emmie, I hope you won't mind me saying so, but you're turning into a real old stick-in-the-mud,' said Phyllis, one day in September 1942 when the two of them met in the hospital canteen at their midday break. Phyllis and Emmie had both started their training at the same time and had become quite good friends. Phyllis wasn't the least bit like Emmie, either in looks or in temperament, being blonde and bubbly and very outgoing. But maybe that was why they got on so well, because they complemented one another.

'When was the last time you went out of an evening?' Phyllis persisted now. 'No, don't tell me. I can answer that one. It was three weeks ago when we went to see *Mrs Miniver*. And a right bundle of laughs that turned out to be an' all! I want cheering up when I go to the flicks, not made to feel dead miserable. Oh, come on, Emmie, don't be such an old spoilsport. Come to the Winter Gardens with us and have some fun.'

Fun? Emmie wasn't sure that she considered it to be fun. She speared a piece of vivid pink Spam and swallowed it with a segment of beetroot before she replied. 'I don't enjoy standing at the edge of the ballroom floor, waiting for somebody to ask me to dance. I hate it when I'm left there on my own.' This had happened on the few occasions Emmie had been dancing and she felt like a fish out of water, as though everybody was staring at her.

'Oh, don't talk such tommyrot! Me and Betty'll be with you, and you're just as likely to be asked to dance as we are.

252

You're a great-looking girl, you know, when you do something with your hair . . . and when you remember to smile.'

Emmie smiled now. It was kind of her friend to want to include her; she knew she was a bit of a wet blanket at times. 'All right,' she said. 'Yes, I might go. It is ages since I went out. But I haven't really felt as though I should, not since . . . you know.'

Phyllis leaned across the table, putting a hand on her friend's arm. 'Listen, if you're thinking about your Ruby, then just try to imagine what she would have said. I didn't know your sister, but I'm sure, from what you've told me, that she'd have wanted you to go out and see a bit of life, not sit at home moping.'

'Yes, you're right,' replied Emmie. 'She would. I'll come, then – but there'll be a lot of those Yanks there, won't there?'

'So what? You are a scream, Emmie.' Phyllis gave a hoot of laughter. 'What d'you think they're going to do? Drag you into a dark alley and molest you?' She sniggered quietly. 'I should be so lucky! No, they're just like our lads, when you come to think of it, only a long way from home. It's up to us to make them welcome.'

'Aren't they a bit brash?' asked Emmie. 'I've seen some of them in town . . .'

'Some of 'em, maybe. It takes all sorts to make a world, like my mum's always saying. It makes 'em more interesting, don't you think? Anyway, I'm not going to let you back out, Emmie Balderstone, not now. You're coming, and you're going to enjoy yourself!'

'OK,' grinned Emmie. 'Aye, aye, cap'n!'

Yes, the Yanks were here. The bombing of Pearl Harbor in December 1941 had brought them into the war, and by the summer of 1942 they were in the north of England. Emmie had seen a battalion of them marching through Talbot Square, the flag with the stars and stripes held high; smart-looking men in their greenish uniforms that looked as though they had been tailor-made – a vivid contrast to the coarse material of the khaki and Air Force blue worn by our own lads. Strictly speaking, they were not stationed in Blackpool, but at Warton, a few miles to the south, nearer to Lytham St Annes. Warton was known in military terms as Base Air Depot 2. Thus, the Yanks stationed there became known as the 'BADS'.

'Overpaid, oversexed and over here!' was a catchphrase constantly being bandied about, but how true it was, Emmie, for one, did not know. What she knew about these young men was only by hearsay; the Americans, as a race, were still as foreign to her as they had always been.

This was soon to change.

GI Gene Lawrenson gazed round the Empress Ballroom, at the gleaming parquet floor, almost hidden now beneath hundreds of shuffling feet, the ornate pillars and gleaming chandeliers, the gilded balconies with tiers of red plush seats, to say nothing of the thrilling sound of the Wurlitzer organ. Gee whizz! Gene let out a long low whistle of appreciation. He had seen nothing to compare with this, even back home. The girls were pretty, too, in their summer frocks and white sandals, a lot of them with their hair tightly curled, some with it flowing on to their shoulders, not nearly so shabby as he might have expected, not shabby at all, in fact. His pals had chosen their partners and gone on to the floor whilst Gene, more reticent about making a move, stood weighing up the situation. Dancing was not really his forte, which was one of the reasons he was holding back; all the less time to fall over his partner's feet and feel a fool.

The girl standing by the pillar, though; she didn't look the sort of girl who would be worried by his lack of dancing technique. She appeared a little bemused as she watched the couples dancing past. The blonde girl who was with her looked much more eager to be out there on the ballroom floor, but it was the girl in the green dress who had caught

Gene's eye. She reminded him rather of his kid sister, Maisie; older, of course, but with that same slightly pensive expression. Almost involuntarily he found himself moving towards her.

'Care to dance?' he asked, smiling at her.

Her eyes were a greenish brown, candidly clear eyes with, he thought, a trace of sadness in them, in a roundish face. Her hair was not curly, like her friend's, but longish and brownish, curled under in a sort of page-boy bob. But then she smiled, and Gene discovered that there was nothing 'ish' about this girl any longer. She was lovely, her face transformed by the radiance of her smile. Gene felt his heart turn over as she replied.

'Yes, thank you very much,' she said quietly. 'I would like to dance.'

It was a quickstep and Emmie was relieved that it was a dance she could do quite well. The American lad seemed very nice. He had eyes as blue as her sister Ruby's had been, and fair hair cut short in what they called a crew cut. He didn't seem pushy at all; he just smiled at her once or twice as they danced round to the strains of *Run, Rabbit, Run*, the tune that had been popular since 1939, but was still a great favourite with the dance bands and ballroom organists.

'D'you come here a lot?' he asked her now. 'I know it's a kinda corny thing to ask, but it's my first time, you see.'

'Mine too,' replied Emmie. 'Well, the first time for ages. I'm not much of a dancer,' she went on, rather apologetically. 'Quicksteps and waltzes, that's about my lot, and the old-time; I can do those.'

'Old-time?' Her partner raised his eyebrows quizzically.

'Yes – the Military Two Step and the Barn Dance and the Veleta. They're good fun because they're all the same steps, you see, and you don't have to try to follow your partner.' She laughed as she stumbled over his feet. 'Like I'm not doing now.'

He squeezed her hand. 'You're doing just fine, honey. I

don't know these old-time dances. Of course I wouldn't, would I, coming from the New World? But I guess I can learn.'

The music came to an end and Emmie applauded, like all the folks around her, before turning to her partner. 'Thank you,' she said, making to walk off the floor. She didn't want to linger; it was doubtful he would ask her to dance again. She hoped he would, but . . .

'Here, what's the hurry?' His hand on her arm detained her. 'Don't go dashing away. I'm just getting to know you. Tell you what; let's go and have a drink, then you can tell me all about yourself. Then maybe we can dance some more. Don't worry, honey,' he added, as she looked at him a little hesitantly. 'I'm not trying to make a pass. You look a kinda nice girl, that's all. And I'm feeling a bit lonesome.'

Emmie smiled at him again. 'All right,' she said. 'Thank you.'

She asked for a ginger beer and was surprised to see that he chose the same drink, then they sat on the little round stools and chatted. It was very easy to talk to him. Emmie learned that his name was Gene, short for Eugene, Lawrenson and that he came from San Francisco in California. Emmie knew where it was; she had been good at geography at school. It was fascinating to meet and talk with someone who actually came from a foreign country, although you couldn't really call Americans foreigners; they spoke the same language and now they were our allies.

'Emmie,' he said, looking at her eagerly. 'That's short for Emily? Emma? Esmeralda?'

'No.' She gave a grimace. 'It's Emerald, I'm afraid!'

'Gee, that's a beautiful name,' said Gene sincerely. 'And it suits you so well, too. You must have been born with green eyes.'

'No.' Emmie laughed. 'It was just lucky that they turned out to be green. My two sisters were named after jewels as well – Pearl . . . and Ruby.'

'That's cute,' said Gene. 'Real cute. And I shall call you Emerald, if you don't mind. Emmie's far too ordinary for a special girl like you.'

By the end of the evening, it was inevitable that the two of them should arrange to meet again. He now knew all about Ruby (the reason that Emmie had been looking a little sad earlier that evening), about Pearl in the Land Army, the rock factory, and Emmie training to be a nurse. She in turn, had learned that Gene was twenty, two years older than herself, and that the war had interrupted his training as a lawyer. Now how could Mum fail to be impressed with that? thought Emmie, making up her mind to invite him to her home very soon. She knew already that Gene Lawrenson was going to become very important to her.

'I'll walk you home,' he said, when she had collected her coat and met him outside the cloakroom. 'Where do you live?'

'Near Stanley Park. It's not all that far.' A little shyly she tucked her hand into the crook of his outstretched arm.

'This way?' Gene turned right when they came out of the entrance.

'Yes, that's right. But I don't want you to get lost, or to be late. What time do you have to be back in camp? It's a long way, isn't it?'

'Don't worry about me, sweetheart. I'm a big boy now.' He patted her hand. 'They're pretty free and easy and I'll be back long before midnight. And I know that all roads thataway lead to the sea, don't they?' He jerked his thumb to the right. 'I can't get lost. I'll just catch a tram along the seafront, then I may be able to hitch a lift in one of our lorries. No sweat.'

Emmie decided that one of the chief differences between the British and Americans was that the former always had to be worrying, whereas the latter seemed to take everything in their stride. Gene certainly did seem to be a very calm, unflappable sort of person. Emmie felt she could relax totally in his company; just as she had been able to do with Davey. But why on earth should she be thinking about Davey now?

She didn't think about him for long, however, because she and Gene had so much to talk about. Their taste in literature was similar, both of them liking Jane Austen, John Galsworthy, and the poet, Keats; Emmie agreed that she would try the American novelist Scott Fitzgerald, a favourite of Gene's, whose works she had not read. They also liked the same composers, Mozart and Tchaikovsky and, in a lighter vein, the songs of Irving Berlin.

Not that their talk was all erudite. He made her laugh with the catchphrases he had already picked up from the British; 'Turned out nice again', 'Don't you know there's a war on?' and 'Can I do yer now, sir?' What on earth did that mean? he wanted to know. So she told him about Mrs Mopp and *ITMA*, which was her gran's favourite programme.

It seemed to be no time at all before they were outside her house, and when they stopped at the gate Gene held her very gently and kissed her softly on the side of her mouth. 'See you on Monday then, outside the Winter Gardens.' They had already made this arrangement. 'Goodnight, Emerald. I'm so glad I've met you. See you soon, honey.'

'Yes, see you soon, Gene,' she replied. 'I'm glad too,' she added, still a little shyly. After all, she had only known him for an hour or two, even though it seemed like for ever.

She stood for a moment and watched him walk away. He turned to wave and she waved back before opening the gate. Never had she felt so happy, or so overwhelmed. What on earth was happening to her? She supposed she was falling in love.

They met whenever they could, their meetings determined by Emmie's shifts at the hospital and Gene's passes from the camp. As the autumn of 1942 drew on, bringing darker and colder nights, they went dancing, at the Winter Gardens again

258

and also at the Tower and Palace ballrooms. Neither of them was very keen on dancing, but it was somewhere for them to go and they could hold one another closely. Had their courtship started in the summer they could have enjoyed the beauties of Stanley Park or taken long walks along the promenade. But a cold and dismal November was not the ideal time to wander hand-in-hand along the sands or to find a secluded spot under the pier in which to embrace. The sands, after dark, were supposed to be out of bounds, but this was a rule made to be broken. Courting couples often made their way there, even in winter, but Emmie knew that for her and Gene to do so would be to cheapen their relationship. He didn't suggest it and for this she was thankful. They understood one another so well, almost as if they had grown up together.

Only once, on a chilly October night, had he drawn her into his arms in the darkness of the colonnades, near to North Pier, and begun to kiss her passionately. His hands had strayed beneath her camel coat, gently caressing her breasts, and she had leaned towards him, wanting him to embrace her even more intimately, wanting to prove to him how much she loved him. Then he had broken away.

'No, sweetheart. We mustn't. This isn't right. Not for you, Emerald. Not . . . for us. We mustn't spoil it.' She knew what he meant. Further along the prom she could see a couple behaving very unrestrainedly. She turned away, embarrassed. 'Come on, I'll walk you home,' he said. 'It's getting late anyway. We don't want your ma to be worried.'

Her mother had met Gene and seemed to like him, although it was difficult to tell with Rachel. She remained aloof, slightly distanced from the situation, as though she didn't take at all seriously the friendship of her daughter with an American GI.

Emmie supposed that this was only to be expected. Her mother was still grieving, though less frenziedly now, about Ruby, and she would not want to think of her youngest daughter getting involved with a man who might, eventually, take her away. Because this was what was going to happen. Gene had asked Emmie if she would marry him, when the war was over, and without any hesitation she had said yes. They both knew without any doubt that this was the way it must be. But, for the time being, it must be kept a secret from her family, most particularly from her mother. Rachel would only tell her that she was too young, just as she had told Ruby.

'I like your new boyfriend,' said Gloria one afternoon when she came round, as she still did, to borrow some books. 'He looks a bit like Cary Grant, doesn't he, except for his hair.'

Emmie laughed. 'You're only saying that because he's an American. Yes, I suppose he might be like him, just a bit. At least it's better than saying he looks like Mickey Rooney,' she teased. That was what Gloria had once said about Davey.

'Oh yes, Davey,' said Gloria. 'D'you still write to him?'

'Now and again,' said Emmie evasively. 'I told you – he was never my boyfriend.'

'No, not like this one, eh?' Gloria grinned at her, rather too knowingly, and Emmie felt herself blushing. Gloria was growing up quite a lot. She was twelve now, a tall, very attractive girl with her long dark hair drawn back in two bunches. She had passed her scholarship examination and was now at the Grammar School that Emmie herself had attended. And doing very well there, from what her Aunt Sally said.

'I'm not keen on his name, though,' Gloria went on. 'It's a girl's name, i'n't it? Well, it is here anyway.'

'It's spelt differently,' said Emmie, smiling. 'G-E-N-E, short for Eugene. I can't say I like that, but Gene's a very popular name in America. Anyway, never mind about him. You're too nosey by half, young lady! Tell me what's been happening to you. What about school?'

'Oh, I'll tell you about that later,' said Gloria dismissively.

'But I've got loads of other things to report.' She settled herself more comfortably on the large cushion on the bedroom floor. 'D'you remember Mr Catchpole? You know, that fellow that Doreen and Susan lived with before they came to us? He was . . . well, he was doing something that was wrong – to Doreen and Susan – and your gran got them away, to live with us.'

'Yes, I remember,' said Emmie guardedly. She had heard a little about the sordid story and what she hadn't heard she had guessed. 'Well, what about him?'

'He's run off with a civil servant.'

'He's what! How d'you know, anyway?'

' 'Cause I heard your gran and Auntie Sally talking about it, and when I asked them what they were going on about, they told me. Auntie Sally doesn't believe in keeping secrets from me, you know. Well . . .' Gloria stopped to take a breath '. . . when Doreen and Susan left, Mr and Mrs Catchpole had some of those civil servants from London to stay with them – two ladies. And Mr Catchpole's run off with one of them.'

'You're sure?'

'Yes, honest. Auntie Sally said so.'

'Well, fancy that.' Emmie couldn't think of anything else to say. 'Poor Mrs Catchpole.'

'Oh, you don't want to worry about her. She's an old cow!'

'Gloria!'

'Well, she is. She was real horrible to Doreen and Susan, not letting them listen to the wireless or read comics or anything. Oh, and you remember those other two evacuees we had . . .' Emmie smiled to herself. It was as though Gloria had forgotten that she, too, had been an evacuee. Still was really, although nobody, not even Rachel, now thought of her as one. 'Wendy and Michael Cooper – you know, they came from Salford when I did. Well, their mam's got married again.'

'How do you know?' Emmie asked for the second time. Really, Gloria was a mine of information this afternoon.

' 'Cause I had a letter from our Monica and she told me. He's a lot older than Mrs Cooper, Monica says, and he's got a ladies' dress shop in Manchester. She'll like that, Mrs Snooty Cooper; she liked dressing up as though she was Lady Muck.'

'And how's your friend, Wendy?' asked Emmie.

'Don't know.' Gloria sounded pensive and she was silent for a moment. 'D'you know, Emmie, she was my best friend when we came to live here.'

'Yes, I remember. You both came to see us, that first week. She was a shy little thing.'

'And now I never hear from her at all. It's my fault, I s'pose. I should have written to her.'

'Don't worry, Gloria. These things happen. We make lots of friends as we go through life, and sometimes – well – we grow apart from some of them. How's your sister and her family?'

Gloria shrugged. 'All right, I suppose. I haven't seen any of 'em for ages. Sometimes I think they've forgotten all about me, and then Monica suddenly decides to write. It's like . . . it's as though Salford and Monica and all of them was something that happened ages ago, when I was a little kid. I don't often think about them now. Does that sound awful, Emmie?'

'No, I don't think so,' said Emmie gently. 'Like I said, you've made a lot of new friends.' Emmie didn't remind the girl that Salford was where her true family lived and that was where, sooner or later, she might have to return. Emmie knew that her Aunt Sally was closing her mind to this, just as she, Emmie, had sometimes done. She was very fond of Gloria and would miss her if and when she returned home, but not nearly so much as her Aunt Sally would.

It was her grandmother who eventually provided Emmie and Gene with the privacy they both desired. Ellen had invited the young couple to tea soon after they had met, and having

262

taken to Gene straight away, in a few weeks' time she invited them again.

'That's a young couple in love if ever I saw one,' she remarked to Sally, after they had been to tea for the second time. 'And I'll tell you something; I feel sorry for them. Where do you suppose they go when they want a bit of a kiss and a cuddle?'

'Honestly, Mam, I don't know!' Sally sounded a little shocked at her mother-in-law coming out with such a remark. 'It's not really any of our business, is it? What do other courting couples do? Find a park bench or a tram shelter, I suppose.'

'It's winter, Sally,' said Ellen, 'or it will be very soon, and I can't see our Emmie necking on a park bench. Isn't that what they call it now?' She was aware of Sally's astounded look, but she hadn't forgotten what it was like to be young. 'And I'm sure our Rachel isn't providing them with any home comforts, apart from the odd cup of tea and ham salad. She won't talk about it, you know. She's trying to pretend it isn't happening.'

'You can't blame her, Mam. Not after Ruby . . .'

'No, I know that. But the next time Emmie brings that young man of hers here I'm going to put a fire in the front room and let them have a bit of time to themselves. We don't need to say anything to our Rachel.'

'Mam, be careful. Don't you think you might be encouraging them to do something they shouldn't?'

'What, with us in the next room? Not very likely, is it? Besides, our Emmie's a sensible sort of girl, always has been, and you've only to look at Gene to know you can trust him. No, you can be sure Emmie'll not let her heart rule her head. But they need somewhere to be alone together. Anyway, that's what I'm going to do. Don't look so worried, Sal. It'll be all right . . .'

Emmie and Gene were delighted with the haven of warmth

and seclusion and Emmie knew, without being told, that she mustn't tell her mother about it. Gran hadn't said she must keep it a secret; to do so would have seemed as though she was encouraging Emmie to be deceitful, but Emmie understood what was in her grandmother's mind, and she kept quiet.

They didn't go there every time they met. That would have been presuming too much on her gran's hospitality, but about once a week they would find themselves on the commodious sofa in Ellen's front room, able, at last, to give full rein to their emotions. Not entirely, however. They were always conscious of Ellen, Sally and George in the next room, and Gloria asleep upstairs. They knew there was a point beyond which they dared not go, but they also knew that one day the temptation, and their love for one another, might prove too strong.

It was the week before Christmas when Gene told Emmie he had some bad news for her. In January he was to be posted to Burtonwood, near Liverpool. He had grown very skilful at the reassembling of planes and was to become a flight engineer.

She clung to him in desperation. 'But when will I see you? Will you be able to come to Blackpool?'

'I don't see why not, sweetheart,' he assured her. 'It's not all that far, is it? And maybe your gran might let me stay here if I can get a weekend pass. What d'you think about that?'

Emmie was dismayed. 'I think you'll forget about me when you get to Liverpool,' she blurted out. She didn't really mean that at all, but his news had been such a shock.

'Forget about you? Don't be stupid, honey. I love you more than anything else in the world. I thought you knew that.'

'I love you too, Gene, so much. I don't want you to leave me.'

They clung together, their kisses and embraces growing ever more ardent. For the first time they were alone in the house. Ellen, George and Sally, and Gloria, too, had gone to a concert at the church hall. Emmie had been aware of her gran's hesitancy as they departed and her concerned glance at her, then at Gene. She knew what Gran was thinking. Be good, I trust you, Emmie . . . but she wouldn't embarrass her granddaughter by saying it.

Emmie knew that what they were doing was going against all the principles that had been instilled in her. But there came a point when all principles were swept aside by the overwhelming power of love . . . and it no longer seemed wrong. Emmie was fully aware of what might happen, what might be the outcome of this, but at that moment she didn't care. She cared for nothing but Gene's arms around her, his lips upon hers, his hands caressing her body, awakening sensations she had never known before. What might happen tomorrow didn't matter. There was only this glorious moment . . .

Chapter 19

'Did you and Ralph fall out?' Millie asked Pearl, one day when they were topping and tailing turnips in the big barn. It was the first reference Millie had made to their friendship for ages, although Pearl guessed that she must have wondered about it, and been puzzled by the lack of progress between them over the preceding months.

'Not exactly,' replied Pearl. 'We're still good friends – *only* friends, mind you. It was never . . . serious, you know.' She was trying to answer casually. She ignored Millie's raised eyebrows and her look that said quite clearly, Pull the other one!

'Very well, if you say so, although I reckon that Ralph was dead keen on you. You were a fool, you know, to give him the brush-off.' It was the first time Millie had voiced an opinion; it now seemed so long ago when Ralph had asked Pearl to marry him. It *was* a long time ago; more than a year.

'All right, I admit it,' Pearl retorted. 'Ralph did ask me to marry him, ages ago, but I turned him down. I wasn't ready! I decided I didn't want to marry him and that's that. Anyway, he's back with his old girlfriend now, isn't he?' She sighed. 'He might have been "dead keen" once, but that's water under the bridge.'

Over the next few days, however, Pearl was aware that Ralph was regarding her thoughtfully. She had become used to his – not exactly indifference – but a certain detachment in his manner towards her. He was always polite: he could even be said to be quite friendly at times but since she had turned him down he had kept his distance from her, mentally if not physically – this was not possible when they worked so closely together – and never once had he referred to his proposal. For all she knew he now regretted it.

'You're feeling quite well, are you, Pearl?' he asked eventually. He had stopped by the stall of Primrose, the troublesome cow who, to her relief, Pearl had eventually managed to master.

'Yes, of course I am. Why do you ask?' she replied, trying to sound cheerful and unconcerned.

'I thought you looked rather pale, that's all,' said Ralph. 'A bit under the weather.' He was regarding her steadily as if waiting for her reply.

'I'm perfectly all right, thank you.' Embarrassed, Pearl turned away, concentrating again on the milk issuing from Primrose's udders into the bucket at her feet. Why didn't he just go away and leave her alone?

But he stood his ground. 'I'm glad to see you've won the battle with this one.' He put a hand on Primrose's flank. 'Awkward customer, isn't she? But I told you she'd be OK if you sang to her, didn't I?'

So he had, ages ago. Pearl looked up and smiled at him, a trifle unsurely. She was remembering how kind and considerate Ralph had been when she first arrived, helping her to settle into her new surroundings; she would never forget that. 'Yes, so you did, Ralph,' she replied. 'And it did the trick. We're quite good pals now, Primrose and me.'

'I hope that's what you and I can be, Pearl,' he said. 'Good friends, I mean.' He hesitated, then, 'I've been concerned about you. I know you were badly shaken by the death of your sister. It's my job to keep an eye on you. My family are responsible for you, aren't we? Besides, there's not very much that I miss, Pearl.'

She had no answer to that except a teary nod of gratitude and she turned again to her work.

'Well, I've cleared the air,' said Ralph awkwardly, 'and as

I was saying, I hope you and I can be friends again. Just friends,' he added hastily as she looked up to smile at him. 'Nothing more than that. You made that very clear . . . and I respect your decision.' They regarded one another unwaveringly for a few moments. Then, 'See you later, Pearl,' said Ralph as he walked away.

Pearl stared after him. She didn't know whether to be upset or pleased that he cared. Cared in a purely unemotional way, of course, because she worked on his farm. That was what he had just implied; he was concerned because it was his duty to be so. Millie's words of a few days ago came back to her. 'You were a fool to give him the brush-off . . .' Well, whether she was or whether she wasn't – and Pearl, for the life of her, couldn't imagine why she was even thinking about it – one thing was certain: Ralph would never propose to her again.

Autumn gave way to winter. The root and corn crops were gathered, the sheep brought down from the summer pasture, and the cows now 'lay in' ready for milking instead of being fetched from the fields. The river rose and flooded the low lying land, then the first snow came. The countryside, if you could stop thinking for a moment about how cold you were, was breathtakingly beautiful.

Pearl travelled home for Christmas across the Pennines, and after the train had crossed the Lancashire border the snowy landscape gradually gave way to the usual browns and greens. In Blackpool there had been no snow at all as yet.

She was glad to be home, but it was a sad sort of Christmas, inevitably, because it was the first one without Ruby. They all gathered at her gran's, as usual, on Christmas Day; Grandma, George, Sally and young Gloria, Mum and Dad (home for a few days' leave), herself, and Emmie with her American boyfriend, Gene Lawrenson. Pearl thought he was a very pleasant lad and Emmie was obviously head over heels about him, as he seemed to be about her. However,

Emmie's young face, in unguarded moments, looked stricken, but maybe it was just because in a few days' time Gene would be moving to another camp. Pearl knew that love brought its heartache as well as its joy.

She found she was looking forward to returning to Yorkshire. In spite of the cold and the gruelling work she knew that was where she belonged. Perhaps, if she were to meet him halfway – maybe a little more – Ralph might be persuaded to change his mind. Now, wherever had that thought come from? It had taken Pearl completely unawares and she tried to quell it. But still it persisted and when she boarded the train a few days later it was still there. She knew that in returning to Yorkshire she was returning home. The thought brought a twinge of guilt. Blackpool was her home; she had never imagined wanting to live anywhere else. But she couldn't wait to get back. Would Ralph be looking forward to seeing her, as much as she was to seeing him? And how could she let him know?

As soon as Ellen opened the door and saw Emmie's anguished face she knew that something was badly wrong.

'Gran, I've got to talk to you.' Emmie hurried through the door and Ellen closed it quickly behind her because of the blackout regulations. There hadn't been an air raid for ages, but it was better to be safe than sorry. 'To you and Auntie Sally,' Emmie went on, following Ellen into the living room. 'She is in, isn't she?' she added, looking round the room.

'Sally? Yes, of course she is,' said Ellen. 'She's just gone upstairs to say goodnight to Gloria.'

'And Uncle George? He's gone out, has he, to one of his meetings?'

'Yes, George has gone to his Liberal Club.'

'I was hoping there'd be just the two of you.' Emmie sat down on one of the fireside chairs, looking pleadingly at Ellen.

'Why, whatever's the matter, dear?' Ellen crouched down

269

at her side and took her hand. 'Is it Gene? You haven't had some bad news, have you?' Emmie shook her head. 'It's not your mum, is it? Or your dad?'

'No, none of them,' said Emmie. 'It's me, Gran. I'll tell you when Auntie Sally comes down.' And as Ellen looked into her youngest granddaughter's frightened green eyes she knew at once what it was that Emmie was about to tell her; her intuition was sure. She sat down in the opposite chair and waited.

Sally came down in a moment. 'Hello there, Emmie. How nice to see you!' She breezed into the room, then stopped as she saw Emmie's troubled face. 'Whatever's the matter, dear?' she said, just as Ellen had. She squatted on a low pouffe near the fire. 'Not more bad news, is it?'

'Depends on which way you look at it, I suppose.' Emmie gave a little half-smile, although Ellen could see that tears were not far from the surface of her eyes. 'I'm . . . I'm going to have a baby.'

Sally didn't answer, not at first. Then: 'You could be mistaken perhaps, love?' Sally spoke now. 'How long is it since . . . you know?'

'When did I have a period? December, and now it's February. I've missed two. Oh Gran, Auntie Sally . . .' She gazed imploringly at them, first at one then the other. 'What am I going to do?'

Ellen didn't know. Get married, she supposed. That was the obvious solution, if Gene was serious enough about her. The poor kid. Ellen, also, was beginning to reproach herself. That night, before Christmas, when she had left them alone, that was when it must have happened. What a fool she had been. 'Have you told your mother?' she asked. Surely Rachel must know.

Emmie shook her head again. 'No, have I heck as like!' For the first time her voice sounded a little more spirited. 'I daren't. She'll kill me!'

Ellen got up and knelt on the floor at her granddaughter's

feet, taking hold of both her hands. 'You've got to tell your mother. You know you must. And of course she won't kill you! I think she might even understand.' Ellen was looking back to a certain incident in her own daughter's past and was thinking that if Rachel upbraided Emmie about this very human error then she would be guilty of hypocrisy; it would be a case of the pot calling the kettle black.

'And what about Gene?' asked Sally gently. 'Does he know?'

'No, not yet.'

'Then you must tell him, love. He's very fond of you, isn't he? Well, I know he is. I've seen the two of you together and it's obvious that you care for one another.'

'Yes, he loves me, and I love him. We didn't mean to, you know. We didn't mean . . . to do that. I don't know how it happened. We just got carried away.'

'Yes, it's easy sometimes,' said Ellen, half to herself. 'The important thing is, he'll marry you, won't he?'

'Yes, we were going to get married, after the war. But now I don't see how we can. I'm only eighteen, and he's twenty, nearly twenty-one. Mum would say I'm too young, like she did about Ruby. Anyway, I haven't told her, have I? I daren't.'

'Don't be silly now.' Ellen clasped both her hands tightly around Emmie's. 'You've got to tell her. Tell your mum, then write and tell your Gene. It'll all be all right, you'll see. You're both young, but you love one another, and it's the only solution. I was married at seventeen, you know, Emmie, the first time.' Ellen didn't add that it had been a disastrous marriage, but this one, she felt sure, would not be. It wasn't ideal for the poor kids, but they weren't the first to give way to temptation and they assuredly would not be the last.

'Now, I'm going to make us all a nice drink of cocoa, and when your Uncle George comes in I'll get him to walk home with you. Don't worry, you don't need to tell him anything. I'll tell him later, but you know what your Uncle George is like. He's an old softie at heart. Cheer up, love . . . and just

271

pluck up all your courage to tell your mum. It'll all work out, you'll see.'

No time like the present, thought Emmie as she entered the house. She would tell her mother now, before she went to bed. She had to be at the hospital at eight o'clock the following morning, so there would be no time then. Besides, it would only get worse and worse if she kept putting it off.

Rachel was sitting by the fire reading a magazine. She looked as though she hadn't moved since Emmie went out a couple of hours earlier. She looked up and smiled. 'Hello, dear. I was just waiting till you came in before I made a drink. Would you like one, or have you had something at your gran's?'

'No, I mean, yes; I've had a drink. Mum . . .' Emmie stood on the hearthrug looking resolutely at her mother. There was no other way. She had to pluck up courage and tell her now. 'I've got something to tell you. I'm . . .' She gulped, then came straight out with it. 'I'm going to have a baby.'

Rachel's smile vanished, her expression changing in an instant to one of horror and disbelief. 'You're *what*! No, no, you can't be. Tell me I'm hearing things.' She put her hands to her ears, at the same time shaking her head. 'No, it can't be true. Did you just say that you were going to have a baby? You can't be.'

'Yes, I am, Mum,' said Emmie. 'I'm sorry . . . but, yes, I am.'

'You're sorry! I should damn well think you are sorry.' Rachel's eyes were blazing with fury. Emmie couldn't remember ever seeing her so angry. 'It's a bit late to be sorry now, isn't it? You should have thought about that when you were . . . Oh, it's disgraceful. I can't bear to think of it. It's you and that American, I suppose, that Gene?'

'Of course it's him,' said Emmie indignantly. 'Who else did you think it could be?'

'I really don't know, Emerald, because I feel I just don't

know you any more. How could you? After all I've done for you. After I invited him – that lad – into our home. That's the way you repay me. You go and behave like a . . . like a tramp. A little trollop, that's what you are!'

'I'm *not* a trollop! How dare you say that?' Emmie didn't feel afraid now she had taken the first step; besides, her mother was being ridiculous and she was determined to stand her ground. 'I've said I'm sorry, and I *am* sorry if you're upset, but I'm not sorry that we . . . that Gene and I . . . did that, because we love one another. I'm not a tramp. You know I'm not and it's awful of you to say that. It isn't what Gran said, and Auntie Sally—'

'Your gran? And Sally? You've been round to tell *them*, before you told me, your own mother?' For a moment Emmie felt scared again as she looked at her mother's face, pale with anger, but she bravely replied.

'Yes, I did go to tell them. And d'you know why? Because they understand, that's why.' Emmie found that she was shouting, which she hadn't intended to do, but the loudness of her voice helped to give her confidence. 'Gran and Auntie Sally are always ready to listen to me. They understand why I want to do things, like leaving school, and training to be a nurse. You've never liked it, have you, Mum, because I didn't go into the Sixth Form and to university or somewhere . . . so that you could swank about me, about your clever daughter. Well, I didn't, did I? I met Gene and I'm going to have a baby, and . . . and we're going to get married. And you can't stop me!'

'You cheeky young madam!' Emmie was taken completely by surprise as her mother leapt from her chair and landed her a stinging blow across her cheek. 'How dare you speak to me like that! Get married? Huh! We'll see about that. Has he asked you then? Does he know about . . . this? I'll bet he doesn't even know, does he? Or care,' Rachel added in an undertone.

'No, he doesn't know, not yet,' said Emmie, taking a step

back, away from her mother's wrath. 'But I'm going to tell him. And of course he'll care. It's very wrong of you to say he won't care. I didn't mean to shout at you, Mum. I didn't mean to be rude.' She put her hand to her smarting cheek. 'But there was no need for you to hit me. I've only said what was true.' Her voice was quieter now, but there was no trace of friendliness or forgiveness in the look that she levelled at Rachel. 'I sometimes think you don't really care about me at all, unless I'm doing everything that you want me to do.'

'I think you've said enough,' said Rachel coldly. 'I don't want to hear any more. I'm thoroughly ashamed of you. You've let me down badly. As if I haven't had enough trouble with Ruby and everything.'

'Yes, I know,' answered Emmie. 'I'm sorry.' Although she couldn't see what Ruby had to do with any of this. As if Ruby's death could have prevented her from loving Gene.

'And for heaven's sake stop saying you're sorry. I don't believe you're sorry at all. You'd better get off to bed.' Rachel's glance was frosty. 'You've to be up early in the morning.' She turned her back on Emmie and disappeared into the kitchen.

Emmie was too stunned even to cry. She had feared that her mother might be angry, but this chilling condemnation beggared belief. Wearily she dragged herself upstairs, realising that she hadn't yet taken her coat off. She flung her clothes into a heap on the floor and crawled into bed. She had expected to lie awake, but her mind was so exhausted with it all that in a few moments she was asleep.

Rachel didn't see her daughter the following morning. The shame of it! Her brilliant daughter, of whom she had had such high hopes, turning out to be no better than one of the factory girls!

In high dudgeon Rachel set off to see her mother. Ellen was on her own, Sally and George both having departed for work, and Rachel was glad about that. She could do without

Sally's tolerance and the way she would try to be oh so understanding – of Emmie, of course, not of her, Rachel. It still rankled, what Emmie had said about Sally and her mother, how they cared . . . and she didn't.

'Well, this is a pretty kettle of fish, isn't it, Mam?' she began. 'I just couldn't believe it when she told me. Our Emerald, of all people . . .'

Ellen listened, saying very little, while Rachel went on and on in pretty much the same way as she had to Emmie the previous night. '. . . I'm so disappointed in her – well, more than disappointed, I'm furious with her. I had such plans for her, and now she's let us all down.' She stopped, aware that her mother was looking at her curiously; sadly, but with a tiny flickering of a smile. 'Well, aren't you annoyed with her, Mam? For goodness' sake, she's only eighteen. It's not a scrap of good you sympathising with her. She needs a damn good hiding.'

'Hold on a minute, Rachel,' said her mother calmly. 'I think you're forgetting something, aren't you? Think back. How old were *you* when you told me you were expecting Harry Balderstone's baby?'

A flush, both of guilt and annoyance, tinged Rachel's cheeks. Trust her mother to bring that up. She, Rachel, hadn't forgotten, but it was ages ago. Besides, it was different. 'That's got nothing to do with it,' she retorted. 'I was older anyway.'

'Not all that much. You were twenty.'

'And I'd been friendly with Harry for ages, all the time he was in France. Anyway, I wasn't pregnant, was I? It was a false alarm.'

'Oh, so that makes it all right, does it? Because you got away with it, then it doesn't matter? Whereas your daughter – who has only done the same as you did – is a wicked girl who needs punishing.'

'I haven't said that, Mam.' Rachel hung her head, beginning to feel ashamed. 'I was cross with her, I'll admit.

Perhaps I shouldn't have said all I did, but it was such a shock.'

'It was a shock for me, too, all those years ago,' said Ellen quietly. 'It's always a shock, but you'll get over it. You must, for Emmie's sake. It's only your pride that's hurt, Rachel, and you'll have to pocket your pride. Do you really think it matters a damn what the neighbours might think, or your friends or family, or anybody? It's your daughter that matters and you've got to give her your full support. If you don't, then nobody else can. Pride is a far worse sin, my dear, than the one she's committed and don't you forget it. You must forgive her – show her you care about her – and help her to get on with her life.'

Rachel could feel the tears pricking at her eyelids, then the next moment they were running uncontrollably down her cheeks. 'Oh, Mam,' she cried, 'I didn't mean it. I didn't mean to go on at her like that. But I've had so much, I can't stand any more. First our Ruby, and now this. Oh Mam, what else is this war going to do to us?'

'I don't know, love, but whatever it does, we've got one another. And we've got to stick together and help Emmie now.' Her mother was at her side, her comforting arms holding her as they had when she was a child; and Rachel knew that her own daughter, whatever she had done, was deserving of the same sort of love and assurance.

'I'll sort it out with her, Mam,' she said now. 'I won't be angry any more.'

Emmie's mother was waiting for her when she came home from the hospital. She didn't even wait for Emmie to take her coat off.

'I'm sorry about what I said,' she began. 'It was wrong of me to say those things about you, and I'm sorry.'

It was the first time Emmie could ever remember her mother apologising and she was so relieved that she felt like hugging her. But she didn't. They had both said some very

276

wounding things and it would take a little time for everything to get back to normal between them. But at least they were talking. 'It's all right, Mum,' said Emmie. 'I know you were upset.'

'And I do care, you know – about you, as well as Pearl, and Ruby.'

'I know you do, Mum.'

'Well, you'd better write to Gene, hadn't you, and see if he can come over for a weekend. Don't worry; I won't be cross with him. And then we'd better see if we can arrange a wedding. Another wedding . . .'

Her mother actually smiled, though rather sadly, and Emmie knew she was thinking about Ruby's wedding, the one that had never taken place.

Chapter 20

Pearl was bemused. She had returned to Yorkshire fully
believing that, with a little signal from her, she and Ralph
would be able to resume their friendship at that deeper
level, where they had left off, the day she had turned him
down. He would take the hint, surely, if she smiled at him
a little more, went out of her way to help him and be near
him, and, above all, showed him that she enjoyed his
company. The fact that he now had another ladyfriend,
Nora, from a nearby farm, didn't figure largely in Pearl's
strategy. If he had been serious about Nora he would have
done something about it by now, wouldn't he? Got engaged
or at least asked her to marry him. But Nora, a red-
cheeked country girl – a typical farmer's wife – didn't
seem to be on the scene all that much. When Ralph did
invite her for tea, the pair just seemed like good friends
rather than a courting couple.

Yet despite her gentle scheming, Ralph appeared un-
moved. A few weeks into the New Year – 1943 – she was no
closer to him than she had been when she went home at
Christmas. Sometimes she thought she detected a gleam of
something or other in his eyes – amusement, awareness,
perhaps, of what she was up to – but the next minute it would
have gone and he was talking to her quite normally. But
only, to her chagrin, as one farmworker to another.

He had been sympathetic about Emmie, but optimistic.
'It's wartime,' he said consolingly, 'and these things happen.
It must be a shock for your mother, I can see that, especially

after . . . your other sister. But it's a new life coming into the world, isn't it? And your mother's sure to be thrilled about that – her first grandchild. They're getting married soon, you say?'

'Yes – the middle of March.'

'Do you want some time off to go to the wedding?'

'No, thanks all the same, Ralph. I don't think so,' said Pearl. 'It's going to be a very quiet affair – in church, of course – Mum wouldn't have stood for a Register Office, not under any circumstances, but there won't be many people there. Just Mum and Dad – if he can get some leave – and Gran, and Sally and George. Oh, and Gloria – you know, our little evacuee. She's going to be a bridesmaid, apparently. Not a fancy, dressed-up one because Emmie can't wear white, but I expect Gloria will be thrilled about it. She's a nice little kid. I don't know what we'd do without her now.'

Ralph smiled understandingly. 'Sure you don't want to be there?'

'No, I'm not due for any leave and it wouldn't be fair. I'll have a few days at Easter, like we arranged.'

'OK then. If you change your mind just let me know.'

As it happened, Pearl was to go home a few weeks before Easter. It was the very beginning of March when her mother made a long-distance call to the farm, the first time she had ever done so, asking for Pearl to come home at once.

Emmie felt as though she were in a dream throughout the month of February. Gene had come over as soon as she had told him the news. Suitably contrite, but at the same time assuring Rachel of his love for her daughter, he had said that of course they would get married, just as soon as it could be arranged.

Together, Rachel and Emmie had chosen a nice turquoise-blue suit, and a hat to match, from Sally Mae's dress shop, for Emmie to be married in. (It had taken some of Rachel's, as well as Emmie's, allowance of clothing coupons.) And Sally was making a dress of a slightly darker shade of turquoise for Gloria to wear. She was to be the bridesmaid and Marvin, Gene's mate from the camp, the best man.

Emmie had felt slightly embarrassed at meeting Gloria again. She knew that Sally would have told her why she and Gene were getting married in such a hurry. As Gloria had said, Sally didn't believe in keeping secrets from her.

'Would you like to see my suit?' Emmie asked, as a way of breaking the ice. 'The one I'm wearing for the wedding.'

'Ooh, yes please,' said Gloria, as Emmie opened the wardrobe door. 'I bet you're real excited, aren't you?'

'Mmm . . . sort of,' said Emmie, as she removed the tissue-paper covering from the suit, holding it out for Gloria's inspection. Excited was not really the word to describe how she felt. Bewildered, slightly incredulous, would be nearer the mark.

'Gosh, that's super!' said Gloria, gently fingering the silky rayon crepe material. It was more of a dress and blouse than an actual suit. A skirt might have been somewhat tight when it came to the day, although Emmie had noticed very little change in her figure as yet, just a slight thickening of her waistline and swelling of her breasts. And she seemed to have escaped the dreaded morning sickness, only ex-periencing a tinge of queasiness, usually in the evenings. This dress was very pretty, ideal for any wartime wedding, with a neckline opening low to reveal a cream blouse underneath, a dainty bow trim at the waist and a gently gathered knee-length skirt.

'You'll look beautiful in that, Emmie,' said Gloria, gazing at her enthralled. 'Can I . . . d'you think I could come to the wedding, with Auntie Sally and Uncle George, and your gran? I've heard them say that you're not having many people there,' she added, 'so I wondered . . .'

'Of course you'll be coming,' said Emmie. 'As if I'd leave you out – what an idea! As a matter of fact, I was wondering if you'd like to be my bridesmaid? Auntie Sally has been making you a dress as a surprise, Gloria. I can tell you that now!' She hugged the ecstatic girl.

'I've never ever been a bridesmaid,' Gloria breathed, 'not even when our Monica got married and me brothers, an' I never thought I would be. Thanks ever so much, Emmie. What'll your mam say? Have you told her?'

'No, not yet,' replied Emmie. 'But I don't see why she should object. It's my wedding, isn't it, so I can ask who I like to be my bridesmaid. And I'd like *you*.' Gloria was nodding raptly, smiling first at Emmie, then at the pretty dress on its hanger.

'Gloria . . . you know I'm having a baby, don't you?' said Emmie.

'Yes,' said Gloria, quite unconcernedly. 'Auntie Sally told me. She said that you and Gene loved one another very much and that was what had happened. That you were having a baby.'

'You know about babies then, do you . . . and all that?'

''Course I do. I'll be thirteen next birthday, y'know. They told us a bit about it at school ─ in Biology, like; mostly about frogs and birds and things, but I already knew a lot of it. Me mam was always having babies, and our Monica's got three. An' I think I know how they get there. I've seen dogs, you see.'

Emmie smiled, a little embarrassed by Gloria's forthrightness. No doubt her young friend knew more about the facts of life than she had done at twelve years of age!

Anyway, it wouldn't be long now till the wedding day, and then she and Gene would have one night together at least before he had to return to camp – under her mother's roof, she supposed, which wasn't ideal, but they had no choice. Elaborate white weddings and glamorous honeymoons were not for couples who had transgressed, as they had; or for very few couples, for that matter, in wartime.

There was no problem about Gene getting permission to

marry as he was now turned twenty-one, and Emmie supposed he had written to tell his parents, far away in San Francisco. That was the part that seemed most unreal, that one day, when the war was over, she would be going there to live with Gene as his wife. It was something that she and her mother had never discussed and Emmie knew that Rachel must be closing her mind to this fact. All that mattered now to Rachel was to get the young couple married as soon as possible. Fortunately Emmie and her mother were quite good friends again and there had been no more recriminations.

It was the beginning of March when the letter arrived. Rachel handed it to Emmie when she came home from the hospital.

'Here you are, dear. Another letter from Gene. It beats me how he finds time to write all these letters . . . or think of things to say. You only saw him at the weekend. Still, it shows he's thinking about you.' Her mother's smile was sympathetic and Emmie felt glad about that. Little by little Mum was coming round.

She glanced at the envelope. 'No, I don't think it's from Gene,' she said. 'It's not his writing.' Hastily she tore the letter open and scanned the contents. Then, 'Oh no,' she breathed, her voice the merest whisper. 'No, no, not Gene . . . He can't be . . .' The sheets of paper fluttered to the floor as Emmie collapsed in a dead faint.

Rachel was at her side in an instant. 'Emmie love, whatever is it?' She cradled her daughter's head and shoulders in her arms. 'Oh Emmie, speak to me, love! Thank God,' she sighed, as Emmie's eyelids flickered and she opened her eyes again. She was coming round. For one awful moment Rachel's anguished mind had feared that she was dead. The letter must have contained something dreadful, though, for her to have passed out like that.

Rachel reached for the letter and glanced at the signature at the end – Marvin Weber. Marvin . . . that was the young man who was to have been Gene's best man. And now he was writing to tell Emmie that Gene had been killed. 'Oh, my poor darling,' wept Rachel, stroking her daughter's hair as she quickly scanned the pages. It had happened on a training flight. The crew had been having some problem with the plane and Gene had gone up with them ... Rachel remembered that he had been training to be a flight engineer. But a training flight, for God's sake! There would have been more sense to it if it had been a bombing raid. It would still have been tragic, but it would have been easier to understand. The plane had got into serious trouble and had crashed on the return flight, very near to the camp. All the crew had been killed.

Marvin, as Gene's best mate, was the one who had to tell Emmie. They had promised one another, he and Gene, he wrote, that if anything was to go wrong then they would pass on the sad news. No, Emmie would not have been notified officially, thought Rachel. She was not a relative; the couple had not even been officially engaged. They were just getting married in a hurry because a baby was on the way. And now that baby would have no father.

All these thoughts ran through Rachel's tortured mind as she read the letter, still cradling her daughter in her arms. Emmie had come round and was now crying quietly. Gene could never have anticipated that Marvin might have to carry out his grave promise, not so soon, at any rate. Gene should not have been in any real danger; he was only doing his training, not yet engaged in bombing missions. Just as Ruby should not have been in peril of her life, working in a store room. Oh, the sheer wicked waste of it all! This accursed war!

Pearl listened horror-struck to her mother's voice coming through the telephone wires. She had to ask her to repeat her words because she couldn't grasp the enormity of what Rachel was saying. Gene ... killed? And could she, Pearl, come home? No, there wasn't anything she could do, not really, but Rachel needed her and so did Emmie. Her father wouldn't be able to get leave – it wasn't really a family bereavement – but if Mr and Mrs Butterfield could see their way to letting Pearl come home for a few days . . .

'My dear, whatever is it?' Mrs Butterfield took one look at Pearl's face when she returned to the farm kitchen and immediately she was surrounded by such care and concern that it was difficult to stem her tears. But she tried, telling them as calmly as she could what had happened, asking if she could possibly have a few days' leave as her family needed her.

'You're due for leave anyroad at Easter, aren't you?' said Bill Butterfield gently. 'You can tek it a bit earlier. Dearie me – that poor lass. You tek as long as you like.' He looked at Mrs Butterfield and she nodded vehemently. 'You're a good worker – you are that – and it's about time you had a break.'

'Thank you,' said Pearl. That, from Bill, was praise indeed. She was aware of Ralph's solicitous glances although he said little while his parents were present. But it was Ralph who ran her to the station the next morning in the farm truck.

'Take care of yourself, now,' he said as he put her case down on the platform. 'I'd best be off, though. I won't wait for the train to come in, if you don't mind. There's work to do, an' I told the old man I wouldn't be long. Take care,' he said again. He hesitated, then, as if obeying an impulse, he put his arm round her shoulders and kissed her cheek. 'Tara, luv. I'll be thinking about you.' Then he was gone and Pearl, in spite of her sadness, felt an uplifting of her spirits.

When Pearl had been at home for the best part of a week, Emmie went to stay with her mother's cousin, Charlie, and his wife at their small-holding in Woodplumpton, near Preston. They kept poultry, as well as having a market garden, and it was felt that the country air and a complete change of surroundings would be beneficial to her.

George had phoned the camp the day the letter arrived, as he had done about Ruby, to make absolutely sure that what Gene's mate, Marvin, had written was to be believed. And, alas, it was. Emmie had expressed no wish to be present at Gene's funeral and Rachel felt that this was for the best. They had no idea, indeed, when the funeral would be. It would be a military affair, no doubt, arranged by the camp authorities for the five young GIs who had died, so far from home, while seeking to serve not only their own country, but the little island they had pledged themselves to help. What a tragic waste of young lives, thought Rachel. And when, oh when was something good going to happen to their family?

It was Rachel who answered the knock at the door at about six o'clock in the evening. She had not long been in from work – she had taken a day or two off to be with Emmie, but had now returned – and Pearl was busy in the kitchen preparing their meal. She looked uncertainly at the young man standing on the doorstep; an ordinary sort of fellow – not in uniform, which was rather surprising – lean-featured, but very healthy-looking, with fair hair flopping across his brow under his brown trilby hat, deepset grey eyes . . . and a most pleasant smile. Even before he spoke she had made a guess as to who this might be.

'Hello,' he said. 'I know I've come to the right house, because you're so much like your daughter. You're Pearl's mother, aren't you? How do you do, Mrs Balderstone?' He held out his hand. 'I'm Ralph Butterfield, Pearl's friend.'

'How do you do, Mr Butterfield. What a lovely surprise.' Rachel eagerly shook his hand. 'There's nothing wrong, is there?' she asked. So much had gone wrong lately, but surely there couldn't be because he looked so cheerful.

'No, not at all. I've come to take Pearl back. I thought I'd be company for her on the return journey. And . . . I wanted to see you.'

'Well, come in, come in. Pearl will be delighted, I'm sure.'

She noticed he was carrying a small case. 'You're staying? Well, of course you must be. How silly of me. We'll be only too pleased to put you up for the night. Or two? Pearl said she'd go back on Saturday, didn't she?' Today was Thursday.

'I don't want to presume, Mrs Balderstone,' said Ralph. 'I intended putting up at a boarding house, but the train was late so I decided to come straight here.'

'You'll do no such thing,' said Rachel emphatically. 'I won't hear of it. Pearl – look who's here. You'll never guess.'

There was no mistaking the astonishment and delight on Pearl's face at seeing Ralph, or the quiet pleasure that Ralph showed at seeing her. It was only after they had eaten their meal and Pearl was making up the bed in Emmie's room that Ralph told Rachel his real reason for coming.

'Mrs Balderstone,' he said, leaning forward earnestly. 'I've come to ask you if I may marry your daughter. Mr Balderstone's not here, so I'm asking you instead.'

To say that Rachel was surprised was putting it mildly. 'Well, of course you may,' she stuttered. 'This is wonderful news! But shouldn't you be asking *Pearl*, not me? She's well turned twenty-one, you know, and she knows her own mind.'

There was a twinkle in Ralph's eyes as he replied. 'I'm not so sure that Pearl does always know her own mind. I asked her once before, you see, and she turned me down. I'm a proud sort of fellow, Mrs Balderstone, and a stubborn one an' all – I'm not ashamed to admit it; Yorkshire folk can be a bit pig-headed. Anyroad, I'd made up me mind I'd never ask her again, and I think she knows it an' all. So I'm asking you instead. Please may I marry your daughter? I do love her very much, and I'll take good care of her.'

'Yes, of course,' said Rachel, bursting out laughing. It was the first time she had laughed in ages. 'But hadn't we better wait and see what she says about it? She's here now . . .'

'What's going on?' asked Pearl as she entered the room. She looked at Ralph's amused smile, and at her mother . . . actually laughing. 'Am I missing something?'

286

'No, not a lot,' said Ralph. 'I've just asked your mother if she'll agree to you and me getting wed, that's all. And she's said yes.'

'You've *what*!' Though Pearl tried to stop it, a grin spread all over her face. 'But don't you think you'd better ask me,' she stammered, 'before you start arranging my life for me?'

'Ask you?' said Ralph. 'Not on your life! I'm not going to risk being turned down again.'

'I've something to see to in the kitchen,' said Rachel, making a hasty retreat. And Pearl, seeing the roguish grin on Ralph's face, knew that what he said was true. He wouldn't ask her again; it was what she had feared all along. But she was going to marry him and that was all that mattered.

'Ralph, I'd love to be your wife,' she said. The next minute his arms were round her and his lips came down on hers in a kiss that both of them knew meant, This is for ever. When Rachel re-entered the room a few minutes later she hastily withdrew again. They hadn't even seen her and she had plenty of jobs to do.

When Pearl and Ralph departed for Yorkshire a day and a half later she was wearing an engagement ring, a small cluster of rubies and diamonds in an old-fashioned setting that had belonged to Ralph's grandmother. He had let his parents into the secret and Amy Butterfield had insisted that Pearl should have the ring, a family heirloom. Pearl knew that both Bill and Amy would welcome her as their own daughter.

They were to be married in October at the village church near to the farm in Wensleydale. They had decided they must wait until after Emmie's baby was born in September. It could be upsetting for her sister, Pearl had pointed out, if wedding plans were going ahead too hastily when hers had been so cruelly wrecked.

It had been Pearl's own idea that she should wear the dress that Sally had made for Ruby. She was a practical-minded girl, not given to superstition, and it seemed to her to be

287

fitting, somehow, as though they were including her sister in the celebrations.

'So long as you don't wear the same headdress and veil,' said Sally, pinning a seam down the centre back so that the dress would fit the slightly slimmer girl. 'Ruby was going to wear mine, you know. I'd lend them to you gladly, love, but I think perhaps . . .'

'It's all right, Auntie Sally,' said Pearl. 'I'm going to borrow Mum's. We've already sorted that out. And would you ask Gloria if she'd like to be my bridesmaid? It must have been very disappointing for her when Emmie's wedding didn't take place.'

'Yes, it was, but she was sad, more than disappointed,' said Sally. 'Sad for Emmie, like we all were. Gloria's a very thoughtful girl. Thank you for asking her, Pearl. I'll tell her when she comes in from school. And she can wear the turquoise dress I made for her, if that's all right with you? I've got some material left, so I can make it into a full-length dress if I put a frill round the bottom.'

'It's the first time I've been to Blackpool,' said Ralph, the night before they went back. They were standing on the lower promenade watching the sun sink behind the sea, painting the clouds in glowing colours of rose pink and fiery orange and setting a million golden coins dancing on the darkening waves. 'To tell you the truth, I'd never fancied it much. All fish and chips and kiss-me-quick hats, I thought it'd be.'

'And sticks of rock,' said Pearl, laughing. 'You mustn't forget the rock.'

'Oh aye, the rock,' grinned Ralph. 'We'd best not forget Hobson's Rock – The Only Choice. Yes, I never thought I'd take to the place, but I'm changing my mind. I've never seen such a glorious sunset anywhere.'

'Not even in Yorkshire?' said Pearl, snuggling closer to him.

'No, not even there.' Ralph bent to kiss her. 'Blackpool's a grand place, I'll admit it. But Yorkshire's going to be your real home from now on, isn't it, luv?'

'I'm not complaining,' said Pearl.

Chapter 21

Emmie's baby, a boy, was born on 17 September 1943 at her own home. The birth was comparatively easy and she was soon ready to receive visitors.

'What are you going to call him?' they all asked – her gran, George, Sally and Gloria – as, one by one, they peeped reverently at the tiny infant, cocooned in blankets, fast asleep in the cot at the side of Emmie's bed.

'Lawrence,' said Emmie, without hesitation. 'I'd really like to call him Gene, but I suppose it's too American. Gloria once told me it sounded like a girl's name.' She smiled at her young friend. 'But as Gene's surname was Lawrenson I thought I'd call him Lawrence.'

'Very nice too,' said Ellen. 'It's something a bit different. We've never had a Lawrence in the family.'

'I'd like his middle name to be Benjamin,' said Emmie, smiling now at her grandmother. 'I never knew my grandfather, Ben – well, my step-grandfather he'd have been, wouldn't he? – but everyone speaks so highly of him. If my little boy is called after him – and Gene – then I don't think he'll go far wrong.'

'Thank you, dear,' said Ellen quietly, finding that her eyes were beginning to fill up with tears. 'I think that's a lovely idea. God bless you, love, and the baby. Lawrence Benjamin. He's going to be a blessing to us, that little boy, I can feel it already.'

Ellen was more relieved than she could say that this baby had arrived safely. Ever since she had heard of Gene's death she had been tormented by the idea that 'things go in threes'. She knew it was a ridiculous superstitious notion, a relic from Victorian times, but she had found herself waiting on tenterhooks for a third death to occur, until she chided herself for being stupid. Then, as time went on, she managed to convince herself that they had already had their three tragedies, if she counted George's accident. George, Ruby and Gene. Yes, they had had more than their fair share of sadness in this family. Now, for a change, maybe things might start to go right for them. The birth of this beautiful baby seemed to be a good omen, and then there was Pearl's wedding next month. Life, suddenly, seemed much more full of promise and Ellen felt, at last, that she might dare to look forward to the future without fear.

Emmie hadn't minded being left at home whilst the rest of the family travelled to Yorkshire for Pearl's wedding. For one thing, it was a long journey to make with such a small baby, and for another, she knew that witnessing a marriage ceremony would have been upsetting for her. She was now much more at peace with herself and her situation. All her family were being so kind and helpful towards her that she felt she owed it to them to be cheerful and optimistic, outwardly at least. Someday, maybe, she might be able to start again with her career where she had left off and become a fully qualified State Registered Nurse. Who could tell what the future might hold? For the time being she had to live one day at a time, just as everyone else was doing, hoping and praying that the war would soon come to an end.

It was whilst her family was away in Yorkshire that Emmie had a visitor. She opened the door one afternoon to a figure in the familiar Air Force blue. Familiar because in Blackpool, even in the fourth year of the war, the RAF lads were everywhere. This one was – Davey Clarkson!

'Hello there, Emmie. I just thought I'd come and look you up.' He was as cheerful as ever, and any embarrassment she might have felt at seeing him again soon abated.

Baby Lawrence was asleep in the large pram which Emmie had wheeled into the living room. It was warmer for him down here than upstairs in a chilly bedroom. That was what she told herself, but really it was because, even though he was now a month old, she couldn't resist having a peep at him every few minutes.

'Did you know . . . ?' she began, motioning towards the pram. It was impossible not to notice it; it dominated the living room.

'Yes, I know about the baby. A little boy, isn't it?' Davey smiled easily. 'My mother told me. That's one of the reasons I've come. To see the baby – as well as you – and to bring you this. Mum's made them for you. She hopes they'll fit him all right.'

Emmie was touched beyond words as she drew from the brown paper bag two pairs of tiny bootees, one white and one blue, beautifully knitted in fine wool and threaded with satin ribbon. 'They're lovely, Davey,' she breathed. 'It's so kind of her. So many people have been so very kind, I just can't believe it.'

She had written to tell Davey, when she first met Gene, what the situation was; that she had become very friendly with a young American and therefore it might be as well if she didn't write to him, Davey, quite so frequently, just every now and again. It wouldn't have been fair to let him think that the two of them might have a future together when the war was over. She hadn't written to tell him she was expecting a baby, nor about Gene's death, but she supposed she shouldn't be too surprised that he knew. News – especially news such as this – travelled fast on a local grapevine, even though her family and Davey's didn't live in the same area.

'Why shouldn't folk be kind?' said Davey, taking off his greatcoat and sitting down in an easy chair. 'It was a bad do about your boyfriend, Emmie. I was so sorry to hear about that – and your sister. But I believe your other sister's getting married? This week, isn't it?'

'Yes, that's why I'm on my own,' said Emmie. She laughed quietly, shaking her head. 'Goodness me, there's not much I can tell you, is there, Davey? You seem to know it all already.'

He nodded. 'It's great to see you again, Emmie. It really is. You don't mind if I stay for a little while, do you? I've made myself at home, you see.'

'No, of course I don't mind. It's good to see you, too.' She smiled warmly at him. 'You're on leave, I take it? Just a forty-eight-hour pass, is it?'

'No, rather more than that this time.'

'Why? You're not preparing for something special, are you?' She was instantly alert, and apprehensive. 'You're not going to fly?'

'No, nothing like that. I'm a flight mechanic, that's all. I just tinker about with the planes; I don't go up in them. I was due for a spot of leave though, so I'm here for the best part of a week. Now, are you going to make me a cup of tea, or am I going to sit here for ever with my tongue hanging out? While you're making it I'll take a peek at this baby of yours.'

'Of course.' She grinned at him, feeling a spontaneous lifting of at least some part of her sorrow. She remembered that Davey had always had this effect on her. 'Don't wake him up though, will you?'

They chatted for more than an hour, about inconsequential things – mutual friends, their families, the fun they had had on the St John's Ambulance course; never once touching on the more serious war news – and Davey left her with the promise that he would call and see her again before he went back to camp. She knew that her mother would have returned home by that time, but it didn't matter. She had an idea that Rachel, with her changed outlook, might be quite pleased to welcome Davey.

One Saturday afternoon at the beginning of November, Gloria

was mooching around the Blackpool Woolworth's, feeling a bit flat after the excitement of Pearl's wedding, when she caught sight of a familiar figure. Her heart missed a beat as she stared at the lad in RAF uniform standing by the next counter, the one that sold men's things like razor-blades and shaving cream. Yes, it was Arthur, her stepbrother, rather fatter in the face and more broad-shouldered, but it was definitely him. She hadn't even known he was in the RAF, but he would be about the right age. She was thirteen so he must be nineteen or thereabouts.

As he turned towards her the light of recognition dawned in his eyes and he hurried over to her.

'Well, well, well, if it isn't my little sister. Our Gloria. Hiya, kid. How yer doin'?'

'I'm very well, thank you, Arthur,' she replied. 'How are you?'

'Me? I'm just fine and dandy, darling. And all the better for seeing you. Haven't you grown up, though? Strike a light, I hardly recognised you! And talk about posh! Crikey, where d'you learn to talk like that, as if you've got a bloomin' plum in yer mouth?'

'Shurrup, Arthur. I don't talk posh,' said Gloria, a little testily. 'I just talk the way they do here, the people I live with at any rate. 'Course, you wouldn't know, would you? I haven't seen any of you for ages. Or heard from you.' A slight hurt at her family's treatment of her had resurged on seeing Arthur. There had been no news from Salford for a long time, not from any of them, even Monica.

'How's me mam?' she asked now. 'And Rose and Lily and Vinnie? An' our Frankie?' If Arthur had joined up, then it was likely that her brother, Frankie, had as well.

'Frankie's in the Army,' replied Arthur. 'Stationed up in the wilds of Yorkshire somewhere.'

Gloria nodded. 'And what about our Monica? She used to come and see me, but she hasn't been since . . . oh, I can't remember when.'

'They're all OK, I suppose,' her stepbrother shrugged. 'Don't see much of 'em meself. To tell the truth, I was bloody glad to get away from all them kids, an' I never did see much of Monica.' After all, Gloria reasoned, Monica was only his stepsister, and Daisy Mulligan was not his real mother. 'Me old man's still working on the bins,' he went on. Bill Mulligan was the one that Gloria hadn't bothered to ask about. 'And Daisy – yer mam – well, she's not been too good lately, one way and another. Come on, our kid, let's go and have a cup of tea somewhere and I'll tell you about 'em all. I'm sure this Auntie Ellen whoever she is won't mind you having a quick cup o' tea with yer brother,' he said, placing his hand companionably under her elbow and leading her out of the store.

Lockhart's café was just across the road and they sat at a window table overlooking the narrow Bank Hey Street, crowded with Saturday-afternoon shoppers.

'What's up with me mam then?' asked Gloria, in between sips of her tea. 'You said she hadn't been too well.'

'Yeah, well – I'm afraid she's up the spout.'

'What?' Gloria frowned, wrinkling her nose. Daisy was too old, surely? She couldn't be pregnant at her age.

'She's too old to be having a baby,' said Gloria in a quiet little voice. She had gone quite cold at the thought, though she wasn't sure why.

'Let's see, how old will she be?' wondered Arthur. 'I've never really thought about it all that much.'

'Our Monica's about thirty now,' said Gloria, 'and she's the eldest. So me mam must be getting on for fifty, mustn't she?'

'A bit younger than that, I reckon. She probably started having kids when she was only a kid herself. She looks older though. Always has done. That's having to put up with my old man, I daresay.' Arthur gave a coarse laugh. 'He's enough to put years on anybody.'

'So when's the baby going to be born?' asked Gloria, still in a state of shock.

Arthur shrugged. 'Dunno exactly. In a week or two I reckon. Like I said, she weren't too good. High blood pressure or summat. Her legs were all swollen and she were supposed to rest. Fat chance of that, with all them kids.'

'But I expect our Monica would help her?'

'Oh aye, happen so. As much as she could. She's got three of her own though.'

'Sam and Len must be at school now, aren't they?' asked Gloria. All these things were going on, back in Salford, and she hadn't heard so much as a whisper.

'I 'spect so,' replied Arthur, very off-handedly. 'I've told yer, kid, I don't see much of 'em at all. I hope Daisy'll be all right. She was always OK with me, I've got to say. She's not a bad old girl. I've told her, she should tell me dad to tie a knot in it . . . Oh sorry, luv. Have I offended you?' For Gloria had cast her eyes downwards and could feel herself blushing.

'Aye, you were always a bit of a Goody-Two Shoes, weren't you?' Arthur grinned. Then he sighed and said, 'But you're a real pretty girl though, honest you are. I always knew you'd grow up to be a real smasher. How are you, kid, honestly? You're happy here, are you?'

'Yes, I'm very happy, Arthur,' replied Gloria. 'Salford seems . . . I dunno – a long way away. A long time ago.'

'That's their fault, i'n't it, not yours? I was going to look you up when I first came to Blackpool, about two months ago. Then didn't get round to it. I thought I might run into you,' Arthur went on. 'I'm glad I have. An' I'm glad you're happy here. They wouldn't know you back home now. You're not scruffy little Gloria Mulligan any more, eh?'

'No.' Gloria felt sad all of a sudden, about lots of things. 'I'm sorry about me mam not being well. I'll write to her, I think. I'll tell her I've seen you.' She stood up. 'I'd better be going, Arthur. Thanks for the tea.'

'I'll walk you back. Where is it you live?'

'King Street. It's only up this road and round the corner. I'll be OK on my own, honest.'

Dusk was creeping in early on this November afternoon and Gloria knew that she should have been home a good half-hour ago. Ellen would be getting worried, although Sally would not yet be back from work. She helped at one of the shops on a Saturday afternoon, as it was their busiest time. She knew it would be churlish and unreasonable not to walk back with Arthur but she insisted that he should leave her at the end of King Street, and after she had bade him a hasty goodbye she hurried the rest of the way home. Ellen would, no doubt, be looking out of the window and Gloria wanted to explain about meeting her stepbrother in her own good time.

'I think they might have let me know about me mam, don't you, Auntie Sally?' asked Gloria. She had told them the whole story, about how she had met Arthur in town, after they had all finished their teas.

'When the baby's born they're sure to let you know,' said Sally. 'Maybe your mum didn't want you to worry about her. Or maybe she just wanted it to be a nice big surprise.' But Gloria was right, thought Sally. Of course they should have let her know. You would have thought that Monica, of all of them, might have written, but they had seen neither hide nor hair of that young woman for ages. Which suited Sally just fine, if she were honest, but she did so hate to see Gloria upset.

Gloria recounted what Arthur had said, about her mother's blood pressure and swollen legs and how she was worn out looking after the kiddies. 'So I 'spect she's been too busy to write,' she said finally. 'I think I'll write to her instead.'

'I think that would be a very nice idea,' said Sally gently.

'That poor woman,' Ellen sighed, when Gloria had gone to bed, 'having a child at her age. It doesn't bear thinking of, does it, with all the others she's got. She's probably too embarrassed to write and tell Gloria.'

'I doubt it, Mam,' said Sally. 'I can't see Daisy Mulligan

being embarrassed about anything. No, the poor woman's probably too exhausted to think straight. But I do think Monica might have let us know.'

Gloria duly wrote her letter, but there was no reply. She didn't mention the fact and neither did Sally nor Ellen, but they could see she was disappointed when, each morning, the postman failed to deliver the expected letter. And then, early in December a letter from Salford arrived, but it was addressed to Mrs E. Hobson, not to Gloria. Ellen, feeling a premonition about it, hid it away and didn't open it until Gloria had gone to school. As Sally and George had already gone to work she was on her own when she read it.

Dear Mrs Hobson and Sally, she read. *I am sorry to tell you that my mother, Daisy Mulligan, past away yesterday. She was having a baby and there were complicashuns. She died soon after the baby was born and the baby died too which is a blessing I supose. It were a little boy. Could you brake the news to Gloria please? You will know how to do it. The funeral is on Friday but we don't think its any use Gloria coming she would be to upset. I'm sorry I haven't been to see her for a wile I've been very busy. Anyway I'm coming to see you on Sunday. I hope that's OK. I'll get the 10 o'clock train. So I'll see you then. Yours sinceerly, Monica O'Brien.*

Ellen's stunned reaction, once she had digested this terrible news, was that here was the third death, the one that all along she had been anticipating, but not knowing who it might be. She couldn't face up to telling Gloria on her own, so decided to wait until Sally came in from work. She managed to snatch a few minutes alone with her daughter-in-law.

'Good gracious,' said Sally, hastily scanning the letter. 'This is dreadful news. That poor woman . . . and all those children left behind. How ever are we going to tell Gloria? Poor girl. It is her mother when all's said and done.'

'Gloria'll be all right,' said Ellen, putting an arm round

298

Sally's shoulders. 'You'll see. She's a tough little thing. I know she's got a gentle, caring side too, but it isn't as if she really knew her mother all that well, from what she's said. And she hadn't seen her for ages. And can't you see, Sally?' she added excitedly. 'It might mean she can stay with us now. That man isn't her real father, is he?'

'No, but there's Monica,' said Sally slowly.

'She's only her sister, and she's got three kiddies of her own,' Ellen rushed on. 'Look, Sal, I'm really sorry about Daisy Mulligan, but it might turn out to be all for the best in the long run.'

'Best for us, perhaps,' said Sally thoughtfully. 'Not for Daisy. Although, come to think of it, she didn't have much of a life. Maybe she's better out of it all. I don't know, Mam.' She sighed. 'What's worrying me at the moment is telling Gloria.'

Ellen had been right. The girl looked serious, sad even, on hearing the news, but she didn't cry. She didn't say very much at all except to wonder what would happen to all the children.

'They'll be all right. They've still got your dad – Bill, I mean,' said Sally. 'He'll make some arrangements, won't he, for somebody to look after them while he's at work? And they're all at school now, aren't they, most of the time?' He was their real father after all, thought Sally. Surely he would face up to his responsibilities. At all events she didn't want Gloria to be worrying about it.

'I don't know,' replied Gloria dispiritedly. 'I don't know whether our Vinnie's at school yet. He's only four. I don't know much at all, do I? About any of them. Anyway, our Monica's coming, isn't she? It'll be nice to see her again.

'What's the matter with me, Auntie Sally?' Gloria asked the next day. 'I'm sorry about me mam an' all that, but I can't cry. Not like I did when Ruby died, and Emmie's boyfriend – an' I didn't know him very well. I'm awful, aren't I?'

'No dear, not at all,' said Sally, giving her a quick hug. 'It's probably because it doesn't seem very real to you. You were only a little girl, weren't you, when you lived in Salford, and now you're quite a grown-up young lady. It must seem a very long time since you lived there.'

'Yes, it does.' Gloria nodded. 'I 'spect that's what it is. And now I live here, don't I, Auntie Sally?' She looked anxious, frightened almost, for a moment.

'Of course you do, love,' Sally said reassuringly. 'This is your home now.'

Monica O'Brien arrived soon after midday the following Sunday. To their surprise she was on her own and she quickly explained she had left her three children in the care of a good neighbour. Ellen had cooked a big enough leg of mutton for all of them – she had a very obliging butcher – but it didn't matter as it would now last for a day or two.

Sally was aware of a certain edginess in the young woman's manner. She had greeted Gloria warmly and the rest of the family politely, but she seemed somewhat ill-at-ease. Sally put it down to her recent bereavement. She was dressed almost entirely in black; black dress and cardigan, black shoes and hat, except for her tweed coat, on the sleeve of which was stitched a little black diamond.

Conversation was stilted during the meal. Gloria tried to tell her sister about the Grammar School she had been attending for over a year now, but Monica seemed pre-occupied and Gloria nowhere near as voluble as usual. And, in turn, accounts of what was happening in Salford – Sam and Len, Rose and Lily at school, even news of Doreen and Susan Aspinall and their twin brothers – seemed to have little impact on Gloria. That was only to be expected, thought Sally. The girl couldn't pretend to show a great deal of interest in what her sister was saying when she had left her alone for so long. Rather strangely, Monica had, as yet, made little reference to her mother. Ellen, Sally and George had expressed their sympathy as soon as they saw her, and she had spoken briefly about the funeral. It had all gone off very nicely, she said. The church had been nearly half full of friends and neighbours and Father O'Leary had spoken very kindly about Daisy.

It was when the meal was over, George had departed for a fishing trip, and all the women were sitting round the fire, drinking the habitual cup of tea, that Monica brought up the subject of her mother again. It was Sally, mainly, whom she seemed to be addressing, although her glance – an uneasy glance, Sally thought – took in them all from time to time.

'I'm sorry,' she began, 'that Mam didn't keep in touch more with Gloria here.' She cast an apprehensive look at the girl. 'You must have thought it were a bit odd. But it weren't easy for her. You see . . .' She stopped abruptly and Sally noticed that the cup and saucer on Monica's lap were shaking. She put them down on the floor at her side. 'You see, she's 'ad 'er 'ands full with the kiddies an' everything. And then with the last 'un on the way, well, it were the last straw. It were all too much for her.'

'We understand that, Monica,' said Ellen quietly. 'But I think Gloria has been a little disappointed that *you* didn't contact her rather more than you have done.' Her voice was gentle, but there was a hint of censure in it.

'Aye, well, happen I should 'ave. I know I should. But Mam kept insisting that our Gloria had settled down here an' it would only upset the kid if I kept coming over.'

'But . . . a letter now and again, maybe?' ventured Sally.

'Well, happen, but I've never been much of a letter-writer. And, like I'm trying to tell yer, I've always had to take notice of what me mam said. If you'd known Daisy you'd understand what I mean. Well, she's not here any more, is she? So I decided . . . I decided it was time for me to come and sort a few things out with you.' Again, it was to Sally that Monica was speaking.

'What sort of things?' asked Sally fearfully.

301

'I might as well come right out with it,' said Monica. 'I won't beat about the bush. There's no need, really, for Gloria to stay here any longer, is there?'

Sally didn't answer. She was stunned; so, too, it appeared, were Ellen and Gloria, for a deathly hush fell on the room.

'I meanter say,' Monica continued determinedly, 'it's quite safe in Manchester now. There 'aven't been no bombs or owt for ages and nearly all t'kids have come back. So, I've come to tell yer . . .' she took a deep breath '. . . I'd like her to come back home.'

It was Gloria who spoke first. 'But I can't, Monica. Not yet. I've got me new school – I've been telling you about it; weren't you listening? – and all me new friends. An' anyway, the war's not over yet, is it? They might start dropping bombs again and—'

'Hang on a minute, Monica,' said Sally. 'You say you want Gloria to come home? What exactly do you mean by home? Your mother's gone now – and, believe me, we were all very, very sorry about that – but that was Gloria's home, wasn't it? With Daisy. I'm sure your stepfather has quite enough to think about at the moment, hasn't he, without an extra one to look after?'

'I'm not going back there!' yelled Gloria suddenly. 'I hate him! Don't make me, Monica! Auntie Sally, I don't want to go!'

'Hush, darling, hush,' said Sally, wanting to take the child in her arms, but knowing that she mustn't. 'You don't have to—'

' 'Course you're not going back there,' interrupted Monica. 'As if I'd let you do that! No, you're coming home with me, aren't you, to live with us, me and our Sam and Len and little Kathy.'

Gloria was shaking her head frenziedly. 'No, no, I can't, Monica. Not yet. I live here now.'

'The child's right,' said Ellen. Sally, for the moment, couldn't trust herself to speak. She felt she might burst into

302

tears. But Ellen seemed to be well in control of her emotions. 'Gloria has come to regard this as her home, Monica. You said you didn't want to unsettle her. Well, you would be doing just that, wouldn't you, if you insist on taking her away now.' Ellen's tone was forceful, almost angry as she continued. 'You've admitted you've not been in touch for a very long time. And, quite honestly, I feel that you have no right now – no right whatsoever – to come here and say that you expect Gloria to go home with you.'

'No right? Let me tell you I've every right!' The look that Monica levelled at Ellen, then at Sally, was unfathomable, until she spoke again. 'And shall I explain why? It's what I've come to tell you anyroad, now me mam's gone. Gloria's mine. She belongs to me. I'm her mother!'

Chapter 22

Again, a deep silence fell upon the room. And, again, it was Gloria who broke it. 'You what? What yer talking about, Monica? How can you be me mother? You're me sister!'

Monica shook her head. 'No, love. I'm your mother, honest I am. Mam looked after you, that's all. She had to, y'see, 'cause I were only sixteen when you were born and – well – it were the only thing to do.'

Sally, watching Gloria intently, saw that the girl was staring at Monica open-mouthed. Her grey eyes, so like those of the young woman opposite her, were wide with an amazement that was akin to fear; and then she looked away, down at her tightly clasped hands as though she were afraid to look any more.

Monica was looking at Sally now, almost helplessly. She shrugged her shoulders, spreading her hands wide in a gesture of resignation. 'What else could I do? I were only a kid an' I had to do as me mam said. I always had to. She were a tartar, our Daisy.' Her voice was not belligerent now, more sad and wistful, and Sally, in spite of the anguish she was feeling, felt sorry for her.

'And so your mother adopted the baby . . . Gloria?' asked Sally.

'No, she were never adopted proper, like. There was nowt like that. Nowt official. I'm her mother – me name's on t'birth certificate – but me mam brought her up as though she were her own kid, me little sister. Then she married Bill after me dad died and started all over again.'

'But you got married yourself, didn't you, a few years later?' asked Sally. 'Why didn't you take Gloria with you then, to live with you and your husband – Gerry, isn't it?'

'Dunno,' said Monica, shrugging again. 'I just didn't. Happen it were because of Gerry. I didn't tell him at first, although he knows all about it now. And she was part of me mam's family by then. Me mam had always looked after her so she went on doing it, though I tried to do what I could to help her. But she never let me forget, you see – me mam, I mean – that I'd done summat wrong. I daresay that's why she insisted on hanging on to the kid, just to spite me. She could be the devil incarnate at times, could Daisy.'

Monica glanced across at Gloria who was refusing to look at her. To Sally's consternation the girl had turned quite pale. 'Anyroad, it's all water under t'bridge. I should have stood up to her, but I didn't, and that's that. But I want to make it up to her now, to our Gloria.'

'No,' said Gloria. 'No.' She looked across at Monica, her eyes full of bewilderment. It was obviously too much for her to take in at this moment. She shook her head disbelievingly, then she looked away again.

Sally longed to go to her, to put her arms around her and tell her it would be all right, but she was too stunned herself to know just what to do. She knew that Monica cared about Gloria; she had felt all along that the young woman was the only one who was really concerned about the girl's welfare. All the same, Monica couldn't walk in now, as bold as brass, after an absence of God knows how long, and insist that Gloria went home with her; even if she was her real mother.

'I can understand how you feel, Monica,' she said now, trying to speak rationally. 'It must have been awful for you, all these years, knowing you couldn't have any real say about what was happening to your little girl. I could tell when I met her that your mother was a very domineering sort of woman.'

'Aye, she was that. Especially with me,' said Monica with

305

feeling. 'I 'ad to do penance for me mistake time and time again, believe you me!'

'Was it not possible for you to have married the young man?' asked Ellen. 'I know you said you were only sixteen, but I was married at seventeen, the first time. Not that I was . . . you know,' she added hastily.

'Oh no, you wouldn't be, would you?' said Monica, a trifle sarcastically. Then: 'Sorry, I didn't mean to be rude. No, I couldn't marry him. Could I heck as like! He were a Grammar School lad; that's why Gloria here's so brainy.' Monica looked anxiously at the top of the girl's dark head, the only part of her that was visible. 'He was going on to college or somewhere, an' his parents were horrified. He couldn't be bothered with the likes of me. Besides, he weren't a Catholic, and me mam would've put her foot down there, even if he'd said he'd marry me. So when the baby was born me mam pretended it was hers. And then, as time went on, everybody stopped thinking about it. She was just little Gloria Mulligan and I was her big sister.

'But it's going to be different now, kid,' Monica continued, looking at Gloria. 'We can let everybody know now that I'm yer mam an' we can be a nice happy family. You and me, our Sam and Len and little Kathy, and Gerry when he comes home. I know you've been happy with Mrs Hobson and Sally and George, but we always knew it was only for the time being, didn't we, love? And the war will be over soon . . .'

'Not so fast, Monica.' Sally broke into the young woman's chatter. She had the impression that Monica felt she must go on talking and talking until she had won Gloria over. 'You're trying to rush things, aren't you? And this is something we can't dash straight into without thinking carefully about it. Gloria has tried to tell you she's got her new school here, and her friends, and us – George and me and Mam here. She's come to look upon us as her family. And we've been a real family to her, though you may not want to admit it. We've

306

cared about her and she's never gone short of anything while she's been here.'

'Oh aye, you don't need to tell me that!' replied Monica, with more than a hint of derision. 'Like a bloody palace 'ere, i'n't it, compared with what she's been used to back 'ome. You've learned 'er to talk posh, an' she's got fancy clothes, an' fancy friends an' all, I shouldn't wonder. But she's still little Gloria Mulligan from Salford, though she'll be Gloria O'Brien from now on, and you must've known she'd have to go back one of these days. You've no business giving her big ideas, letting her think that this is her real home – 'cause it's not!'

'It's Gloria's home as long as she's here, Monica,' said Ellen steadily, 'and it always will be, whenever she wants to come back.' Then Ellen went on to say, in her usual composed manner, 'But I do think you should give some thought to her schooling. She's doing very well at the Grammar School and it would be a shame to disrupt her studies now. How would it be if we were to wait till the end of the school year, next July? By that time the war may even be over, and at least it will have given us all plenty of time to look at things more rationally. As Sally says, we can't go rushing into something as important as this without thinking properly about it.'

'I've thought about it every day of me life, for the last thirteen years,' shouted Monica. 'Haven't you got the sense to see that? I've longed and longed to have me little girl back. And now there's nowt to stand in me way, I'm damned if I'm going to let you two stop me. I've got right on my side, I'll have you know. I'm her mother! And we've got grammar schools in Salford, too, y'know. Oh no, I didn't go to one meself, but I shall make jolly sure me daughter does. They'll find a place for her, don't you worry. There's a Catholic grammar school – the Convent of Our Lady – not all that far away, an' I'm pretty sure I'll be able to get her in there.'

'A Convent?' said Sally. 'A Catholic school?' Of course, the child had been baptised as a Catholic, but during the years she had been in Blackpool this fact tended to have been forgotten. Gloria had never referred to it, not since the very beginning.

'Aye, a Catholic school.' Monica nodded decisively. 'And that's another thing; I haven't reckoned much to her going along to yer Methodist chapel, but I knew it were best to keep me trap shut about it. But it'll be different now.'

'That's what you keep saying,' Sally broke in, 'that it's going to be different. But, can't you see, it's going to do Gloria a lot of harm if things are too different, too soon. It must have been quite a shock for her already. Why don't we all just calm down and give ourselves a breathing space? A few weeks, maybe, to help us get used to the idea. Then we can see how we feel.'

'To give you the chance to get yer claws into her again?' scoffed Monica. 'No, thanks. I told you, I've got the law on my side, an' if I say she's coming back to Salford with me, then that's what she's doing.'

Sally started to panic. She tried to speak slowly and calmly, in the way Ellen always seemed able to do. 'You can't mean that you want to take Gloria with you now . . . today?'

'Perhaps not today,' said Monica grudgingly, 'but soon – happen next week. It'll give her a chance to get her things together, and I can get her room sorted out.'

'You won't have much space for her, will you? Not with your other three children?' Sally was grasping at straws now.

'Oh, we'll manage, don't you worry,' said Monica. 'She won't have to sleep three to a bed like she did at me mam's, if that's what you're thinking. She'll have her own room, even if it's only a box room, and me landlord's going to see if he can get me a bigger place. I'll do me best for her.'

Sally could feel everything slipping away. 'Then let her stay till after Christmas,' she whispered. 'It's only a few weeks.'

'Oh no. I want all me family with me at Christmas,'

retorted Monica. 'All except Gerry, that is. God knows where he is. But I've waited a long time for this. A real family Christmas.'

Gloria hadn't spoken for ages. Her eyes were no longer downcast. She was looking first at one, then at another of the three women as they sat there discussing her future. It was Ellen who came to her rescue. She smiled encouragingly at the girl before turning to the others. 'Don't you think we should give Gloria a chance to speak for herself? Here we are, all of us, saying what we think, and Gloria's quite old enough and sensible enough to make up her own mind, isn't she?'

Sally could have hugged her mother-in-law. Of course, it had to be Gloria's own decision, if only Monica could be made to see it that way. And, given the choice, Gloria would be sure to decide to stay in Blackpool. How many times over the past few years had she said, 'I like it here, Auntie Sally, with you and Uncle George and Auntie Ellen,' or, 'I don't want to go back,' or even, 'I don't think about them very much now.' But Sally would make sure they kept in touch far more than they had been doing; Gloria could go over to Salford every few weeks – perhaps every time there was a school holiday – or Monica could come over here. It was by far the best plan for Gloria to stay here and continue her grammar school education, until she was sixteen and took her School Certificate Examination. Sally had it all worked out in her own mind.

'I think that's a great idea,' she said now, 'to ask Gloria what she thinks. It's the only sensible solution, isn't it? Do you agree, Monica? That we should let Gloria herself decide what she wants to do?'

'S'pose so,' said Monica, but rather resentfully. She turned to her daughter. 'D'you hear that, Gloria? We'll do what Mrs Hobson has said, and Sally. We'll let you decide. What d'yer want to do? D'you want to stay 'ere in Blackpool, or d'you want to come back home with me, to Salford? You can come back and see 'em, though,' she added. 'I can't say fairer than that. Mrs Hobson's said, hasn't she, you'll always be welcome?' Sally couldn't help but notice the warmth of Monica's smile and the affectionate look she gave the girl. She really did care for her. 'Come on, kid,' Monica went on, rather more brusquely. 'Let's be 'aving yer. What d'yer want to do?'

Gloria's mind was in a turmoil. She could hardly believe what she was hearing. Monica was her mother? At first her mind refused to accept it. Monica was making it up. Now that Daisy was dead she was telling a silly story so that she could persuade Gloria to go back and live in Salford. But, as Gloria listened, she realised that it must be true. Monica *was* her mother . . . And if she was, then it made sense of a lot of things that Gloria had found so perplexing before.

Monica had been the only one of the family who had ever cared two hoots about her. Gloria had always known that, but now, more than ever, she recalled the odd little kindnesses that Monica had performed through the years; the affection – somewhat brusque at times, but affection nonetheless – that Monica had shown her. The time she had turned up at the station with those mint humbugs when Gloria had been going away as an evacuee; the birthday cards and little presents when none of the rest of the family had bothered; the visits, infrequent though they might have been, that Monica had made to Blackpool; and, above all, the extra-ordinary bond, the feeling of kinship, that there had always been between herself and the woman she had thought of as her big sister, 'our Monica'.

Monica should have told her the truth years ago, not let her go on believing a lie. Why hadn't she done so? Gloria wondered. And Monica had neglected her for a lot of the time while she was living here in Blackpool. Gloria knew that Auntie Sally thought so. For months and months she hadn't even bothered to write. And Gloria loved it here in

310

Blackpool. She was so happy with Auntie Sally and Auntie Ellen and Uncle George. And she had Emmie and baby Lawrence, and all the friends she had made at the Grammar School. Her home was here now. How could she possibly live in Salford?

They had given her the choice, though. They were leaving it up to her to decide what she wanted to do. Gloria knew only too well what she *wanted* to do: she wanted to stay here in Blackpool.

She looked first at Monica then at Auntie Sally and Auntie Ellen, all of whom looked as bewildered as she herself felt. Auntie Sally appeared unbelievably sad, but there was just the tiniest glimmer of hope in her eyes, hope that Gloria would decide to stay in Blackpool; that, given the choice, how could she decide to do anything else? Gloria knew only too well what Sally was thinking, and it was what she wanted to do, oh, so very much.

But Monica was her mother. Gloria hadn't wanted to believe it at first, but she knew now that it was true. And her home, surely, should be with her real mother. She took a deep breath before she made the decision that she knew might well affect the whole of her life.

The few seconds before Gloria replied seemed much longer, as she looked at each of them in turn. Then, her glance finally resting on Monica, she said, 'I'll go with you, with . . . our Monica. I'll have to, won't I? You're my mother, and I've got to be with my mother, it's only right.'

Sally couldn't help protesting. 'Gloria, don't go because you feel you've got to. If you decide to go it has to be because you really want to.'

'Look 'ere, that's not fair!' Monica rounded on her. 'We gave the kid a choice, and that was your idea, so you can't go sticking yer oar in now 'cause you think she's made the wrong one.'

'I'm not,' Sally protested. 'I just want her to be sure.'

'Auntie Sally?' Gloria turned to her now. 'D'you remember telling me, ages ago, that it wasn't always what we *wanted* to do that was important, 'specially in wartime. It was what we knew we *must* do. Like Pearl joining the Land Army and . . . and Ruby,' she faltered, 'going into the WAAFs. Well, I know I've got to go back to Salford, 'cause it's where I live really, and 'cause Monica's me mam now. But I'll come and see you, Auntie Sally, and you, Auntie Ellen. I won't ever forget you.'

Sally couldn't answer. She knew that if she tried to speak she would start to cry. It was Ellen who replied. 'I know you will come and see us, Gloria. We'll be very upset if you don't. Are you sure about this, dear?' She ignored Monica's exasperated 'tut'.

'Yes, I'm sure,' said Gloria, although she didn't sound sure at all. 'I want to go . . . with me mam.'

'Not today,' said Sally weakly. Gloria didn't answer, but Monica spoke up.

'No, not today,' she said briskly. 'I'll come back for her next week. I'll get a school sorted out for her and make her room all ship-shape. And it'll give her a chance to say her goodbyes here.'

'I still think it would be better if she stayed here till after Christmas,' said Sally, trying desperately to control her quaking voice and to stem the encroaching tears. 'Then she could finish the term at school.'

'No,' said Monica. 'She's said she's coming with me and that's what she's doing. Next week.'

'I'd better not stay for Christmas, Auntie Sally,' said Gloria, 'because if I do, it might be harder.' Her voice faltered. The plaintive look that Gloria gave her convinced Sally that the girl did not want to go at all. But Sally knew that she had lost.

Once again, it was a rather sad Christmas and a very quiet one with several familiar faces missing round the table when they met, at Ellen's, for the festive meal. There were only six of them; Ellen, George and Sally, Rachel, Harry and Emmie. And baby Lawrence, of course, asleep in his pram most of the time, but bringing a smile, now and again, to the serious faces around him, providing a much-needed ray of hope in what was, on the whole, a sombre festival.

Ellen had tried her best with the festive food, and the decorations which came out year after year; the paper bells that opened like concertinas, the streamers suspended from the central light fitting to each corner of the room, and the fragile glass baubles – each year there was another one broken – and somewhat tarnished tinsel which decorated the artificial tree. But no amount of paper streamers or glittering baubles could lift the weight of despair that had descended on Sally since Gloria's departure. Dispiritedly she pushed the last bit of plum pudding to the side of her dish. It was delicious, as Ellen's homemade puddings and pies always were, but she felt that it was choking her. Her heart was too sad, her mind too full of memories.

She found herself remembering that first Christmas of the war. It had been a happy time, even though the threat of the unknown had hung over them all. They had had the three evacuees then, Wendy and Michael Cooper and Gloria, and despite the small squabbles and disagreements they had seemed like a big happy family. No, Sally recalled; Wendy and Michael had gone home for Christmas – and had never come back – but Gloria had made a world of difference to that first Christmas meal of the war. To Sally, at any rate. Even then, she knew she had been looking upon the little girl as the daughter she had never had, and the close affinity they had shared had grown and deepened over the years. What a fool she had been to believe it could last for ever.

Not only had Gloria gone, but her beloved niece as well. Sally had just been starting to recover from the shock of Ruby's death – although she would never forget her – when Gloria had been taken from her. Not by death, of course, but to Sally it felt almost as final. It was no use deluding herself that the girl would keep in touch. She might, for a while. She would write; she would, no doubt, come to see them, but Sally had no illusions about Monica O'Brien. The young woman had got what she wanted now and she would make sure that Gloria was left in no doubt as to where her loyalties must lie. And who could blame her? If Sally were the girl's mother she knew she would react in just the same way.

Gloria, Ruby . . . and Pearl, too, was missing from the Christmas table. But that was for a happier reason. Pearl was spending Christmas with her new husband and in-laws at the farm in Wensleydale where she was no longer a Land Girl, but a farmer's wife. So the war had brought a little joy, here and there; Pearl's marriage and Emmie's baby, though he had been born out of much grief and heartache. So much grief, for so many people, far more grief than joy. That was the way of it in wartime.

'Come on, love; try and cheer up a bit.' George put his hand over Sally's and held it tightly. He didn't ask her what was the matter. There was no need. Gloria's sudden leaving had affected him, too. 'We've got to look forward,' he whispered, 'not back. It's the only way to get through this lot. What do you bet,' he continued, in a louder voice to the rest of the family seated round the table, 'that this time next year the war'll be over?'

'D'you reckon?' said Harry. 'It feels to me as though it's going to drag on for ever. I've seen precious little action since I joined up, I can tell you.'

'Nor do you want to, Harry,' remarked his wife, sharply. 'Let the younger men take part in the action. I've told you, you're doing an important job looking after the inner man. The Army marches on its stomach, you know.'

'You reckon it's important, do you, serving out bangers and mash, Spam and chips? Yes, well, happen it is. Somebody's got to do the cooking and it might as well be me.' Harry was the Sergeant in charge of the cookhouse at his camp, a job assigned to him because of his trade in 'Civvy Street', that of a sugar-boiler and rock manufacturer. 'I'll be glad when they get moving, though. There are enough rumours flying around.'

'More than rumours, surely,' said George. 'After the meeting of the Big Three, things must be on the move. They've reassured Stalin, haven't they, that the Second Front in Europe will be opened next year. And now we've got Eisenhower as Supreme Commander . . .'

George was the expert on war news. His avid perusal of the daily papers and his continual tuning-in to the news bulletins on the wireless tended to aggravate his wife and mother. They were glad, however, that his interest was now more objective. No longer did he want to be up and doing; he had accepted his limitations, eventually, with what seemed to be a good grace, or that was the impression he tried to give.

'Come on,' said Ellen now, rising to her feet and beginning to stack together the pudding dishes. 'Let's leave the fellows to their war-mongering. I don't know about you, but I think I've heard enough of it.' She grinned cheerfully at Rachel and Emmie, before turning to Sally with a look of quiet understanding. 'We'll go and tackle this washing up, shall we? Then we'll make a nice cup of tea and listen to the King. His Majesty always puts heart into us, you can say that for him.'

'You've heard from Gloria, have you?' Emmie asked Sally in a quiet voice, as they dried the dishes. 'Apart from the Christmas card, I mean. I know you got a card last week. I didn't like to ask you at the table, Auntie Sally, in front of them all. I know you're still upset.'

'Yes, I've had a letter,' said Sally. 'Well, *we've* had a letter, I should say. It was to all of us. She didn't say much. She said she was well, and Monica was well. You know the sort of thing; "We are all well here, as we hope you are." All very stilted. It didn't sound like Gloria at all. She didn't say she was happy.'

315

'I don't suppose she can be very happy, do you,' said Emmie gently, 'catapulted into a whole different way of life? It must be confusing for her.'

'Yes, it must, but I hope she's settling down.' Sally sounded wistful. 'She said she'd been with Monica to see the boys in their Nativity play ... I noticed she called her "Monica", though, not "Mum" or "Mam" or whatever.'

'Did she mention her new school?'

'No, she didn't. She just wished us all a Merry Christmas and said she hoped she'd see us soon. She didn't say when.' Sally could feel her voice breaking and she hastily put her apron up to her eyes, dashing away the tears. 'I'm sorry, love. I mustn't give way like this. I've got to try and get used to it.'

'It's all right, Sally.' Emmie put an arm around her. There were times now when her niece called her 'Sally' and not 'Aunt' and Sally was glad of this. It made them feel closer, and they had both lost so much. 'Perhaps I shouldn't have asked you about her,' Emmie went on. 'I didn't mean to upset you – but I miss her as well, you know, almost as much as you do, I think. She was a lot younger than me, but we got on ever so well. And she was delighted about Lawrence, wasn't she? She said he was the bonniest baby she'd ever seen, and I think she meant it. She was really good with him. She nursed him a few times when she came round; like a real little mother, she was. And she said, could she change his nappy? So I let her. She knew what she was doing all right.'

'She would,' replied Sally meaningfully. 'She had enough practice with her little brothers and sisters, Daisy and Monica's kids. Those two, Sam and Len, they're her brothers, aren't they, not her nephews? That's what she used to call them, so proudly – "my nephews". Half-brothers, at any rate. What a muddle it all is. I still can't take it in properly. I hope Monica doesn't make a drudge of her, but of course they're not babies now. Kathleen, the youngest one, must be about three and a half. I remember Monica was expecting her that

316

time we went over. Oh, what's the use?' Sally shook her head despondently. 'I keep going over and over it in my mind and I can't make any sense of it. I really felt that that little girl was mine, but I was just deluding myself, wasn't I?'

'She'll keep in touch, Sally,' said Emmie. 'She thought far too much about you to ever forget you. She told me, many a time, that she wanted to stay here.'

'But when she was given the choice, she chose to go,' said Sally. 'That's what I find so hard to accept. I can't get over that. Anyway, that's enough of my troubles.' She tried to smile cheerfully at her niece. 'How's Davey? He's home on leave, I daresay. Are you seeing him?'

'Yes,' said Emmie, a little guardedly. 'Mum's invited him to tea tomorrow. He'll be going back the next day, I think. Don't start jumping to conclusions, will you? It's nice to see him. He's a great friend ... but I'm scared, after what happened to Gene. I'm afraid to let myself fall in love with anyone again, Sally. I'm afraid that if I love somebody too much they might just ... disappear.'

'Yes, I know the feeling,' said Sally.

Chapter 23

Gloria pushed the things she thought she would need into the bag she had brought from Blackpool, the one Auntie Sally had given her when she was leaving. Underwear and socks, a couple of jumpers, a cardigan and a skirt, an extra pair of shoes. These few items would be enough to be going on with. She could collect the rest later or they could be sent on, when it had all been sorted out with Auntie Sally and Auntie Ellen. Because Gloria was determined that she was not coming back to Salford ever again.

She hid the bag at the bottom of the wardrobe, out of sight, and the letter she had written to Monica in her dressing-table drawer. She had her plan all worked out. In the morning, instead of going to school, she would catch a bus going in the opposite direction, to Victoria Station. She would have to wear her school uniform, but she would take off her hat and put on her red beret when she got to the station so she wouldn't look so conspicuous. She always made her own bed and tidied her room in a morning, so Monica wouldn't be likely to find the letter until later in the day when Gloria failed to return from school. By that time she would have arrived in Blackpool. She knew that what she was planning was wrong and Monica would be upset, but she couldn't stand it any longer. That awful school and those awful girls . . .

It hadn't seemed too bad at first, the idea of coming back to Salford. More than anything it had seemed unreal, like something in a dream or something that was happening to somebody else.

She had managed to get through that awful last week in Blackpool, so very much aware of the tears that Sally was trying hard to hide, and Ellen's quiet sadness and George's resignation – which fooled no one – by pretending she was a character in a story. Anne of Green Gables, perhaps, when she had to go and live with Mrs Hammond and her eight children, before she came to live with Matthew and Marilla. Anne had survived by having a vivid imagination, and so could she, Gloria. But saying goodbye to everybody had been dreadful, especially to Emmie, and then to Auntie Sally; but what lay ahead was an adventure and Gloria knew that she was, really and truly, looking forward to seeing Sam and Len again, and little Kathleen. They would have grown so much and she had always liked children.

The strangest thing had been feeling so much in awe of Monica. It was so awkward, finding out she was not who she thought she was.

'I don't know what to call you,' she had said, when they were settled in the train heading for Manchester. They had a compartment to themselves at first, although it was very likely that the train would fill up at Preston. Gloria didn't know whether to be glad or sorry that the two of them were on their own. Other people around them would have meant that they didn't need to converse, and Gloria felt so tongue-tied.

'Go on with yer, you silly chump!' said Monica, laughing. 'You'll call me what you've always called me – Monica. I'd feel daft if you started calling me "Mam" now. So long as folks realise that I am, that's all I'm bothered about.'

Things began to seem rather more real by the time they arrived at Victoria Station. There was no mistaking the reality of the bomb-damaged city. This was no dream or part of a story. Gloria stared in astonishment through the carriage window at the piles of rubble, the boarded-up shops and open spaces covered with weeds where there had once been houses. There had never been anything like this in Blackpool.

Only once had they been bombed properly, when Seed Street had 'copped it' and Uncle George had lost his leg. How they must have suffered in Manchester, Monica and her mam – her grandmother, she corrected herself – and all of them, whilst she, Gloria, had been safe and sound, away from it all. That was the purpose of evacuation, of course, but she couldn't help feeling a little guilty.

The streets of Manchester, when they emerged from the station, looked drab and grey. So they had seemed to her when she had visited the city that time with Sally and Doreen and Susan, when Monica was expecting Kathleen; but they looked more so now, neglected and shabby after four years of a wearisome war.

'Cat got yer tongue?' said Monica, giving her a nudge. 'Come on, snap out of it. Can't have you going all broody, love.'

'I'm just trying to work out where we are,' said Gloria. 'It looks so different. There was a row of houses here, wasn't there?' The houses had gone, but the pub still stood on the corner.

'Aye, some of the familiar landmarks have gone,' replied Monica. 'But it's not too bad in Salford. Our street's still all in one piece, thank the Lord. Hey up, there's a bus coming. Stir yer stumps an' we might just catch it.'

Monica's house was pretty much as Gloria remembered it, although she had obviously made an effort to tidy up. No amount of housework though could disguise the stained wallpaper, peeling paintwork and threadbare carpets and curtains. Gloria couldn't help making a comparison with her home – which was no longer her home – in King Street. She chided herself; she knew that Monica didn't have the money that Ellen and her family had to spend on furnishings and decorating. Neither, Gloria tried to tell herself, did Auntie Ellen have three little kiddies running about messing things up.

When she met the three children – at least the two boys –

Gloria understood even more what a battle Monica must have. Sam and Len were at school when they first arrived and Kathleen was being looked after by a neighbour, but it wasn't long before they made their presence felt. Sam and Len burst into the house like a couple of miniature tornadoes. Coats and caps were flung on the floor as they tore into the back kitchen demanding slices of jam and bread.

'We're starving, Mam.'

'It were a rotten old dinner. Nasty 'orrible meat with all fat on it an' rice puddin'.'

'Lumpy 'orrible cold rice puddin'. Ugh!'

Monica laughed good-humouredly. Gloria was to discover that little seemed to daunt her, which was perhaps just as well. Daisy, on the other hand, had always seemed harassed by her brood of children. 'All right, you can have a jam butty each. Just one, mind, or it'll spoil yer tea. We're 'aving a special tea today 'cause Gloria's here. You remember Gloria, don't you? Well, she's come to live with us now. Isn't that nice?'

'I don't remember 'er,' said Len, stuffing his mouth with the thick greyish-looking bread and bright red jam. It oozed out on to his chin and dribbled down on to his jumper.

'Well, I do,' said his brother, likewise gobbling down his snack. 'Hiya, Gloria. You used to live with me gran, didn't yer? Me mam told us. She died, y'know, me gran. And then you was an evacuee or summat.'

'Yes, I came to see you once,' said Gloria. 'Do you remember?' She felt rather nonplussed. In her memory they hadn't been quite so dirty. They were still bonny little lads, as they had always been, round-faced and dark-haired with engaging grins; at least Sam was grinning although Len was still eyeing her somewhat suspiciously. But they were so scruffy, with grimy faces, tousled hair, food-stained jumpers and holey grey socks concertinaed round their ankles. Just such an unkempt little girl had she once been, Gloria recalled with a jolt, before she went to live in Blackpool. She smiled at them both. They were her brothers; she had to get to know them. And of course little lads were always scruffy, much more so than little girls.

''Course I remember. I telled yer, didn't I?' said Sam. 'Anyroad, yer living with us now, aren't yer? Me mam said so. You can play football with us, can't she, Mam? Our Kathy's no good. She yells if the ball 'its 'er, but she's only a girl.'

'Gloria's a girl, too,' Monica laughed. 'A big girl. I shouldn't think she'll want to play football, but I 'spect she'll do a lot of other things for you.'

Gloria thought that Kathleen was a lovely child, not at all like her boisterous brothers in temperament. She was placid and affectionate and she took to Gloria almost at once, although she was rather shy at first. Her clear grey eyes, dark hair and slightly longish nose made her look the image of her mother. (Monica's hair was no longer bleached blonde, but her natural dark shade.) And the image of Gloria, too, as Monica was quick to point out.

'She's the dead spit of you when you were a nipper, our Gloria. Can't you see it? We're like peas in a pod, ain't we, the three of us? Anyroad, if she grows to be like 'er big sister, then it'll suit me fine.' Monica put an arm round Gloria's shoulders and gave her a peck on the cheek, then she drew away quickly as though embarrassed. Gloria remembered that she had never been a sentimental sort, given to hugging and kissing and all that . . . like Auntie Sally was.

''Ere, make yerself useful,' said Monica that first afternoon. 'You can butter this bread. An' it's real butter today, mind, in your honour. We'll be back to marge tomorrer. An' I'll open a tin of corned beef as I've been hoarding. You like corned beef, do yer? We'll have some chips wi' it and beetroot. And I've gorra tin of sliced peaches. What d'yer think of that, eh?'

Monica loved to prattle away about something and nothing and Gloria found she was doing far more listening than talking. 'The lads usually come 'ome for their dinner, but they 'ad to stay at school today. Didn't go down all that well, did it? I reckon you'll have to stay at school for yer dinner, though, when you start at the High School. It's a bit far to get back 'ere.'

'The High School?' queried Gloria. 'I thought you said I was going to the Convent?'

'Oh aye, so I did. But they hadn't got room for you there, love. At least, that's what they said. Happen it's for t'best. They seemed a snooty lot to me. Anyroad, they've found a place for you at the Girls' High. You don't need to start till after Christmas, though. You can 'ave a bit of an 'oliday first.'

There was so much to get used to, so much that was very different from her previous life, and as the days went by it seemed less and less like something out of a dream or a story in a book. This was harsh reality, but it was her life now and Gloria knew that she had to adapt, to accept things as they were. She had been very good at that when she was a little girl; now it was not quite so easy. But she had known, when Monica had come to Blackpool with the startling revelation of her parenthood, that she had to go with her mother. She hadn't wanted to go, and she hadn't believed for one moment that Ellen and Sally really thought that she did, but she had known that she must. And here she must stay.

What a silly, dreamy little fool she must have been, she recalled, that time she had 'wished upon a star', believing she could stay in Blackpool for ever and ever. There was another song that said 'Wishing will make it so'. Well, it wouldn't. Gloria had grown up a lot since she had seen that film about Pinocchio and the Blue Fairy, and she knew that no amount of wishing would get her back to Auntie Sally which was where, in her heart of hearts, she really wanted to be. Nor would praying about it.

Gloria had tried to say her prayers in the huge ornate building where Monica sometimes took her on a Sunday morning. But it all seemed so strange; the gold and the glitter, the sweet sickly smell of incense, the big statue of the Virgin Mary smiling down at her, and the even bigger one of Jesus suffering on the Cross. Gloria remembered, vaguely, that she had seen all these things before, when she was a little girl, but they seemed alien to her now after the homely feel of the chapel she had attended with Ellen and Sally.

She was glad Monica hadn't managed to get her a place at the Convent. She was sure she would have felt like a fish out of water there, just as she did in the church. The Girls' High School would be OK. Maybe she would meet some of her old friends there from the Junior School as well as making some new friends. As the New Year started – 1944 – she began to look forward to that. She must try to look forward to something. At least if she was at school she wouldn't be taking care of Sam and Len and Kathy all the time, which was what she seemed to be doing now. Monica had never spoken a truer word than when she had said, 'Gloria'll do a lot of things for you.'

She was sure that Monica didn't mean to put on her quite so much as she did, but as the days went by Gloria found herself doing more and more for her younger brothers and sister, just as she had done for Rose, Lily and Vinnie when she had lived with Daisy. At first it had been, 'Just look after t'nippers, will you love, while I pop out to t'shop?' Monica was continually 'popping out to the shop' for things she had forgotten. She collected her rations once a week from the grocer's where she was registered, but apart from that her shopping was very haphazard. Or, 'Just wash their 'ands and faces, will you, love, while I pop next door to see Mrs Jackson? I forgot to ask her summat.' And Monica's 'popping next door' to see a neighbour was usually of an hour's duration or more. Not that you could blame her, thought Gloria. Monica had managed single-handed for so long, it must be nice for her to have someone to help with the chores. And so, little by little, Gloria found that she was washing the children, peeling the spuds, drying the dishes, laying the fire, just as she had used to do when she had lived in Salford before.

She had seen Bill Mulligan and his family only once. He seemed to be coping quite well. Rose, Lily and Vinnie were sometimes looked after by a neighbour when they were not at school; a war widow with just one son, the neighbour served behind the bar in the local pub of an evening, and it was Monica's opinion that her stepfather would soon be ' 'anging 'is 'at up there'.

As soon as she and Monica walked into their old home, Gloria thanked her lucky stars that she wasn't still living there. By contrast, her life with Monica began to seem not too bad.

'Well, well, well! Fancy seein' you. That's a turn up for the book, ain't it?' Bill's prominent pale blue eyes leered at Gloria, travelling from her head to her feet and up again. 'Grown up, 'aven't yer? I wouldn't 'ave known yer.'

Gloria felt uncomfortable. 'Hello,' she said awkwardly, not adding 'Dad' or anything. 'It's a long time since I saw you.' Honesty prevented her from saying it was good to see him again. 'I was sorry to hear about . . . my grandma.'

'Aye, well, we've got to carry on as best we can. Your grandma, eh? I'll bet that took the wind out of yer sails, didn't it, this 'un turning out to be yer ma? 'Ere, mek yerselves a cup of tea if you want one. I'm just getting meself ready to go down t'road.' He turned back to the sink and started lathering his face with a shaving brush.

To the pub, thought Gloria, remembering what Monica had told her. To see his new ladyfriend.

'What about the kids, Bill?' asked Monica. 'Yer not leavin' 'em on their own, are yer?'

'You mind yer own bloody business, lady!' Bill didn't turn round, but scowled at Monica through the broken mirror propped up on the windowsill. 'Our Rosie's plenty old enough to look after the rest of 'em.'

'She's only eight . . .'

'Aye, like I said. Plenty old enough. She's been doin' it ever since the old woman died. She's got to do 'er bit. Anyroad, it's nowt to do wi' you.'

'Where is she now?'

'Our Rose? 'Er and Lily are getting t'nipper to bed. Owt else yer'd like to know? Where's yer own kids anyway, seein' as how yer so concerned about mine?'

'They're at Mrs Jackson's, my next-door neighbour's,' replied Monica frostily. 'I said we wouldn't be long, and I don't ever leave them on their own.'

'Aye, well, you've got yer own nursemaid now, 'aven't yer, young Gloria 'ere. She'll have to come and look after my lot now and again, if you're so worried about 'em.' Bill turned round now to leer at Gloria again and she hastily looked away.

Monica ignored his remark. 'We won't bother with a cup of tea. Come on, Gloria. Let's go upstairs and say hello to Rose and Lily, then we'd best be off.'

The two girls were very much as Gloria had remembered them, stolid-looking children with the lumpy features, pale blue eyes and sparse ginger hair of their father. They took as little interest in Gloria as they had ever done although they knew who she was. She didn't know what to say to them. They had always been silent children and were no more communicative now. They answered Monica, however, at her anxious questioning, that they would be all right on their own. They were used to it now and they knew they had to knock on the wall for Mrs Smith next door if they were in any trouble.

Vinnie, now aged four and a half, showed much more animation on seeing Gloria. He sat up in bed, surveying her with keen interest. 'Who are you?' he said.

That's a good question, thought Gloria. Who am I? And who is he? And who are Rose and Lily? She used to think they were her half-sisters and brother. She frowned, trying to work out the complicated relationship. She supposed they must be her . . . half-aunts and uncle, if they were Monica's half-sisters and brother. But that was ridiculous, a little boy like this being her uncle.

'I'm just Gloria,' she replied eventually. 'I used to look after you when you were a baby.'

He nodded at her then slid back between the grimy bedcovers. Monica and Gloria soon took their leave, and Gloria felt that she didn't ever want to return, even to see Vinnie, though she had always been fond of the little lad.

Monica had got her the correct uniform for the Girls' High School; the round felt hat, the blue and white tie, and the blue and white striped scarf. Apart from that, the same clothes that she had worn at the Grammar School in Blackpool would suffice as the colours were basically the same; white blouses, navy blue skirt and whatever coat you chose to wear. Hard and fast rules couldn't be adhered to in wartime. Gloria guessed that it might have proved too expensive for Monica to buy the uniform for the Catholic School, which was green as opposed to blue, a colour they tried to insist upon in spite of clothes rationing. Maybe that was why Monica had decided against this school, thought Gloria. At all events, she was relieved. At least she would look just like all the other girls, and she set off on the first day of the new term with very little fear. She had never found it hard to make new friends.

To her surprise Gloria didn't know many of the girls. The High School took pupils from several schools, not just those from Gloria's previous Junior School. In Blackpool she had been in the top form, but here she found herself in the lowest one, 2C. 'Just until we see what you can do,' the headmistress explained. Gloria didn't take to her. She seemed aloof and disinterested. She had hoped she might meet up again with Wendy Cooper, but Wendy was now living in Didsbury, a much posher part of Manchester. The Aspinall girls, Doreen and Susan, were at the High School, but Doreen was in a different form, 2B, and, to Gloria's amazement, hardly acknowledged her when she saw her. Susan was only a 'first former' and though she waved to Gloria in the yard the years didn't mix overmuch.

Right from the start Gloria felt an outsider at this school though she was at a loss to know exactly why. It was a combination of factors, she supposed. She had started in the middle of a school year. Friendships had already been cemented and 'cliques' formed, and none of them seemed to want to include Gloria – probably because they soon discovered that she was way ahead of them in ability. She was soon right at the top of the form in weekly tests and this was resented, especially by the ones who had previously held this position. They ganged up on her. They called after her in the schoolyard or on the way home.

'You think you're "it", don't yer, Gloria Mulligan?' (Monica hadn't got round to changing her name, for which Gloria supposed she was thankful.)

'Oh, look who's here, girls. Old Clever-Clogs!'

'Smartypants, Smartypants! Look at 'er, trying to let on she hasn't heard.' Then they would shout even louder.

They made fun of her because they said she talked 'posh', and for some reason her name, Gloria, sent them into fits of malicious laughter. It was obviously a name that was not much heard in their environment, amongst all the Jeans, Joans, Barbaras and Margarets. And, her persecutors soon discovered, it was an easy one to parody.

'Glor-or-or-or-ria, in Excelsis Deo,' they chorused after her in the yard. (Christmas was not long past and this carol had featured in their school nativity play.)

Or, 'Glory, glory, hallelujah!' they chanted repeatedly in sing-song voices.

There was no sense at all in their mockery, nor any reason why they should be ridiculing her in this way. Gloria knew that she had done nothing to deserve it, but she also knew that once this sort of jeering against an unfortunate victim started in a schoolyard it could sometimes snowball out of control. Neither did there have to be any real reason for it. Some girls, who at first may have paid little heed, got carried along by the ringleaders, egging one another on in fresh taunts and insults.

Gloria's answer to it all was to try to ignore them and not to retaliate. This wouldn't have been her reaction at one time. The Gloria Mulligan who had gone to Blackpool as an evacuee would have given as good as she got, even stuck up her fists and taken a swipe at them. But not any more. Gloria was a tall girl, but she was quite slim and she knew she was no match, physically, for some of these rough, tough lasses. Neither did she want to engage in a slanging match with them as Daisy had used to do with her neighbours over the backyard wall. Her years away from her natural environment had shown her that this was not the way everybody carried on.

There were a few girls who rallied round her, but they were the more timid, reticent ones who were unable to make their presence felt amongst their more dominant form-mates. Gloria hadn't told Monica how unhappy she was. Monica's answer would have been, 'Give 'em a clout, duck. Show 'em what you're made of.' And there were too many of them. Neither did she want to report them to her form-mistress or one of the other teachers. It was an unwritten code of practice that you didn't sneak on your class-mates. Children in Junior Schools were known to tell tales on one another, but in the Senior School, never; certainly not at the High School. And the teachers, strangely, seemed unaware of what was happening.

It was the leader of the 'gang', a hefty girl with muscles like a prize-fighter, who came up with the cruellest jibe of all. 'Hey, d'yer know what?' she said one day to an admiring audience. 'D'yer know what me mam calls the closet under t'stairs where she keeps all her rubbish? She calls it the Glory

329

Hole! Hey, that's a good 'un, i'n't it? Glory-hole, Glory-hole . . .' They fell about, giggling and shouting. And the name stuck. Poor Gloria became 'Glory-hole Mulligan'.

Eventually she knew she couldn't stand any more of it. That was why she had decided to run away. All her plans were made; her bag was packed, her letter written. All she had to do was make her getaway in the morning.

She got up earlier than usual. She had been awake for ages; she had an idea it was the sound of little Kathy crying that had woken her and then she couldn't get to sleep again. It was only half-past six by her bedside clock when she put her feet out on to the cold linoleum. Shivering in the icy temperature of a February morning she pushed her feet into her slippers and made a grab for her woolly dressing gown. It was pitch dark outside as she peeped through the curtains and blackout blinds, but by quarter-past eight, when she intended to set out on her journey, it should be coming lighter. She had a funny, churned-up feeling in her stomach as she crept downstairs to boil a kettle for her morning wash.

To her surprise Monica was already in the kitchen, rocking to and fro in the fireside chair, holding a fractious little girl in her arms. Kathy was crying piteously and Gloria could see that her face was covered with bright pink blotches.

'You're up before yer breakfast, aren't yer?' said Monica, sounding much more cross than she normally did. 'Well, now you're 'ere you can give us an 'and with our Kathy. Just look at 'er, poor little mite. Had me up half the night, she has.'

'What is it?' said Gloria. 'What's the matter with her?'

'What does it look like? Measles, I reckon. Or German measles. One or t'other. 'Ere, you 'old 'er for a bit, while I mek us some toast. Then you can look after her later while I nip along to t'doctor. And see that the lads get off to school in good time, won't yer? It won't matter if you're a bit late for school, will it? You can tell 'em you had to help yer mam with the little 'uns.'

Gloria nodded. 'OK, Monica. I'll look after her. Come on, Kathy, there's a good girl. Shhh . . . shhh . . . Don't cry. Mummy'll get the doctor and he'll soon make you better.'

Later that morning, before she set off for school, Gloria unpacked her bag and replaced her clothes in the dressing-table drawers. Then she tore the note she had written into tiny pieces and flushed them away in the outside lav. She knew she couldn't run away to Blackpool, not now, perhaps not ever. How silly she had been even to consider it. She might have known that something would happen to stop her. Poor little Kathy had a bad dose of measles and Monica needed Gloria to help with her. Monica said she didn't know how on earth she had managed before Gloria came to live there.

Chapter 24

Monica knew that her daughter was not happy. She had been watching her anxiously for a couple of weeks or more now. Then when Kathy started with the measles she thought perhaps that was what was ailing the girl. Maybe she was coming down with a dose of it, too. But no, Monica reminded herself; Gloria had had the measles when she was five, just after she started school. The girl's lassitude and general low spirits must stem from something else. And it had been getting gradually worse since she started at the High School.

Monica wasn't one to pry. She didn't believe in continually asking, 'How do you like your school?' or 'Have you a lot of homework tonight?' She knew the answer to the last question, anyway. Gloria always seemed to have a lot of homework. She settled down to do it each evening at a corner of the kitchen table after she had helped to get the kiddies to bed. Monica sometimes felt guilty about Gloria helping her so much, but the girl didn't seem to mind. Besides, she, Monica, deserved a bit of help, surely, after being on her own for so long. She had always believed that a girl should pull her weight in the house. Goodness knows, she'd had to do so when she lived at her mother's.

But her conscience also told her that Gloria had her studies to do, and when her daughter was in bed she sometimes took a peek at the books she had brought home from school. Algebra, Trigonometry, Physics, Chemistry . . . subjects that Monica had never even heard of, some of them, let alone studied. And the books she had to read, supposedly for

enjoyment – *Silas Marner, Jane Eyre, A Tale of Two Cities* . . .
Monica leafed through the pages and just as quickly shut
them up again. She'd never be able to read boring stuff like
that, not in a month of Sundays. Apart from the local paper
and her *Woman's Own*, Monica didn't do any reading at all.
You could wear your brain out with too much reading and
studying. Maybe that was what was wrong with Gloria . . .
but she didn't think so. Her homework didn't seem to pose
any problems. She never sat chewing her pen or gazing into
space. She just got on with it, quietly and methodically, never
asking for any help. Not that there was anyone *to* help. A fat
lot of assistance she, Monica, would be able to give. Most of
it was like double Dutch to her.

Eventually, when Kathy was on the mend and Monica felt
less harassed, she decided to ask Gloria what was the matter.
'How are you getting on at school?' she asked, one evening
when the children were in bed and Gloria had closed the last
of her homework books. It was a question she had always
refrained from asking because it was a sphere that was
beyond her comprehension, all this Mathematics and English
Literature and stuff. But she was sure it was mainly from the
school that Gloria's unhappiness stemmed. 'I don't mean the
work,' she added. 'You seem to be able to do that as easy as
winking. But there's summat else, isn't there, love? You're
not happy there, are you?'

'It's all right,' said Gloria, shrugging slightly. 'It's not like
the one in Blackpool – the Collegiate School – but I can't
expect it to be, can I?' The girl looked more dispirited
than Monica had ever seen her, with dark shadows beneath
her eyes. Monica guessed that she wasn't sleeping well
either.

'What d'yer mean, it's not like the one in Blackpool?'
probed Monica. 'It's a grammar school, ain't it, for the ones
that are clever? An' I know you can do the work. So, what's
up?'

'It's partly the work,' replied Gloria. 'Oh yes, I can do it all right. That's the trouble. It's dead easy. Too easy, 'cause they've put me in the bottom form.'

'You? In t'bottom form?' Monica was indignant. 'But you're a clever lass. I don't believe it.'

'I told you, Monica,' said Gloria, a trifle edgily. 'Don't you remember me telling you? They put me there just for the time being, they said, to see what I could do. Well, I can do it, all of it, but they haven't moved me, and . . .' Gloria looked down, shaking her head dejectedly. 'Oh Monica, it's awful . . .'

'What is?' asked Monica. And then, as Gloria didn't answer, 'Come on, love, I know there's summat badly wrong. You can tell me, can't you?'

Gloria looked at her plaintively. 'It's the other girls.'

'Why? What's wrong with 'em?'

'They don't like me. They don't like me at all. And I know I shouldn't say it, but I don't like them either. I hate them! Some of them, anyway,' she added more calmly. 'Some are OK, but I haven't got any proper friends.'

'Well, blow me down!' said Monica. 'I would never've thought it could be that. Not with you, love. You were always such a friendly little girl. D'you remember how you looked after that little kid, Wendy Cooper? It must be them that's to blame,' she went on loyally. 'What's up? Are they snooty, like?'

'No, not at all,' said Gloria. 'Not the ones in my form anyway. No, they think it's *me* that's snooty. They say I talk posh – an' I don't, do I, Monica? Not really – an' they think I'm stuck up 'cause I can do the work dead easy. And they make fun of me name.'

Monica listened aghast as Gloria poured out her tale of woe. Once she had started she didn't seem able to stop. The poor kid; Monica had had no idea she was so desperately unhappy and she blamed herself for not getting to the bottom of the problem earlier.

'And I don't know how I'm going to be able to stick it,' Gloria continued. 'I'm only in the second form, so it'll be another three years, and then the Sixth Form. That's if you let me stay on, Monica. I might not even want to,' she added dolefully. 'I used to think I'd want to, but I hate it so much I reckon I'll have had enough by the time I'm sixteen. Three bloomin' years!' She sighed deeply. 'Even if they move me into another form I still won't like it. I miss my friends. I never thought I could miss 'em so much.' Again she looked across at Monica, such a pleading look. 'But I've got to get used to it, haven't I?'

Monica stared thoughtfully at her daughter for several moments before she tried to reply, her heart almost bursting with the love she had for her. She found it incredible now that she could have left her alone for so long, but that had been mainly Daisy's fault. Monica hadn't wanted to 'upset the apple-cart', but once she had claimed Gloria as her own she had been determined to make up to her for her years of neglect. All the while Gloria had been speaking Monica had been thinking hard. Three more years at school, then the Sixth Form. (Monica hadn't really considered that.) She knew she had to do her very best for this clever child. There could be no leaving school at fourteen for Gloria as she, Monica, had done. And everything was so damned expensive. The bits of uniform she had bought already had cost what seemed like a fortune, and it could only get worse as Gloria grew older and bigger and needed new items. But she would do it; she would have to, because she had taken the girl away from the place where she had been so happy and now she had to make amends for that. What was the use, though, if Gloria was so miserable? Monica had known all along that she hadn't really wanted to come back to Salford, that she had been doing it out of a sense of loyalty. She loved her; over the last couple of months Monica had come to love her daughter even more. But maybe the best – the only – way to show that love was by . . . letting go.

Monica opened her mouth to reply, but the words didn't come.

'What's wrong?' said Gloria. 'Why are you looking at me all funny?'

Monica took a deep breath. 'I think you want to go back to Blackpool, don't you, love?'

The flicker of joy that immediately lit up the girl's face brought a stab of pain to Monica's heart, but it had given her her answer. 'Could I?' said Gloria. 'D'you really mean it, Monica?' But then, before Monica had time to reply, the look of elation left Gloria's face. 'No,' she said. 'How can I? I can't go back. I've come here, to live with you. You're my mam, aren't you?'

'I'll still be your mam, even if you go back to Blackpool,' said Monica. She smiled sadly. 'Nothing'll ever alter that now. I know I neglected you, but it won't ever happen again, I promise. I'll come and see you every few weeks, or you can come and see us. You'll have to, won't you, or the kids'll drive me barmy. "Where's our Gloria?" they'll be asking. They'll miss you, and so shall I. But it's what you want, isn't it?' Monica hardly ever cried, but she felt very close to tears now. Even more so when Gloria dashed across and gave her a hug.

'Oh Monica, I do love you, really I do. But it was better before, wasn't it, when I thought you were me sister? I can't seem to get used to you being me mam. But what about Sally and Mrs Hobson?' She hadn't called them 'Auntie', Monica noticed, most probably out of consideration for her mother's feelings. 'They might not want me back now. It might not be convenient. And the school as well – the Collegiate – they might've filled my place.'

'Now don't you go making trouble where there is none,' said Monica. She stroked Gloria's dark head as the girl knelt at her side on the hearthrug. 'She's very fond of you, is that Sally, and the other one, Ellen. If they weren't I wouldn't dream of letting you go back, I can tell you. Now, how about you writing to 'em and asking 'em if you can go back to Blackpool? You can tell 'em why, 'cause you're not too happy

336

at that there school. That's the real reason, isn't it? It's because of the school?'

But Monica knew, deep down, that there were other reasons as well. Gloria had hit the nail on the head. It had been better when they were sisters. This more complicated relationship was proving to be something of a strain on both of them despite the affection they had for one another. And it could get worse when Gerry eventually came home. How might he react to having a grown-up girl about the house, who was not his daughter? Monica could foresee trouble. 'Happen it's best if I write to them,' Monica decided. 'I'll do it tomorrer . . . then you can start getting yer bits and pieces together. You're not going back to that bloomin' High School, though! I'm not 'aving any daughter of mine treated like that. If they come snooping – sending t'School Board fellow round – I'll tell 'em you've caught measles off yer sister. And when you've gone off to Blackpool I'll write and tell 'em where they can stick their bloody High School. The cheek of it!' Mother and daughter grinned conspiratorially at one another.

The war news was good. Sally was trying to take more interest than she had previously done when George read out bits to her from the newspapers, and she listened conscientiously with him and Ellen every evening to the nine o'clock news. She knew that she must try to look forward, to be optimistic about the future, but the dark cloud of depression that had settled around her following Gloria's departure had never lifted.

Everyone knew that this would be the year when the Second Front was launched – D-Day, Deliverance Day – the start of the liberation of Occupied Europe, and, it was hoped, the year of victory. There was an air of expectancy throughout the nation which had been sadly lacking until now, the definite feeling that Britain was going to win the war. People in general were taking more notice of what was going on overseas; the successful landing in January of 50,000 British and American troops at Anzio in southern Italy, and further afield, in the Far East, news of the British troops gradually gaining ascendancy over the Japanese. Japan, according to George, would be the stumbling block, the one that would hold out the longest and prevent the war from coming to a speedy conclusion.

Yes, Sally was trying desperately hard to show enthusiasm at the hopeful news, but all she longed for, still, after an absence of two months, was news of Gloria. She wrote to the girl every week, chatty cheerful letters about what was going on in Blackpool. About Emmie and baby Lawrence; about Pearl in Yorkshire, now expecting a baby in the late summer; and little inconsequential items of news about church bazaars and concerts and the work of the WVS (which Sally, as well as Ellen, had now joined). Sally wasn't sure whether or not she was right to natter on as she did about things that were happening here. It might only serve to unsettle Gloria, but she had to keep in touch and she had to find something to write about.

Gloria's letters back were humdrum accounts of what had been happening in the day-to-day routine at Monica's house. Kathy had measles; Monica had a cold; Len had fallen in the playground and gashed his knee; they had started reading *A Midsummer Night's Dream* at school . . . There was nothing about whether she was happy or not. Reading between the lines Sally guessed that Gloria was feeling as miserable as they were.

The news, when it came, was too wonderful to comprehend. As Sally stared at the writing on the envelope she had, at first, experienced a feeling of panic. This was Monica's handwriting, not Gloria's, and the letter was addressed to her, Sally, not to Ellen. Previously Monica had addressed her letters, infrequent though they had been, to Mrs E. Hobson, obviously believing that the older woman was the one in charge. Something must be wrong, thought Sally. Gloria was ill, she had had an accident ... Feverishly she tore at the envelope and pulled out the sheet of cheap lined paper. She stood in the hallway, her hands trembling slightly, as her eyes quickly scanned the words.

Her cry brought Ellen and George hurrying from the living room. Sally was leaning against the banister rail, tears streaming down her face. But, as she held out the letter to her husband and mother-in-law, they could see that her tears were ones of joy.

'She's coming home,' she cried, smiling as she had not smiled for months. 'Gloria ... she's coming back. Here – read this.'

The letter was quite brief and to the point.

Dear Sally, I am writing to ask if Gloria can come back to live with you. Not for ever I don't mean but it would be a good idea if she finished her studdies at that grammer school in Blackpool. She's not happy at the school here and I don't like to see her unhappy. I am writing to you becos I want to ask you to take speshul care of her for me. I know you think a lot about her and she thinks a lot about you. I haven't been a very good mother but I'm trying hard and this is the best way I can show her I love her by letting her come back to Blackpool. It was your idea anyway weren't it that she should carry on with her studdies at that school and you were right after all. Best wishes to Mrs Hobson and your husband, Yours sinceerly, Monica O'Brien.

'It's like a miracle,' said Ellen. She cast her eyes towards the ceiling. 'Don't ever tell me that He doesn't listen.'

'Yes, happen He does ... sometimes,' replied George, a huge smile cracking his face, 'when He wants to. But it's good news all right. I've missed that little lass. I have that.'

Sally could only smile and smile at them, her heart too full for words.

Red, white and blue bunting was criss-crossed along the avenue from lamp-post to lamp-post, Union Jacks fluttered in the trees and from top floor windows; and in many windows, also, were pictures of the King and Queen or Winston Churchill. The latter had been defeated in the recent parliamentary elections, but no matter, he was still, to many, a national hero. The avenue near Stanley Park where Rachel and Emmie and little Lawrence lived was holding a VJ party. The neighbourhood was normally a genteel one, not much given to jollification and wild behaviour, but the news on 14 August, 1945, of victory in Japan was a cause for celebration if anything was.

Many communities had held parties in the late spring, when victory in Europe had been declared, but the weather was warmer now, much more suitable for an out-of-doors festivity. The children were on their long summer holiday and many of the servicemen had already returned home. Harry, unfortunately, was not one of them, but Rachel was expecting to hear news of his 'demob' very soon. Demobilisation had started at the end of June, but only for 'Class B' servicemen who had priority of release, such as builders and others who were urgently required for postwar reconstruction work in Britain. Harry's work as a rock manufacturer was obviously not considered to be of such great national importance!

But the end product was very popular all the same, thought Rachel happily, as she made her way round the long trestle table placing a stick of red, white and blue striped rock into the eager hands of each child. She stopped for a moment at the high-chair where her grandson was sitting, impatiently spooning red jelly and ice cream into his mouth, brushing aside any assistance from his mother. He was going to be an independent little lad and no mistake. He had proved to be a real blessing to all the family. And a child in whom they could put their hopes for the future, Rachel thought, as she placed her hand on his sandy hair. She had been disappointed – no, more than that, she admitted – devastated, when her hopes for Emmie had been so cruelly dashed, but who could tell what this bright little boy might not become? A doctor, a lawyer (like his father) – a Member of Parliament, even.

Emmie was now engaged to her Davey. He had not yet been demobbed, but as soon as he was, they would be married, and Rachel was delighted about that. As she was about her two little grandsons in Yorkshire. Pearl had had twin boys a year ago, and though Rachel didn't see them as much as she would like to, she knew they were well and happy.

Grief and joy; the war had brought a goodly share of both. But nowhere was the joy more apparent than on the face of her sister-in-law, Sally, as she and Gloria – just like mother and daughter – set about clearing the tables ready for the fun and games that would soon take place. That evacuee girl; what a poor, neglected little mite she had been, not the sort of child you would want to take into your home at all. But her mother and Sally had done it, Rachel reminded herself, and now Gloria was as much a part of the family as any of them.

Sally had been apprehensive at first that Monica might change her mind, that she might miss Gloria too much and insist on her returning to Salford. But that hadn't happened. Monica had kept in touch, as she had promised, seeing her daughter every few weeks. But Blackpool was the place that the girl now thought of as her home. She would be fifteen in October, time to start planning her future, and Sally knew that this girl whom she loved so much could go far. The Sixth Form, university, maybe . . . But as she glanced across at the little family group of Rachel, Emmie and two-year-old Lawrence, Sally recalled how the loftiest of ambitions could be shattered. It was sufficient for Sally to have her adopted daughter – for so she thought of her – near to her and to know the girl was where she wanted to be.

'Look at little Lawrence,' Sally said now, as she and Gloria stacked the discarded cups and plates on to a tray. 'My goodness, he's going to lead them a merry dance before long! Just look at him!' They both laughed as the sturdy little figure ran off down the avenue as fast as his chubby little legs could carry him, his mother and grandmother in hot pursuit.

Sally smiled at Gloria. 'Your little Kathy would've enjoyed the party, wouldn't she? If I'd thought about it earlier we could have asked her to come over.'

'Not to worry, Auntie Sally,' said Gloria. 'They had a party of their own in May, and Monica says they're going to have one in the next street on Saturday.'

'Why don't you visit Monica next week?' Sally suggested. 'You haven't seen them since you broke up from school, and in another couple of weeks you'll be back there again. Then you'll be too busy with your homework and everything.'

'I might,' said Gloria. 'Yes, that's a good idea. P'raps I will – if you don't mind, Auntie Sally.'

'Mind? Why should I?' Sally grinned at her. 'I know you'll be back, don't I?'

'Yes, I'll always come back,' said Gloria.

A Mersey Duet

Anne Baker

When Elsa Gripper dies in childbirth on Christmas Eve, 1912, her grief-stricken husband is unable to cope with his two newborn daughters, Lucy and Patsy, so the twins are separated.

Elsa's parents, who run a highly successful business, Mersey Antiques, take Lucy home and she grows up spoiled and pampered with no interest in the family firm. Patsy has a more down-to-earth upbringing, living with their father and other grandmother above the Railway Hotel. And through further tragedy she learns to be responsible from an early age. Then Patsy is invited to work at Mersey Antiques, which she hopes will bring her closer to Lucy. But it is to take a series of dramatic events before they are drawn together . . .

'A stirring tale of romance and passion, poverty and ambition . . . everything from seduction to murder, from forbidden love to revenge' *Liverpool Echo*

'Highly observant writing style . . . a compelling book that you just don't want to put down' *Southport Visitor*

0 7472 5320 X

HEADLINE

Where the Mersey Flows

Lyn Andrews

Leah Cavendish and Nora O'Brien seem to have little in common – except their friendship. Nora is a domestic and Leah the daughter of a wealthy haulage magnate but both are isolated beneath the roof of the opulent Cavendish household.

When Nora is flung out on the streets by Leah's grasping brother-in-law, the outraged Leah follows her, dramatically declaring her intention to move to Liverpool's docklands, alongside Nora and her impoverished family. But nothing can prepare Leah for the squalor that greets her in Oil Street. Nor for Sean Maguire, Nora's defiant Irish neighbour . . .

'A compelling read' *Woman's Realm*

'Enormously popular' *Liverpool Echo*

'Spellbinding . . . the Catherine Cookson of Liverpool' *Northern Echo*

0 7472 5176 2

HEADLINE

If you enjoyed this book here is a selection of other bestselling titles from Headline